BLOOD IN
THE WATER

AND OTHER SECRETS

BLOOD IN THE WATER

AND OTHER SECRETS

JANICE LAW

WILDSIDE PRESS

BLOOD IN THE WATER AND OTHER SECRETS

Published by Wildside Press LLC.
www.wildsidebooks.com

"Secrets" originally appeared in *Alfred Hitchcock Mystery Magazine,* July, 1997. "Lions on the Lawn" originally appeared in *Ellery Queen Mystery Magazine, Mar 2002.* "The Summer of the Strangler" originally appeared in *Alfred Hitchcock Mystery Magazine,* October 2001. "My Life in Crime" originally appeared in *Alfred Hitchcock Mystery Magazine*, July/Aug 2007. "Lying" originally appeared in *Ellery Queen Mystery Magazine*, March 2002. "Blood in the Water" originally appeared in *Ellery Queen Mystery Magazine*, August 2000. "My Famous Relative" originally appeared in *Alfred Hitchcock Mystery Magazine,* November 2005. "Perfection" originally appeared in *Alfred Hitchcock Mystery Magazine*, December 1995. "The Blind Woman" originally appeared in *Ellery Queen Mystery Magazine* August 2002. "The Meeting at the Café Visconti" originally appeared in *Ellery Queen Mystery Magazine*, March 1995. "Pigskill" originally appeared in *Ellery Queen Mystery Magazine.* "The Archeologist's Revenge" originally appeared in *Ellery Queen Mystery Magazine*, September/October 1998. "Star of the Silver Screen" originally appeared in *Ellery Queen Mystery Magazine*, December 1996. "The Ghost Writer" originally appeared in *Ellery Queen Mystery Magazine*, September/October 2002. "Tabloid Press" originally appeared in *Alfred Hitchcock Mystery Magazine*, February 2000. "My Demon Lover" is original to this collection. "The Man Kali Visited" originally appeared in *Alfred Hitchcock Mystery Magazine*, August 1995. "The View From Above" and "To Beauty" are original to this collection. "Ideas in My Head" originally appeared in *Ellery Queen Mystery Magazine,* September/October 2007. "The Paradise Garden" is original to this collection. "The Helpful Stranger" originally appeared in *Ellery Queen Mystery Magazine*, April 2001.

CONTENTS

Introduction 7

Secrets 9

Lions on the Lawn 19

The Summer of the Strangler 28

My Life in Crime 39

Lying 47

Blood in the Water 59

My Famous Relative 71

Perfection 84

The Blind Woman 95

A Meeting at the Café Visconti 105

Pigskill 117

The Archeologist's Revenge 124

Star of the Silver Screen 137

Ghost Writer 146

Tabloid Press 160

My Demon Lover 173

The Man Kali Visited 183

The View From Above 191

To Beauty 200

Ideas in My Head 210

The Paradise Garden 220

The Helpful Stranger 231

INTRODUCTION

I used to tease my students that the public works overtime for mystery writers, and it is true that many of these little stories were inspired by something in the press (or, more rarely, on television). However, in every case the incident was selected because it struck some personal chord, and one of the chief pleasures of the short form is that one can so easily indulge one's interests. Thus my love of gardening shows up in the *Paradise Garden*, combined — smoothly, I hope — with a passion for folk and fairy tales. A key detail in *Secrets* came from a news item, but the narrator's neighborhood adjoined ours and, as a child of immigrants, I found her fears and ambitions easy to understand.

The young teacher in *The Helpful Stranger* is saddled with difficult students as I was early in my career, while the protagonists of both *The Ghost Writer* and *Ideas in My Head* know the trials and tribulations of the less than glamorous writing life. An interest in archeology shows up in *My Famous Relative*, itself inspired by an exhibition at Chicago's Field Museum, and in *The Archeologist's Revenge*, whose plot came from a little British news item, but whose atmosphere owes much to a small bark house displayed at the University of Connecticut.

Just how these disparate ideas come together is something of a mystery even for the writer. As the exasperated screen writer in *Ideas in My Head* says, you can feel an idea coming. "...you have this feeling that one is in the vicinity, that you just have to watch and wait and you'll find yourself sitting down at the computer typing..."

That, in fact, is most of what writers do, namely staying alert for ideas wherever they might show up and writing as soon as the Muse tips her hand. Naturally, like most divas, she has to be courted with lots of work and research. Details have to be checked and various bits of criminal and other lore – from typical insurance frauds to the dietary habits of pigs to types of large watercraft – have to be assembled, whether one is writing a novel or a short story.

But the short story has the advantage of compression. Because one does not have to know all about, say, parasailing to make a vacation diversion or the Late Riverine Archaic to suggest an academic specialty, the short story encourages all the writer's nosey interests. Another benefit is that one does not have to keep company too long with psychotics like Bren of *Lying* or with irritating folk like Vern of *Blood in the Water*, both interesting enough on a short term basis but, at least for me, not so good for the long haul.

Characters in novels, on the other hand, represent a long term commitment and can overstay their welcome unless selected carefully, but the denizens of short fiction are literary mayflies. They hang around for a week at most, and if they have a good story to tell all is forgiven. If not, they can be replaced easily, and so the form encourages experimentation with different personalities, different voices, different sorts of plots.

The mystery genre is particularly flexible in this regard, ranging easily from gritty realism to psychological suspense to the edges of the supernatural. One can be serious, edging up to tragedy as in *The Blind Woman* or to dark comedy as in *Pigskill* or to real mystery with a capital M in *The Man Kali Visited*. This is a genre for the easily bored and one that challenges the writer to keep going to the typewriter, now, the computer.

But besides lots of time at the desk and an alert eye for ideas, writers need publication. It is safe to say that there would have been far fewer of these stories written, never mind printed, without the encouragement of the editors of *Alfred Hitchcock's Mystery Magazine* and *Ellery Queen Mystery Magazines*, Linda Landrigan, the late Catheen Jourdan, and Janet Hutchings. I owe their passion for variety a debt of gratitude.

—JANICE LAW

SECRETS

My first and only failing grade in school came in sixth grade, when Miss Solway asked us to write a paragraph about a secret. Patty Tolliver set to work about a surprise birthday party for her dad. I could see "birthday party" and "hiding presents" and the rest of the story emerging in her big curling script. Eric Rodriguez printed out something about fireworks in steeply angled lines. His letters grew smaller and messier as they approached the right edge of his paper, then swelled again into big, assertive words with each new line. Even Jon Hansem, the slowest kid in the class, was hard at work, but my mind refused to function. I sat sweating at my desk and turned in a blank page.

At the end of the period, Miss Solway called me up to her desk. She looked disappointed and asked if I was feeling all right. I said I was fine; I just didn't have any secrets worth writing about. Miss Solway was unconvinced: I was considered a good, even an imaginative, student.

"I just couldn't think of anything," I wailed, and though Miss Solway was one of my favorite teachers, I added, "It was a dumb topic, anyway." I was almost twelve years old, and I already knew that there are some secrets too big too tell, like the one about my mother and Mr. Conklin and what happened the July that I was ten years old.

That summer was hot, dreadfully, dreadfully hot. We should have been used to it after three years in Hartford, but we weren't. Days when the thermometer crept up into the 80s and then the 90s, my mother would wipe her face and say, "What I wouldn't give to be back in Ireland now. It was never imagined to be this hot in Ireland."

Of course, other days, Mother "wouldn't have had Ireland as a gift," as she'd say, not with my Dad dead. "Not an honest day's work to be had. Nothing but pride, poetry, and ignorance. It's bad times here, but worse there. You remember that and work hard in school, my girl." I would promise, of course. I liked school and did well, even though I was in the public school and not with the Sisters, who provided a really good education. But Catholic school was out of the question, an unimaginable luxury. Although Mother worked hard, cleaning at the motel and the restaurants, we still lived from week to week. Her pay was usually owed from the moment she got it, and we ate cereal or beans for supper most Wednesdays and Thursdays.

I don't suppose we'd have managed at all if it weren't for Mr. Conklin, our tyrant and savior, who was a distant relative of my late father. Mr. Conklin owned a triple decker house near his "Irish Pub." He also owned a motel and a snack shop at the shabby end of Park Street, where the Puerto Rican section stopped and the Portuguese, new immigrants like ourselves, were moving in. Their children went to the big, frightening city schools, rough and full of black people, Mr. Conklin said, while we had the top apartment of his triple decker just over the city line in an old Irish-Italian neighborhood. The schools in the suburb were much, much better Mr. Conklin said, as "they damn well should be, considering the taxes." Both the apartment and my admission to the local elementary were the direct result of Mr. Conklin's intercession. It was understood that either could be withdrawn at a moment's notice.

Stout and red faced with a pug nose and a loud, jovial voice, Joseph P. Conklin was a sentimental bully with unsettling moments of gaiety and kindness. He brought me a doll once and occasionally chocolates for Mother, and he sang "Danny Boy" every St. Patrick's Day as the restaurant was closing. But even in his best moments, I was leery of him. I hated it when he wanted me to sit on his knee and tell him how I was doing in school. Fortunately, his interest was usually focused on his property: the restaurants, his triple decker, and his motel. He hiked his profits and kept his costs down by employing illegal immigrants like Mother, for whom he had originally gotten a visitor's visa.

As relatives, Mother and I actually occupied a privileged position; we were given the apartment and protected from the school authorities. In exchange, Mr. Conklin paid Mother less than the minimum wage and visited every Saturday around five o'clock on his way to the restaurant. If it was nice weather, Mother would send me out on the big front porch of the triple decker, where I would watch the traffic and try to spit on the drooping heads of the hydrangeas that flanked the front steps far below. If it was bad weather, Mother would tell me to go down and see Annie on the first floor. Annie was a stooped, arthritic old lady with a close and cluttered apartment and a fat gray neutered cat. She was lonely for company and never minded my visits. We would sit companionably, watching her old black and white tv or crocheting, until I heard Mr. Conklin's smart patent leather loafers descending the stairs. Then I would tell Annie I had to go to dinner.

Upstairs, Mother would set the table and lay out dishes without saying much. When we first came, she'd cried and talked to her saint and said Aileen — this was Mr. Conklin's wife, who'd had polio and was in a wheelchair — would put a stop to it; later on, she was flustered and ashamed; finally, she was bitter. That was when she realized we were trapped. Mr. Conklin relied on that. "You're nobody," I heard him say to her once. "Nobody knows you're here. You're invisible and be damn glad you are or Immigration'll have you back on the blessed Old Sod before you can pack your bags."

Working in the restaurant and the motel and being visited by Mr. Conklin changed my Mother. She lost the prettiness I can see in her old photographs, and she lost the playfulness and sweetness that she had when my dad was alive. She grew tired and silent and tough. I was not tough — not then and not for many years. That July I was still afraid of the dark people at the far end of the street and of the sirens and night noises and of Mr. Conklin, who held our lives in his clean, meaty hands.

Since Mother was out working during the day, I spent afternoons in the local park, where there was a pool, picnic tables, a playground, and an organized recreation program. Whenever the swim team or adults had the pool, the rec department supervisors encouraged us in messy arts and crafts and group singing. Eventually, some of us formed a chorus, and the plan was that we would sing for our parents and for the local convalescent home at the end of the summer.

Everything about the chorus was wonderful: the rehearsals under the maple trees during the hot afternoons, the smaltzy songs like "It's a Small World" and "Frere Jacques," the giggling groups of gossipy, self-important little girls. The only difficulty came when the chorus voted to wear dresses for our concerts. I had a skirt for Mass, of course, but for the concerts a dress, preferably a pretty sundress, was essential, and for weeks I teased mother and scoured the newspaper ads for sales. Finally, she announced that she'd gotten some material. Secretly I would have preferred something from Caldor's or Ames, but the material she pulled out of the bag — light blue with small pink and yellow flowers — was soft and pretty.

"With a ruffle," I asked. "Can we have it with a ruffle?"

Mother smiled. I look at her pictures now and think how pretty she was, how very pretty before she grew tired and overworked and tough. Once she had liked nice clothes, been flirtatious, carefree, popular; she understood the importance of a ruffle. Mother started the dress early the next morning, before she went off on the bus to clean at the motel, and she finished it late the same week, after she came in from mopping up the snack bar. On Saturday morning, I found the dress waiting for me, a pinafore style with ruffles around the arm holes and two pockets on the skirt.

I put it on. It was not just a perfect fit but a perfect, transforming, dress. I was undersized, bony and plain. In the dress, I seemed dainty; the effect was charming; I was enchanted.

"Take it off and hang it up," said Mother, "you'll have it dirty before the day's out. It has to be kept for good."

I hung the sundress up in our closet, but as soon as I came back from the park, I ran to look at it, to stroke the ruffles and spread out the skirt.

And when, just around four, the phone rang and Mother had to go out on an errand, I could not resist trying on my dress again.

I dragged a kitchen chair into the bathroom and climbed up to look in the mirror of medicine cabinet. I was standing there admiring myself, when I heard the knock on the door, followed by the sound of a key turning in the lock.

"Are you home, Patsy?" Mr. Conklin was the only one who ever called my mother, 'Patsy.'

"Patsy?" I heard him walking softly through the living room and down the hall. For a fattish man, he had a light tread.

I didn't want to see him, and if I hadn't been afraid of dirtying my dress, I'd have slipped under the bed. In my moment of hesitation, he appeared in the doorway.

"Where's your mother?"

"She had to go to the store," I said.

"Don't you answer the door when someone knocks?"

I shook my head.

"Where are your manners?" he asked.

"Who else visits you every Saturday?" Then he laughed. "But there'll be boys around soon enough," he said, looking at me more closely. "Very pretty." He reached out and touched the ruffle. "I must be paying Patsy more than I thought."

I flinched away from him. "Mother made this for me," I said, almost in tears. His remark spoiled my happiness. I wished I'd never put on the dress; I wished Mother would come home; I wished he was dead.

"There, there, now," he said, hitching up his light summer pants and sitting on the edge of the bed. "Who's your pal? eh? Who brought you that Barbie doll?"

I bit my lip and didn't answer.

He ran his finger along the ruffle again, then smoothed the front of my dress. "I don't have a little girl of my own, you know," he said. "Wouldn't have been as pretty as you, anyway. Your Mother, now, there's a pretty woman. I met her on a visit to the Old Country. She wasn't much older than you and she was one of the prettiest girls in Belfast; that's the truth."

He took my arm although I tried to ease away. "Come sit here for a minute," he said. His voice sounded different, soft and sort of sticky, like something Mother would say was 'too sweet to be wholesome.' "Since your mother is out."

"You called her," I said, frightened by sudden knowledge. "You asked her to get something for the snack shop."

"Did I now? And me with a car and going out anyway as I always do on a Saturday evening? Would I do such a thing?"

"You called her," I said, stubborn despite my fear.

"You're a clever girl," he said, settling me on his lap. "Maybe we should send you to the Sisters at St. Bridget's. Would you like that? Wear a nice little uniform, they do. Gray blazer," he said, running his hand down my dress again, "little maroon tie, little maroon and gray kilt, little gray knee socks. Just to here. Wouldn't you like that? Lots of nice Irish boys and girls at St. Bridget's."

I stopped trying to squirm away from him. "I like my school," I said, "but I'd like St. Bridget's better."

He laughed. "I just bet you would. I just bet you would. Well, it depends if you're good." He was stroking my knee, and I both did and did not know what he meant. I'd heard a fair bit out on the porch on those warm evenings.

"We'd have to ask my mother," I said.

"Oh, your mother can't afford St. Bridget's. Never in this life! Don't imagine your mother can afford to send you to the Sisters."

"My mother decides," I said.

He laughed. "Does she now?" I could see the veins in the whites of his eyes; I could smell his aftershave, and something else, a raw, dangerous smell.

"I want to get down now," I said.

"Not yet," he said, sliding his meaty red fingers under my dress. "Not if you want to get to St. Bridget's."

A minute later, I started to scream.

"Shhh," said Mr. Conklin, and when I didn't stop, he yelled,"Shut up, shut up, you little bitch!"

I wasn't tough like my mother. The scream wasn't under my control, it went echoing around my head and burned between my legs and poured out like blood from a wound. I couldn't stop, not even when he slapped me. The scream was so independent, so beyond my control, that at last it even frightened Mr. Conklin, who did up his pants and hurried down the hall and out the door.

Mother came home just minutes later. I was sitting on the bed. My dress was torn, and there was blood on my legs. Mother took one look at me and her face went white. She wrapped her arms around me, cursing and sobbing at the same time. When she stopped, she said, "I'll fix that bastard. He'll never hurt you again."

Taut with anger and pain, her face was almost unrecognizable, and I was nearly as frightened of her as of Mr. Conklin. "I promise," she said. "As God is my witness."

"No," I said, "no!" I had an intimation of disaster, loss, some terrible punishment. Good or bad, Mr. Conklin was the chief power in our small universe.

"You'll see," Mother said, "I won't bear this." Then she sat back on her heels and looked at me. "It's got to be a secret. God forgive me, you've got to keep this a secret. The police would tell Immigration. Do you understand that? We can't tell anyone what that bastard did."

I nodded my head. I didn't want to tell anyone. I had no words for what had happened. "A secret," I said.

"A deep, dark secret," Mother said grimly.

Sometime after ten P.M. the next Friday, Mr. Conklin died behind his fast food restaurant. A stab wound stopped his heart so suddenly that he was dead before he hit the pavement. The papers made much of the speed of his passing, and for years, I carried an image of Mr. Conklin, tumbled like a large, ungainly bird from the sky and dying in mid-fall.

That night my mother was late coming home from work. The city sounds made me nervous — the sudden shrieks and eerie lights of police cars, fire trucks, and ambulances, the accelerating hot rods with their booming radios, the hoarse, quarrelsome voices of men drifting back from the bar — and I was still awake at eleven o'clock when I heard her footsteps. I ran to unlock the door.

Mother's weary face was bloodless. "I'm sorry I'm so late, Darling," she said. "I had to wait and lock up. Mr. Conklin didn't come back from making the night deposit."

"I hope he never comes back," I said.

Mother gave me a sharp look. "Be careful what you wish for," she said, then she went into the bedroom and began to pack our cases.

Mr. Conklin looked out at us from the morning paper. His picture made him seem younger and more benevolent than he ever looked in life. The accompanying story told us about his violent end. I was thrilled and horrified by his death, by the unlooked for fame of one of our acquaintances. These were sensational and superficial emotions, but I was genuinely sorry and frightened about leaving our apartment.

"My job's gone," Mother explained. "We don't exist. There never were any papers, agreements."

I asked about school, about the park chorus, our concerts; Mother looked me in the face and shook her head. I felt suspicion dawn in a shiver of anxiety which grew stronger when we caught the morning bus to Boston without saying goodbye to anyone, not even to Annie. Once in Boston, the MTA took us to the South End, where we started calling ourselves Malloy instead of O'Brien and quietly disappeared into the Irish community. We put down a security deposit on a shabby apartment, and a very distant relative of Mother's found her a job in a sweatshop sewing curtains.

That fall I attended a real urban school, where I learned to smoke and swear and became outwardly tough. Inside, I was frightened of a lot of things, all related to secrets and to July: men, sex, sudden death, Immigration. Underneath were even deeper fears, more terrible because unacknowledged: the fear of guilt, police, and discovery, the fear, worst of all, of being separated from Mother, whose protection, I sensed, was both sure and terrible.

It was several years before I learned that my particular horrors were not unique. Fear and loss were the common experiences of my class-mates, and the art of keeping secrets was so essential to our survival that, though we could not forget old fears, we could push them down relentlessly. I put away my suspicions and learned to live with ambiguity. When I graduated from high school, I joined the Army, where I became a citizen and trained as a nurse. Amid the suffering of others, I at last grew really tough, tough enough to ask Mother the question that had haunted my youth.

It was on another summer day, and tough or not, I would probably not have dared ask if we hadn't gone to Hartford. I'd had attend a lec-ture at the Medical Center, and Mother said she'd ride along and visit a friend who lived nearby in Farmington. When I picked her up after the program, she suggested driving down to Park Street to see the old triple decker. At once, my childish fears returned. I stopped in the parking lot and looked at her.

"If it's not out of the way," said Mother, handsome in her dark navy dress. For years, she had worn only dark colors, black, navy, deep purple, somber shades that gave her a vaguely european air. The rich ladies who patronized the bridal salon where Mother worked thought her taste dis-tinguished and sophisticated.

I shook my head. "Is it wise?" I asked.

Mother gave nothing away. "Who do you think will notice us?" she answered.

Of course, she was right. I parked near the house, and Mother got out on the sidewalk and looked up at the big solid building with the flaring eaves and the prow-like porches. Blue-gray vinyl siding covered the dark wood shingles, and Mother approved. "Saves the painting," she said. "Clean looking. Young Joe must be up on all the latest."

"Young Joe?"

"Mr. Conklin's son. He must be just a few years older than you are. Aileen's probably turned everything over to him by now. It was her money, part of it, anyway. Her people owned some grocery stores, you know."

I did not know and I thought Mother might say more about the Conklins, but she took a last look up at the apartment and got back into the car. "I've never been so hot as in that third floor flat," she said. "Remember how hot it used to get?"

"Yes," I said.

"Go on down Park," Mother said. "We might as well stop by the snack shop, too."

She spoke so casually that I felt guilty for all the years of suspicion and apprehension. Nonetheless, I drove down town carefully, nervously alert for stop signs, traffic lights, and squad cars. Next to me, Mother looked out the windows and remarked on changes in the neighborhood. The Portuguese shops had mostly gone, leaving a mix of Indian and Southeast Asian businesses: Bombay Foods, a Vietnamese market, shops that promised to speak Khmer, Vietnamese, Hindi, or Laotian. The old snack shop had been transformed into the New Thai Palace Restaurant, and Mother said, "Turn in. There's room for you to park."

I pulled next to a van labeled "New Thai Palace — Restaurant, Catering, Takeout," and shut off the motor. The late spring evening was mild and pleasant. The sun turned the bricks of the restaurant to gold, and the sky was a peachy shade of pink. Mother stepped out of the car and walked around back of the restaurant where a big exhaust fan whirred out the smell of hot oil and spices. Beyond a brown board fence, children were shouting and playing, and, on the sidewalk, two women in saris and dark sweaters pushed their children in strollers. Mother studied the restaurant, the garbage cans, the little open porch that led into the kitchen. Long ago, Mr. Conklin had been seized by some swift and terrible force right at the foot of those steps.

For years I had wondered about the precise agent. Now that I was on the verge of discovery, I found I'd rather not know.

"Please let's go," I said.

Mother seemed surprised that I was nervous. She, herself, was perfectly composed, a fine looking woman somewhere in middle age, her hair still dark, her face only faintly lined, old hardships and weariness visible only in her eyes. The days of sweatshops and exploitation had eventually ended in Boston, where she had turned her toughness into such elegance that men admired her and were afraid of her. Six years ago, she had married a brave one who owned a fancy funeral home and had become comfortable and happy.

"There is no danger," she said as she walked back to the car. "I told you that years ago."

I remembered the hot apartment, panic, fear, and pain — and Mother's contorted mask-like face. "You said you'd fix Mr.Conklin."

"I wanted to comfort you," my mother said, looking at me calmly. "But people are different. You would have been happier not knowing. You lack the taste for vengeance. It is a shame you never went to the Sisters. They would have approved."

"I would have suspected anyway," I said. "We packed right up and left."

Mother gave a slight shrug. "We'd have gone immediately in any case. Aileen hated me; she'd have had us out of the apartment before his funeral."

"I was terrified you'd be questioned," I said. "For years, I worried that someone would come, that you'd be taken away, that somehow . . ."

"We didn't exist," said Mother. "If he told me that once, he told me a hundred times."

"But the knife, the fingerprints, the other workers? There must have been evidence. Look at this place — where was there to hide anything?"

Mother got back in the car and fastened her seat belt before answering. "I didn't have a plan," she said. "I've been told that makes a difference, not planning, I mean. I don't even know all that was in my mind when I went out the door after him. It was around ten-fifteen; He was going to the night deposit but first he stepped out for a smoke — one of those vile cigars. There was a boning knife on the counter, sharp as a razor. I picked it up because I wanted him to know I was serious. I was desperate and hot and sick and my heart was breaking. He'd gone too far. I wanted to tell him that he was never, ever to touch either of us again."

"What did he say?"

Mother's face grew dark and reflective. "He laughed," she said. "He had trampled my heart; he had hurt the one person I had left, my only treasure, and still he laughed — you see what it is to be rich and powerful. Then he said that I was looking older, and I understood everything. We were nothing to him, nothing at all, and he was thinking of you for a replacement."

"I was ten years old," I said in a small voice.

"There was really nothing else to do," Mother said. "I was surprised he took such a long time to fall."

I imagined the night parking lot with the moths swirling around the security lights, the long shadows, the urban smells of hot asphalt, exhaust, and garbage cans, and my mother, young then and frightened, standing by the stair with a knife in her hand.

"Everyone thought it was a robbery," I said.

"So it was: the day's takings from two restaurants," Mother said with a slight smile. "The police blamed the gangs, the Puerto Ricans, wild kids from the project. What else could they do? He'd managed very carefully, and very few people knew me."

"But the knife?" I asked. "What about the knife?"

"You don't know restaurants," she said. "Restaurants are full of knives. I rinsed off the boning knife in the sink and threw it in the dishwasher. As far as I was thinking at all, I figured the staff would unload it the next morning and put it back in the rack as usual."

"Of course," I said. I realized that my brave and decisive mother was untouched by fantasy. While I had been tormented for years by fears of discovery and loss and guilt, failure had never crossed her mind. She was a woman without imagination. "But didn't he have a wallet? Didn't he used to carry something for the money?"

Mother opened her pocket book and pulled out a battered green leather zippered purse which I'd seen a thousand times without recognition. "No matter where you discard things, they're apt to be found," she said calmly.

I was dazzled by the simplicity of her strategy, which had required only nerve and silence. Until now. I could not decide whether her guilty secret had finally and irresistibly resurfaced as guilty secrets are supposed to do — or whether she felt a satisfaction that demanded recognition. I realized uneasily that the parish gentlemen who admired and feared my mother were right. Life had made her desperate, and then it had made her remarkable. Mr. Conklin had been hit by a force quite out of his reckoning.

LIONS ON THE LAWN

Lions. Lions on the lawn. No, no, not lawn. Lions on grass, in grass. Is grass right? Leaping, jumping, hunting. Hunting is right, but another word, like plant, plant stalks, stalking lions on the lawn, on grass. Forgotten words. Could be worse, have the idea still, ideas. Awake? Yes, tv flickering:

." . . the lionesses are hungry. They move out across the veldt to the watering hole . . ."

I sit up: living room, tv, low sun. Time. Time to move using the whatsits name? Frame? Frame for walking, walker. Yes, I'm awake again which beats the alternative and ideas are dropping into place and words, some of them, enough of them, are there for use. But what's the time?

Right hand on useless left, turn watch: 4:25 pm. Five minutes. Time to get up, to concentrate. Hard with one hand, one arm. When I think of the work I did, the loads I could carry, the strength effort. Effortmore? Effortleast? Effort. Make an effort. Up. One hand, one foot. Two feet, leg better than arm, arm better than hand. Straighten up, step, another. Vastness of the rug, vast as lawn, as grass, no, no, as veldt, veldt where lions hunt. Are there lions today? We'll see.

The chair's by the window. A tricky maneuver, like parallel parking, like sliding heavy trucks and big sedans into tight spaces neat. Lining up, lining up walker, feel chair, easier on the right side, guess on the left, drop. Ah hah!

Take a breath. Well done; motion's good. I can see the street; ideas all in place, and words coming easier. There are days, moments of days, times of days, when I think, this will work. I'll beat this, stroke or no stroke, so hang on a bit, hang on.

The window overlooks an old house fitted up with picture windows. It's the office for the lumber yard and hardware store. Front door opens onto parking spaces. Good as tv, really, to watch who comes in and out. Who's driving a new truck and who's got a junker. Who's laying in the paint and lumber and hardware and supplies — and who's in the office trying to raise some credit.

Sitting smack by the window I can see the far corner of the yard and watch them loading ply and 2 x 4's and planks. Trucks come out further up the street, but the drive right under my window leads to employee parking. That's my interest. Time?

Turn wrist with right hand. Slow. Everything is slow. Is time my friend or my enemy? How much is left? I'm prepared either way; I've had a good life, a long life, oh, yes. But there's always going to be something left undone, isn't there? If you've got nothing you're leaving undone, you've overstayed your time.

And yes, there she is, right on time. Black, curly hair, black eyes — maybe Puerto Rican? The red coat today; she always looks snappy in that red coat.

I lift my hand and smile — I think I smile. Ellen says, Yes, yes, you can smile, but I don't know. Left side a problem all the way up and more up than down. Ellen says I smile okay, and I choose to believe her.

I smile and the pretty woman in the red coat waves back. The day I don't smile at a pretty girl is the day you can put me in the box and nail down the lid. A nice girl, too.

I watch until she gets to her car. Just a habit of mine. I can't say how it started, but it gives the day another landmark besides meals and evening news and the Discovery Channel.

She pulls out and I check the street one last time. No lions today. Her car's a bit of a worry. I'd rather it was newer, faster. You can't be too fast with lions around.

She needs a fast car, I tell Ellen when she arrives to give me supper. Actually that's just what I try to say but it doesn't come out so well. Just a lot of grunts and howls. She brings me the pad and pencil but it's too much effort to try to print. And what would I tell her? The car would have to be explained, and the lions, one lion in particular. I point to the window and try to smile.

"Been flirting with Kim Alvarez again? I've seen you waving to her. At your age, too!"

This is a little joke between us. To Ellen I'm an awful man for the ladies. She fusses about me and I give her extra time off and never notice the housecleaning.

"She's a nice woman. Has her troubles like the rest of us."

I perk up at this. Ellen brings me tells. No, no, wrong word again. I'm getting tired. Tells me words. Papers, newspapers. Tells me news. I look up and nod my head so that she knows I'm interested.

"Her husband was Jimmy Alvarez — you know, the policeman who was shot. A drug raid went wrong or something."

For a minute raid means nothing and then drugs and policeman come into a kind of focus. I grunt and wave my hand, and Ellen puts one hand on her hip and concentrates. "A year ago maybe, maybe less. They raided a house on Milk Street and something went wrong. Shots were fired and he was hit. Very sad. And terrible for her. They have a three-year old."

Talk, talk, I think, but time for dinner — Ellen has to get home. My man needs his dinner, too, you know, is what she says. My dinner is heated up turkey, gravy and canned beans and mighty good. Ellen helps me into my pajamas and says good night. I try to concentrate the way I could before the stroke when I read the newspaper every day and remembered things like drug raids gone bad. Something was nasty about the Alvarez shooting. Contraband? No, but C, something with a C. Controversy, that's it. The Alvarez shooting was controversial in some way. I fall asleep on this triumph.

So now it's important that I'm at the window every day, even if there's not much I can do beyond watching Mrs. Alvarez get safely to her car. Four-thirty she comes out, waves, and hurries into the parking lot. I put an OK mark on the calendar. I mark each day, awkwardly, because I was a lefty and my right hand doesn't like the pen. End of the week, I look back at the record and check how many lions.

The man stopped by on Monday. He's a big guy with a smooth, hard face. A muscular face is how I'd describe it like he's done a lot of heavy frowning and scowling. Looks like muscles elsewhere, too, the kind for show that you don't get with honest labor. He went into the office but just for a few minutes. So he could have been anyone, no lion at all.

But then Wednesday he was standing on the sidewalk when she came out. He put his hand on her arm, and she pulled away and ran to her car. I saw that and it figured. He'd been hanging around too much for a guy who wasn't in the market for nails or lumber.

Thursday I didn't see him but the car was there. A Ford, one of the big new ones. I know cars, drove limos for a while, but I couldn't stand sitting cooped up. His car is HXT 030. This time I wrote it on the calendar in big letters and pointed it out to Ellen.

"License plate?"

Ellen's quick.

I nod.

"Someone bothering you?"

Shake my head. Point out the window.

She goes and looks but there's nothing. Mrs. Alvarez has gone home, and he only comes when she's at work. He's in the grass. He's hunting. Ellen frowns and looks uncertain. She finally brings the pad and a pen.

Hold pen straight. Press down so it doesn't shoot away at an angle. Bothering Mrs. Alvarez comes out as Boting msAlVEez.

Ellen looks at this, looks at me. "Mrs. Alvarez? Listen, her husband was a cop. If she doesn't know the police, who would? We best stay out of it." She puts on the nature show for me. Eagles of the World tonight.

Eagles soaring with eyes like search lights. Tired. I forget the cops, the drug raid. Jimmy Alvarez. Words gone, ideas gone, memory going into holes like swiss cheese. On the screen, a monster eagle, big as a nightmare, fishes in Siberia, and I remember why the Alvarez shooting was controversial. It was a friendly gun, no, no. A minute, a minute more. Another eagle lands on what looks like a small ice berg. An eagle of the mind that tells me, friendly fire: another cop shot Jimmy Alvarez. Ellen had forgotten to mention that.

The next day I pick up my portable phone. Ellen has it programmed: her number; Ginny, my daughter's number; Kevin, my son's number; 911 and Meals on Wheels. This makes her feel good, although I can't really use the phone. I can listen to Ginny and Kevin all right; awkward calls, their voices, unanswered, are affectionate but uneasy. As for the rest, I don't know what good 911 would do me.

Still, Ellen means well. You won't need the phone book, she said, and she put it in the kitchen, the Long March. So, up. Walker. Today I re-member walker without trouble. That's a hopeful thing. One day a word is gone, the next it's back. Forward march to the kitchen. Get the phone book. Drop it. Drop it again. On the third try, hang the damn thing over the bar of the walker. Good thing we have a small town, a thin directory. Change direction, hard as turning a sixteen wheeler. Back to the chair and the big project of sitting down. Then, no paper. Exhausted.

I maybe fall asleep — I sleep easily and often — but I'm visited by eagles hunting. Hunting means lions, and I'm alert again and consult the book. Print small and wobbling. No good. Try the Yellow Pages. Ah! Nice black type and good sized, too: Bradford Lumber, Your Place For Wood. I write the number on the calendar.

Late on the Monday afternoon he's back: HXT 030. I can see the car, panting with exhaust, parked just up the street. He's waiting. I press in the numbers.

You have reached Bradford Lumber. For the yard, press one, for hard-ware, press two, for the billing office, press three.

Press three. Hear Mrs. Alvarez. "Hello. May I help you? Bradford Lumber."

I hang up and call again. Three times. This must make her nervous. I can tell from her voice, and I feel bad. But then I see her pass the corner window on her way to the front door.

She must have seen his car, because at 4:30 pm, she leaves with the boss, Henry Johnson, who's not all muscle like the hunter but big enough to give you pause. HXT 030 starts to get out of his car, sees Henry, and drops the idea. Henry walks Mrs. Alvarez to her car as HXT 030 drives away. I have the eagle eye all right.

So that's how it is. Every day, I watch for lions. When he drives up, I press in the numbers and her phone rings. She doesn't always go to the door; she knows the signal now, but I'll bet she can't guess where it comes from. She should call the police. It bothers me that she doesn't.

One day Ellen arrives early. The windows are open, and I hear the horn, then voices. Ellen has a good loud voice when she needs one.

." . . blocking the drive way. I need to get in. I have a client . . ."

Lower voice in reply. A man, not too pleased. I get myself up and turn the walker and look through the glass in the front door. Ellen's signalling to get into the drive and giving a big guy in a familiar dark Ford what for.

." . . police business doesn't need to block this driveway," she says and HXT 030 pulls away.

"So," she says when she comes in. "You don't have to worry. Police business."

I must not look convinced.

"Police. He's plainclothes, maybe undercover."

Ellen is fond of thrillers and cop shows and knows all the lingo.

"But even if he's on a stake-out, he doesn't need to block your driveway. What if you were taken ill?"

I nod, but I'm worried. How to watch both the front and the lumber yard. I wonder if "safe days" just means he's out of my sight. There must always be lions on the veldt. Always.

Just before Ellen leaves, Kevin calls. He tries to call while she is here so he can get a report. "Your dad has a little more energy," Ellen says today. "He's taking more interest."

I smile and nod to encourage her. She does not mention what the interest is, and I smile about that, too, before she gives me the phone.

Kevin tells me how he's doing at work. How Timmy is managing on the baseball team, that Patty's joined the band. I've gotten used to listening without answering, and it's nice in a way. I get to hear him thinking, which you don't always do when you're flapping your mouth.

"Games, remember all the games, Dad? Soccer, hockey. You used to time for the hockey team. Remember the air horn? That was the height of my ambition: to operate the air horn at the rink." He laughs and I laugh, too.

When I hang up, I grab the walker and set out for the hall closet. Thump down the walker, step, thump, step, thump: a journey. I open the door, a tricky maneuver, then I'm faced with the clutter of forty plus years and two kids. If Bess were alive, this would all be tidy.

I stand and think about Bess for a bit, before I take an old hockey stick and start poking here and there. Down come baseball gloves and garden tools and winter scarves the moths have been after and mouse traps and floor polish. Ellen will have something to say when she sees this.

And then, there it is. A blue and white can . . . canster . . . canister! My old air horn. I get it off the top shelf with the hockey stick and tease it out into the hall. I nudge it over toward a kitchen chair where I sit down so that I can — yes! — pick it up. Daily life's an epic if you live long enough.

Rink, smell of chemicals and ice, sound of skate blades and thump of pads against the boards. Kevin, rosy faced beside me, clutching the air horn. Is it time, is it time yet? My eyes on the stop watch, counting down, seven, six, five, four . . . Kevin holds the horn away to the side as he's been taught . . . two, one. A hoot that would take your head off. His smile. Pure joy.

I give the can a shake and push the trigger, quick and gentle. Nothing. Shake again. Push, harder this time. Nothing. I set it on the table and start writing a note for Ellen.

The next day, she's not sure this is such a good idea. She's thinking neighbors and the tenants on the second floor and Social Services. Anything I want that she doesn't gets the same response: You don't want Social Services involved, do you?

Careful, I tell myself. Don't mention HXT 030 or I'm out of luck. I point to the phone and shake my head.

"That's true," Ellen says.

I point to my throat, my mouth.

"Yes," she admits, but first she tries to push the Lifeline Button the local hospital distributes.

I point to the phone, the weak link in all these plans. She argues it out with herself and then I write down the name of the sporting goods store, and she promises to bring me a new air horn. Which she does. The same brand, even, and at the slightest touch it gives a shriek like a steam locomotive. I put it by the window, because by this time there's been a new development.

I almost missed it. HXT 030 hadn't been around for a while. I'd maybe see the car passing, driving by, but no more office visits. No more standing out on the side walk. He was hidden deep in the grass until the evening *National Geographic* repeated Sea Turtles, Wonders of the Spring. Grand reptiles, no doubt, but I prefer fur and feathers.

A warm night. I get the side window open and sit down to listen to the starlings and sparrows in the hedge.I don't bother to put on the light. Eyes closing. Outside, twittering and the occasional car passing, and inside, a memory of large olive colored turtles paddling over reefs. Paddling, slowing, braking. A car stops. Two car doors open and then I'm right awake. Something makes me grab the walker and begin the big project of getting up and turning around. It's him: right there on the sidewalk, standing beside a guy I know, a suburban psychopath named Gippy Dorgun, who got chucked off our local junior hockey team for going after a ref with his stick.

That was the better part of twenty years ago and I remember it like yesterday — better than yesterday, to tell the truth. I've forgotten a lot since then, but Gippy's learned nothing except the value of a good lawyer.

They're talking quietly together right there on the driveway of the lumber yard. I can't make out the words, but I see Gippy nod. It is him, I'm sure. You don't forget someone skating toward you with his stick over his head.

Arrest? Maybe an arrest? Could I be wrong, wrong entirely about HXT 030? I'm sure I'm not, and yet I worry even after I see the big fellow clap Gippy on the shoulder, as if something's been settled. They get into the car and drive away.

The next few days there's nothing. Nothing out front of the lumber yard, nothing so far as I know out front of my house. No voices in the night. Maybe I was wrong, dreaming. Maybe there are only sea turtles, drifting placid, not lions. Still, I keep watch every afternoon. It's warm now; I sit on the porch looking both ways. With my air horn.

Red behind my eyes, green circles, green like turtles, bleaching out to pale yellow, to the grass, no, no, to the veldt, the lions. I hear lions and open my eyes. I doze in the afternoon, especially in the strong spring sun. The pretty vines haven't really leafed out yet on the porch; the roses took winter death. Is that the right word? Would Bess have called it winter death? She was the gardener.

A squeal of brakes, a car door opening but not closing, Gippy Dorgun on the sidewalk heading toward the lumber yard office. Friday afternoon. Payday. A hockey stick in his hand? No, no, that's at the rink, long ago. But I'm awake, and he's carrying something. A friendly gun? Friendly fire. I reach down for the air horn. Smooth side of canister. I squeeze the trigger.

Gippy stops at the door. Memories for him, too. Ice and the rink and the sound of the horn. He skated pretty well; he was just psychotic. I hit the horn again. He goes inside anyway, which is what psychotics do. A minute later a cop car roars up and neighbors look out and the go car, the going car, the getaway car, which I guess it is after all, peels off, leaving rubber all down Station Road, before horns and squeals and a shriek as a pickup truck turning into the yard loses some essential metals.

There's a shot and another. I keep up with the horn until a guy in uniform runs over to the porch and says to knock it off, the excitement's over. I try to ask about Mrs. Alvarez, but everything comes out wrong. I wave my hands and grab a pencil and take special care and get Mrs. Alvarez OK? printed out mostly all right.

The cop gives me a funny look, as if he doesn't think I'm all there. People do that when you can't speak. Fortunately Ellen arrives and takes over the way she does. "His friend, Mrs. Alvarez. He's worried about Mrs. Alvarez. She works in the lumber yard office."

It's a good hour before Ellen can find out that Mrs. Alvarez bolted as soon as she heard the "siren."

Ellen looks at me and says, "We'll hear from Social Services for sure."

But I have some ideas about why a siren panicked a cop's wife, and I write down, Lion kills with friendly fire. A message with a good many errors in it.

"Lion?" says Ellen, worrying I've maybe taken another bad turn, a mini-stroke, an aftershock.

Tired from all the excitement, that's for sure. From cops and shots and Mrs. Alvarez running like a wildebeest. HXT 030 I write on the pad. And that's as clear as anything I've ever written.

Ellen grabs the paper, my she's quick, and tears it up. "Say nothing," she said. Then, "You saw a gun."

It takes me a minute to figure this one out.

"You saw a man with a gun and you let off the air horn to warn everybody. That's all." A significant look.

I nod. That's okay with me, if Mrs. Alvarez is safe.

"The police will come," Ellen said. "Maybe the guy in the car, too. You understand?"

I do. And he does. While Ellen hovers over me, fussing at the cops and giving me warning looks, I labor to print out lion gun.

"He saw the gun," Ellen tells them quick before I can scratch out more.

She adds I've had a severe stroke, that I've lost words. On this big hint, I close my eyes and drop my head, while Ellen tells them how well I manage and describes my rehab. I can tell she's worried about the air horn, Social Services, and grumpy neighbors, but the police are pleased. Except for HXT 030, who is Detective Brannak. Even with my eyes half closed, and words all gone to hell, I can tell that.

But what can he do? Alert Septuagenarian Helps Foil Lumber Yard Heist. Right in the local rag. Ellen is thrilled. The kids and grand kids are impressed to death. I've been a good citizen, an eagle. One of the alert.

So's Mrs. Alvarez and that gets me thinking again soon as I hear the news from Ellen. I sent her to get new batteries for my TV remote and hoped she'd come back with gossip. She didn't disappoint me.

"She's gone, left town, left her job, gone," Ellen repeats, full of surprise. "Gone back home to Puerto Rico with her baby! What do you think of that?"

Ellen doesn't approve, but I think it's smart. A wise decision for a moment when Gippy Dorgun's dead and Detective Brannak's still a cop in good standing.

Gives me something to chew over, that's for sure. Did Brannak get her husband killed? Was he trying to romance her? Did he plan to shut her up permanent? Was he always a lion or have I been dreaming. I can't decide. Maybe I should have ignored good advice and printed out Gippy Dorgun's name and HXT 030 and seen what the cops would say to that.

But I may find out yet. I still see lions, and I keep my air horn handy. He's out on the veldt, and I'm the one he's watching now.

THE SUMMER OF THE STRANGLER

It was hot. A Bermuda High had stalled over the Connecticut River valley for the better part of a week, trapping a big dome of stagnant air in which exhaust from thousands of commuters' cars and SUVs hung like a giant plume of cigarette smoke. Everyone was exhausted and short tempered, sick of the heat which showed no signs of ending, sick of the gritty smog that insinuated itself into eyes and noses; sick of being inside, if there was air-conditioning; sick of the still air, if there was none.

In the evenings, the humidity stayed ferocious but the heat dropped, and people cautiously opened their windows and sat on porches and balconies and walked along the edges of the parks. The edges, note, and under the lights. When they came back to go to bed, they checked all their windows and doors, shut their porch sliders and locked them, too, because that summer there was something outside worse than 98% humidity and record-breaking heat. Everybody, especially women, knew all about the new security drill.

"Lock doors and windows; use security bars; check the identity of everyone who comes to your door; screen phone calls." Debra Aken knew the routine by heart: the words came unbidden to her mind as she moved the newspaper with the big, black Strangler's Seventh? headline off the beauty salon chair and sat down to let a variety of expensive potions do their work. Tall and well built, devoted to the gym and fitness, Debra was not a nervous woman, but even she had found herself taking precautions, checking the dead bolt at night, and nagging Lance about locking the French windows and the sliders that opened to the patio.

Of course, Lance was hopeless at that sort of thing; details were not now, and never had been, his forte, a personality trait which Debra alternately found irritating and endearing, but which had secured his devotion. Yes, she thought she could say that. She thought she could.

"Frown lines, frown lines," handsome Mr. Jose warned as he went by with another customer, and Debra gave him a smile that showed all her teeth and shut him up. She wondered why the hell she'd come to the beauty salon anyway when it was pressing 100 outside. Did she really need the works — streaking, setting, styling? It was in the back of her mind that Lance with his chronic disorganization, domestic helplessness, and fiscal impracticality could damn well take her as she was.

She lifted the latest chapters of his new novel from her briefcase. The books were all much the same, sexy, violent, convoluted, and profitable. Lance came up with the plots, characters, and raw, very raw, copy. She put his effusions into recognizable English, cleaned up the spelling, and caught inconsistencies, for her husband was quite capable of changing his heroine's last name from one chapter to the next and of altering the hero's car within a paragraph or two. Once the manuscript was readable, Debra conducted negotiations with the publisher. She and Lance were a team, and they were very successful.

Chapter seven of *Deadfall* began with the hero, Matt Dillard, an ex-CIA agent turned Silicon Valley Entrepreneur — all Lance's characters were involved in Big Espionage and Big Business — at play with his chief rival's wife, the glamorous, sexually voracious, Cynthia Lamont. Debra tidied up three dangling participles and altered a misplaced modifier which suggested that Matt was caressing the wide screen tv instead of the bodacious Cynthia.

Debra wasn't sure how she felt about Cynthia, a clever and aggressive woman with a big mane of streaked and styled hair. She tried to remember if Cynthia had preceded or followed her own coiffeur changes: of such small details is our fate comprised. Cynthia had been around for two, no, three books. A glorious, full figured, modern, mature woman. And her prototype? Well, the illustration on the jacket cover had been based on a family photo of Debra, herself.

But now it seemed to Debra that Lance was stressing Cynthia's age, the maturity of her beauty, the necessity of her devotion to the gym. It was a rather too subtle characterization for Matt to find a blond hair on his cashmere jacket and to notice that it had a black root. Terrible sentence, anyway, Debra thought and scratched it out.

The scene gave her a bad feeling, just the same, and she put aside her pencil and began flipping ahead to see if there was more about Fiona, "the Venus of Rodeo Road;" really that was trite. Fiona was raven haired, blue eyed, just nineteen, and, yes, she was certainly becoming more prominent. By chapter eight she was in bed with Matt and, by nine, she seemed to have supplanted Cynthia, entirely.

Debra closed the manuscript and stared at the ceiling, asking herself, would he dare? Did he intend? Was this serious? It was a curious fact of their marriage that her husband often communicated his intentions and interests via his copy. And that was funny, because, while every critic that had ever deigned to open a Lance Aken had labeled it unrelieved and cliched pulp, a discerning eye could see that, in fact, he put a great deal of his life into his work. He really did, and Debra figured he was popular because readers knew that, even if the critics did not.

Could this be serious, she asked herself again, as Jose unwrapped the bleached strands of her long, thick, hair. He fussed with his comb and blow dryer, inflating her locks, making her into Cynthia, who was about to be displaced by the Venus of Rodeo Road, AKA Gwen Romani, Lance's current mistress.

They'd met Gwen at the annual book and author festival, where Lance had been the keynote speaker and the big draw. Gwen was a literary groupie with a degree in English and a face and figure to die for. She was twenty-five, not nineteen like the old lecher's Venus of Rodeo Road, but Debra had to admit to twenty years on her. This vision of youth and spring had worked in publishing, longed to return to the world of books, "absolutely dreamed" of being an editor.

She thought Lance's books were "wonderful," a "breath of fresh air," "the living thing;" she'd had enough of overly refined, overly theoretical "so-called literature;" Lance's were "real." Debra had struggled to keep a straight face through all this, but Lance ate it up. He was at the age to want to be serious, or rather, to be taken seriously, though, thank God, he was sensible enough not to change his style. Gwen offered, Debra belatedly saw, the best of both worlds: she burbled on about "literature," but she didn't expect him to change a line.

Debra glanced at her Rolex, a very nice one with very nice diamonds, a gift from Lance after a previous indiscretion. She thought that she might stop by Lux, Bond, and Green; she felt like diamonds, something expensive. She'd seen a handsome choker in the window, but that was maybe too dowager empress. She needed young diamonds at the moment, perhaps a tennis bracelet. Perhaps. Sporty diamonds suggested flirtatious youth, but the calculation of compensatory gifts is a fine art; Debra didn't want to settle too cheaply.

She got home, hot in spite of the Mercedes' air-conditioning, the super cool of the salon and the almost glacial confines of the jewelers', to find her husband sitting by the pool checking her latest corrections and drinking a vodka cocktail red as blood. Debra dropped the chapter she'd finished on the glass table beside him.

"How's it going?" he asked.

"Slow," she said, though she knew as well as anybody that the correct response was *terrific*. "I only finished seven."

"Well, you have a tendency" — a pause in which Debra felt her temperature rise by several more degrees — "to overwork some of the copy."

"Since when," asked Debra, "have I overworked anything?" Definitely, a tennis bracelet would be a mere bagatelle!

Lance's blocky features took on a sly and cagey expression. He looked like the Marlboro Man and schemed like Casanova. "I thought I might let Gwen have a look. You're so busy, and she's got plenty of time in between job hunting."

"She's got blue eyes and sexy tits," Debra said and cleaned manuscript, drink, pencils and pens off the table. His favorite Waterford crystal glass shattered on the tile with a satisfying crash and the manuscript pages, spidered all over with her neat script, spun languidly through the humid air to land on the aquamarine surface of the pool.

Even over their straining air conditioners, neighbors three houses away heard angry voices and the bang of the house door slamming. Debra stamped up the stairs, swearing still. She charged into Lance's office with murder in her heart. Downstairs the door banged again, as Lance followed her inside; he knew her habits.

She'd thrown the finished copy of the manuscript out the window and had begun wrestling the computer into its assorted components, when she saw the day's paper again. The Strangler's Seventh? headline fairly jumped off the page, cutting through her hot, red anger, bringing a shock of realization, and stopping her momentarily, so that Lance arrived in time to save his monitor and his hard drive, though his modem was wrecked and his printer was already upended on the floor.

"This is too much," he said. "I damn well don't have to put up with this, Debby. I really don't."

She looked at him with narrowed eyes. "I suppose your books just happen by magic. You type half a day and, presto, semi-literate verbiage becomes polished copy."

"Editors," Lance said, his voice corrosive, "editors are a dime a dozen. I can afford any editor I want. But can you get yourself another best selling author?"

In that moment, Debra understood everything: him and Gwen and herself. She even had an inkling of what she was going to do next: she had no choice.

The next day she visited the local library. They all knew her there as writer Lance Aken's devoted research assistant. Debra found a table in the periodicals section, picked up the whole summer's worth of papers, and began to read everything that had been written about the Strangler. She started with the earliest account, "Woman found Dead in Sigourney Street Apartment," and continued right up through a pretentious Sunday magazine rumination on the Strangler as a projection of our hidden fears.

What Debra was interested in was the Strangler's MO. Of course, the police would have concealed some crucial detail: she had watched detective shows and understood (really, it was just common sense) that certain things would have been withheld. But she also figured that there would be a margin for error, especially in this heat, especially with the growing panic and paranoia, especially when, yes, the Strangler might, indeed, be the projection of our hidden fears. Debra smiled grimly when she thought of that.

He struck at night. The first killing appeared to have been at dusk, but usually, the victims were surprised late at night or in the early hours of the morning; the hours of birth and death and very suitable, Debra thought. Typically, the Strangler gained access via an unlocked slider or porch door; several apartments had been entered through unlocked windows, and, in one case, the killer entered through the front door, but that was in the early days. No one opened her door now without a careful inspection through the peep hole and a precautionary check-up call to the pertinent utility or repair company. Any late night stranger could expect a woman home alone to call the police.

Once inside, the Strangler throttled his victim with a nylon stocking and ransacked her lingerie drawer. Debra wondered if the Strangler brought a stocking with him or if he trusted to luck. There were lots of other questions. Had he visited the chosen apartment earlier? Did he scout neighborhoods? Were his victims pre-selected or did he operate at random and pick his targets by chance? The police claimed not to know.

What they did know was that the murders were clustered in a semi-circle west of the river and that all the victims were under fifty years of age, single, and living in apartments, condos, or, in two cases, single family houses with access via backyard decks. The Strangler thrived on carelessness, on cheap locks and loose window fittings, on the anonymity of suburban apartment complexes, especially of "garden apartments." Debra smiled again, for they'd been to see Gwen at her apartment in the Sedgwick Elms complex.

At the time, Debra had considered the visit a pain in the ass, a typical example of Lance's weakness for flattering women. Gwen had come by with some books that he had promised to sign. She had the first two Matt Dillard novels, brand new, Debra noticed, and two of his early books, *The Money Changers* and *Blood Beach*, both clearly second hand. She was thorough, Debra saw, and Gwen moved up in her estimation, although Debra was still pleased to be able to tell her that Lance was away on business.

She should have put the books out in the trash, but that was in retrospect. Instead, Lance had come home to sign the title pages with funny remarks, for he was surprisingly witty off the cuff, charming with audiences, quick and amusing. His writing was another matter. Lance Aken prose bogged down unless strictly, strictly edited, and even then, you could scarcely say the novels bubbled. Scarcely.

"Of course we'll bring the books over! No bother. We're out anyway." That was Lance on the phone, being charming, being agreeable. Debra had gone along to make the situation clear to Gwen Romani, who was gushing and clever and had worked in publishing and wished so much that she could afford to work as an editor again.

Debra leaned back in her chair and stared at the holes in the acoustic tile covering the library ceiling. Probably asbestos laden, she thought, and then she tried to remember the exact layout of Gwen's small, neat apartment, and how the intercom buzzer worked. It seemed important to know. Debra remembered geraniums, pink and white, and lots of bookshelves and yet another of Lance's early novels on the coffee table. Where were the doors located? Debra could see the couch and two doors to the right of the hall and straight ahead, visible through a sliding door, the pink and white flowers and a single chair on the minuscule deck.

The Strangler would enter through the deck, approach the couch where Gwen sat reading her newest Lance Aken novel, loop a stocking around her slender neck, and — Debra's hands clenched on the library table and jerked apart. It was very pleasing to imagine this scene and maybe it would happen.

For Gwen, who was so careful about cultivating rich, successful authors, might be careless about other things like her personal safety, like locking her windows. Maybe her beauty would attract the Strangler, and once he was inside, how hard could it be? Debra found herself thinking several times a day about the Strangler and mentally directing him to Gwen's apartment in the Sedgwick Elms complex. If he'd eliminate Gwen Romani, Debra would be quite willing to consider him a public benefactor.

In late July, Lance had speaking engagements in Tulsa, Dallas, and Houston. Debra declined to go. They were still on bad terms and the heat out west was even worse than in the Connecticut Valley. Besides she still had a dozen chapters to edit, and Lance had sense enough not to mention Gwen Romani's editorial talents again. He planned to be away for a week.

The first night he was gone, Debra got into her car right at dusk and drove slowly toward Gwen's neighborhood. She had no plan in mind; she just wanted to see how it would feel to roll down those leafy suburban streets where deep shadows were punctured in every yard by a security spotlight. When she got within two streets of the Sedgwick Elms, she parked and stepped out of the car. Her hair was pulled back with an elastic; she wore a black top and black shorts and running shoes like a serious jogger — and like the Strangler, too, Debra thought, who would, of course, wear black.

Her feet made a steady thump along the sidewalks in the quiet suburban night. She ran back to the boulevard, orange tinged with high intensity lights, noisy with traffic, with motors and stereo systems, the air tainted with gasoline, fries, and pizza. Another corner brought the sudden darkness of heavy street trees and the shadows of the thick screen of pines around the Sedgwick Elms.

Debra could hear voices; the complex had a pool, well lit at night, and a couple tennis courts which echoed with the hollow thock of the rackets, the shouts and laughter of the players. The black clad Strangler would wait until later, until there would be no one to see him glide along the shadow of the hedge and around the utility sheds to the back of the complex where Gwen Romani lived. He would pick out her apartment, he just had to.

When Debra got back to her car, she was damp with sweat, thirsty, and exhilarated. She liked the sound of her own footsteps and the way her shadow surged ahead, dwindled to nothing, then rushed forward again. She liked the glimpses of lighted windows, of other lives, the half-caught sounds of laughter, of agreement, of anger. She hadn't been running after dark because of the Strangler, but that was when she'd seen herself as prey. Now that she'd stepped to the other side, Debra had no reason to feel frightened.

She began to go running every evening, later and later. It was too hot during the day, far too hot, and although these excursions were foolish in several ways, they were irresistible. The fantasy that she was preparing for something, for something which she carefully left unnamed, was almost as good as action.

But though she passed the Sedgwick Elms almost every evening, Debra was unable to get a clear look at the decks and the windows. The day before Lance was scheduled to come home, she went into the office, searched the shelves for his early editions and found three copies of his first novel, *A Dynamite Idea*. *A Dynamite Idea* hadn't done terribly well when it was first published but it was now a collector's item. She wrapped it up and called to see if Gwen was home.

"For your collection," she said, when Gwen opened the door. Debra was dressed in her running clothes. "I was just passing."

"Surely you don't run at night," Gwen exclaimed.

Debra smiled. "It's so hot during the day. You're lucky to have the pool. And your deck."

"The sun is on it until almost four."

"But now," said Debra, moving to the back of the apartment. "Now it must be pleasant. You're up a little, too. I prefer second floor apartments, don't you?" She stood at the sliding door, looking at the catch, at the type of lock. Gwen, the good hostess came over and slid the door open.

"And you have a screen. You can leave it open and get the air."

"Not likely," said Gwen. "Security's lousy here."

"Really?"

"And for what we pay," said Gwen.

Debra made a sympathetic face and checked the height from the ground: the Strangler would manage that easily, she thought. She smiled and agreed with Gwen that most realty management companies were criminal.

Back at home, Debra took a screwdriver and experimented with the catch on their sliding door. The hardware looked to be a better grade than the Sedgwick Elm's but did not prove durable. She stood out on their patio and looked at the sprung latch with considerable contentment.

When Lance returned, Debra stopped her evening runs, but she found herself thinking about dark sidewalks, the thick row of pines along one side of the Sedgwick Elms complex, and the ease with which a jogger blends with the unremarked life of a street. She felt that she had two lives, one in which she was Debra Aken, editor, researcher, agent, a woman who went to Mr. Jose's salon every other week and had her groceries delivered from La Epicerie, and the other, in which she ran the shadowed streets of their suburban town like a maenad, hair flying, eyes wild, possessed by violent, not to be examined, emotions. This latter woman understood the Strangler and breathed his air.

Lance was working hard on the new novel, and Debra was kept busy editing. They said very little about their own situation, united as they were in their desire to get the project done, to meet their deadline, to be finished with *Deadfall*, which Debra, at least, was beginning to find wearying. She sensed the crisis would come when the book was finished, when she'd managed to extract another large advance and another favorable contract. That was when Lance would make his move, and Debra intended to be ready.

She might have continued to bide her time, if she hadn't received the e-mail. Was it a Freudian slip or a calculated gamble which had led Gwen to write daken@aol instead of laken@aol? Debra had opened the message and scanned it perfunctorily before she realized what she was reading. "I wouldn't ordinarily want you to rush a single word," Gwen wrote, "but the sooner you're done, the sooner we'll be together." That was the heart of it; the rest was an unsavory (and rather ungrammatical) mix of sex and sentiment, in which the Gwen expressed herself with more vigor than Debra would have expected. She sat at the machine seething. Should she hit the forward button and send this straight to Lance and let him know that she knew everything? Should she call him in from the yard — he was fond of sitting out by the pool with his laptop — and show him what had come up on her screen?

Once she would have; Debra was fearless where her own interests were concerned. But now she felt the temptation of the night streets, the shadows leaping ahead and racing behind, the security spots piercing the black foliage, the sounds of cars passing, and the rhythmic thock, thock from the tennis courts behind the Sedgwick Elms.

She carefully did not plot any course of action; the future remained unknown, unknowable, and she was content with that. But it was a nervous, alert contentment. Debra knew that she was waiting for something, and that something arrived when Lance announced a trip to New York for a meeting with a programmer who knew a great deal about computer espionage. Matt Dillard needed help to unravel a key problem in *Deadfall*, and Lance said he'd stay overnight and take his friend out for a really good dinner once the plot details were sorted out. Debra said that sounded like an excellent idea.

Her husband took an afternoon train into the city, and Debra changed into her jogging clothes as soon as the sun set in red and smoggy glory. It was full dark by the time she parked her car. No one noticed her running along the sidewalk — faster than normal, all her muscles alert — nor remarked on a woman alone moving quickly through the Sedgwick Elms parking lots and behind the hedge of trimmed pines to the scrap of lawn overlooked by the decks. She stood on the grass until her eyes grew accustomed to the harsh contrasts between the security spots and glowing windows and the shadowed grass and black leaves of the trees. The first floor neighbor was out; the apartment dark. Debra felt her legs tense as if anticipating the effort of stepping up onto the first floor deck, balancing on the rail, and reaching for the floor of the deck above. That's what the Strangler would do, before a brief operation with the screwdriver — which had been bouncing and bruising her leg with every stride — opened the glass slider with a click.

She stepped back and ducked around the hedge. She would take the easier route and hit the buzzer. "I was just passing," she said, when Gwen opened the door. "Out for a run."

Gwen did not look particularly pleased to see her. "You're still running at night!"

"The heat," Debra said.

Gwen stood in the doorway unmoving.

"I thought we might talk," Debra said, and added, "business."

Gwen stepped aside and held the door open. When she turned to snap the dead bolt, Debra reached into the pocket of her black running shorts for the nylon stocking.

* * * *

She was back in her own living room just over an hour later with nothing but a slight scrape from climbing over the railing around Gwen's deck. Debra took the stocking out of her pocket and laid it on the coffee table, her hands trembling a little from excitement. Her legs felt stiff, as if she had run an exceptionally long way. Excitement and fatigue, that was all, which was sort of amazing, considering. She looked at her watch, 10:15, almost exactly an hour since she'd backed the Mercedes out of the garage to change everything: her life, her attitude, her future.

Debra was a little surprised that she didn't feel more than an admittedly unseemly exhilaration, but then she supposed that a good many lies are told about all strong emotions. We imagine what we'll feel at intense moments, based on what we've been told by books and movies. When the real experience comes, we often discover that everything is quite, quite different and that we don't feel anything like what we're supposed to.

Without doubt, what Debra felt was satisfaction, a satisfaction increased by the fact that on some level the events of the evening were the Strangler's doing, not hers. The door locked from the inside, the catch on the slider sprung, the victim's own stocking taken from her emptied lingerie drawer: those were the Strangler's trademarks, his fault.

Debra went into the kitchen and opened a celebratory bottle of white wine and poured herself a glass, which she drank quickly, standing by the sink. The yard beyond was dark; she had not bothered to put on the outside lights, being now, herself, a creature of the darkness. She poured another glass of wine. As she was corking the bottle, she thought she heard a rustle, a click, and walked into the living room but found nothing amiss amongst the handsome lamps, the fine oriental carpet, the matching modern sofas, the quiet purr of the air-conditioning. The rustle must have been one of the shrubs rubbing against a window. The rhodies were getting overgrown and lanky enough, perhaps, to catch a stray breeze, though the night had so far been as still, stagnant, and humid as most that summer.

Back in the kitchen, Debra took another long drink from her wineglass. She was thirsty, as well she might be. She took the cork out of the bottle and topped up her glass. She would drink the whole thing, and it was just too bad she hadn't anything better on hand than this quite mediocre Chablis. Champagne was what she really needed. Champagne and a shower; then she'd better wash her running clothes and her sneakers, too. She carried her drink into the living room, thinking that she'd turn on the shower as soon as the washer filled up. Then she'd lie on her bed, finishing the wine and remembering the night shadows under her running feet and the rush of power she'd felt in Gwen Romani's apartment.

As Debra walked down the hall toward the laundry room, she remembered the stocking, which would also have to be washed. She returned to the living room, but the coffee table was bare. The stocking was gone, and she was struck by the absurdity of that absence. She had carried the stocking home in her pocket and placed it like a trophy on the coffee table. Could it been knocked off? She searched the floor but saw only the red and cream arabesque of the rug.

She felt her pockets, then went into the kitchen and swept her hand along the black granite counters, as if a pale nylon stocking would not be obvious against the stone. She reached for the phone on the counter, then thought better of that. In the excitement, she might have laid the stocking anywhere. Perhaps she had even left it in the car. Perhaps she had simply been mistaken. The car was an idea in any case, she thought, and she stepped into the hall.

But this time, Debra was in no doubt about the sound. It was a rapid step, behind her and to her left, followed immediately by a sudden blow to her throat that took her breath and brought her hands up, clawing in panic. She tried to scream, to protest, to explain that this was all wrong, but she could not get out a sound. So she was able to hear, quite distinctly and clearly, a male voice. It was soft and seductive, surprisingly mild, far milder than hers had been when she had struggled with Gwen. "I've been waiting so long for you," the voice said, "and you even left me a stocking."

MY LIFE IN CRIME

It started the day Billy J showed up at school in a real leather jacket and a pair of Nike Zoom LeBron II's. The leather was class, man, but LeBron II's! The coolest shoes on the planet. I'm not the biggest kid on court, but I got a killer outside shot and I'd sure fly with shoes like those. As I kept telling Mama, all I needed to take my game to the next level was better equipment. But Mama, who wasn't my mom at all but my grandmother, had old fashioned ideas and was all the time telling me that Payless sneaks were good enough if they 'kept the wet off my feet.'

So there I'm dreaming of LeBron II's with the special support straps that would lift my game, when in comes Billy J, fresh from a trip to Sportslocker and the top leather shop in the mall. He's wearing a four hundred dollar bomber jacket and my LeBron II shoes. Mine. Are me and the guys interested? Do we want to know how this could have happened when Billy J's so dumb the corner dealers won't touch him for a runner? Sure we do. Fortunately, Mitch, who lacks the cool and self-restraint that gives me a bigger game than you'd expect from my size, comes right out and asks him.

Billy J, moving and styling like some new born rap star, says, "It's the settlement."

And being that dumb, he tells us the rest, starting with how his cousin knows a guy who knew another guy, plus confusing legal and medical stuff with relatives' contacts we don't need to bother with here. Some of my guys are losing interest before Billy J gets to the point, but I still got one eye on the LeBron II's and I keep my ears open. The deal was pretty simple once Billy J finally spits it out. The night of the accident, his brother Wesley drives the family car along South Main at 8 P.M. "Eight exactly," says Billy J. "No later, no earlier. Super important." He goes on about this til we get the picture.

Anyway, Wesley's on his way to his night shift at McDonald's, and he has his sister Meghan with him, giving her a lift to a friend's house. They're rolling along Main, right at the speed limit, which impressed Billy J, "Cause my brother's a speed king," when "Boom! Bang! Crash!"

Billy J's got minimum verbal, as you can soon tell from talking with him. What's happened is that the guy who knew the other guy who's some far off Billy J relative has come out of a side street and lost his brakes and piled into the back quarter panel of the Billy J family car.

"The bullet car was done professional," says Billy J, like this is some sort of job, a career path like Mr. Dawkins is always going on about, how we need a "career path" to take us from where we are to someplace none of us can imagine. Perhaps I can put out down "bullet car driver" next time.

"They hurt?" I ask.

Billy J gives me a look. It's a scary thing, I tell you, to see a loser like Billy J in fancy gear with a scornful look. "I told you, done professional. Not a mark on them."

"How you get money for that?" asks Kev.

"Whiplash," says Billy J and nods his head. "The doctor said Wes was one bad case and Meghan was almost worse. They've had to have therapy and everything."

"You got to pay for that," says Mitch. "How they get health insurance?"

"Ain't nothing wrong with them," says Billy J. "And the auto insurance pays for everything."

"Sure, you say," says Kev. "I don't think there was an accident. I think you lifted that jacket and run out of the mall."

"No way. You ask my Aunt Bessie. She 'bout hit the roof we didn't add her daughter as a jump in."

"I wouldn't want to jump her daughter," says Kev and everyone laughs.

"A jump in ain't even in the car. Just on the accident report. I'm telling you them insurance companies got the money."

Kev and Mitch weren't impressed, but I could sort of see how it worked. Course you had to have a doctor, and a lawyer was good, too, cause nobody in their right mind would take Wesley Durfen's word for anything with cash involved. Major connections required, and even with the LeBron shoes, I'd probably have forgotten the whole thing, if other guys around hadn't started sporting fancy gear. Then the Ramondis got a hot tub and Hector's dad got his teeth done. Tanya Morris managed a new car and her brother-in-law got a set of tools and started doing cut rate roofing jobs.

Pretty soon everyone at school and around the basketball court is talking settlements and the finer points of rear end crashes. I learn a whole lot about whiplash injuries and back pain and rear quarter panel damage — human and automotive. One night when Mama is complaining about the electric bill and telling me for the millionth time I can't get a cell phone, I come right out and say, "What we need is a settlement."

"We're already next to a housing project," says Mama. "A settlement's more than I need."

The thing with Mama is you're not always sure if she's onto you and making a joke, or if like most folk her age, everything new and big's passed her by.

"I'm talking about an insurance settlement. Like everybody's been getting."

"You're talking about a bunch of no good gangbangers," says Mama.

"Mr. Ventilla's no gangbanger. He got his teeth fixed cause he was in a car accident."

"He gets hurt in an accident, he deserves to get his teeth fixed," says Mama, refusing to see what's right in front of her.

"It wasn't an accident. Hector was in on it, too, and I saw him last month with one of those cool little Kawasakis."

"He'll have a real accident with that," says Mama, which I thought was likely but wouldn't admit. "Then where will he be? Wishing he'd left the damn thing alone."

This is off topic for sure, but that's how Mama talks til you find yourself blocks away from cell phones or a way to tap into insurance. I spell out the details for her about Billy J and the lawyer and New Life Chiropractic, Inc, a little storefront down on River Street that's all of a sudden doing business like Walmart. I'm getting into whiplash and why it's the best injury of all, when Mama cuts me off.

"I don't want to hear another word more now or ever," she says. "We don't have much but we're going to live honest."

She stuck to that, although when she had to cut back her hours cleaning at the motel, we had lots of bean and rice dinners, and I had to put my can money and circular delivery cash into groceries instead of a cell phone or LeBron II's.

"Be up to LeBron III's," says Mama when I complain. "You get yourself a better pair by waiting."

I grouse to Kev and Mitch, but they aren't much better off. Kev's dad's been gone even longer than mine and Mitch's working the Walmart loading dock. "We gotta get ourselves a settlement," says Mitch.

"Mama'd about kill me. She'd tattoo my ass," I says, and 'cause neither Kev nor Mitch has initiative, the settlement stays just so much bull around the court and in the hallways. Then one day Mama's home from the Hampton Inn one day before I get back from school. I open the door and I can tell right then that something's wrong. The apartment feels different, like the air has gone out of it, and it's quiet in a different way, too. Not the quiet of the tv or my boom box waiting to be turned on or the frige opened and a soda cracked. Something else was waiting.

"Who's there?" I call. I'm maybe even a little nervous. You don't always know what you come home to in our neighborhood.

"That you, Davis?" Mama's voice sounds different, like when she took pneumonia three winters ago.

She's lying on the bed in her room looking very white and very old. I never think of Mama as being any particular age except when she's sick. "What happened? You get the flu that's going around?" I'm worried, but I'm also thinking now I can't crank up the boom box and have Mitch and Kev over.

"Maybe. Probably that's it," Mama said. But she doesn't sound convinced. "I've got this pain."

I forget my afternoon plans and start to get worried. When Mama says she hurts, it's something serious.

"Should we go to the ER?" I ask.

She doesn't know. She says yes and then no, and I have a bad feeling about deciding either way. Finally, so I don't have to be the one, I says I'll ask Mrs. Perez. She's our next door neighbor, a little short woman with neat black hair, who has a night shift job in the hospital laundry. By default, she's the medical resource for our block. Mrs. Perez comes in, takes one look at Mama, puts her hand on her forehead, which I hadn't thought to do, and says, "I drive you to the ER."

"I don't want to bother you," says Mama.

"I drive you and Davis stays with you. I gotta be here for Luisa getting home." Luisa's in the elementary and gets home later cause of the bus routes.

So we get into Mrs. Perez's ancient Subaru. Mama looks green and winces every time we hit a pothole. In the ER, we meet Dr. Patel, an intern, who has a round brown face that gets serious when he talks to Mama, and we get a referral to an oncologist, which sounds like a funny specialty but which turns out to be as bad as you can get. It's like Mama says, you think you have worries, then you get real trouble and you realize things weren't so bad before.

Now I got to come home every day after school, pronto, to shop and do the dinner; no hanging around the basketball court, working on my outside shot and my quick moves to the hoop. I gotta consult with Mama on the shopping, of course, because I'm too young to get a regular job and she's had to quit at the motel. "Just for a few months," she says. "Til I get over the surgery."

I don't know about that, but in the meantime, we're living on welfare. Mama scours the coupons and flyers and gets on me to take the bus out to the big supermarket instead of shopping the Jiffy Mart or the Vietnamese market. A trip like that takes up the afternoon, and I usually make it on check day.

Mama has regular visits to the hospital for her chemo, too. I go with her unless its during school time, 'cause Mama's dead set on my staying in school. I have feelings both ways; I feel I should go and make sure she gets there in the old car and has somebody to be with her when there's needles and doctors. On the other hand, I hate the smells of the hospital and the tight feeling in the air like everybody's facing some bad scary thing, which they are, for sure. Things I don't even want to think about too much.

Anyway, Mama gets through the chemo and starts with the radiation. "Do me up like that new meat, doesn't ever go bad," she says, sounding like herself. But in the meantime she can't go back to the Hampton Inn and making beds and cleaning, and she keeps mentioning my Aunt Rita, who lives outside of Jacksonville. Mama keeps saying things like how nice Aunt Rita is and how kind and how she has a boy, Brian, just about my age.

Last thing in the world I want is to go to Jacksonville, Florida and live with Aunt Rita, who I don't know — or her kid, Brian, either. What we need is a settlement and we need one now. We got an old junker of a Ford that Mama used to drive to her work and now takes to the hospital. It's ideal for the purpose, but Mama won't consider it and I'm not old enough for my license.

"She'll never do it," I say to Billy J. I'm so desperate, I've talked to him about the lawyer and the chiropractor and getting the job done professional.

"Up front money for that," says Billy J.

"If I had money I wouldn't need a settlement," I says.

He says he'll think about it, like this is some big favor. I'd about given up hearing anything, when, one day when Mama is feeling ok, and no radiation on the schedule, and the shopping is done, I'm down at the court, missing everything because I'm so out of practice, and this guy comes over. He's skinny with a yellowish face and a thin moustache and he's smoking a green cigar. His waist is so little his pants are all bunched around his belt, and he doesn't look like much except for his arms which are ropey with muscle like he's lifted serious weight.

He watches me for a while, then raises his chin and gestures to show he wants to talk to me. Privately.

I'm not enthusiastic. He's no bigger than I am but he gives off a kind of warning vibe like a video game villain with a pulsing bad aura. I come over to the fence.

"You Davis? Friend of Billy J's?"

I says yeah and there he is: Victor, the guy who makes accidents happen, who has arrangements with lawyers and chiropractors, who can do serious rear quarter panel and axel damage without creating fatalities. He's some kind of foreign, Viet or Thai or maybe some weird Indian-Hispanic. I don't know what I expected a bullet car driver to be like.

But this is it: thin, smelling of cigar smoke, with narrow eyes and a cold stare.

We sit on a bench in the park. He doesn't like it that I can't drive. He doesn't like it that Mama won't cooperate. He's ready to blow off the whole idea, when I mention we just gotta have a settlement cause Mama's a cancer patient, fifth floor, Central Oncology unit. I don't know why I added all that — guess it just made it sound more official, as if there's anything more official than cancer.

He gets interested at that. "Sympathetic victim," he says. Then he asks a lot of questions about what kind of car and when she goes out.

I said for a regular schedule of radiation. And Mama was always, always on time.

"Better if you was driving."

"I'm not old enough."

"Not even for a learner's permit?"

I shook my head.

"I'll think about it," he says. "But we do this, I want 25% — of everything." He reaches out and takes hold of my shirt in a way I don't like, but I know we have no choice. This's our one chance and we have to take it.

Well, I start seeing him around our street and get so I recognize his car — a big heavy Chevy Caprice, practically vintage. More than once I see him parked on a side street near the hospital. Then one day, just before Mama finishes with a round of radiation, the Caprice is idling at the curb as I walk home from school. The passenger side door opens. "Get in," he says. "We gotta set this up." Just like that.

I get in. It's dead simple. Mama's radiation appointments are set at 3 P.M. She's always on West Walnut heading for the hospital lot by 2:45; Mama hates to be late. Victor's in the Caprice on Chapel Street and the accident goes down at that intersection. "Very tricky," he says. "Thirty percent."

"You said twenty-five," I says, but I already sensed there isn't much point in arguing.

"Mid day," he says. "Traffic. Cops. Very tricky."

I can see that. "But nothing'll go wrong," I says, half wishing I was home and had never met him.

"Thirty percent and nothing goes wrong." He smiles and I swear he had pointed teeth.

"When?" I says.

"Today."

I hustle home and get ready to go with Mama. I'm all the time watching the clock, nervous she's going to be late — or worse — early. It's not one of her good days; she sits in the car for a minute, kinda collecting herself. She says radiation softens your brain and she is sometimes forgetful. She looks awful, too, pale in that soft doughy way old people get, which scares me when I let myself think about it. But this is why we need a settlement, so Mama isn't all the time worried about bills and paying the pharmacy, and so I don't have to live with Aunt Rita and her son Brian.

"We gotta go," I says. "You want me to drive?" I don't know if she knows I can, thanks to Kev's older brother who lets us practice with a junker down on the river road.

Mama shakes her head and puts the key in the ignition. "You worried about something?" she says. "You got them big tests coming up at school?"

I wish. "No, nothing's wrong. I just wish your radiation was over and you were all better."

She puts her hand on my knee for a minute, just a minute, but it tells me everything I don't want to know and a few things I need to remember. Then the car pulls away. I look out the window, counting down the streets. I wish this was over. Washington, South Adams, Jefferson; Chapel's next. I gotta be alert, cause Victor's gonna pull out in front of us and swerve and clip the rear on my side. I repeat that to myself a couple of times. I'm thinking how very cool it will be, the crash and all, when suddenly Mama hits the brakes and jerks the wheel so she misses the gray green Caprice that's suddenly filling my window.

Our Fairlane swings into the oncoming traffic; Mama's struggling with the wheel, trying to get us back in the right hand lane. I shout 'cause there's this oncoming delivery truck, and Mama, who's about got no muscle left between the chemo and the radiation, pulls the wheel but can't get it round before the impact. Squealing tires and brakes, shattering glass, twisting metal. Not the crash I'd imagined, not a video game crash, but a shock that unhooks all your bones and wets your jeans and brings blood into your mouth where it sloshes around with your heart.

I realize I'm yelling and moving, but Mama's not. She's leaning over the steering wheel and her car door is caved in. I start struggling to get my seat belt off and unhook hers and I'm starting to pull at her to get her out, when someone yells, "Leave her, leave her. You'll hurt her worse."

I don't know what to do, but I keep talking to her, telling her she'll be all right. There are sirens and a cop comes, and I'm telling him she'll be late for her radiation, Memorial Hospital, Fifth Floor, Oncology Unit. The cop gets on his phone and calls for an ambulance, though we're only two blocks away, and I'm thinking I can walk, we can walk, when the cop comes and puts a blanket around me, though I hadn't realized I was cold, and has me sit down on the sidewalk. That's what a real crash does to you and I guess why they call it a bullet car.

They keep me in the hospital overnight. I keep saying I need to see Mama, but it's the next morning before they take me down to her room, which isn't a real room at all but a glassed in place like a big fish tank full of monitors and machines. This is worse, ten times worse than the oncology waiting room. A doctor's there, not the intern we know, Dr. Patel, nor the gray haired oncologist, but another doctor, a short African with an accent. He says I can talk to her for a minute. Only a minute.

"Mama," I says, taking her hand, "Mama, I'm so sorry."

She opens her eyes and though she squeezes my hand, I can see she's already gone a long way off. I want to tell her about the accident, about the settlement, about the biggest mistake I ever made, but she shakes her head slightly. She has something important to tell me; she opens her mouth, struggles and finally whispers, "Hall closet, your birthday." Then she presses my hand again and closes her eyes.

The doctor puts his hand on my shoulder. Only a minute.

I see Mama several times after that but she doesn't speak again, and I don't feel right telling her anything that would upset her. The day she died, the doctor sat me down the day and said she could not have survived, anyway. Her cancer had metastasized. I knew what that meant from reading the little pamphlets in the oncology waiting room. All the radiation and all the chemo in the world would not have saved her.

A week later, I'm packing to go south, when I remember the hall closet and what was so important that Mama told me that last, instead of anything else. I open the door. There's a rolled up quilt on the floor and underneath it, a shoe box. I know what's inside before I lift the lid, and it makes me feel sick and glad and sad all at once: a pair of Nike Zoom LeBron II's. My size.

I keep them under my bed now and the only time I've ever hit Aunt Rita's boy Brian was when I found him with his feet in them. I feel funny about those shoes. I can't bear the thought of putting them on and playing in them, and at the same time, I can't bear the thought of her saving up for them and giving them to me, and me not using them. So they're in the box and 'bout every night, I lift the lid and push aside the tissue paper and take a look at them. Sometimes that's all I do; sometimes I put them on and even lace them up. Whenever I do, my old life with Mama and Kev and Mitch and Billy J and settlements comes back to me, along with my short life in crime.

LYING

Three days before finals, I'm trying to catch up on stuff I would of read weeks ago if it wasn't for the unreal stress I've been under. It's 1:30 A.M. and I'm falling asleep over Emerson. He's going on the way he does about self reliance and individuality and living your own life and lots of similar ideas that are pretty unreal at the moment, when all of a sudden I read that lying is a 'sort of suicide in the liar,' and before I can stop myself I've run my highlighter over the text so that it glows the vivid yellow of caution lights, safety clothes, and police barricades. Bad things.

I wasn't always so impressed with Emerson or so hung up on lying, but now I have a more than academic interest in whether or not he's right. That's because everything started with a lie, not even a serious one, nothing personal, more like a disguise. "Like a party mask," Bren said, as she stood in the door of my room wearing a t-shirt and cutoffs with her hair wrapped in a towel. She was dying her sandy hair red and some of the brownish dye was dripping down her face like blood.

"You gotta live a little," Bren continued. "You gotta go on Spring Break at least once. I've told you these tickets are dead cheap. I know you've got the money."

That was when we were digging out from under the great northern winter. Snow that started in early November was still piled two and three feet thick on campus, and the walks were ankle deep in slush. The dorm heat hadn't worked right since we came back for spring semester, and when Bren mentioned Florida and the beach, I could almost feel the sunshine.

"I don't know," I said. I was thinking of tuition and next semester's books and of what to tell my parents.

"You deserve a break," Bren said, shifting her long legs impatiently. It's a bit hard to describe Bren, because after all that's happened, I naturally see her differently. If I look back to that afternoon, I see she's tall and rather thin, not pretty, exactly, more interesting looking. Her nose is too big and her face is bony. But she's got terrific hair and big, dark, wild eyes that she paints up with blue and brown eye shadow, and there's something about her, something in the eyes and in the easy, loose jointed way she walks, that really gets men going.

At least, that's what I thought. Now, I'd say it was something else, the edge she carried of irresponsibility and danger. Maybe that's what attracted me to Bren, as well, so that against my better judgment, I agreed to room with her and then to share an apartment with her and then, that day in early March, to part with $119 for a special cut rate, spring break flight to Florida.

"It'll be great," Bren said. "Travel gives you another soul."

"I thought it was language," I said. "I thought it was learning a language that gave you another soul."

Bren laughed. "You just kill me, Jen. Learning a language teaches you a lot of words. Travel's immediate. Mind expanding. You just gotta go with it. You just gotta get into the whole experience."

My idea of travel was to get somewhere equipped with warm water and cool guys. Bren's was somewhat more complicated. She was in favor of the warm water and the guys, all right, but she wasn't kidding about getting another soul. The first thing she said we needed was vacation names. I thought that was a dumb idea, but she brought it up again later, when we were in the plane. Our seat backs were upright and the tray tables closed for the queasy, stomach dropping final approach, when she says, "So what's your vacation name?"

"Nom de vacance" drops into my mind, courtesy of three semesters of French. Maybe Bren was right, all I'd learned was words; or maybe not, cause the idea sounded better in French, where it carries echoes of *nom de guerre* and *nom de plume* that make it seem kind of legitimate. I said to her, "Sabine."

"Sabine," she said in this phony francais accent, "woman of mystery. Sabine What?"

The image of my faithful dictionary came to mind, and I said, "Sabine Garnier."

"Great. And I'm Danielle. Danielle — give me a French surname."

"Belleville," I said.

"Danielle Belleville," she said, excited by the idea and enthusiastic the way she gets. "And we're students from Montreal. We're English majors down to practice the language. How's that?"

"Terrible," I said. I could see embarrassment and misunderstandings, but Bren was going on about what a neat idea this was, and I had difficulty convincing her that there was no way. As we whooshed along the runway, she reluctantly agreed we'd be UMass students.

"Since you're too chicken," Bren said. That was always her way when she was trying to do something crazy: make like it was somebody else's cowardice rather than her own stupidity. I see that now.

By three o'clock, we were on the beach: white sand, bright sun, blue water — not too warm, but pretty nice. Across the road was a strip of motels, interspersed with McDonalds, Taco Bells, and Burger Kings, where seedy little clubs played punk and metal, and souvenir shops sold tacky Spring Break t-shirts and over-priced sun oil. The scene was already packed with guys in college t-shirts and baseball caps, and the smell of beer mixed in with the salt spray and the perfumed sunblock. Bren and me flopped on the sand and gratefully soaked up the rays after five solid months of winter.

When the high rise shadows started fingering across the beach, we hit the Tiki Huts back of our motel, where they were selling draft beer and margueritas. I think somewhere along the line we got a burger, or maybe pizza slices, before we left the brilliantly lit strip for the dark night shore where boom boxes were thumping like electronic thunder and guys were dancing around a little bonfire and couples were making out on the damp sand.

I wound up talking with a guy from Penn who was big on environmental science. I guess I wasn't really cut out for having another soul, especially after beer and margueritas, because I had trouble keeping my name and story straight. Bren was high on the whole thing, though. She was dancing on the sand in her bare feet with her long red hair down around her face, and Penn couldn't take his eyes off her.

I momentarily wondered why she asked me along. Moral support? Company? Not likely. If you'd asked me then, I'd have guessed that it was because I set her off nicely: pleasant, conventional, pretty Jen to complement wild, original, irresistible Bren. Right now, sitting with Emerson, I think it was something else. I think I let her know what ordinary and normal were; I think I maybe helped her find the boundaries, which, otherwise, she wouldn't have recognized.

So that was spring Break: your basic budget saturnalia, party all night and recuperate on the beach come morning. After a couple days, I had burned shoulders, a sour stomach, and a semi-permanent hangover. Bren was flying. She was up all night, slept all morning, swam all afternoon. She was in her element, the permanent party. But though she kept saying that everything was fabulous, I sometimes noticed that her eyes were strange, as if she was reflecting the sea and the night beach. I'd like to know what Emerson would of thought about that.

After four days of excess, I was ready for moderation, but not Bren. We were on the beach this night, about one A.M. I guess, and I said, "I'm wasted. I'm going to bed."

Bren began teasing the way she does when she wants something, and as I started toward the street, she came running after me. "You gotta have a last drink," she said. "A beer with Doug and Pete."

I said that I was already seeing in triplicate, and Doug, disappointed in Bren and hanging with me as compensation, said he was ready to call it a night, too. Doug was a quiet, good looking guy who liked rollerblading and wanted to get into the magazine business.

Bren insisted he really did want a drink, and as she went on about it, laughing and leaning on his shoulder, pally, pally, I could see that he was going to agree. His friend, Pete, short and cheerful in a kind of alcoholic and unfocused way, always wanted a drink: no problem there. We went over and bought a last round of beer.

I knew this was a mistake almost instantly: I could feel my teeth starting to fur and perception becoming uncertain. But though my focal point had been shifted, I somehow made it up to our "efficiency suite," a concrete box no bigger than a dorm room — designed to make students feel at home, Bren said. "Efficiency suites" come equipped with a bath, a fridge, a hotplate, and a balcony. The latter is the chief tourist brochure selling point.

Not too much later, I heard voices on the balcony and then Bren banged at the door because she'd lost her key and had to use the john. I got up, pretty well blind, to let them in, then collapsed again, totaled by that last Bud. I don't remember else anything until Bren woke me.

"Sabine!" I didn't respond. 'Sabine' was a lifetime ago.

"Sabine!" She was shaking my shoulder. No response from me.

"Jen," she tried, and this time I found myself facing a big, dangerous blank.

Bren was about to fill it up. "You gotta help me," she said.

All quiet, but the street lights were on, which meant maybe 3:30, 4 A.M. Maybe 5. I didn't know. I didn't care. My head was throbbing and my burned shoulders itched. "Leave me alone."

"You gotta get up, Jen!"

Bren's voice was remote, but persistent. Also sober and that came through as scary, somehow, because I finally opened my eyes and sat up. What I saw was a guy lying on the floor near the door. It took me a minute to register that I knew him, that I'd seen him before, that it's my sort of friend Doug.

"You gotta help me with him," Bren said.

"What's the matter with him?" But I already knew it was something bad, that it was more than just alcohol.

"He's dead," Bren said.

I can tell you I just freaked out. Death was impossible on general principles; that was the first thing. But I also had in my mind that Doug didn't belong there. That he'd had been on his way to his motel. He'd told me that. And so I'd gone to bed and later I'd opened the door for Bren and someone whose name I couldn't remember but who was not Doug. I knew that much; my problem was that my thoughts were kinda like one of those swirl desserts. I had bits of ideas and images all mixed up, coming together at surprising points and drifting apart in odd, unexpected ways.

I thought that I might be dreaming, that I was in one of those dubious states where you're tempted to things you wouldn't normally do because you're almost — but not quite — sure you're dreaming. That's what I thought, but it didn't stop me from screaming — or trying to, because Bren got her hand over my mouth before I could get out more than a squeak.

"You know it's true," she said. "You can see the blood."

I looked down to see blood smeared on my t-shirt. Some more of it had come off on the sheets. If this was a dream it was a real bad one, and all of a sudden it seemed important to remember the other guy's name, because he was the one who'd come upstairs.

Bren had a different story and she was relentless with it. She and Pete — Pete! That was his name Pete! — were down by the Tiki Huts. He'd passed out, totally hopeless, and she'd come upstairs where she'd found Doug. She knew just what had happened.

"What had happened?" I asked. I didn't understand anything. Rational thought was beyond me.

"You caught him just right. Hey, I don't blame you." Bren put her arm around me. "You know what these guys are like. Spring break, drunk outa their minds. He thought you'd passed out. But you fooled him. You must of picked up the bottle. This one," she said. She jumped off the edge of the bed and brought back a big green glass bottle of Apollinaris water. I watched it like a poisonous snake.

"Bam," she said. "You were absolutely in the right. Hit him in the temple. Bam!" she said again with a kind of contained relish.

I was stunned. Could someone die that way? From a single blow with a bottle? I felt that the universe had made a mistake, that the normal rules had suddenly ceased to apply, that these new rules had never been intended for me.

Bren didn't have any doubts. "Just the same, you're in trouble now," she said, fixing me with her large wild eyes.

"I didn't do it," I said. With the enormity of the thing collapsing on me like a psychic black hole, I couldn't think of anything to do but start to cry.

"Of course, you did it," said Bren, roughly. She gave me a shake. "Or Sabine did it," she said in a softer voice. "Yes, I think we'd better say Sabine did it." She gave a little giggle, the first sign that she might be nervous, too.

"The police," I said. I was incapable of forming the rest of the idea.

"Do you want to be arrested?" Bren thrust the bottle into my hand. "That's it," she said. "That's what killed him."

I dropped it onto the sheets and stumbled off the bed. I wanted to be out of there, back home, safe in my other life, and I was headed for the door when Bren stopped me.

"Don't panic," she said, suddenly calm again. "No one needs to know. I've taken care of you. I've taken care of everything."

And she had. I was amazed then; thinking about it, I'm even more amazed now. We were packed and the bathroom cleared, wet swimsuits stuck in plastic bags, cosmetics tucked away. She'd even emptied the wastebaskets and retrieved our discarded airline tickets, though I didn't find that out until later. "Put on your jeans," she said, "and take off that shirt. The sheet, too. We can't leave anything behind."

"They'll find out," I said. You can probably see I was hardly thinking like a criminal.

"Not if we're careful. If we're careful there's no reason for them to come in here at all."

I didn't believe this. "Anyway, we can't leave Doug," I said. He was lying on the floor wearing a remote expression. He had a little blood around one ear and a little more was smeared into a red moustache. Otherwise, he didn't look greatly changed and yet he was already gone, transformed. The phrase "dead meat" came into my mind and I almost threw up.

"Doug's going to fall," Bren said. "Doug's going to have fallen off the balcony. You need to help me with him."

My disordered imagination presented sudden profane shouts, nosey management, humiliating and dangerous discoveries. "Someone will hear."

"The place is dead," Bren said. She got up and grabbed Doug by the arms. "You gotta help me."

I opened the door and she pulled him out onto the balcony, then I picked up his legs, bare and hairy and ending in dirty sandal clad feet. He was heavy, limp and unconvincing, like an inadequate prop, and we struggled to hoist him onto the rail. We were dripping with sweat in the close, humid night, before we got him balanced the right way and tipped him over. He fell, crashing through the palms, banging a metal table, and overturning a chair, before he hit the cement with a sickening ripe melon thud.

I remember that sound and how it was succeeded by a totally unexpected silence. Bren waited a moment, breathing hard, before she stepped back into our room and said, "Let's get out of here." She picked up the bags, stuck mine in my hand and stuffed the sheet and the bloody t-shirt into a plastic carry bag that she put into her own backpack. There were a few spots of blood on the floor and she pulled off a lot of toilet paper and wiped them up. She washed off the water bottle, too, and stuck it in my pack over my protests. "It'll be hot today; we'll drink it up."

I thought I'd gag.

"Leave nothing," Bren said.

I looked around the room, sure that every atom would betray us.

"Who's to say he was here?" Bren asked. Nobody but Sabine and Danielle. They're both gone now. Say good-bye to them." She giggled again, before grabbing my arm and hustling me out the door.

By the time we got to the bus station, the reality of the whole thing was beginning to sink in. The new reality, that is, where I'd killed a casual acquaintance, putting myself on the run, in disguise, in deep shit. The new reality had a distinctly surreal edge, visible in the greenish lights of the bus terminal, the mists hovering over the swamps and housing developments, and the gray early morning before the sun exploded like a searchlight out of the deep green Atlantic. We got out in Miami and sat exhausted with our packs under a pavilion on the boardwalk and watched ghostly white Caribbean cruise liners returning with festive strings of lights on their superstructures.

Later, we waited out the heat of the afternoon in the shade of the big hotels and bought a cheap dinner, which I couldn't eat, before getting on the bus for the airport. Thirty-six hours after Bren had waked me up to confront disaster, we were back on campus; Danielle and Sabine had never existed and, as Bren said, I'd "lucked out."

That was one way to put it, if you can call stomach cramps, near terminal anxiety, and attacks of terror and guilt luck. I spent three days in bed. When I got up, I haunted the library and the newsstand, checking the out of town newspapers, and for weeks I was on the Net every night, looking at the South Florida newspaper websites and at Wisconsin papers, too, because that's where Doug's hometown was. Even after the story died down, I kept waiting for "new evidence" to develop; for some Hercule Poirot to put together the significance of one missing bed sheet, two girls with *noms de vacance*, and a boy who'd tumbled, perhaps not accidently, over a motel balcony.

During the next year, I changed my mind about what happened three times. I started out feeling innocent, then I was convinced I was guilty, and then, just recently, when I'd almost adjusted to being dangerous, depressed, and depraved, and had sworn off every known alcoholic beverage, I started to have doubts again.

By that time, we were living in our new apartment, the top floor of an old three decker in town. Actually, I moved last summer, because I wanted to get away from Bren and bad memories. She wasn't happy about that. First, she got mad and complained I was ungrateful, and then, when I moved out, she stopped paying rent and got herself evicted and showed up at my door with her wok, her backpack, and her sleeping bag. What she was also carrying, which I could see perfectly well, was a big load of knowledge — and obligation. Innocent or guilty, I'd of waked up in that motel with Doug on the floor and nothing but trouble ahead of me. I owed her and there was nothing I could do but open the door and tell her that the sofa was hers.

Actually, it worked out better than I'd expected. I started some serious study, worked on my denial skills, and pretended I was still a normal student. Bren kept a low profile. Her share of the food budget was always beer, and she was out, two, three nights every week. Most weekends, she simply disappeared, leaving her textbooks untouched in the living room.

Bren's absences kept my anxieties to a manageable level, until she arrived home one day a couple weeks ago all bright and happy. She'd gotten a ticket off some Frequent Flyer miles her brother had accumulated, and she was going to take a little pre-exam break. This was two weeks before finals, when even the party animals were getting reacquainted with their classes. "I need to get away," she said, as if she'd been working non-stop, instead of blowing off the semester. "Away from school. I'm going to New Orleans! Party City, here I come!"

I think it was right then that I began to doubt her version of events. I don't know why but I did. Maybe it was just that disaster had made me more skeptical, so that I saw the nervous edge to Bren's fascination and the way she both attracted and repulsed men. Maybe it was just because, for the first time since we'd come home, I'd seen her excited and careless again, and because her eyes seemed wild and secret and peculiar, the way they'd been on the beach and in those terrible moments when she'd waked me up to disaster.

I didn't say much more than "Have a nice trip," but as soon as she was gone, I started to have questions, and then I started to have ideas. I began to wish I had Pete's address, his last name, a way of checking events. I began to wish I'd believed in myself from the first and called the police and trusted to innocence. And since that was impossible and fear had, at the very least, made me an accessory, I did the next best thing and began to check the New Orleans Times Picayune.

I found the item the day Bren returned : "Visiting Businessman Found Dead in Bourbon Street Hotel." He'd fallen from a sixth story window and police were trying to trace a young woman known only as "Sabine."

The name jumped right off the page to hit me in the stomach. When I got hold of my self, the first thing I remembered was the motel room, with Bren leaning over my bed, saying, "Sabine did it. I think we'd better say Sabine did it."

I sat there in shock, staring at the screen, and I'd just barely gotten breathing again and the story printed out, when I heard Bren rattling open the door and dropping her bags on the kitchen floor. I could be wrong, I told myself; it could be a coincidence, some kind of cosmic error, but I had no time to decide. I snatched the sheet out of the printer and clicked off the website.

"What you doing?" asked Bren. Her eyes were brilliant, dark and intense, and her hair, which she had prudently allowed to return to its non-descript sandy hue, was now a startling white-blonde.

"What's with the hooker hair?" I asked.

Bren laughed and fanned out her pale mane. "Great, huh? New Orleans is for blondes." She pivoted on one foot and did a couple dance steps. Bren, I've got to say, was a brilliant dancer. "So, what's with the Net?"

Right there I was nervous. Bren had tuned out school like it was a foreign language. Now all of a sudden she was interested. I wondered if she'd gotten a glimpse of the Picayune's web page logo, or if she was going to reach over and snatch up the print out lying face down on the desk and ask "what kinda neat stuff is this"?

"American Lit," I said. I was getting better at lying. Much quicker. "Last minute paper. I was looking to see if there was anything new on the Whitman website."

Bren shook her head. "You gotta watch that stuff, Jen. Too much radiation; bad for the cells."

Was this a warning, or just Bren being funny? Maybe you can imagine my state of mind. But she turned away, bored with technology, and headed toward the kitchen. "We got any beer?" she asked. "God, I'm thirsty."

"As always," I said under my breath and realized that she hadn't been completely sober since we got back from Florida. I folded up the print out of the New Orleans story and stuck it into my desk drawer. I've taken it out every day since then and read it over, trying to figure out what Bren's done and what she might do and what I ought to do about both.

My big hope for a while was graduation: I'd graduate and leave school and never see her again. That seemed a reasonable plan, especially since she was going to have to take summer classes and probably another whole semester to get caught up.

But since she's come home, Bren's been going on about how I ought to stay in the area or, better, get an apartment in the city. I'm an English major with a minor in graphic design. I've got computer and layout skills and should be able to get work. The subtext of all this is that Bren will be along for the ride at my expense. This is what she expects; this is what she thinks I owe her.

Behind all this gratitude and obligation, there's a threat of exposure, though Bren still makes like I'm her best friend, like she just can't bear to see me go. What she doesn't know is that since I've stopped feeling guilty, I've got a weapon of my own. In fact, I've got several weapons, courtesy of some extracurricular research on the Web and in the local newspaper files.

The problem is that I may be too chicken to use them, because if I do, what will happen then? Bren's brave — or maybe just reckless — and in either case, she's bigger and stronger than I am. That's why I'm sitting out here on the porch, catching up on Emerson and trying to define Transcendentalism and make sense of the Over Soul: I'm really waiting for Bren.

Two A.M., I hear a car stop. A door slam. Bren's feet on the stair. She's an original, all right, marching to her own drum. Emerson would have approved the premise; I wonder if he'd have approved of her conclusions. Or of mine.

I call through to her. She comes out onto the porch where I've been working. She's been drinking, but I was counting on that. Has she had enough? I've got to decide quickly. I've got to act the way Bren did that night at the motel, decisive with no regrets. I decide. "Want a beer?" I says.

"Sure. Why not?"

I push over a bottle of Sam Adams and the opener, too. I'm well prepared.

Bren notices and gives a funny smile and my heart begins to pound. I am basically not brave. I'm counting on fear to make me reckless. "You're working late," she says.

"Finals," I says, like she's not a student, like this is all news to her.

"You gonna pass?" she asks.

My heart jumps again. It's like she knows, like she understands the real test, the real situation. I gotta be sneaky. I gotta lie. "Probably," I says. I go on for a bit about Emerson, about the difficulty of the essays and the wonderful lines. This is the kinda stuff English majors get to say, and Bren lets me babble, though she gets up and helps herself to another beer to get through it. That's cool; I've laid in a supply. "His writing's great in the details," I says finally, "not so much in the big picture."

"God is in the details," Bren says.

"So physicists say. In literature, I'm not so sure."

"You like the 'big picture,'" she says, "but the 'big picture' is just an accumulation of small stuff."

"Little lies," I said like some kind of Freudian slip.

"Is it?"

"You lied to me," I says then, right out. God that's dumb, but I'm nervous as hell.

"Everybody lies," Bren says. "You lie, too."

"I didn't have anything to do with Doug," I says. "I didn't kill him. I know that now."

"You don't 'know' that," says Bren. "You don't remember anything."

"I know I didn't do it," I says.

She gives a funny, superior little smile; before she ditched school altogether, Bren took a lot of philosophy. For a minute, she looks tempted to go on about 'knowing' and 'knowledge.' But she doesn't. Maybe she's too drunk. That's what I'm hoping. That's my only chance. "Then you should of called the police," she says.

"There's more," I says. "That frat party two years ago."

"No one was killed," she says quickly. "A cigarette fire. They've made them put in smoke detectors. That little fire probably saved lives."

"One was badly burned," I says. "And you were there."

"Was I? And what am I? Bren the Destroyer? Come off it!"

"So, okay, that was an accident. A mysterious accident. What did you know? You were only a sophomore then."

Bren gets up and goes to the kitchen. She comes back with a half empty bottle of vodka and pours some straight into her glass. She doesn't say anything. So I do.

"New Orleans," I says and I slide the Times Picayune story out from under my notebook and hand it to her. "You were in New Orleans. You were on Bourbon Street. He fell out of a window. You used the name 'Sabine.' How could you do that?"

"Sabine's a killer," she says calmly. "You should know that."

The police in Florida," I says, and then I run out of courage.

"You talk to them?"

"I might. I might talk to them."

Bren laughs and tosses her bleached hair. "You don't have the guts."

"I want you out of the apartment; I want you out of my life. I want to graduate and never see you again and never hear the name 'Sabine.'"

She laughs. "Or what?" she says.

"Or I will go to the police. I think I have enough."

"Okay, sure," she says. "Deal." And then she laughs again and says, "But can you trust me?"

It's all a big joke to her; she's laughing again, and I reach down and pick up the phone. With an extra long cord, I've found it just reaches to the jack in the living room.

Bren's surprised. I can see it in her face. I pick up the receiver and she makes a grab for it. I should of known she wouldn't wait; she always decides quickly. As I jerk the phone out of her reach, she lunges across the table and gets caught off balance. I drop the phone and push her with all my strength. When she stumbles back against the porch balustrade, I push her again. With a gasp of fear and surprise, she tumbles over the edge, then gives a terrible cry, which only I can interpret, as she hits the spiked iron fence below.

I stand on the porch with my eyes closed until I can bear to open them. I look down and see a darkness that I know is blood, and the way the fence is bent, and Bren's open, empty eyes still looking my way. Right then I'm back at the motel and she's saying, "Sabine did it," and, in an odd way, I realize that Bren was right. Now I have done it, and though there's no proof of anything else, there's no doubt about this.

BLOOD IN THE WATER

Vern Lanyon had always said that he knew only two things, boats and babes. Though babes had sometimes created trouble, boats had done ok by him. He owned a nice yacht brokerage and a busy Connecticut marina which appreciated in value when the Pequots went shopping for shore front property. Pretty soon Vern had a waterside condo, a really nice Bertram 54 dubbed Lively Lady, a Lexus in his garage, and lots of five figure credit card bills. The rise in his net wealth was so steep that Vern began to think himself rich enough for politics.

His mistake in this happy situation was venturing too far from his base of knowledge. Vern sank more money than he should have in a hedge fund and then some more into a "sure thing" currency speculation. The currency deal got killed when the Thais blocked conversion of the baht in the Asian financial crisis, and the hedge was hit when the market turned bullish against all reason.

One morning Vern woke up to find himself not just overextended and temporarily embarrassed, but in a major cash flow crisis. To put it bluntly, he was broke. That's when he thought of Sandy.

Not that he didn't often think of Sandy, who was a genuine babe: tall, slim, and nicely assembled with beautiful cornsilk hair and brown eyes. Smart girl, too, a legal secretary with a good firm, but a babe just the same. Sandy's hobby was the theater, and seeing her perform planted the idea which blossomed out of Vern's cash flow nightmare.

Wakening to disaster, he remembered the play. The venue was nothing fancy, just a school auditorium with friends, family, senior citizens, and high school drama students corralled to see *The House of Bernado Alba*. Vern, personally, had gone prepared for the worst, but he agreed to attend because he liked Sandy. She was a big girl who looked good in cutoffs and a wind breaker; a woman who belonged up on deck in bright weather with her hair blowing round her face. Vern could almost get romantic about Sandy — or, at least, about the look of Sandy.

So, there he was, being a good guy and swelling the crowd, when she walked on stage: black lace, collar to her chin, skirt to the floor, talking fancy talk as this Spanish spinster, a Spanish virgin, for God's sake. What was astonishing to Vern was that she was completely believable. Completely. She'd become someone else.

He was impressed at the time, but though he recognized an unsuspected talent, that's all he saw. Protected by a good cash flow and a favorable position in the market, Vern had been safe from ideas. When calamity changed that, one thought blew up like a mushroom cloud. At first, of course, he dismissed it, put it aside, recognized the lunacy of it.

But the idea lingered around the edges of his mind, teasing and pestering him with the hope of a solution, until one night he broached the subject to Sandy.

They were at the Oyster House, a marble, mahogany and cell phones bistro with the best clam chowder south of Boston. The Lexus was gone, and the bank owned the co-op, but as long as he had plastic, Vern intended to eat well. "I got a proposition for you," he said.

She made a small, salacious joke and they both laughed.

"Not that kind of proposition."

"Is there any other kind?" she asked. Sandy had acquired the cynical edge romantics get when they're disappointed in love. She'd spent five of her prime years on an affair with a handsome Coast Guard officer who was married with three children.

"This proposition is all business," Vern said.

"I thought this was a date." She pursed her lips and her brown eyes darkened. Sandy was ready to be serious about someone. She wanted a house and a garden and small children. It troubled her sometimes that Vern might be her last really good chance.

"It is, it is a date. An important date." Vern took her hand. Though he'd always believed that Sandy was more attached to him than he was to her, he would have to exert himself now. "Every date with you is important," he said.

She watched him, bright eyed, playful but alert. In his nervous state, Vern was picking up on all sorts of irritating and distracting vibrations. He was going to have to be careful.

"So," she said.

"So, listen, you know my situation at the moment. 'A vulnerable position in the market' is how my broker puts it. Temporary, of course, strictly temporary, but worrisome at this moment, with the way things are between us." He looked at her eyes and hoped that was the right note.

"How are things between us?" Sandy asked. The thing with legal secretaries is that they're inclined to cross the "t's" and dot the "i's," especially ones like Sandy who'd had their hearts in pieces.

"Interesting and becoming serious," Vern said. He thought he could say that safely, suspecting, as he did, that Sandy hadn't quite gotten over the man she used to see. She'd mentioned him one night after a few too many margueritas. Sandy had gone on about how she wanted to make a "fresh start."

Not that Vern had paid much attention. All he remembered was that it had been a heavy, serious affair and that the man was married. A classic babe situation was Vern's diagnosis.

"We're becoming serious, right?" he repeated.

"I'd like to think so," said Sandy. "But I didn't think you were ready to settle down."

The very words, "settle down," iced Vern's stomach. "Sometimes you need a reversal to let you see what's really important," he said. "You know what I mean? You get too many toys, you don't always see the essentials."

Sandy inclined her head in agreement.

"The hell of it is, now that I see what I want in life, I've got this major cash flow problem. Way things are going, I don't look able to settle down, as it were, for another decade."

Sandy took his hand sympathetically. "You're a smart guy," she said, "and I make a good living. Between the two of us . . ."

"Sandy, darling," he kissed her hand. "I couldn't do that to you. I'm under a whole landfill of debt." He described his follies in the market, the horrors of selling short in a rising Dow, and then, when he had discouraged her pretty thoroughly, he presented his idea.

"You see, at this point, I might be worth more dead than alive."

"Vern!"

"Listen, a minute. I've still got Lively Lady — haven't been able to sell her for what I paid for her. If I were, well, say I was to be lost out in the Sound. With the insurance on the boat and my personal life policy — you hear what I'm saying? I'm seeing a kind of nest egg for us." Emphasis on "us." "And risk free. I mean, I wouldn't have to be anywhere near the water. Not if someone convincing was to put the alarm in to the Coast Guard. That's the key, someone convincing. Someone like you who can really act up a storm."

Sandy didn't say anything for moment, but, of course, she knew the legal ramifications. Vern was just beginning to worry when she asked, "Who's the beneficiary?"

"Why you, of course. It would have to be you."

"How new's the policy?"

"I don't have it yet. I didn't think I needed a big insurance policy. I wasn't going to disappear at sea when I had everything going great, was I?"

In his irritation, Vern let his voice rise just a little.

Sandy shook her head with what seemed to be regret. "Too big a coincidence. It's got fraud written all over it."

She didn't seem shocked, just practical. Vern could see the problems, but now that he'd actually voiced the idea, he hated to give it up. Before he could reconsider, he heard himself say, "It would be all right if we were engaged. If we were engaged, the policy would make plenty sense."

"Are we engaged?" she asked.

Vern hesitated for a fraction of a second. He wasn't eager to risk his freedom, but he could see from her eyes that nothing less would do. "I'd like that," he said.

"Do you mean it?"

"Yes, yes, I mean it," said Vern, who thought that he was becoming a pretty good actor, himself.

She smiled then, the big, open smile he liked so much. "Well, all right," she said.

Vern kissed her hand.

"But I'll need a ring. It won't be plausible without a ring."

"We need a major ring!" Vern did enjoy shopping. "We'll hit Lux Bond and Green tomorrow. Maybe a party, too?"

"Yes," she said, then "no. No party. Not if you're going to disappear. I'd feel that I was deceiving my family. You know."

This tenderness of conscience made Vern uneasy. "But they'll have to know. I mean, before we do it."

"Oh, sure. Nearer the time I'll tell them. It's just that it will be hard. You'll disappear and be lost, and they'll feel bad and I'll always have to be pretending. Acting."

"You're such a terrific actress," Vern murmured.

When Sandy shrugged and looked sad, it passed through his mind that he had never met her family, the family who would grieve for his loss. He was marrying a woman unknown in certain essential aspects. But then Vern reminded himself that at this stage, their marriage, itself, was still hypothetical. Once they got hold of the money, things could change, might change, would have to change. "Sure, wait til we get the ring and have everything set." He raised his glass. "To insurance," he said, and immediately thought that he should have said, "To us."

But Sandy smiled. "To the depths of the sea," she replied.

# # #

The next day, Vern began to put his plans in motion. Fortunately, with running a marina and selling yachts, he had acquired useful contacts. Guys who pay cash for fast boats and sail them into the wee hours have esoteric knowledge: like where to get a new identity cheapest and the easiest way to leave the good old U S of A and emerge with a new name and new papers in our friendly big neighbor to the north. Stuff like that.

In the busyness of these preparations, Vern buried the rest of his reservations and scruples. If it worried him once in a while to be relying so much on Sandy, well, he reminded himself that she adored him. Besides, he was going to be a new person, too, with new possibilities, no debts, and a very nice chunk of money. He told himself that he could make this scheme work, absolutely.

When everything was ready, Vern rehearsed the plans with Sandy, who listened without making any comment. When he was done, she remarked, "I've told my mother we're engaged."

"Good," said Vern.

"She was pleased," Sandy said, "after — you know." She meant, of course, the Coast Guard officer, that mysterious married hunk whose name, occupation and identity Vern had forgotten — if he'd ever known them.

"Sure. That's great." Considering her melancholy expression, Vern wondered if Sandy might rethink their marriage, though probably that was wishful thinking. "This will work. Everything will be fine." He took her hand. "And listen, there's a storm front coming in end of the week. Is that perfect?"

Sandy gave a little half smile. "I guess," she said.

The front arrived Thursday right on schedule and, at first, blew up such wind that Vern was worried the Sound would be too rough. It wouldn't do to look suicidal with a million dollar policy at stake. Eight hours later, the storm had begun to track east north east, and the high winds lightened, leaving cloud and rough water behind. Vern called Sandy and alerted his friend Norm, who had a nice little boat shed up on a very small, quiet creek.

This boat shed was the ultimate destination of Lively Lady, and once she was safely moored, Vern took his phony papers and his newly dyed hair and got himself first to Montreal and hence to Quebec City. There he switched on the motel cable and watched a big green and yellow blob devour the east coast.

Some poor sucker in a rain parka was doing a standup on the Rhode Island shore. Rain spotted the camera lens and sluiced down his face as he went on about gale force winds and thirty foot seas. The storm had changed track at the very last minute. Couldn't have been better for Lively Lady's disappearance, thought Vern. Couldn't have been better.

A couple hours later, he tuned in again to the news that a fishing boat out of Nantucket had capsized, a surfer had drowned off Newport, and a private yacht was overdue out of Stonington. The seas were so brutal even the Coast Guard boats were having trouble. It would be no surprise at all if a boat like Lively Lady were lost forever.

This was absolutely perfect, and in his excitement Vern called Sandy early. He let the phone ring twice, hung up, called again, let it ring three times, hung up and waited for her to go to the convenience store pay phone and call him back.

He went through this routine a dozen times over the next three days before he finally got the call. In the meantime, waiting dulled his excitement and sharpened a latent vein of anxiety.

"Vern?" She sounded tired and upset. "Vern?"

"Victor, darling. Please remember not to call me Vern."

A silence. Ominous.

"Is everything okay? We couldn't have asked for more from the storm. A boat can sink in a blow like that and never be found. Perfecto, eh?"

"Ideal." Sandy said, but her voice had a strange, flat, shocked quality as if all the electricity had gone out of the line.

"So what's the problem? Insurance will be in your face, sure, but you've just got to be tough. They're not going to have the ghost of a complaint."

"It's more than that," Sandy said, and Vern could hear tears. "One of the rescue ships got into trouble. They lost a man and another was hurt. I was on the beach that afternoon. I was the one who told them you were out. It's all so bad, Vern."

"Well, shit, Sandy, that's tough, but don't take it personally. I mean they'd have been out, anyway, wouldn't they? It's their job to be out. Fishing boats, windsails, yachts, surfers. I'm sure it wasn't just Lively Lady on the water."

"You didn't see the waves. I told them you were lost and a lot of extra people went out and now everyone's angry," she said. "The police say they're going to look into your finances. They don't really believe-"

"Listen," said Vern firmly, "they're paid to be suspicious."

Silence.

"Of course you're upset. Of course, you are." And thank God for that, Vern thought. Upset was good. Plausible, believable. As long as Sandy didn't go overboard on the guilt thing. "If you weren't upset, it would look pretty funny, wouldn't it?" Vern went on in this vein as the silence got longer and longer. "They can't touch you," he said. "Keep your mouth shut and they can't touch you. There's not the slightest proof. You want us to get married, don't you? You want us to get the money?"

Finally Sandy stopped sniffling and agreed to these propositions. Vern hung up feeling only semi-nervous, but it was late August, four full months, before Sandy called again. By that time, Vern was working at a marina along the St. Lawrence and beginning to worry about getting himself to a warm water port. Then one night the phone rang, and when he lifted the receiver, he heard the sound of traffic in the background. Instantly, he could smell the exhaust from the Clam Shack and diesel fuel and later summer heat on tarmac: the convenience store parking lot, Sandy on the phone, insurance.

"We've done it, haven't we?" asked Vern.

"Yes," said Sandy.

"We've really done it!" he exclaimed and whooped over the line like an Apache. On the other end, Sandy was quiet, but Vern did not notice.

"I need to see you," she said when he had congratulated her, exclaimed about their good fortune, credited his own brilliance. There were things to straighten out, Sandy said, fiscal manipulations and complications, a new account in the Bahamas, other details. She was precise and organized, all business. Vern would be best not to return to the States, certainly not to Connecticut. Especially not by boat. Sandy was very explicit about that. "Don't even think about it," she said.

In his euphoria, all this was minor stuff. "Hey," Vern said, "I've got to take a boat down to Nassau next week, and I'm supposed to pick up another crewman. How about it? A little holiday for you. Fly to Quebec, we sail to the islands. It's an easy trip. Get our cash and we're on our way permanently, baby."

Sandy said something about her job.

"This is a new life," Vern said. "After all that's happened, you need to get away, to make a fresh start. That's what you wanted, isn't it?"

"Yes," said Sandy, but her voice was odd. "Yes, I wanted to make a fresh start." She began to cry.

"I know it's been tough," said Vern. "It's been tough for me, too." He'd been lonely in Quebec, he told her. He couldn't wait to see her.

* * * *

She arrived by plane a week later, thinner and paler than he remembered, her eyes hidden behind sun glasses. She had five thousand dollars in cash with her, which was helpful, and from the way Vern felt himself relax when she stepped through the doors at the gate, he realized he had been half afraid she might not come. She could have cashed that big check and lost his phone number. She could have, but, fortunately, there she was. Gorgeous as ever in a white summer dress and a red jacket, still in love with him, and set to make a fresh start as his wife. Vern put the latter thought aside and swept her into his arms.

There was a moment's awkwardness, then she laughed at his hair — bleached blond — and his full beard and his French sailor's shirt.

"You wouldn't have recognized me, would you?" he asked when he put on the wire rimmed aviator glasses he'd affected.

"Not at first glance," she admitted.

"So there's nothing to worry about. Vern Lanyon's dead, gone and forgotten."

Sandy nodded, agreeable to the death of Vern Lanyon, to the trip, to everything he suggested. Vern felt how foolish he'd been to worry. And really, who wouldn't like the boat, a big, handsome Hatteras, beautifully fitted, that was being run down to its new owner in the islands? Vern had everything prepared in anticipation of her arrival, and they left at dawn the next morning, cruising into the cool, golden light of the seaway. All down the Canadian coast, they slept on board, remaining on the water except to put in for gas and food.

Vern was a touch nervous when they reached the States, but in the mass of late summer yachtsmen, no one gave them a second glance. Just the same, Vern was pleased with his preparations, with the success of his disguise, with the foresight which had obtained papers for Sandy, too. "It's your ultimate role," he joked. "A completely new life."

"For how long?" she asked.

"Long as you like," he said.

"And then take on another life, maybe," she said. "When we're tired of this one."

Vern decided she was teasing and passed the remark off with a smile. But she'd suggested a possibility. Oh, Sandy was fine. Easy to take, good with the boat. There's nothing wrong with Sandy, Vern told himself a couple times a day. Of course, she was quieter than before. She didn't make the little dirty jokes she used to make. And she liked to sit on deck at night, staring at the white wake of the boat.

There were other things, too, if Vern had troubled himself to count them up, like the day they stopped at Cape May, and Sandy disappeared for twelve hours. Just disappeared without even her wallet and seemed surprised when he questioned her, when he was concerned. She'd gone for a walk, she said, and perhaps she had, because Vern saw no sign of Coast Guard boats or police. Only his nervousness had magnified her absence, which was an odd thing, sure, but not quite enough to make a reasonable man worry.

Especially not when they were sliding down the edge of the continent towards a fortune. The days took on a heavier warmth, losing the bright crispness of the north in languid humidity. The sea warmed up enough so that they could swim even out from shore, and they got in the habit of taking a dip every afternoon. Sometimes they saw dolphins and one day, off Ft. Lauderdale, the black fin of a shark.

"Nothing to worry about," Vern said. "They come for blood. Otherwise they're really not that dangerous."

Sandy got out of the water, anyway, and lay sunbathing on deck, her eyes sweeping the water. When he was finished swimming, Vern sat beside her on the warm boards and talked about what he wanted to do, about the kind of boat he'd like to buy, about the possibility of starting a charter business in the islands. "I'm going to stick to what I know from now on."

Sandy was noncommittal. She was already finding the endless, hot, blue and gold days oppressive, and she could not see herself crewing a boat or whipping up meals in a galley kitchen for the paying customers.

"I can't go back," Vern said. "You said so yourself. Not for a few years anyway. Got to get myself established in a new business in my new identity. That's the key."

"And what about me?"

"You've just got a big insurance settlement. What's more natural than that you should invest your money? Buy into a company, say? It just needs to be something I understand like boats. I understand boats just fine."

"I was thinking on a personal level," Sandy said. Her voice was quiet, uninflected. There were disquieting moments when Vern remembered how she'd looked on stage as that vindictive Spanish virgin and sensed that she was now giving a slightly imperfect performance.

He shrugged. "We get married, of course, if that's what you want." That was, Vern thought, the easiest way to divvy up the money.

"Or maybe a different life?" Sandy suggested.

"Sure, maybe a different life. We divide the money, you have a different life if you want."

"Or if you want," said Sandy, and they proceeded to quarrel without really saying what they thought — or maybe without really knowing what was in their minds. They were not, after all, the same people any more.

That night, Sandy sat up on deck in the early dark for a long time. Later, preparing some vegetables in the galley, her knife slipped and she cut her hand. Blood mingled with the cubed carrots and celery, the garlic and tomatoes, and spotted the blond maple counter. Vern grabbed a dish towel. He was wrapping her hand up and putting pressure on the shallow, fast bleeding wound, when he realized that she hadn't made a sound, hadn't moved. She was watching the blood with the detached, concentrated expression of a surveillance camera.

"Hey," said Vern, grabbing her shoulder. "You're not going to faint, are you?"

Sandy's eyes came back into focus. "Sight of blood," she said. "I've never done that before. Ouch, what a stupid thing to do." She gave the old Sandy smile, and Vern got some bandaids and relaxed.

The weather held — Vern thought he had never seen such perfect conditions for cruising — and they reached Freeport on schedule. Sandy was sick of fish and wanted to find a butcher shop. Vern had in mind to do some banking; he wanted to transfer some money, to begin pulling down that big new account, but she said, "Let's wait until we look at some boats, at something big." There was a nervous, enthusiastic note in her voice. "Just like you wanted."

And Vern, knowing that was safest, agreed. He worked around the boat, putting everything in order, while Sandy set off to find a steak. She returned two hours later, hot and tired, with a large package.

"You bought the whole cow?" asked Vern.

"A steak and a surprise," said Sandy, and she packed everything away in the galley refrigerator.

The following day, heading toward Berry Island, they stopped in the Channel to swim. They'd gotten fond of isolation, of the vast blue green open water, of the great depths below. Vern liked to dive straight down as far as breath would take him, then rocket back up on the edge of fear. The water was very clear, and once in a while, they would see the white of a sail or a hull on the edge of the horizon.

Vern shook the brine out of his eyes and looked for Sandy far out from the boat — she was a strong swimmer. He saw only empty water and the gentle roll of the waves. He turned, isolation and a thousand little hints and feelings breeding alarm, to see her starting up the ladder of the boat.

He waved and she called back, "I've taken a cramp."

"Need some help?"

"I'll be fine as soon as I get out of the water." She reached the deck and began massaging her left calf.

Vern ducked under the surface, the sudden cold of the lower water washing away his anxiety. There's nothing wrong with Sandy, he reminded himself, before he struck out for the horizon with his flashy crawl. Vern was fast but not good for any distance. He was ready to turn back when he heard the rumble of the motor, and the pleasant frisson of the deep turned into something else.

He shouted to Sandy, then swam briskly toward the hull. Sandy was standing at the helm in her floppy hat, her eyes hidden by the brim and by her sun glasses. She could be anyone, Vern thought, but he was an optimist, so he called again and waved to the woman who adored him. The boat hung suspended in the emerald water with nothing wrong at all except for the sound of the motor. Vern swam into the shadow of the hull. She had lifted the ladder, but he could perhaps scramble up the side.

"Sandy!"

She looked down at him, her face blank, indifferent, her voice steady and uninflected. "I did for you. And what did it get me?"

Vern was indignant. "It got you well over a million dollars!"

"He was killed," Sandy cried, her voice turning hoarse and strange, a stranger's voice, carrying a stranger's inexplicable passions.

"Who?" demanded Vern. "Who are you talking about?" In his present distress, he had forgotten Sandy's former lover. Vern's only thought was that she'd had a breakdown, taken some sort of fit.

"The only man I ever, ever loved."

"You're going to marry me. I thought you loved me," Vern protested, but Sandy ignored him.

"How was I to know he'd be on that cutter?" A wail of grief and desolation. "How was I to know? Of all the boats, out of all the Coast Guard bases! How was I to guess?"

"Christ, Sandy, you couldn't know," said Vern, who was wondering how any of his was his fault. If she couldn't keep track of what's his name, how was, he, Vern, supposed to? The whole situation was bizarre, nonsensical, and he was tired of treading water. But when he tried to reach the stern, Sandy eased the boat away and brought it around again. Sandy could handle the Hatteras very nicely.

"I wouldn't have done it except for you," she said. "It was not the sort of thing, I'd ever have thought of. The seas were terrible, but I insisted they go, because my fiance was out. My fiance," she added bitterly, "who wants the money and the single life. Don't deny it!"

In the water and beginning to gasp for breath, Vern thought it best to remain silent, though a preference for the bachelor life is hardly a capitol offense.

"They were hit by a huge wave. He was slammed against the rail and hurt and swept overboard."

"No one's fault," Vern gasped. "No one's fault." And then he asked her to let him come aboard. She needed help, he said. She'd had a bad shock, how bad he hadn't realized. He should have realized. She should have told him. But now he knew, and they could work something out.

Sandy shook her head. "I loved him," she said. "I wanted to get away from him, but I loved him. You didn't know I was still seeing him, did you? I was, I was. But after a while all I wanted was to start fresh."

Vern pleaded with her and tried to distract her, as he paddled about. The water felt cool, almost cold, in the shadow of the hull. Above him, Sandy didn't answer; she held her head stiffly as if she was wearing an old fashioned, high collared dress.

At last Vern risked everything. "Listen," he said, "there are yachts passing all the time. When I get picked up, Sandy, and I will get picked up, what will you say?"

In response, she lifted a dark red plastic bag like a lumpy balloon. Before he could cry out, Vern saw the flash of the boat knife. Liquid spurted onto the water, making soft, red fans.

"I'll tell them sharks came while we were swimming," said Sandy. Her voice had gone dead, dead and uninflected, as if Vern was of no concern to her. "I know how to act. I know what to say. I've had practice with a dead fiance."

She threw the plastic bag into the water and put the motor into gear. Vern shouted once, twice. Then he began splashing after her, churning through the wake, exerting all his strength, because, though he'd never catch up, he could already see the fins.

MY FAMOUS RELATIVE

As long as I can remember, my famous relative, Professor Jonken, was an important person in my life. When I was a child, his portrait, placed above the buffet in the dining room, literally loomed overhead, and all the romance archeology has ever held for me was summed up in that image. The great man stood in front of a massive stone work deep in jungle. Feathery sepia colored boughs closed off the sky; the walls, perfect, yet barbaric, stretched high overhead. A serape clad worker stood to one side, leaning on a pickax, his face in shadow, while the professor, himself, wearing a slouch hat, a shirt with lots of pockets, and pants tucked into high boots, held center stage. The camera caught him as he looked up from his notebook. Tall and commanding, with strong features and light eyes, he was a prince in the wilderness, and everything around him breathed mystery and adventure.

How I longed to step into that clearing. To touch the stonework and discover what lay hidden behind the exotic foliage was an almost irresistible desire. Especially after illness damaged my right leg, I cherished the picture as my imaginative escape route. I spent hours dreaming of jungle expeditions and devouring maps and geographies and tales of exploration.

Later, I grew interested in the personality, as well as the adventures, of this intriguing figure, and what I discovered only enhanced his appeal. Intelligent and fearless, Petrus Jonken was further distinguished by the great sorrow of his life, which completed his romantic image in my eyes and won my impressionable heart. As befitted my age, his tragedy was conveyed obliquely at first.

"Poor Uncle Petrus," my mother would say. "He didn't have a very happy life, for all his great discovery." And later, "It was his wife's death. He never got over losing her." And finally, when I was maybe twelve: "She was lost on his third expedition. A great mystery — she disappeared and was never seen again. You can imagine," Mother said. "Not even a grave to visit, unless you consider that whole place a tomb with all its altars and bones and whatnot."

"It must have been dreadful for him!" I was on the verge of tears, so closely had I identified with my gallant relative, whose strength and skill had carried him places that I, with one severely crippled leg, could only dream of.

"Hard? It broke his heart, your great-grandmother said. He was never the same. He worked on, of course. But he was never the same. It's difficult to get over things when there's so many questions."

"What questions?" I asked.

"What had happened to Alice, of course."

I somehow knew better than to point out that was only one question and contented myself with the romance and tragedy of my illustrious great uncle. The magic of his image led me to my profession, and though extensive field work was out of the question, I gained a modest reputation for my skill at interpreting artifacts and for mining neglected museum warehouses for new patterns and insights.

At first, I was scrupulously careful to avoid treading in Uncle Petrus's footsteps, though I must admit that bearing the famous Jonken name didn't hurt my career. I started out in Caribbean archeology then moved over to Mesoamerican pottery. Having achieved a degree of eminence, I was hired by my famous relative's alma mater and found myself, junior but tenured, with access to all his papers and collections.

Even then, a kind of delicacy, part professional and part personal, kept me aloof from these treasures. But as my interests began to converge on his most famous discovery, I was the logical choice when the university decided to mount a major exhibition of Petrus Jonken's life and work.

This was a massive project, because the great Jonken Bequest had never been fully catalogued. Successive generations of students and scholars had explored bits and pieces, producing monographs on the pots and textiles, and on the metal work and the fabulously detailed architectural drawings produced by his expeditions, but no one had tackled the whole, sprawling Edwardian treasure.

Amos Brisco, the energetic museum director, young and recently hired like myself, had plans for a new approach to the material. "Life and work," he told me, his dark features glowing. "We need to convey the passion and excitement of the man. And to make his work accessible."

The museum, I did not need to be told, relied a great deal on student groups.

"Plus — and this may be difficult and why I pushed very hard for your involvement, as I know you're sympathetic — we want to be inclusive. Though Jonken's the very peak of American archeology, he didn't do it all by himself. We want to get a feel for the contributions of the local people."

In my fascination with Uncle Petrus, I had not, to tell the truth, seen the natives as much more than local color, but I understood Amos's point completely. Another scholarly possibility!

"I'm betting Jonken had a number of native informants and collaborators who were more influential over time than the boy who first took him into the ruins," Amos continued, "though he's usually the only name mentioned."

"Jonken's diaries may help out there. I was surprised to find they've hardly been touched."

"Who's had the time until now? But the big NEH grant makes this project a priority, and we'll be able to employ some grad students —"

I nodded my head. We could both envision one or more fascinating dissertations based on the Jonken papers, and we soon found two promising students, Kristen Boisvert and Matthew Dinatale, for the transcriptions. The plan was that I would supervise their work and the cataloguing of the still quite chaotic bequest, while Amos arranged for the displays and explanatory documents and handled the grant money. I offered to begin examining the diaries, myself, to give him a head start, but it was really to satisfy my own curiosity that I found my way into the yellowing pages and copperplate script of Uncle Petrus's records.

These were kept in a high and grandly proportioned storage room constructed to the architectural taste of the last century. The long windows were equipped with yellowing blinds to protect the shelved volumes, while the even more perishable manuscripts and diaries were stored in massive flat files. I can still remember my emotions when I unlocked the first drawer.

I'd come up alone to do the initial inventory, and as the drawer slid open, revealing an assortment of green and buff leather bound books and untidy bundles of photographs and letters, I was returned for a moment to my childhood dining room and the mysterious jungle with my princely relative. There in the Special Collections room, I recovered the sense of mystery and adventure I'd felt as a child whenever I looked at Uncle Petrus's photograph.

Jonken had left two different sets of diaries: the green bound work volumes, meticulous notations of every detail of each expedition's discoveries, with — yes — records for every worker and, more to the point for Amos's exhibition, notations about whoever turned up any significant artifact. One of the students could manage a roster, surely, and perhaps we could coordinate the names with some of the faces in the photographs. This was excellent news already.

I put Kristen onto that, and only two days later, she had the first tentative ID — Hector, mentioned as uncovering an outstanding silver mask, turned up in one of the browning photographs holding just such an artifact. Amos was delighted and snatched the just catalogued photograph to have it enlarged for the exhibition. Very soon we had a growing list of Jonken's local collaborators, and the work diaries were yielding other useful insights.

As there was more than enough material in the green volumes to occupy both graduate students, I reserved the little personal diaries for myself. I was naturally anxious to learn about the man who had played such a large role in my life, and I wasn't disappointed. Reading his accounts, admiring his vigorous and exact style, wondering at the omnipresent reports of fever, I knew I hadn't been wrong to see him as one of the warriors of archeology.

Nothing deterred him, not floods, not sickness, not disease-bearing insects, venomous snakes nor hunger; not difficulties with workers nor backbreaking labor. Through every hardship, he displayed an exuberance, a joy, in archeology, first, and then in all the flora and fauna of the jungle. Here was a man who had been born for discovery and adventure and who was alert to everything in his environment.

Including his collaborators. I found especially enthusiastic references to Henry Devolt, one of his students, and, in affectionate tones that surprised me just a little, to Jose Antonio and Ernesto, two of his long time local contacts. The latter, especially, seemed to have been not just an employee, but a confidante, a friend. When I passed their names on to Kristen, she nodded her head.

"Jose Antonio is mentioned dozens of times in the records. He seems to have had a gift for knowing what was important. It's nice to know Jonken appreciated him." Kristen took out the steadily growing folder of catalogued photographs. "We don't know for certain," she said, pointing to a slim figure posing beside a possible observatory building with slit windows, "but we are pretty sure this is him. There are references to his helping with the preliminary surveying of this site."

Jose Antonio looked familiar, somehow, the jaunty angle of his sombrero, the elegance of his serape, something distinctive about his sandals. As soon as we finished our meeting, I went into my office and consulted the walnut framed photograph that I had transported from our old dining room. There was Petrus Jonken, the Prince of the Wilderness, and the man on the other side of the stone work was Jose Antonio. I took out a magnifying glass. He was a mestizo, whose sharp features were at once exotic and familiar to one who had studied the artifacts of his ancestors.

Knowing his name changed the balance of the image, and I began to read the diaries with a greater alertness for the other personalities. I had seen my famous relative as alone, virtually, in the wilderness. Now I saw him as the leader of a small community, a little masculine fraternity, that worked through sweltering days and relaxed at night around campfires, swapping stories and information — and, in his case, dreaming always of the discoveries which might move him closer to his goal, the location of the great city he was convinced was lost in the jungle.

Jonken returned, thin and ill, from the first expedition, but no sooner had he recovered than the jungle exerted its fascination. It was painful to read some of his New England entries, where despite a prestigious post and an affectionate family, he was restless and almost desperate to return south. The second expedition, the one that came tantalizingly close to his goal, ended only when he had to return to raise money for continuing the work.

Jonken's financial struggles were clearly of historic importance, but I thought those might be left to Amos with his keen appreciation of the rigors of fund raising. The third expedition was my real interest, the one when Jonken returned with the young wife who vanished in a dangerous paradise and darkened his life.

I must confess I approached the records of the third expedition with some unscholarly preconceptions. Uncle Petrus's romance had been the story of my childhood, and I expected the diaries to follow the script: a young couple, much in love and enthralled by the romance of a lost civilization, enjoy a idyllic adventure cut short by her tragic disappearance.

Except for Alice's loss, nothing in the diaries was quite as I'd expected. Of course, the bride was prominent during the trip down from New York. Petrus records "tutoring" her in the basics of archeology and drilling her on Spanish verbs and the essential vocabulary of the aboriginal language — not my idea of a honeymoon. I began to suspect that for all his courage and charm my famous relative had been a pedant.

Once they reached the jungle, Alice dwindled into invisibility, with the diary again dominated by references to the sites and artifacts and his native informants. More than half way through the records of the fatal expedition, I couldn't help contrasting the amount of ink devoted to Ernesto with the few references to Alice — and not very tender ones, at that. She suffered a fever, she complained of illness, she disliked the heat, while the sounds of the jungle night, which Petrus had missed so passionately up north, grated on her nerves.

Alice was clearly not a wilderness person, and I couldn't help wondering if I would have shared her reactions. Twice Petrus records sending her with Jose Antonio back to the nearest city for supplies, trips, arduous in themselves, which reassured her that she was not entirely stranded.

Meanwhile, Ernesto remained prominent, though I could not determine his official role. He did not turn up in the daily work records that Kristen was compiling, nor did he make any discoveries or find any artifacts that might account for his substantial weekly stipend. His only function appeared to be to encourage Petrus's conviction that they were near some great ceremonial center. Only late in the third diary, when I discovered a reference to his absence, an absence which apparently upset Petrus, did I learn Ernesto's profession. He was away, Petrus wrote, to conduct a highly important religious ceremonial.

"Does that mean he was a priest?" Kristen asked, when I showed her the passage.

"I don't think so, not a Catholic priest, anyway. Then he'd have been Father Ernesto. No, I think this is the old, pagan religion. There are still pockets today and, of course, a good deal was grafted onto Catholicism."

"The reason he might have known about interesting ruins," Kristen suggested.

I nodded. "All records agree, though, that a young boy guided them in at last."

"Ernesto might have been elderly," Kristen said, "or handicapped in some way." She spoke quickly as if I might be offended. I wasn't; I scarcely thought of my limp.

"Are there any pictures of such a person?"

"We haven't found anything yet, but not all the natives approved of photography."

I had known, but not considered, that, remembering as I did, the striking photograph of the handsome man I now knew was Jose Antonio. A priest, a believer in the old ways, would more than likely have been suspicious of modern devices — and archeological digs as well. Yet Ernesto consistently encouraged Petrus in what a good many people, both locally and back in New England, considered a delusion and an obsession.

Theirs was a curious relationship, but questions about Ernesto were soon lost in the greater mystery. On the morning of November 9th, the diary notes that Jose Antonio had not appeared for work — atypical behavior from the records Kristen was examining — and then, apparently that evening, Alice was discovered missing. Petrus wrote, "A terrible thing has happened." A single line; no details. I can't say how odd and disquieting I found his brevity.

The next day, Ernesto was consulted, and they formed a search party. The diary records the various distances and directions of their searches, which even included a short trip downriver, all without success. A week later, Petrus journeyed to the nearest telegraph post to send the sad news back to Alice's family.

The diary gives this account in a terse and straightforward style, as if Petrus had lost his emotional nuance and grasp of colorful detail along with his wife. Indeed, the diaries, and his literary style, never quite recover. There is only one entry that I feel speaks from the heart, and that comes much later, long after the great breakthrough discovery: "There are devils here and I have made my bargain with them. God, how I regret this hellish business."

Coming as it did from a man who had hitherto regarded the jungle, despite all its discomforts and dangers, as the outskirts of paradise, this gave me a bad feeling. By then, however, we were deeply involved with the exhibition. Constrained by the terms of our grant, we were all run off our feet, and when Matt came to me with news of an anomalous skeleton, I only went down for a quick and distracted look.

I saw four dusty skeletons inside the large wooden crate, three of them curled up as if they had died in their sleep. They had been shipped north with their modest grave goods — archeologists of that era having few scruples about tomb robbing — and I guessed the corpses had been workers in the great city.

"There's a photo," said Matt. I'm sure these three are the same grouping.

As far as I could determine, he was right, except for the presence of a fourth body, lying supine, with a damaged breastbone and some broken ribs.

"Jonken or one of the shippers could have made a mistake," I said.

Matt shrugged. The crate was numbered, the photo corresponded. To tell the truth, both of us felt there was something not quite right about the skeleton, slightly lighter in color, and both longer and narrower than typical of people who live at altitude. But Amos had been after us for burial material and here it was. Knowing only too well how carelessly the Jonken Bequest had been treated and how downright chaotic some of the storage rooms were, I made a command decision.

"We'll take this one out," I said. "Someone must have stuck it in the box after the fact. I suspect it's from a whole other collection."

If Matt had any reservations, he suppressed them. "This group will be ideal for the exhibition."

"Ideal," I agreed, but just to salve my scholarly conscience, I had him box up the rogue remains and put them on the top shelf in my office. "When I get a minute, I'll see if I can find where it belongs."

Meanwhile, I plowed on with the diaries, without uncovering the secret of Alice Jonken's disappearance. By the time I'd skimmed the later books, I felt further than ever from understanding Petrus. But there was so much to do that I found little time for pondering my famous relative's enigmatic personality. Our exhibit was ambitious, and the catalogue, extensive. If Matt and I felt a trifle guilty about our description of the burial exhibit, we put our doubts aside, and, on the whole, the exhibition turned out to be a model of its kind and modestly groundbreaking.

Before the opening, I did make an attempt to locate some of Alice Jonken's relatives, but the American branch had been recently extinguished with the death of a elderly second cousin. I saw no need to pursue the matter further. That left me, I believed, the only descendant of any exhibition notable.

I was wrong. About a month after the opening, and two months after selected material had been put up on the museum's website, a Dr. Fuentes stopped in at my office. A handsome, dark haired, sharp featured man perhaps a decade my senior, he had courtly, old fashioned manners. He had already visited Dr. Brisco, he said, to congratulate him on "this admirable exhibition" but he especially wanted to meet and congratulate me.

As I thanked him, I noticed his eyes strayed to the framed picture behind my desk. To tell the truth, Uncle Petrus's enigmatic personality had given me mixed feelings about the photograph, but it had been so long a part of my life that I felt as uneasy moving it as keeping it in place.

"The source of the very handsome poster image," Dr. Fuentes remarked.

I took a rolled up copy from my desk drawer — the poster had been a popular souvenir. "You might like one," I said. "The photo enlarged very well, thanks to the graphics department."

"Thank you. This is one of the best photographs of my grandfather as a young man."

"He was Jose Antonio? I thought there was something familiar about you. You know, this photo determined my profession. In a sense, I grew up with your grandfather and my great-uncle."

"Though you never met your Uncle Petrus, I do not think?"

I shook my head. "But your grandfather. I am so glad he survived. His disappearance —"

"Disappearance?"

"From the expedition site. The same day, if I'm reading the diary right, that Alice Jonken vanished."

"Might we sit down?" Dr. Fuentes asked.

"Oh, please. Would you like some coffee or tea?"

He settled on coffee. The department secretary rustled up some cookies and brought in everything with matching cups on an elegant tray. I could scarcely conceal my surprise, but Connie has a keen sense of occasion and she wasn't wrong about this one either.

"I noticed the diaries were included in the exhibition. It was very gratifying to see so many of Jonken's workers and informants recognized at last."

I told Fuentes that he must give Dr. Brisco most of the credit. "His ideas won us the grant."

"But the diaries?"

"That was mostly me — and Kristen Boisvert. She plans to do her dissertation on Jonken and his collaborators. She will be thrilled to meet you."

"It will be my pleasure. Our department at the Universitidad is a direct result of my grandfather's apprenticeship with your great-uncle. And now we two sit here with puzzles and questions, yes?"

"Yes," I said — and suddenly understood why he had come. In spite of years of archeological study and the cultivation of scholarly detachment, my heart stuttered. "Why did he leave so suddenly," I asked, "when he was so gifted and so interested?"

Fuentes had the answer for that. "And what happened to her, when she was so young and full of life?"

"It was the same day, wasn't it?"

He nodded. "My grandfather was literate. Your doctoral candidate will discover his family was of modest means, not poor by the standards of the time. He had prospects."

"He has a certain elegance in the photograph, I've always thought."

"You are perceptive. Unlike the others, he was not in desperate need of the work. When his situation no longer pleased him, he was free to leave."

"Alice Jonken was a wealthy young woman. She did not enjoy the jungle and I do not think she was as entranced with archeology — and maybe with Petrus — as she'd expected to be."

Dr. Fuentes raised his eye brows.

"The diaries, which are very lively and detailed — at least until her disappearance — mention her only infrequently."

We sat quietly for a moment, each thinking our own thoughts, and glancing, almost involuntarily, at the photograph over my desk. After a moment, Fuentes unrolled the poster I had given him. "I was struck," he said, "by the shadows. Perhaps they have been distorted in retouching."

In the enlargement, it did seem that the shadow of the photographer was more prominent.

"My thought," he said, "is that while this was labeled as a picture of your great uncle with worker (until your fine exhibition, of course) the photographer, was actually looking at my grandfather. What do you think?"

I compared the poster with the photograph. Once this detail had been pointed out, I had to agree. The shadow of the camera and the photographer indicated a subtle inclination toward Jose Antonio. "That might account for Jonken's questioning expression," I said. "Of course, we cannot be sure Alice took this particular photo — although she did take some."

We sat silent again for a moment. It was a painfully awkward situation, as each of us had suspicions it seemed impolite to raise.

Finally Fuentes said, "My grandfather was supposed to take Alice downriver that day."

"He had taken her to the nearest city several times," I said.

My visitor looked surprised.

"It's in the diaries. I have the transcriptions if you would like to read —"

"That actually strengthens his story. We thought perhaps a romantic interest, although he never said that. It was clear, however, that they were friends. On the day he waited for her, but she never showed up, and he left."

"But why didn't he return to the campsite and help in the search?" I could not conceal an accusatory note.

"He never intended to return. He was leaving for good. He said that he was frightened by Ernesto."

"Ernesto? A much older man, is that right?"

"Yes. What the people called a *brujo* — a sorcerer. You rightly identified him as a priest of the old religion."

"Your grandfather believed in his powers?"

"He believed in Ernesto's power over Petrus Jonken. If there was trouble between the young Jonkens, you can be sure it was because of that man."

That was something I hadn't consciously articulated, but I felt it was true. "He encouraged Petrus about the city — and he turned out to be right."

"My grandfather was sure Ernesto knew all along where the ruins were. He just wasn't willing to tell."

"What changed his mind?"

"I was hoping you knew that. I think he was waiting for something, perhaps something that would excuse, or exorcise, the guilt of bringing a foreigner to the sacred site."

"What would that something be?" My voice sounded small as if I'd lost the air under my diaphragm.

"Some sacrifice," Fuentes suggested. "As in the old days."

There was another long silence. I waited until I could no longer resist the idea which must first have insinuated itself on the day Matt called me downstairs. "Are you good on bones?" I asked, and when he said he was, I told him there was an anomaly in the collection.

We took the box down to the laboratory. As we opened it, I smelled the dust and the faint earthy scent of old bone.

"There," I said, "you can see the length of the leg and arm bones."

The body was damaged, too, the breastbone, split, and the ribs, broken. Matt and I had believed — or pretended to believe — that was shipping damage, but in the clear white light of the lab, I was unconvinced.

Fuentes pulled on gloves and began to examine the bones, handling them with care, even tenderness. On the way downstairs he told me that he'd done volunteer forensic work in both Guatemala and Bosnia. I did not want to imagine what he had seen or the immense catalogue of suffering he had amassed. I, personally, have a fearful imagination, which, doubtless, will keep me from doing anything of great significance.

Now and then Dr. Fuentes gave a soft grunt, but he did not speak until he had completed his examination and was completely sure in his own mind about the conclusions.

"We would have to do carbon dating to be sure, but I believe this to be a modern skeleton — it's certainly nowhere near as old as the rest of the bones. She was in her early twenties, a well nourished woman who had never done hard manual labor. The teeth are excellent, only two missing. Caucasian. My guess would be she was of Scandinavian extraction."

My heart skipped a beat. Alice Jonken's maiden name was Grieg. "Do you know how she died?" I asked.

"She was strangled."

I was astonished. "You can tell that?"

"One of the easiest deaths to spot. See here, damage to the thyroid cartilage and here, this little bone? That's the hyoid bone. A broken hyoid bone is the defining sign of manual strangulation."

"That couldn't have happened in shipping?"

Dr. Fuentes gave me a sympathetic look but shook his head. "The bone, maybe," he said, "but the damage to the cartilage cannot be accidental."

"But then the skeleton was surely crushed in transit?

He shook his head. "The mutilation was post-mortem, thankfully. Most unusual."

I felt sick, and to keep down nausea, I kept talking. "When I saw that damage, I thought we had been wrong. I mean, wrong about the bones not belonging." Thank God we had not put them in the exhibition! Amos, a non-specialist with an eye for publicity, would certainly have been tempted.

"You were right to wonder, but take a look."

He handed me a magnifying glass and directed my attention to the deep and irregular scratches on the split breastbone.

"Messy," I said, but I was thinking of Uncle Petrus and trying to bring the Prince of the Wilderness into some relationship with the mutilation before me.

"Done with a stone knife. No, no," he replied to my question, "modern steel knives give quite a different cut. This was an obsidian blade, probably. Obsidian can be made razor sharp, but the flaking leaves it jagged."

"Human hearts for the sun god," I said, half to myself. "The gods were fed on blood; without blood the world would end."

"A common belief these days as well." Dr. Fuentes spoke sadly, and I thought that he had reason to know.

"She was murdered as a sacrifice? As the price of the city?" And Uncle Petrus, my archeological prince, had perhaps paid…

"Remember that whoever strangled her may not have made these marks. We cannot go beyond the information of the body. And we have no positive ID for the bones."

"If the skeleton really came from the expedition," I said, "who could it be but Alice Jonken?"

He had no answer for that.

"One of the three killed her," I said. "And Ernesto —" I couldn't finish and ran to vomit in the laboratory sink.

"If there is no proof," Fuentes said carefully when I'd recovered myself, "It is as easy to do harm as good."

I agreed that it would be a great scandal — even a century later.

We did carbon dating on the bones to confirm the age, but neither Dr. Fuentes nor I felt that we were required to go further. I had a quiet word with the provost who found a spot for the bones in an obscure mausoleum owned by the university, and over the strenuous objections of some of my colleagues, I arranged to repatriate the majority of bones in the Jonken Bequest. It didn't seem right to treat them differently.

I've gone back to my specialty, collections and archives, and constructed a little scenario, entirely without proof except for the photograph. I've had it enlarged again, in segments this time. I really think Fuentes is right. Alice did take the picture. At another order of magnification, you can see her long hair, distorted, true, but unmistakable in the cast shadow.

Maybe José Antonio strangled her, a crime of thwarted passion, but he was a slight, short man, while Jonken was tall and strong. Regretfully, I'm betting on Uncle Petrus with his cold, bright, questioning glance. I think he's asking if she's leaving — and taking her funds with her — or if she's fallen in love with his handsome archeological apprentice. I think maybe Fuentes' grandfather gave him an edited version of their story. There's something else, too, that would never stand up, but which gives me the chills every time I look at the enlargements. I think the camera caught Ernesto, as well.

You need to get the image up to the highest magnification possible and then the clever technician has to manipulate Photoshop like the wizard he is, tinting, sharpening, adding pixels like fairy dust: and presto! there's an old man, crouching out of sight, huddling, I believe, from the lens. He's visible there in the deep shadows and he's holding something. I see a line of reflected light, and, though the graphics maven is uncertain, I'm sure it's a knife.

So there they all are, all the actors in place and the only question is how they got themselves arranged. Who was guilty of her killing, I do not know, but from that one *cri de coeur* in the diaries, Uncle Petrus must have discovered and been horrified at her mutilation. I am convinced that he stowed the bones years later in one of the crates destined for the Jonken Bequest.

Why did he do that? Guilt or remorse or a slyness almost beyond imagining? Maybe like Ernesto, he had a sense of ceremony, a concept of what was due to old ways. In any case, sure the skeleton was Alice, who had funded Jonken's glory and darkened his life, I had the provost promise they would read the burial service for the bones. It was the least I could do for her.

Someone will find out eventually, I'm sure of that. Someone like me, who trolls the storerooms and pokes into old papers, will come up with the right questions. But the evidence lies safe in the ancient cemetery next to the Green, just a stone's throw from where my famous relative came to rest. I'm not exactly proud of what I've done, but I owe Uncle Petrus such a lot, and concealing evidence does not seem so very bad in this case. But that is the most I'll do for him. After this, he and his papers and his bones are on their own.

PERFECTION

Even if she had passed the point of absolute perfection, Eric thought that Vanessa was still beautiful. Some women are beautiful into old age: the dying Izak Dinesen's skull remained splendid, and Lillian Gish had transformed a soulful childish prettiness into an almost equally lovely and ethereal maturity. But Vanessa, would her beauty last? That was a question of some moment with Eric, and, though he wasn't sure, he thought not. Vanessa's prime had been early and spectacular: she had been the most delicious, the most perfect, ingenue ever. Even now, some of her early films could bring him to tears, like the moment in *Melody in D* when she begins playing "The Moonlight Sonata" for her dying teacher. Vanessa had learned enough of the piece so that her hands could be filmed, and Eric remembered the difficult rehearsals, the tears, the thousand adjustments of sound and light. But when he watched the film, all that was forgotten. What lived were Vanessa's rapt concentration and her dreamy, smiling expression, accompanied so beautifully by Beethoven's repeated figures.

Or *Last Dance*, her debut film. The clothes were ridiculous now, all those baggy slacks and blazers and limp print dresses, and the trendy plot was sadly mildewed. Eric had had a hand in the rewrites, and even he couldn't say that he'd improved it. But Vanessa! Amazing! Even there, still a little too plump, hair overdone, stuck in a tertiary female role, that was her, not Vanessa Wagner, the aspiring young actress, but Vanessa, a personality destined to be a first magnitude star. Eric hadn't known that on the set. He'd spent most of his time trying to straighten out the plot and generating new dialogue for its overpaid and under-disciplined stars. One night he'd had a glimmer when he caught the rushes for her scene, but he hadn't really understood until the film came out. Then the whole world knew. Vanessa was one of the deities, invisible to the human eye, but instantly recognized by the god of their profession, the camera.

What followed was a string of hits both artistic and commercial: Bordighera, a big Italian co-production; *Blood Moon*, a spectacular thriller; *Illegal Separation*, a comedy, not Eric's personal favorite, but her all-time money maker, and its sequel, *My First Husband*. Oh, there were joys in each, little moments, gestures, expressions, turns of phrase so perfect he sometimes wanted to shout at the screen, "Stop there! Not another word! Nothing more is required."

As for the important dramatic works, *Melody in D*, *The Undelivered*, and *Lion Spring*, Eric believed he could live in any one of them very happily. If he could step into the golden savannah of Lion Spring, or the rehearsal halls of Melody, or even the bleak hospital ward of *The*

Undelivered, he would have reached the outskirts of paradise. Vanessa's perfection was his delight, and he would have it there forever.

Of course, his darling had her faults — even on screen. Eric was not so besotted as to be absolutely uncritical. Quite the contrary. He had for years functioned as her artistic conscience — and as her coach, too, for Vanessa was dreadful at learning lines. More than a few of her scenes had to go out as shot, not as written. In fact, she wasn't a particularly well trained actress. She'd had the usual classes and some drama school, but her art was basically intuitive, and she had no head for analysis. Characterizations either came to her quickly and easily or they were destined to be stillborn.

Eric had understood that almost at once, and that awareness had made him invaluable to her. His role, as it developed, began with sorting through masses of scripts and proposals. He eliminated the chaff and then listened while she read scenes aloud from the rest, always alert for the hesitations and awkwardness which sent up warning flags, or, happier, for the sudden rich modulations in her voice that signalled inspiration. What a joy it always was to see her jump up and move around the room, script in hand, to see another person, not supplant her, but modulate her, for Vanessa was a star, and all her characterizations were simply facets of her screen personality.

Gradually, their on-screen and off-screen lives merged into what the tabloid press liked to call a "power partnership." Eric tailored material for her, and, with it, Vanessa earned fortunes, which he prudently reinvested in the rights to promising novels and screenplays. All of this managing, investing, and adapting reduced Eric's own writing, but there could be no complaint about the results, either financial, artistic, or indeed, personal. They were a happy, as well as a glamorous, couple.

This is not to say that the marriage was perfect — how could that be imagined? Eric was quite aware that his wife had personal, as opposed to theatrical, weaknesses, weaknesses both venial and serious — or, better, for he liked the old Catholic classifications — mortal. This, he thought, was as good a time as any to sum them up. Under the venial sins, he listed a love of praise, possibly inseparable from her profession, a tendency to drink too much when things were going badly, and the habit of taking lovers from among her leading men.

Another husband might have regarded the latter as a serious, even a mortal flaw, but Eric was complacent. As part of her fantasy screen life, Vanessa's loves were inseparable from that larger, more important existence. Then, too, her lovers were always either demi-gods of the screen or rising and charismatic newcomers. Pleased with her exquisite aesthetic and theatrical taste, Eric regarded her romances as mere peccadillos.

But there was a more serious failing in his darling, and Eric's face, very handsome still if increasingly fleshy, underwent a subtle rearrangement at the thought. This was her newly acquired passion for "growth" — as if a great star were a plant rather than a constellation, which must remain in remote, unchanging perfection. The fact was that, quite suddenly, Vanessa had changed. She had decided she wished to act. She felt she needed to study; she aimed to undertake abstruse, challenging works that Eric foresaw would lose her audience. She even talked about going on stage, which showed, he thought, just how bad her judgment could be. In the theater, she would be just another actress, not so young any more, prettier than most but less talented than many. She didn't seem to understand that her real gifts existed only in a delicate symbiosis with the camera or to suspect that they were ultimately untranslatable. Vanessa Wagner was an attractive person of moderate talent; Vanessa, the bankable star beloved by millions, was not only the creature, but the creation, of the screen.

This was somewhat delicate to explain to his darling, particularly when she was in a nervous or a headstrong mood.

"I'm tired of being an idol," she said, quite unconscious, Eric noticed, of the arrogance. "I'm sick of staring at the camera and letting my eyes tear. I'm too old for this."

Eric protested. Her last stills were ravishing and with the lighting in *Demon Lover* —

"Any lower lights," she said, "and they wouldn't have known who was who. Don't think I don't know why."

"That's nonsense," Eric said. "A few lines around the eyes — Darling, those can be taken care of."

"You see, you admit it," she said, inspecting her face critically in the big mirror over the mantel. "Though the neck is still good."

Vanessa, he had to admit, was realistic about her physical assets.

"Flawless," he said. "You have great films in you yet."

"But only for a little while," she said. "I want to be ready. For the transition."

"Transition?" Like some damned piece of machinery, Eric thought. "What transition?"

"Don't be silly," she said, laughing now, "I can't keep playing romantic leads. Eric, I'm going to be 37 this year."

"Thirty-three," he said quickly. He had revised her biog, but she had no head for details and kept forgetting the corrections.

"Whichever. It's not to late for me to improve my craft. To land good character rolls. To position myself as a serious actress."

Eric jumped up in exasperation. It was all so logical and sensible — Vanessa was a good deal more practical than he cared to admit — but it was unendurable. "How can you think of it? How can you think of it when you've been a major star for fifteen years? Character rolls? Bit parts? It won't work! Even Garbo. Garbo, the greatest of all. What happened to her? She tried to change and it was disaster, an embarrassment. She quit one film too late, because she was tempted to compromise. It can't be done. This is all nonsense. It's unendurable," Eric said.

"For whom?" Vanessa asked.

In reply, his voice rose; he gave examples and reasons, but he was aware all the while that she wasn't listening. She was concocting other plans even as he described the new property he'd found — the heroine was 28, a wonderful age and still very plausible. He had some other ideas; he'd write something just for her. She was right, no more juvenile leads; he knew exactly what was needed, a mature character, who was still romantic and glamorous. She'd see, she'd see. But Vanessa was looking out the window and whatever she saw there, she did not confide to Eric.

Thinking it over later in his screening room, he blamed Hugh Greshwin, Vanessa's most recent co-star, a multi-talented young man who aspired to be a director: in short, the very worst of a difficult breed. Eric considered him carefully. Hugh was intelligent, that was obvious, and well read, "intellectual" even, but not greatly talented. There was, as Eric was only too aware, only a partial correlation between creative talent and intelligence.

Greshwin was really Vanessa in reverse, that is, a personality much more impressive in reality than he was on the screen. With his long dark hair flopping into his burning eyes, his quick powerful gestures, his sense of pent-up emotional neediness and anger, he had all the ingredients, one would have thought, for a male star. The idea made Eric smile cynically; on screen, Hugh's pale complexion looked pallid; his smoldering eyes went dead; the emotional charge dissipated. Too bad; he'd better direct.

But not Vanessa. Though that was Hugh's aim, Eric could tell. With her backing, Hugh would get a shot at a film, and, given his abilities, Eric would bet on success. At least for Hugh. But for Vanessa, to whom this Beverly Hills Mephisto was whispering *The Seagull and Streetcar* — next it would be *Sweetbird of Youth*! — what would there be for her but disaster? And even if success, relative success, that is, surely there would be a diminishment, for she'd already achieved perfection.

The whole idea was so upsetting that Eric had promised himself *Melody in D* after he had it out with her, and he was determined to enjoy the film even if nothing had been settled. Even if Hugh Greshwin still lurked in the shadows. Even if there were still decisions to be made. But there were the credits now, the swell of Beethoven on the sound track, and, there, in long shot across the bare wooden floor of a rehearsal stage, his darling, bending gracefully over a concert Steinway, touching the first chords. Now came the tracking shot Eric knew and loved so well, the camera drawn inexorably toward her, then circling to close on her magical face. Perfect, he thought, unbelievably perfect. Nothing must ever be allowed to spoil that.

As he always did after watching a favorite film, Eric felt better, calm enough, in fact, to call Hugh Greshwin and make a lunch date. As he drove north a day later, Eric had reason to feel confident. Over the years, he'd dealt with other aspirants, ambitious for a piece of Vanessa, Inc. — writers, producers, directors, co-stars. They'd all settled for something more tangible, if less satisfying. He was the only one who was devoted, totally devoted, to Vanessa.

He made that clear to Hugh over an expensive lunch. "My first and last thought is always for Vanessa and for her career," he said.

Hugh nodded rapidly, his hair flopping into his eyes. He really should try a different cut, Eric thought, or styling gel. "Nobody, nobody doubts that," Hugh said. "It's a matter of perspective. Vanessa's a major, major talent. Naturally, she wants to develop, to grow as a person and as an actress."

"What's to grow?" Eric asked. "She's one of the few bankable women in Hollywood."

"For now," Hugh said. He talked demographics, the changing audience, Vanessa's age. "She's completely realistic," he said. "She wants to maintain the same control over her career she's had so far. She wants to position herself the right way."

Eric heard this echo of Vanessa's phrases with loathing. "But you have ambitions of your own, I think. Vanessa's co-stars — well . . ." Eric let the phrase tail off, indicative of outer darkness and mere reflected light.

"Oh, direction is definitely my goal. I've had some success," modestly ducking his head and flopping his hair — the phoney — "on screen, but behind the camera is really where I belong."

Eric controlled his nausea and recollected Hugh's background: film school, a well regarded documentary, some regional theater, including direction. Something might be done, but delicately; Hugh was brighter than the usual claimant, at least as ambitious, maybe personally involved.

"There's a project I'm interested in," Eric said after a pause, "that needs a director. Moderate budget, you understand, but potential. A neat little thriller." He mentioned names, possibilities, pitched the story. "I could get bigger marque interest — the script's a gem — but what the hell? It would give you a start."

Hugh's eyes were avid, but when Eric was finished, he shook his head. "I've promised Vanessa," he said.

"What have you promised Vanessa?"

"Why to direct her, of course. We've been talking about *The Whisperer*. Surely she's mentioned . . . Do you know the novel?"

Eric did; he read everything. *The Whisperer*'s heroine was an impoverished Appalachian woman who migrates to Detroit with her five children. Within Vanessa's range? Probably, but risky; the heroine was forty, at least.

"Well, you know then. It's quality product. And the rights are available. Listen, it would be a hell of a package."

"You and Vanessa."

"No, no, I like Baldwin or maybe Nolte for the male lead. I'd direct."

But now it was Eric's turn to shake his head. "You can't practice on Vanessa," he said, laying aside his napkin. "But think over the other proposal. It could make your career."

So the offer was on the table, and Eric could only wait and see. As he drove home, he told himself that it would be all right. A fine property, a chance to direct, Eric's backing — and he would be as good as his word and back the film 100% — what more did Greshwin want? What more could he want? No, Hugh would take the bait and busy himself with his film, and Vanessa would return to her senses.

"Don't rely on Hugh," Eric told her that evening.

She looked surprised. "I'm not relying on Hugh," she said. "I've got my own plans. I'm taking classes. Starting next month."

"Classes?"

"With Madame Skaskevich."

"Jesus Christ!" Eric said. Madame was straight from Leningrad, a Method guru with an impenetrable accent and a yen for hard currency.

"I know exactly what I want to do," Vanessa said and the set of her mouth told Eric that she wasn't kidding. "I'm signing up at UCLA, too. No, no, not the film school. You know, literature and history and things. I'm sick of being ignorant. The business school is good, too. I want to grow as a person. You understand that, don't you, Eric?"

Of course, he told her. Indulge her, he thought. Encourage her, even. She'll get bored with college work. It was a laugh. When had she even looked through the script pile? But Madame Skaskevich! There might be real dangers there. A gift like Vanessa's, so intuitive, so natural — so vulnerable? Eric was beset by waves of anxiety which only increased when it became clear that Vanessa was thriving on her new regimen.

He'd been afraid she'd take on some crazy project; now he began to fear she wouldn't take on anything at all. Her classes were "so absorbing"; her new professors, "all marvelous," and squat Madame Skaskevich with her glassy survivor's eyes and croaking voice, "a genius."

All this Eric endured with remarkable patience. It was only when he learned Hugh Greshwin was also one of Madame Skaskevich's regulars that he felt the decisive moment had come. Vanessa was set to betray, not him — not him, there was never anything personal involved — but herself, her career, her destiny. And the problem went far beyond Hugh Gershwin or even the toadish Madame Skaskevich. The problem was Vanessa. And if Eric wanted to remain within the greater world of her films, it was up to him to save her from herself. That was perfectly clear. Without any more hesitation, he dialed Hugh Greshwin's number and invited him to dinner on the yacht.

Later, Eric would deny to himself that anything definite had been planned. It was something much more subtle than a plan; it was a matter of situation, not of event. The way he arranged things, Vanessa had had every opportunity to come to her senses, and Hugh Greshwin had had a shot at a terrific project. That was all, absolutely, and Eric's conscience was clear. Anything else that happened was beyond his control — although he had been at pains to create a certain situation and, beyond that, a certain atmosphere. Eric would go so far as to admit that — but only to himself.

To Vanessa, he spoke of drama. She expected to see the *Miranda* moored in the usual spot amid the close packed ranks of the marina, and she was surprised when he pointed far down the bay.

"I asked Sven to move her further out. I know, I know, you're not fond of the dinghy — though you managed to get to the Teasdiles last week, didn't you? — but think of Hugh. The drama of it. Walking out to a yacht along a floating sidewalk isn't the same at all."

Eric stretched his arms before the great sweep of San Diego bay. The lighted restaurants and shops behind them, the shadowed hills to their right, and, far away across the intensely blue water, the dusty mountains of Mexico. He wished they could weigh anchor and sail around the green point and straight out into the Pacific, away from classes and Madame Skaskevich and ambitious young men with predatory eyes. But his darling did not like sailing, even though she'd bought *Miranda* for him. Vanessa could barely swim, got seasick in the lightest swells, and confessed to a kind of dread of open water.

For that reason, Eric was sure that once out on the boat, she would be willing to stay there. No sudden sulks and tempers would tempt her into the small, uncomfortable dinghy. Nearer shore was another matter. How many times lately had she taken it into her head to visit the Teasdiles, that viper photographer and his poisonous model-wife?

"I've given Sven the night off," Eric said as he untied the dinghy from their usual slip. Sven knew Vanessa's nervousness on the water, and he was all too obliging about running her here and there. "He needs some time to himself. We don't want to lose him."

"Well, but how will Hugh . . ."

"I'll pick him up. You'll have time to change and see that Jorge has everything ready."

Vanessa raised one eyebrow. She already looked smart and nautical in white slacks and a navy and white striped shirt.

"The star treatment, darling. Heels, neckline, mega-glamour. Let's show Hugh what the business is all about."

"Hugh's not into glamour," Vanessa said.

"We'll see," Eric said. He'd learned very few people are truly immune to glamour — or even to its little cousin, major wealth. "Indulge me. I have something in mind for him. You'll be pleased. It could launch a major career."

"I don't know why you had to move the *Miranda* so far out," Vanessa repeated as they left the marina.

"I told you, darling," Eric said. "It's pure theater. Strictly for your friend Hugh."

And running out later, as they left the little shops and restaurants and the trees with their fairy lights behind and passed the white plank pontoons of the marina and the glistening yachts, Hugh Greshwin was impressed.

"Beautiful night," he said.

"I love the bay," Eric said. "You feel you're alone, don't you? Alone on the sea, even here." Beneath them, the indigo water was splashed by the reflected lights which thinned out and then disappeared, leaving them on the verge of a great darkness before the *Miranda*'s lights took over, bathing the water under her sides in gold.

Vanessa was waiting at the top of the ladder. She was all in white, like the ship, in a long slim dress with a low neckline, a light shawl over her shoulders against the evening breeze. Eric brought the dinghy along side and threw up the line for her. "You remember the hitch?" he called. His darling was quite hopeless about knots.

She fumbled, giggling, with the knot until the boat was fast, and Hugh and Eric could scramble up the ladder to the greetings and laughter of a determined conviviality. Vanessa called Jorge to bring out the cocktail tray, and they sat down with their drinks in the lee of the wind. They could see the white and yellow lights of San Diego, the winking eyes of arriving and departing planes, the faint and mysterious signals of distant ships.

When Eric recalled the evening later, that's what he remembered: light against darkness, points of gold, blue, and white brightness against the amorphous spread of sky and sea. They, that is, Vanessa and Hugh, talked of Madame Skaskevich and of Vanessa's growth and Hugh's plans. Eric listened until the paella was served, splendid like all Jorge's creations, golden with saffron, redolent with garlic, and filled with mussels, lobster, and shrimp. Below, the dining room felt pleasantly warm after the cool breeze on deck. The room was aglow with light, and soft baroque music issued from the stereo system. Hugh admired, and Eric said, "*The Whisperer* wouldn't pay for all this." That was his opening gambit. He stuck to the financial details, to Vanessa's possible losses. And then when she proved stubborn and Hugh Greshwin resourceful, Eric moved on to his other cards, his knowledge of their finances, his control over rights.

It was all very civilized, although Vanessa was upset, he could see that, for on top of three very substantial cocktails, she'd added several glasses of good French Bordeaux. The fact was that tension and disagreements made her nervous. She was a simple and direct person, "transparent to the role" as one of her directors had said, a personality subtle on the screen but easily distressed by malice and maneuver in everyday life. Eric thought she did not appreciate what he'd done along those lines for her sake. She'd always left business to him — "You'll have to talk to Eric," she'd say with a graceful, dismissive gesture. "He worries about all that sort of thing."

That sort of thing being contracts, percentages, residuals: the mundane foundations of her art. He'd done the negotiating, the dealing, the hard bargaining with the shrewd and the ruthless. He'd managed the directors, the scriptwriters, the agents, the producers. Now she wanted to fly away into some artistic empyrean to "grow" as a second rate actress instead of a first rate star. A sense of grievance made Eric sharp, crueler than necessary, crueler than he ever wanted to be, and Vanessa jumped up, grabbed her shawl, and ran up the steps to the deck.

Hugh started to follow, but Eric stopped him. "Vanessa hates business," he said. "She knows it's time for serious negotiations."

"You shouldn't have said. . . ."

"The film," Eric said, cutting off his reproaches. What did Hugh know of Vanessa! Of him! "If you're really committed to *The Whisperer*, we might do something — minus Vanessa, of course."

"She's essential," Hugh protested, but Eric could see he was interested.

"A tad too young," Eric said, "unless you just want a star turn. There are other actresses who'd be available — if you had my backing." He reached over casually and turned up the music: Vivaldi's violins launching repeated, descending chords. Later he would remember an odd perception of inevitability, both in the music and in events.

"Who?" asked Hugh.

Eric mentioned names, possible combinations, possible financing. He could see how Hugh was torn between future hopes and present loyalty. Yes, he was divided; Eric would give him that, but that was not enough. He, Eric, would never have wavered for a moment where Vanessa's interests were concerned. It gave him a kind of bitter satisfaction to think of his own devotion, especially now when he was listening for any sound from the deck, for the sounds that might come, must come, must not come.

"We should see where Vanessa's gotten to," Hugh said finally, tipping his wrist and consulting a large and fancy watch.

"Not until we've decided," Eric said. "She'll expect it all to be settled." He thought he heard a sound then, the sound he had been anticipating and dreading, and he reached over and turned up the volume again. "I love this section, don't you? The start of winter, the hunt, the kill."

"I want to direct Vanessa," Hugh said. "I know she's interested in *The Whisperer*. I think she should be involved in the discussion."

He stood up, but things had gone too far, and Eric could feel events sliding in the descending sixteenths of the violins. "There is another possibility," he said slowly. "We'd planned it as her next big project. It's right for her, absolutely."

"And the director?"

"Not set yet." Eric mentioned the possibilities, a garland of impressive names. "But nothing's decided. If Vanessa really wants you as director. . . ." He let the suggestion trail off and Hugh sat down. Though he was concerned, Eric could see, concerned but not concerned enough, and, in that moment Eric grieved for Vanessa. But somehow he talked on, percentages, arrangements, scheduling, scripts. How avidly Hugh devoured them! On the stereo, baroque violins cut into chords with big clean bites of sound. Eric heard all this as in a dream. Then with the suddenness of baroque dynamics, the violins dropped in volume, and in the relative quiet, there was a scraping sound.

Hugh jumped up and turned off the system. There it was again, from outside, from the side of the hull. Eric ran up the steps to the cool, brightly lit deck. There were the chairs, as empty as they'd left them, and the rail was deserted. On the Pacific side there was nothing, nothing at all, not even the glimmer of a distant freighter. He ran to the bay side, searching without success for the thin white wake of the dinghy against the reflected glitter of the city. It was all clear to him. He could almost see her struggling with the knot and the rope, then, a little drunk and detached from her fear, descending the ladder in her high, delicate heels and stepping out over the water toward the unsteady gunwales of the dinghy.

Beside him, Hugh gave a cry. A limp white triangle was rippling beneath the dark water, rippling and floating, then sliding deeper: Vanessa's shawl. Near it, loose now and scraping against the hull, the dinghy.

They called, shouted, woke Jorge, turned on every available light. Eric grabbed the boat hook and, scrambling down the ladder, secured the dinghy and clambered in. The shawl was only a dim, gray shadow when he caught it at last, his arm soaked to the elbow. He knew then, though he got the oars and rowed around the *Miranda*, shouting until his throat was raw, until the sleek Coast Guard launch arrived, until it was official.

On deck, an officer took down details, organized the search. Eric stood clutching the still dripping shawl. He was shivering in the cold, but, in his imagination, he'd already left the yacht. In his imagination, he is standing at the door of a bare rehearsal hall with clear white light to the left, shadows to the right. A woman is seated at a concert Steinway, and as the camera starts to close, she bends gracefully over the keyboard and begins the first soft notes of "The Moonlight Sonata." Eric feels himself drawn closer and closer, over the dusty plank floor, around the great black fin of the raised piano lid, circling with the camera, until he confronts Vanessa's lovely and expressive face. It is, Eric thinks, perfection.

THE BLIND WOMAN

At the end of Seth's corn field the forest began, thick and dark and mysterious with the occasional whisper of moccasined feet. Once in a long while if the wind was right, he and Abigail might see smoke from new farms far to the east and south. North and west remained primeval, unbroken except for the fields that they themselves had wrenched out of the woods and the rocks with three years of unrelenting work. Seth could feel that effort in every muscle of his back and shoulders.

Stumps from the trees they'd girdled and burned remained in the fields along with a few boulders too big for even the ox team to shift. But for acres around their cabin, the darkness of the forest had been replaced by the tender greens and pale, silky golds of wheat, oats, and maize. Sometimes when Seth went out to check his fields, he'd sit on a stump amid the smells of wood chips and humus and pollen and let the soft colors of cultivation expand in his imagination out to the horizon, erasing the woods with all their mysteries and dangers.

He might not see it, but his sons and daughters would. His son. His child, his children. Then Seth would feel the pain of futility: what if there were no children, no child? What had they done all this for?

Sometimes he lingered so long that Abigail had to call him in to eat. She would open the door of the cabin and step onto the stone stoop — a flat stone hauled in from the fields — and call, "Seth, Seth." If he didn't answer right away, she would call again, with a high, sad, frightened note in her voice. He could hear the change even from the far end of the corn field. Abigail hated the woods worse than he did and some days even the fields, open, pale, rich with life, distressed her. On those days she hid in her dark, square kitchen.

At first, she used to say, "It will be different when we have children. When the babies come, I'll feel different. I need a little life in the house. "But when the children didn't come, when she lost one early and one late, late enough, so that their straw mattress was soaked with blood and her face turned pale as bleached linen, she stopped talking about company or about anything very much at all.

Which had suited Seth, at first. He was a silent man inured to the quiet emptiness of the frontier. It was several months before he realized how silent his wife had become. He hadn't paid a great deal of attention to what she'd said, but he'd been used to the sound, which was to him like a familiar brook plashing and burbling, or the wind in the trees, or their hive of bees. Then the sound stopped and he felt its absence.

Still she worked hard; Abigail was a good worker, a good wife; Seth would never say otherwise. The cabin was clean, not like some with dirt unswept on the floor and plates filthy, pots thick with grease. Their garden plot was neat; their chickens fat, their milk and cream made into good butter and cheese. And yet, her silence, which should have been a comfort, troubled him.

It was as if something, Seth wasn't sure what, had been turned inside out like a skinned rabbit. Even her announcement that she was pregnant again had not lifted his heart. He'd felt a momentary joy, then fear, then the uneasy sense of something wrong. One night he had incautiously remarked that her waist was still slim. After that Abigail no longer let him touch her.

Lately she'd risen every morning ahead of him and once, waking early with the spring light, he'd seen her stuffing a little pillow down the front of her dress. He'd not been able to look at her thickened silhouette without dread since.

As her pregnancy advanced, Abigail began to talk again. She spoke of the child, of the boy they'd have, the boy who would help in the fields and take over the farm. Seth tried not to pay any attention, but though he could ignore the words, he could not shut out the joy and terror and despair he sensed behind them. If he wasn't careful, he might begin to wonder what would happen to Abigail and how they would manage if her mind went.

At the end of mud time in their fourth year, they began to see folks going westering again and others fixing to settle down nearby. Clear mornings working on his crop, Seth could sometimes hear the ring of axes and the crash of trees toppling on new made farms. Ox carts occasionally passed their cabin, and tired men and women stopped to ask for buckets of water from the spring. Abigail always came out to talk to the women, to admire their children, to hint shyly that it was getting near her time. She would stand for a long time watching the wagons creak away into the forest on the trail that was slowly widening into a proper track.

Sometimes she and Seth sold provisions to the travelers: eggs, butter, cheese, salad greens, a little smoked bacon. The money was handy, and the sales confirmed their prosperity and the rightness and luckiness of their decision to take up this raw western land. They were doing right, and plenty others were following in their footsteps.

One cool, wet day they were both in the cabin, sitting close to a good fire. Abigail was knitting and Seth was making the frame of a chair, when they heard a wagon rumble to a stop. Outside, a pregnant woman stood beside a worn out pair of oxen with one hand on their collar. The other held a switch, and she was turning her head this way and that in the misty rain as though listening for something.

"Morning," Seth called from the doorway.

She turned her head but did not look directly at him. Dampness had soaked her bonnet and stringed her long hair down around her shoulders. "Who's there?" A note between hope and alarm. "Is that a house? I thought I smelled a barn."

Seth went out to her, and at the sound of his feet she turned large cloudy eyes toward him, and he realized that she was blind. "My husband's took sick," she said. "I've been following the oxen."

The animals were standing with their heads down, looking ready to drop. "They're near finished," Seth said. "You can't take them much further the shape they're in."

"I been following the oxen," she repeated. Her voice held a stubborn querulousness, as if the state of the team had nothing to do with her.

"They'll need water," Seth said. "We have a good spring."

"God will bless you," the woman replied, but she did not move, and Seth saw that, like the oxen, she had reached the limit of her endurance. Just his luck. They had little enough fodder this time of year for their own oxen and the new pasture was still thin. It was bad luck for them to be landed with her and near her time, too, by the look of her. Seth called to Abigail.

"It's my husband needs help," said the blind woman. She felt back along the ox cart and lifted the canvas flap. A tall, black bearded man was lying wrapped in a filthy blanket. His face had all gone to bone; his closed eyes were dark rimmed and sunken, and the whole wagon stank of fever. He lay so still that it crossed Seth's mind the man might already be dead. "Haven't been able to do much for him," the woman said in a flat, detached voice. "It's hard for me to find water."

Seth felt a resentful fear at the thought of fever. How many farms had she passed? How many folks had told her to keep on going? If he'd had children, he'd have told her the same, Seth thought. As his fear struggled against his better nature, he saw that the woman's bare arms and legs were scratched from twigs and brambles and bitten all over by flies and mosquitoes.

His wife decided the matter by running out to tell the woman she must come inside. "For the sake of your child," Abigail cried with an anxious, almost a hungry, look, as if, her husband thought, she feared these unwelcome strangers might decline hospitality.

The woman allowed herself be led to the cabin, and Seth unhitched the team, took them to the barn, and hauled water for them. When he returned to the cart, half figuring and half hoping that things might be settled, he found the man returned from the dead, groaning and shivering, his whole body shaking. Seth fetched a clean piece of canvas from the house and wrapped the sick man up in it, leaving the filthy blankets in the wagon. He hauled the man, big but much lightened by his illness, into the cabin and laid him on the floor by the fire.

The wife sat with a bowl of fresh milk and a piece of corn bread left from breakfast, eating like a starved thing. When she'd finished the last crumbs, she said that they were Connecticut people, who'd been traveling in a good big wagon train until the fever came. She began to count off names, her voice indifferent. Then they'd lost their only daughter and stopped a day to bury her. The woman's face remained impassive, as if she were too exhausted even for grief, but her cloudy eyes filled with tears. Her husband had thought they could catch up easy, but he went off his head, yelling and singing, and she'd put him in the wagon and followed the oxen. "I find farms by the dogs and the smell of manure piles," she said.

Abigail patted her hand, but Seth turned away, his face dark. Fool oxen could have stopped miles away, he thought, instead of about walking themselves to death and bringing this trouble. It was bad luck, and bad luck came in threes. Everyone knew that.

After lying some time by the fire, the man stopped shivering, and Abigail fed him a little hot water and whiskey which quieted him some. The woman fell asleep in her chair.

"Those oxen can maybe pull by tomorrow," Seth said. "Day after, sure, if I give them some oats."

Abigail's face twisted with anxiety. "Oh, no, Seth! She is near her time. She can't possibly travel."

"We could take her back a way. Get her some help. Jared Tompkins's wife is skillful. We could take her to Goody Tompkins."

"Goody Tompkins is twenty miles or more," Abigail said. "And Goody Tompkins will want to be paid."

Seth shrugged. He thought it would be worth Goody Tompkins fee to be rid of the sick man and the dazed, mole-like woman. And two more oxen to feed. Even if they'd had plenty, even if they'd had more than enough feed, Seth would have wanted them gone.

"We will need to pay Goody Tompkins when our own child comes," Abigail said. She had a shy, nervous smile.

"That's true," said Seth, who understood that he must give in and felt sick at heart.

They tended the dying man all day, while the blind woman slept in the chair. Seth stripped off the man's filthy clothes and Abigail soaked them in a bucket and hung the stained trousers, shirt, and small clothes in front of the fire. Late that night, they were awakened by the sound of awkward steps in the cabin, of someone fumbling and bumping into things, before a high, keening wail raised the hair on Seth's neck and told him that the man was dead.

In the morning, Seth dug a grave at the edge of a clump of berry bushes adjoining the little patch of wild flowers where their last, sad infant was buried. The stranger's clothes were dry, so his wife was able to dress the body. Abigail sewed up the canvas for a shroud, then together she and Seth carried the body out to the grave, and Seth shoveled the soft, damp, black earth over the gray bundle. Abigail brought out the family Bible, and Seth read "I am the Resurrection and the Life." He told the woman that next time a preacher came through, he would ask him to say a prayer.

"God has forgotten us," the blind woman said simply.

They both felt a kind of horror at this, Abigail at the great unwisdom of the idea, and Seth at its possible truth. She put her arm around the woman and hugged her, but Seth felt dismay. Now they had the woman with them permanent; there was no way she could go on alone. They'd have another mouth — maybe two — to feed and not a lick of work out of her. He could see that, for the blind woman sat by the fire on cool days and on the stoop out front when there was sun. Whenever he asked her plans, she said that she'd just followed the oxen, and those famished beasts seemed set to make up for long hunger and neglect by stripping his pasture and getting into his corn.

"She may have folks in the east," he told Abigail. "A woman alone, a blind woman alone, half-witted, too, by the look of it: tell me how she's going to manage to farm."

"She's going to have a child," said Abigail, as if this answered all things. On anything to do with the blind woman, his usually mild and agreeable wife was unyielding. "And," she added, "when my time comes, I'll have a woman to help me. We won't have to send for Goody Tompkins."

It was on Seth's tongue to say, "The wilderness has turned your mind," but he could not do it. The blind woman grew swollen to enormous size, and Abigail, too. They padded around the cabin, swaying on their enlarged hips, stretching their tired backs, grunting when they brought up water from the well.

The blind woman now followed Abigail everywhere, learning the house and garden, finding her way to the chickens and the young pigs. And in another way, Seth saw, Abigail was following her, copying, he was sure, every movement, every adjustment of the woman's heavy body. So though his wife seemed happy, almost as happy as she used to be when they were young and hopeful back east on her father's farm, Seth began to stay out of the cabin. He lingered in his fields during the day and sat out on the stoop after dinner with his pipe.

In the evenings, Abigail knit garments for the children who were to be born. She would need flannel, too, she told Seth, and some new muslin and calico. Her dresses were just about ruined with letting out and the baby, the babies, would need clothes. At first, Seth shut his ears to all this. The blind woman's baby was not his concern; he'd fed her and sheltered her and her team, too, and risked fever for himself and Abigail to do it. But then he looked at the woman's oxen, growing sleek and fat again and thought he might make up some of their losses and solve two problems at once.

Seth proposed selling the team for her in the nearest village. With the money, she could get a trader to take her back east. The blind woman's cloudy eyes gazed just to the left of his face, and she sighed and nodded. Abigail made out a list of household necessities, and early one morning Seth made ready to leave. He brought in a heap of extra wood for the fire and left his great woodsman's ax by the door in case of trouble. Abigail could swing an ax about as well as any man he'd seen.

But now she said it was too big and heavy. "I couldn't hardly lift it now," she reminded him, her expression half coy, half annoyed, the way it always was when she had to remind him of her condition, the "pregnancy" which half broke his heart. Seth took the big ax out to the oxcart and returned with the little hatchet he usually carried when he traveled. He'd already hitched up the oxen, both his own and the blind woman's, before he had misgivings.

"Suppose her time comes," he told his wife. "Or yours. There will be no one."

Abigail said that they would manage, that they would hardly deliver the same day. She laughed at the idea, the first time she'd laughed in Seth did not know how long, and he said that he'd make all the time he could. "Three days," he said, "if I can find buyer right away. They're good looking beasts, I think they'll go quick."

Abigail kissed him, her face alight. "We'll be all right," she said.

Still, he wasn't sure, but though he could see plenty reasons not to go, Abigail was insistent. The longer he waited the more dangerous it would be to go, for suppose he was gone when one or both did deliver? And the babies would need clothes, flannel, some soft plain cotton. It would not do to lose a child to cold. The very thought set her trembling. Seth picked up his switch and told the team to walk on.

As it turned out, he was gone a full week. When he got to the village Seth found that a wagon train was expected soon. He waited three full days for it, and then another to dicker back and forth with the farmer who eventually bought the blind woman's team. Finally, Seth started for home, pushing his oxen as hard as he dared and thinking all the way that anything could have happened, but also, because it was a radiant early June day, that all would be well. He knew that he'd been right to wait for the wagon train, because he'd gotten a good price for the blind woman's oxen. As soon as she could travel, he'd take her into the village and one of the traders going east with furs and skins would see her back home. Seth carefully did not think of his own wife or of their child.

He spotted the thin blue plume of their kitchen fire long before he could see the cabin, and smelling the good, familiar, faintly sour smell of a wood fire, Seth told himself again that the blind woman would leave and that Abigail would be all right. They might even have a child eventually. If not, Seth was beginning to think of asking the minister back in the village to look out for a likely orphan, strong and bright. The wagon trains always seemed to wind up with one or two who'd be glad of a home.

The cabin door stood open to the sun, and white squares of stained cloth were drying on the line that ran from the corner of the cabin to the big elm that reminded Abigail of home. Seth heard an infant crying, briefly, as if shushed and comforted, and felt his heart clench. It was not fair that the blind woman should have a child and not his poor, hopeful, deluded wife. Seth felt how small, how pathetically inadequate, were the few ribbons and the fancy comb he'd bought as compensation; what were such little trinkets to a child, to a future?

This dark thought kept Seth from halooing as he usually did at the first sight of the cabin. Instead, he brought the cart into the yard, and he'd have gone on to the barn with the now eager team, if Abigail had not stepped out on the stoop with a bundle in her arms. Seth stopped in his tracks. Her face was glowing, exalted; her belly, as flat and thin as the day they'd wed. The child stirred in her arms. "This is Adam," she said. "Our son."

"And —," he asked and stopped. He could not name the blind woman thought she suddenly filled his thoughts.

Abigail's face took on a flat impassivity very like their guest's. "She died," said Abigail. "Her time came first, and she died and her child, too. You were right; we should have taken her to Goody Tompkins."

Seth felt a kind of horror mingling with hope, or perhaps it was a hope mingling with horror; he did not know what he felt, what he doubted, what he feared. "And where is she? This weather, we'll have to bury her quick."

"The ground was still soft over her husband's grave," Abigail said. "It was hot and I figured you'd been delayed on the road. I dug down as far as I could before my pains came on."

"Be a nasty job to rebury her." Seth watched his wife's face closely.

"I've been thinking we should put a little porch on the cabin," Abigail said. "We could haul this old stoop over and put it on top of the grave. It'd keep the animals out and be a monument to them."

First thing the next morning, Seth set out to trim up some logs for the floor of the new porch. He got his wedges and split some good pine logs, then shouted for Abigail to find his hatchet.

She stood, wary and puzzled, then pointed to the barn. One of the chickens had gotten egg bound, she said, and had to be killed. Seth found the ax flung carelessly in the back of the barn, its usually gleaming blade discolored and threatening to rust. He had to put it back in order with his sharpening stone before he could trim up the planks.

When he was finished, Seth hitched the oxen to the stoop and dragged the big stone across the yard and past the barn to the grave. He didn't like the way the oxen's cloven hooves sank into the grave, nor the way the thick, flat stone plowed up the soft soil. But Abigail was right: the stone covered nicely. If it were carved, it would be as good as the big fancy stones back home, and by rights it should have been one of the family lying there. He wondered if Abigail had read something over the grave, but decided he did not want to ask her.

"It looks nice," she said. "Nice as you can get out here." She was holding the baby in her arms, rocking it back and forth with a smile on her face. She carried the infant everywhere like a Mohawk squaw, and the baby seemed healthy, though it cried a lot, and Seth wondered how she'd nurse it. He'd seen her dripping milk from Bess, their cow, into its mouth.

A day after he'd moved the stone, Seth was laying the floor of the new porch when Abigail cried his name with a strange, high sound. He dropped his tools and ran into the cabin. She was standing holding the child at her breast, her face filled with a surprise so intense it was almost fear. "My milk has come in," she cried. "It's true what they say. Sometimes it can take a few days."

Seth touched her shoulder and dared for the first time to really look at the child with its matted dark hair and tiny hands and voracious mouth. "Adam," he said. And felt hope.

From that time, the baby thrived like a true child of the wilderness, a noisy, barefoot imp, fearless even in the darkness of the woods. Soon Adam running about the house and finding his way to the chickens for their eggs and to the cow for her milk. When he was barely five, he could already lead the oxen and manage them with the switch.

"He'll make a good farmer," Seth said.

The boy was so bright and cheerful, so happy and eager, that it was easy for Seth to think of present and future happiness rather than of past questions and doubts. How deeply all these had been buried was revealed to Seth one day when a small train of wagons passed through. They were Connecticut people and one man, in particular, aroused both Seth's interest and his anxiety. The stranger was tall and wide shouldered with a black beard and high bony cheeks. They were heading for new land in northwest territory, he said, and hoped to find his brother there.

"Went out before you then?" Seth asked.

The man held up the fingers of one hand. "Five years it's been and never a word. I been asking all along and I'll ask you, too: a big man with a beard like mine and a blind wife and a little girl of eight or nine? They drove an ox cart with one red spotted ox and one dun colored beast."

Seth shook his head. "Course, not everyone stops. And we're a little off the main track," he said.

When they were gone, he wondered why he had lied when it would have been so easy to have set the traveler's mind at rest, so easy to have said, "fever took the man — and they said the little girl, too — and the woman died in child bed. I can show you their grave. We put a good big stone over it." But Adam came running in from the field, whooping and capering, his fair baby hair gone dark now, almost black, and Seth knew he'd done the right thing, though he could not quite have said why.

As for Abigail, her delight in the child knew no bounds. She made the neatest little clothes for him, played with him, sang to him, showed him, with endless patience, all she knew of everything in and out of the house. And Adam was a very likely lad but for one thing: he refused to read, and no matter how many times Abigail sat him on her lap, he never learned his letters.

To be read to was a pleasure he craved, but no sooner did his mother pull out the slate or attempt to trace letters in the Bible or in their battered blue backed Shakespeare, than he was up and away like a wild creature. "He does not need book learning out here," said his father. "And he's young yet."

As Adam grew tall, he became handy with anything to do with tools or animals. Seth could see him taking over the farm in another dozen years, so his mind was at ease for the future. Almost. It was, Seth, sometimes thought, because Adam was their only child that trifles, meaningless in themselves, provoked such anxious fears.

Trifles. The boy could not, no matter how he tried, sight the rifle Seth used to hunt squirrels and rabbits. And more than once, when Adam had been allowed a day away to play with the boys on the neighbor's farm, he returned in tears over the ball game which he could not master. Seth told himself that ball games were children's play, and one could live without squirrel meat.

One bright fall day, Seth and Adam had been clearing rocks and old stumps out of the original corn field, the first, hastily cleared land he'd broken. After they'd loaded up the wagon with some flattish rocks for the foundation of a new shed, he told Adam to go ahead and tell his mother they were coming in for dinner. The boy ran off, his hands slightly outstretched the way he did, as if to caress the tall weeds that grew along the track.

Seth followed with the oxen. He had reached the barn and he was unharnessing the team, when he heard a terrible scream of pain and horror. Seth sprinted around the corner of the barn, fear for his son flooding his heart. Adam stood perfectly still before the cabin, looking straight into the sun with a bewildered expression. His mother was on the porch, her face frozen in anguish. At that precise moment, Seth felt darkness opening inside him.

"Oh, Seth," she cried. "I have been so terribly punished. This is my fault! This is all my doing."

"Hush," he said, for he did not want to know what, in some way, he already understood. "We've known, haven't we, that his sight isn't good? He's still our Adam, who can do most anything . . ."

"It is my punishment," his wife sobbed wildly, her features distorted with terror. Seth opened his mouth, but it was too late to stop her.

"I killed the blind woman for her child," Abigail screamed, "and now she stands again before my face."

A MEETING AT THE CAFÉ VISCONTI

The sun still lit a high, cloudless sky, but the worst of the heat had sunk into the sienna- and ocher-toned buildings, making them glow as if by some subtle, internal fire. The big courtyard of the café was now mostly shadowed, and, freed of the heat and glare, the Bolognese were loitering over a Campari or a glass of mineral water or ordering pretty dishes of ices and biscuits. Michael smelled the smoke of their cigarettes, exhaust from the street, and a woman's passing perfume, all touched with that more elusive smell, the faint exhalation of old stone and old buildings. Overhead, the swifts were beginning to swoop and twitter, while fat pigeons whirred between the tables and looked for crumbs underfoot.

Michael opened his notebook and glanced again at the column of figures. He had done all right. More than all right. The astronomy faculty had liked his presentation, admired the new software, understood the documentation; he had done the translations and now he had the orders sewed up. It was a good feeling, and he was thinking how much he liked Italians in general and the Bolognese in particular when a woman's voice asked, "Do you speak English?"

Sometimes Michael ignored these appeals. His Italian was fluent, nearly perfect; his German was passable; his French, very good; and he could manage in both Portuguese and Dutch. Sometimes he would shrug, smile sympathetically, and shake his head.

"You must be American,," said the voice. "I've got one of the older models. A bit slow now."

She must have noticed his company briefcase. Michael turned to see a nicely dressed woman with faded blond hair pulled back into an untidy knot. She was wearing oversized sunglasses with very dark lenses, and Michael was reflected as a tiny figure against a vast and somber sky.

"That must be the P — ninety-six?" he asked politely. You never know when you may find a customer.

"A generation before, actually. I've got one of the P — eighties." She was somewhere in late middle age, a tall, sturdy woman with the confident smile of someone used to meeting people, used to making friends, or, perhaps, like Michael, used to making useful contacts.

"Really! Bane of our existence," Michael joked. "How can we sell new software when those old dinosaurs are still going strong?"

"Slow but sound," she said.

"A vintage model," Michael admitted. "For personal use. For business applications now, our new line is the only thing to consider."

He could hear himself switching into his sales mode and smiled. "But you're not here on business."

Her expression adjusted subtly, and Michael wondered if he'd given offense. He nodded toward the guidebook and map that lay on her table.

"Travel and business," she said after a moment, and there was a long pause. "You could saw that travel has become my business."

A waiter approached, very bright, neat, and important like all the café staff, and she ordered a San Pellegrino. Her Italian was quite passable, Michael notice.

"I look at restaurants, hotels, tourist itineraries," she remarked. "This is only my second time in Bologna. An underrated city."

"One of the nicest in Italy."

"That is what I think. I think it's ready to be an important secondary destination if presented in the right way. Much more could be done with the university area as a package of entertainment, culture, and history. But not too touristy. That's important for the publications I write for."

Michael smiled at her enthusiasm.

"You're wondering why I spoke to you," she said.

"Americans abroad usually appeal for translations."

"You are" — she hesitated, tipped her head to one side — "thirty-six, thirty-seven?"

"Thirty-six. Thirty-seven soon," he added and instantly regretted it, for she said, "My son's age exactly. He would have been thirty-seven next month. I saw you sitting there, and I said, he's Mark's age. That's what Mark would have looked like. That's what Mark would look like sitting in Bologna at the Café Visconti."

"Your son . . . died?"

"I don't know. I think now that he is dead, but I don't know for a certainty." Her expression momentarily turned vague and distracted, and Michael began to fear eccentricity, mental disturbance, all the anguish of emotional illness.

"I'm very sorry," he said. He would wait a minute, he thought, then call the waiter and ask for his check. He was glad now that he had his briefcase and could use the excuse of a meeting.

"I didn't believe it for a long time," she said in a reflective tone. "There are days when I don't believe it yet. I can understand those MIA families, I really can. Until you have something to bury, you don't believe. It doesn't seem real, does it? Someone is young and alive without a problem in the world and then — he's gone."

"An auto accident?" Michael asked.

She shrugged her shoulders and something about the gesture made him think that she must once have been attractive, desirable. "I don't think it could have been an auto accident. Those are reported. No, he disappeared years ago on a cross-country trip. He'd been camping out, hitching from one town to the next. It was the thing to do then, backpack, hitchhike, 'see the world.' Perhaps you did the same thing yourself."

Michael nodded before he could stop himself. "I traveled around a bit after my senior year."

"You'd have been seventeen," she said very definitely. "You might have been at the same campsites. It's a small world. When I travel, I meet so many people . . ." The waiter appeared with a coaster, a napkin, a little bottle beaded with condensation, and a glass garnished with a slice of lime; he laid them out smartly and was gone with a flourish. ". . . who might have known Mark," she resumed without a break, "who might have seen him, who were the right age or in the right place. Over the long run, that has become comforting."

"There was an investigation, of course . . ."

"No 'of course' about it," she said sharply. "It was strictly after a fashion. You know that was also the time for running away, dropping out. It was hard to convince the authorities that Mark would never just have disappeared."

"You did not accept that."

"Never."

"I supposed you searched, yourself . . ."

"Searched, hired detectives, put up posters, leafleted the entire area. It was in northern Arizona — not a very populous place. I don't think I left anything undone. That's a bad thought, the thought of having left something undone. I still wake up sometimes at night, sit up in bed with my heart pounding, thinking, 'I've forgotten something. What was I supposed to do? Where was it I was supposed to go?' But I haven't forgotten anything." She took a sip of her mineral water and looked around the café and then back at Michael. It was impossible to see her eyes behind the sunglasses. "I can assure you I've followed every lead, every clue."

"I'm sure you have," Michael said. He put his hand on his briefcase, ready to get up, ready to leave.

"Twenty years," she said. "A lifetime. It's been a very curious life. But you'd have a different perspective. Twenty years ago, you'd have been seventeen, and twenty years later my son would have looked like you."

"It's a very sad story," Michael said and shifted forward in his seat. He looked around with his hand half raised, but the alert and efficient waiters were all inside.

"There was a grove of aspens," she said, and as soon as she spoke, Michael felt the shift of some inner tide. "There was a small lake, too. When I first went there, the aspens were turning; I remember little pale gold leaves shivering in the wind and, behind them, mountains the color of lead."

"But you said he 'disappeared,'" Michael said. "No one was to blame, was there? There was no suspicion, no evidence? You've said as much . . ."

She studied her glass for a moment. "There was evidence," she said, "if you looked hard enough. What was hard was to convince the authorities to do something. To convince them that Mark would never have . . ."

"It's hard to be sure sometimes," Michael said abruptly. "It's hard to know what anyone will do in a given situation."

"But some people you just know," she said. "In extraordinary circumstances, yes, that's true. In extraordinary circumstances, who knows what we would do. I look at those poor Bosnians and Romanians sitting in the arcades . . ."

"Some of them are professionals," Michael said. He prided himself on knowing a scam when he saw one. "They're refugees today, Gypsies tomorrow, pickpockets the day after."

"They look miserable enough," she said, "wherever they come from. That is a drawback to Bologna."

"As an 'important secondary destination'?"

Like so many determined and energetic people, she was immune to satire. "What would we do in their place?" she asked in turn. "In their place, with poverty and disaster? That is one thing. But on a camping trip in the West?"

"Sometimes extraordinary things find us in ordinary places."

"That was what I said! I said something terrible must have happened. That's why I believe he must be dead."

"Other things can happen," Michael began. "People have been known to —"

"No, no, you don't understand. Let me tell you . . ."

"I'm sorry. It's been good talking to you, but I really must be going." Even to himself, Michael found his voice unconvincing. "I've got this meeting."

"Not now, surely," she said, imperturbably, relentlessly. "This is the hour for cafés, for aperitifs, for reflection. Especially for reflection. I see you are the sort of man who reflects, who remembers. As soon as I mentioned the lake and the aspens, I saw that you were a man who remembers."

Michael laughed and gathered his forces. "You made me think about camping in the mid-seventies. Evenings in a sleeping bag, listening to Jimi Hendrix, the Doors, and the Stones."

"Yes," she said eagerly, "all that wonderful music. All that loud, wonderful music. Generation-breaking music, but not for us. Mark and I grew up together. Was that an advantage or a disadvantage, do you think?"

Michael shrugged. "My parents were older than average. Quite a bit older."

"I had Mark when I was eighteen. So, you see, I understood him. I understood his generation. The wanting to get way, to experience life, to see the world. Our town was small. The button factory and the cloth mill were still running then. 'Make something of yourself or you'll end up in the mill,' that was what I was told as a girl. And then the sixties came and the new electronics plant and the real estate businesses and it wasn't as hard for a woman to earn a living anymore."

"And Mark's father? What did he do?" Michael asked abruptly, although it was rude, although it would surely delay his departure.

"That's what Mark always wanted to know."

"He didn't know?"

"It was irrelevant, completely irrelevant."

"Perhaps not to him," Michael protested.

"Mark's father was like me, young and foolish. But he didn't have any staying power, and so he became irrelevant."

"Boys need a man in their lives."

"Of course, you had a father. A conventional life. But Mark had his grandfather. My parents were very kind. I had a wonderful life when Mark was small. I had a part-time job with the local travel agent. Twenty-five hours a week. The rest of the time I took care of Mark. We went fishing and on picnics along the river; we went to the swings in the little town park. We never missed the children's matinee at the movie theater or the special programs at the library. That was the happiest time of my life."

"Then he grew up," Michael said. "He got too old for the park and picnics and being perfect."

She took a sip of her mineral water and ignored the implications. "It was an adjustment when he went to school. Though I had to work, so I was away part of the time anyway. And then he did so well, no one could say I hadn't done a good job with him. No one. He started the trumpet in elementary school, then played with the high-school band. Do you play an instrument?"

"As a child." He remembered the shiny, flaring brass mouth, the padded valves, the amazing amount of slimy fluid distilled from puffing out the notes of the "Triumphal March."

She smiled. "And sports. Baseball, of course. That was the big sport in our town. We had an adult team as well. And he insisted on playing football, although he was too light. That was the only thing we ever argued about. I went to all his games, and I suffered through every one of them until his junior year. Junior year, he broke his right leg in a game. I remember that awful sound, that terrible, unmistakable crack. I was in the stands and the sound went right through my heart."

She put her hand to the base of her throat. Her hands were strong and capable, Michael noticed, but spotted with age and beginning to wrinkle.

"After that, I said 'no more,' though I think he played sometimes with the boys after school. I think he did."

"But he was off the team?" Michael asked.

"The leg didn't heal quite right. It was shattered. A bad, bad break. And the local hospital wasn't the greatest — I still regret I didn't insist he be taken to Providence or Hartford. But he was in such pain, and I was scared to death. Do you have children?"

Michael shook his head. "I haven't been married long. We're hoping."

"You will know when you have children. The fear, the regrets. It left him with a slight limp. Most of the time it was undetectable, but when he was tired, you noticed."

"Athletic injuries are so common now," Michael said. "My right knee isn't all it might be." He was aware of a strange, tactile memory, not in his mind so much as in his shoulders: the weight of pads, the last of the old-fashioned leather pads, and the shock of impact, the springy force of bone and muscle and leather.

"Oh yes," she agreed. He could feel how much she wanted to agree with him. "And contemporary lives hare certain parallels, certain points in common. Like you and Mark. The same age, the same desire to 'see the world.' Music as a child, too, and sports? Did you play sports, too?"

"Soccer," Michael said too quickly. "And a little tennis."

"Tennis, too," she said with a smile. Her smiles were beginning to make him uneasy. She seemed to be finding some sort of confirmation from him, and Michael told himself that he was crazy to be trapped in a café by this stranger.

"It's getting late," he said, looking at his watch. "I really do have a meeting."

The old buildings were turning from sienna to a deep, shadowy umber, and the waiters were putting down the umbrellas. The sky had shifted imperceptibly from blue to pink, and her sunglasses reflected an amber and purple void.

"Of course," she said, "of course you must keep your appointment,"

There was a hint of condescension in her voice, and Michael said, "It might not have been the way you remember. It might not have been that way at all."

"But you know nothing about it," she said.

"He never knew his father," Michael said. "You told me that. What boy wouldn't be unhappy? And in a small town . . ."

"Where everyone knows everything? Is that what you think?"

"Children are cruel."

"And adults, too. We are not an attractive species, are we? You think he was miserable, that he ran away, that for twenty years, twenty years! He left his mother wondering what had happened to him. Is that what you think?"

"I don't . . ."

"He wrote me every week," she said triumphantly. "Or called. Called more than wrote. Collect. My phone bills were huge. Hi, Mom, he'd say. I'm in Cleveland or Denver or Mesa. Wherever. I was going to fly to San Francisco and meet him there in two weeks. To celebrate his cross-country trip. Does that sound like alienated youth? I got the records from the phone company and showed them to the police. Week after week, he called. Then new friends, the campsite up in the aspens with the lake and the lead-colored mountains, and he was never heard from again. What do you think?"

"His story might be different," Michael said. "He might have wanted to know —"

"Secrets?" she asked. Her well-shaped hands had rather long nails. Rather long; he had not noticed that. And though the light was almost gone, she still had not removed her glasses. Michael turned slightly. Three of the waiters were back at their station. One was smoking, the other two were starting to wipe up the tables and put away the chairs.

"What do we owe our children?" she asked. "Love, care, a decent life. Do we owe them our history? Yes? Even if it is a terrible one?"

"It isn't for me to say. It was for your son."

"But he's been dead for twenty years. You must answer for him."

Michael felt his chest tighten. He'd developed a touch of asthma after he turned thirty; it acted up under stress or in smoky places. "I would want to know," he said. "He would be a grown man and he'd want to know."

"But by now Mark would have a secret, too," she said. "As you must. By thirty-six, one has had time to accumulate follies and secrets. Isn't that right?"

"But you believe your son is dead."

"Mark has one of two secrets: the secret of his death or the secret of his disappearance." She leaned forward in her chair, and for the first time, Michael caught a glimpse of her eyes, light, lighter than his own, intent, pained, and cruel. He understood that she was not pathetic but dangerous. "I propose a swap," she said.

"I can see you were always manipulative," he said before he could stop himself. "Trading off one thing for another. Trading silence for a 'nice' life. For money, for protection."

"For my son's happiness," she replied quickly. "For a way to live. I was eighteen years old. No, I lied, I was barely seventeen when he was born, and scared to death. At seventeen he was on a cross-country trip to 'find himself,' but at that age I was faced with supporting an infant and myself with all my hopes and dreams ended."

"You should have thought of that before you got into bed."

"Do you suppose that's what he thought?" she asked. "I would be happy if he had, but I think he had other fears. You would understand that. I can see you have imagination. I can see you have an appreciation of what is not ordinary."

"Things happen," Michael said. A little breeze sprang up out of the arcades and chilled his damp chest.

"Things happened up in the aspen grove," she said. "I am an intelligent woman. I didn't know that at seventeen — or even at thirty-four. I've discovered that since. Twenty years is a long time. The works of Shakespeare, the theory of relativity, a treatment for cancer. What can't be done in twenty years if one puts one's whole mind to work?"

"Not everyone can write like Shakespeare," Michael said.

"But maybe there is a task for everyone," she said. "A unique task. My task was always Mark, protecting him, searching for him. You might be interested in how I proceeded."

"It is getting late," he said.

"Yes," she agreed, 'very late. Brian, David, Judy, and one other with Mark. Up in the aspen grove. I spoke to the camp manager. He is a rather sour, indifferent man. He remembered drinking, marijuana, loud music. The night Mark disappeared, he heard shouts in the dark, but he was not one 'to borrow trouble.' That was his phrase, 'to borrow trouble.' He just sat in his office and collected the camp rentals, but he was decent enough to store Mark's gear." She reached into her bag and produced a snapshot. "Judy. It took five years to find her. A fortuitous meeting. You know, it was rather sad about her. She died on her honeymoon in Hawaii — one of the very first cases of attacks on tourists. She left the campsite the same night Mark disappeared. I got these from her."

Michael looked at the photos spread on the table: young men with scruffy beards, shorts, hiking boots, and big rucksacks on frames. He remembered the smell of dust and unwashed socks and hemp. "That was David," she remarked.

"Was?"

"It only took me three years to find David. An unattractive person," she added reflectively. "Not the sort of friend Mark had been used to having. He had a motorcycle accident. I read later that they believed he'd been forced off the road by another vehicle."

"How did you find him?" Michael asked.

"Judy's snapshots. She knew his name. I found his address by contacting very motor vehicle department in the country. It took a lot of time. David told me about the party. There had been a fight, he thought, but he had been too drunk to remember. In the morning, he said, Mark was gone. I did not believe him."

"Perhaps you should have believed him," Michael said.

"But that would have raised other questions. Brian, now, took nearly eight years. He'd gone into camping equipment, working as a mail-order company for serious backpackers and hikers. There are a surprising number of mail-order companies. I paid to have a computer age the image from Judy's snapshot. And, of course, travel is my business. I found him in San Diego."

"How did he die?" Michael asked. His voice sounded hoarse, unfamiliar.

She looked at him quizzically. "He died in a fall," she said. "Ironic for a climber, but he fell down his office stair."

"Four years ago?" Michael asked.

"About that. I'd figured maybe another six or seven years for you, but there is always serendipity. I saw you sitting here when I least expected to, but of course you'd always been in my mind."

"Of course," Michael said.

"And now we must swap," she said. She laid her handbag on the table. It was the size of a small duffel bag and looked heavy.

"Perhaps you do not really want to," he said.

"Perhaps you are afraid," she said. "Afraid to know."

"None of this has anything to do with me," Michael said. "Now Mark . . ."

"Yes?"

"Mark was afraid."

She waited.

"When it happened — and before — he was afraid . . ."

"Ah," she said, "when what happened?"

"The fight, the accident. It really was an accident; it was no one's fault."

"Up in the aspens," she said. "The night of the party."

"That's right."

"He was afraid . . ." she stopped, and, for the first time, hesitated.

"He was afraid of violence, of unforseen craziness and confusion."

"Why?" she asked and bit her lip.

"I think that is what you have to swap," Michael said. The lights were coming on. Their golden pinpoints swam in her dark lenses.

"There is no way he could have known," she said softly.

"There are always rumors, hints."

"In a small town, yes, rumors, hints, whispers."

"And when it happened — we were all drunk, you know — when it happened —"

"It? It?" she demanded.

"You've been there," Michael said. "The loneliness of it, the mountains, the sheet of water with the trees quivering and dancing."

"The campsite was sordid."

"In the mountains, you feel small," Michael said. "The wind comes down and blows your soul away."

"But if he was afraid," she said, "he was afraid of himself."

"He had a temper," Michael agreed.

"But nothing like . . ."

"You were going to say?"

"I was going to day, 'Nothing like his father.' Nothing like."

"Yes he was worried," Michael said and gripped the edge of the café table.

"There was no sign," she said carefully. "There was no sign whatsoever. Schizophrenia develops typically in adolescence. His father — his father was ill from the time he was eleven or twelve."

"A fine father you picked for your son," Michael said.

"'Picked' is not the right word. But that's another story. We were talking about Mark. He was seventeen when he disappeared. True, the danger years, but there was no sign ever."

"But you must understand," Michael said. The night awash in beer, rivalry, anger, a sudden violence —"

"And my son was killed," she said in a cold voice.

"There was blood," Michael admitted; he sounded surprised. Yes, there had been blood. "Even in midsummer, it is very cold there in the morning. The light is bluish and the mountains are the color of lead. You can wake up there and see the very shape of your fears lying in a pool of blood."

"You had killed . . ."

"Let me give you the situation, all right? This guy was in the camp. A stranger passing through. He joined the party that night. He made a pass at Judy, picked a fight. In the morning, he was lying dead in the tent, and the others were gone."

"They would have had ordinary fears," she observed, not unsympathetically."

"They bugged out. Mark had no head for alcohol. By the time he came to, everyone else was gone. He was left to . . . clean up."

"The lake," she suggested.

"The lake is very deep," Michael agreed.

"But not as deep as deception."

"Nor as madness. There was the proof, wasn't there? Proof of what he'd always wanted not to know. Proof of the rumors about crazy Uncle Ben, who'd done something terrible, who was locked up far away, who could never, ever be released."

"You knew all this and yet you left him," she said, her voice dangerous again.

"I'm trying to give you the situation."

"The situation in which he died or in which he 'disappeared'?" She began fumbling in her purse and Michael stood up.

"It was Uncle Ben, wasn't it?" he demanded. "Mark's father was loony Uncle Ben?"

"You see," she said softly, "why it was better not to tell him. You see how much I had to protect him from. You do see that, don't you?"

"Maybe you can see why he had to protect you, too." Michael's whole body pounded with his heart like a great resonating chamber, and a gray mountain light suffused the Café Visconti, bringing with it the inescapable awkwardness of death. "Why life was impossible for him. How could he have told you, for God's sake!"

"He would have told me in the end," she said calmly. "We were very close. I can't expect you to understand that, but he would never have left me wondering and grieving for twenty years. Never. You had an ordinary life, a conventional home. You have no idea." A little black snub-nosed pistol peeked out over the top of her purse. "You are the very last," she said. "After twenty years." She raised the pistol, and full of anger and regret and fear, Michael leaped back from the table and broke for the street. His bad leg slowed him, and she saw that the instant before she saw the car. She jumped up and shouted his name, and he glanced back — she would remember that he did glance back — but he had hidden too well, the past was too terrible, and all alternative futures too full of regrets and recriminations. He was still running when he hit the street.

The squeal of brakes and the thump transfixed her heart and turned her nerves to thorns. After a few seconds, she sat back down and laid the child's pistol on the table. When the carabinieri arrived, the pistol would be lying there, a harmless toy, and she would be staring toward the dark street behind her tinted glasses. She knew what she would say, something about a present for a friend's child, a misunderstanding, a curiously unstable stranger. She knew she would say those things, though she was not sure why she should bother, for now she was not convinced that she had not, after all, made a terrible mistake.

PIGSKILL

Martin met her on holiday — a bad time, if you ask me, to meet a wife. He was in the south of France with gorgeous weather, perfect food, and no more than three words of French, when along came Diane. "I'm from Liverpool," she said, "Luv." That "Luv" should have warned him, but if it did, he closed his ears. Her much-processed hair was golden against the blue water, her bracelets jingled to the hopeful guitars and flutes of the boardwalk musicians. Even "Luv" was heaven; she spoke English.

It was the best holiday of Martin's life: long days on the beach, lazy dinners down the rail line in Cannes, then the trip back in the almost dark, the rail carriage dim, the red rocks of the cliffs diving straight into the sea and marking their entry with a whoosh of breakers. Such nights are like nectar, and Martin wasn't the first to try to bottle that charm for the cold New England winters. Not by a long shot.

Her package tour left from Marseilles, and he went into the city to see her off. "Goodbye, Luv," she said. Her mouth still tasted of the sea, her hair blew against his cheek. "Write," he said. Though she promised, it was not enough. There on Quai Cinq of the main Marseilles station, Martin Forbish did the first of the three very foolish things he was to do in life: he proposed.

Diane, charmingly, hesitated — calculated, he would later say, but one was as deceived as the other. He looked at her and saw pleasure, sunshine, bouillabaisse, strong white wine, and soft black nights behind the long shutters of their room. She saw a prosperous man who liked a good time and could be generous to the woman who amused him. He was a trifle older than she'd have liked and she'd have preferred him blond, but as the train pulled out she thought again. Liverpool meant rain, hard times, sore feet from the shop. At the next station she got off an hired a cab. In her haste, the luggage was left on the train, and when she fell into Martin's surprised arms, her bridges had effectively been burned. They were married in Nice, which their friends thought romantic, and flew to the States.

At the start, things did not go too badly. Diane occupied herself with canvassing the house, with discovering all that was missing and that she could supply by trips to the mall. There was the novelty of company for him, and it was not until the rains of late October were followed by the bitter cold of November and December that the costs of their impulsiveness became clear. Put in simplest form, they were not the people they had supposed. Martin Forbish was not the generous bon vivant he had appeared on the French coast. Rather, he was an intensely cautious, fiscally conservative realtor who spent his days in the excitements of surveying an assortment of rural properties, and, when he was lucky, in the conveyance of wornout farms and scrub woodlot to investment-minded suburbanites.

As for Diane, I regret to say that she was what she seemed — only more so. At home, Martin noticed that she was vulgar, that her clothes were flashy, her makeup loud, her whole style a little cheap. She needed blue skies, white sun, the red rocks and pastel stuccos of Provence. She needed warmth. Undone by travel posters for Miami and Orlando, Diane had expected palms, pools, and heat; instead she found a trim but chilly New England village that was clogged with snow and ice for four months of the year. Before long she was bored — bored with the town, bored with Martin, bored with the shop — so much like the shop she'd left in Liverpool! What was she to do? The answer was as irritating as it was unsurprising: first it was George, who worked in the hardware shop next to her own every so dreary billet at the drugstore. Then it was Peter, who, if no better, was younger, then Alex, who was sweet, and Leonard, who definitely was not. There were nights out for drinks and afternoons out at the motel along the country road.

Things went in this way from bad to worse. Martin took to having a bite of supper after work, and a few drinks, too, in order to get home just in time to plant himself in front of the TV and watch the sport of the season. Diane, who had been reasonably circumspect, began to flaunt her affairs. She came in late, took days off work, left the house in a shambles, and spent the food money on perms and fancy cosmetics. The Martin Forbishes began to quarrel, to curse fate, to regret the soft lights and madcap romance that had raised their hopes beyond reasonable fulfillment.

They could have called it quits, of course, but each had acquired a taste for romance. Diane didn't want to go back to Liverpool leaving behind her "American developer." And Martin, solid Rotarian that he was, did not like to admit that his fling abroad had ended in failure. They soldiered on, each hoping the other would disappear one morning like dirty dishes under a fairy godmother's wand, and each, quite unconsciously, made certain plans for how things might be without the other.

Like other unhappy couples, the Forbishes might have lived this way for years if it had not been for two incidents trivial enough in themselves. The first occurred in connection with Martin's work: a farmer out beyond Pomfret wanted to sell off some land, and Martin went to have a look at the property. It was a narrow strip of scrubby woodlot and low meadow fronting the state road, which was good, and backing up a pig farm, which was not. Martin leaned on the wire fence, surveyed the churned-up earth where several dozen muddy-legged red pigs were rooting and snorting, and shook his head.

"Can't have bacon without hogs," the old farmer observed sagely. "Ain't no smell to good hogs."

"City people," Martin murmured apologetically.

"These hogs," said the farmer, "they're raised the way hogs are meant to be raised. Outdoors, see. Your pig's an intelligent animal. She gets bored indoors, gets bored, too, if you ask me, with all this processed feed. Slop's good for pigs, old bread, too. They like that. Cook it up myself for them a couple times a week." He nodded to a small dark shack which Martin had failed to notice. Before it stood a line of troughs.

"Bread, you mean?"

The old farmer shook his head in irritation. "Bread they eat plain," he said scornfully. "Naw I mean old turnips and cabbage, waste from the butcher. Cook it all up for them. I tell you I've eaten a lot worse than those hogs many a day." He spoke with a relish that Martin found disturbing.

"They eat meat? Pigs aren't carnivorous."

The old farmer laughed. "Eat you, young fellow, right down to the gristle, and crunch your bones." He gave Martin a keen, unpleasant look, as if he could fancy a cutlet or a chop himself. See that gilt," he pointed to a hugh animal with a bristling of white around her snout. "That's Peg o'My Heart; she weighed over seven hundred and fifty pound last time we had her on the scale. You can bet she enjoys a meal."

"They're not dangerous, are they?" Martin asked in alarm. His suburban clients were alarmed by large livestock.

"Naw, not if they're well fed and not molested. And clean. Now they're muddy at the moment, but this is a sweet-smelling animal. You can tell that to any client. If they build a house along here, why they'll hardly even know there's pigs around."

"Well, I'll see what I can do," Martin said, "but it won't be top dollar. You understand that. What with the low ground and the brush to be cleared and your agricultural endeavors —

But the old farmer repeated everything he had said about the merits of his land, the cleanliness of his hogs, and the general level of profit that he considered reasonable before Martin got away, and the visit did not leave the junior partner of Raymer and Forbish in a happy mood. He'd be lucky if he sold that tract within a year, and the thought of the pigs and of their hearty yet somehow insinuating guardian made him shudder. Their round bulk balanced on dainty hooved feet, their small, cold, intelligent eyes, and their disgusting habits, so vigorously depicted by the farmer, touched the pit of his stomach. Perhaps that's why the argument he had that night with Diane turned ugly. They started to shout at each other, disregarding the neighbors. She called him drunken pig and he called her a tramp before disappearing into the den, slamming the door, and turning on the television set. After that, all seemed as usual, but twice in the next week, Martin found himself checking details he had forgotten about the farmer's parcel of land and standing, nervous yet fascinated, watching the pigs. The second time, he brought three hamburgers from a roadside eatery. Though he could not have borne to examine his reasons, he was set to make an experiment.

One of the animals came over to the fence with the peculiar ambling trot of a fat pig, raised its long, sensitive snout, and sampled the air. Martin felt his stomach contract. The hog made a snuggling sound like the clearing of large, nasal passages and fixed its small round eyes on Martin hopefully.

Automatically, his hand opened one of the greasy paper sacks and produced a burger. A second pig came over and leaned against the fence so that the wire vibrated, making Martin nervous. "Here," he said and threw a piece of the burger on the ground. It was gone in an instant. He threw out another piece and then another, separating the meat from the bun, but it didn't matter, they wolfed it down like children on an outing and pressed their big bristly bodies against the wire and snorted and snuggled and demanded more.

"Get away you filthy things," Martin cried, and he kicked at the wire and slammed his fist against the fence post before he ran back to his car. Sitting sweating in the front seat, he had some inkling of the way events were going, and in a passion of fear, knew his danger, knew he had to escape. That night, when he was pounding some veal for dinner, Diane came in. She was in a good mood, and ordinarily, Martin would have postponed unpleasantness, but now he dared not.

"I want a divorce," he said. "I'll pay for your flight back to England."

"You want?" she said.

"We have to get a divorce."

"Well, you picked a fine time. Think you can just say come and then go, do you. What would you say if I told you I was pregnant?"

Martin didn't say anything. Instead he swung the sold steel meat tenderizer straight at her head. It caught her on the temple and she fell to the floor without a word.

For an instant, Martin stood in the middle of his kitchen. Then he dropped the implement with a clatter and bent over his wife. "This is why," he said stupidly. "It can't go on. I didn't mean to hurt you. Surely, you see now it was all a mistake." There were tears running down his face and he talked on for several minutes, explaining, cajoling, apologizing, before he realized she was dead.

He sat back on his heels in shock. He jumped up to call the doctor, an ambulance, the police, lifted the receiver, then let it drop. He ran into the bedroom, ripped a sheet from their bed and covered her up, then sat down at the kitchen table, lit one of his rare cigarettes and tried to stop shaking. He sat there for quite a while, incapable of thought, incapable, almost, of feeling, before he noticed the meat tenderizer and the veal — for two, obviously — waiting on the counter. The thought, stern and overmastering, came to him that everything must seem normal, that everything must be as always. With a feeling of intense relief, he jumped up, put the tenderizer in the dishwasher, threw the veal into a frying pan and prepared dinner. When he had set the table for two as usual and fixed the vegetables and fried the veal, he could have wept with joy; everything was the same. And it would be. Everything would be all right, if he did not think, if he did not remember.

It was dark after dinner, and since the house had been build with an attached garage, there was no problem about putting Diane in the car. Martin loaded in the rest of what he figured he'd need, threw in, at the last moment, a change of clothes, and headed for the farm. A half-hour later, lights off, his car lurched onto the dirt track that ran between the property for sale and the field where the pigs were kept. Martin pulled well into the trees, turned off the motor, and reconnoitered. Then, satisfied, he laid his trouble light down on the floor of the swill shed and went back to the car.

He was in the shed all night, working hard with a kind of blank concentration. He was assisted in this oblivion by the physical difficulties of the operation: the swill kettles were large, cast-iron tubs, heavy and awkward. The fire burned coal or wood indifferently and required constant watching if it were not either to smoke and go out, or flare up with a vehemence that threatened the entire shed. By dawn he was ready, and using a scoop he found in the shed, Martin Forbish began to transfer Diane's mortal remains to the troughs outside. When he was done, he changed, fed his soiled clothes and hers into the fire, and then waited out in the gray, dew-soaked pasture for the pigs.

The sun rose and he had a moment of sheer horror: they weren't coming; the old farmer had gone to modern methods, confined them to the barns, fed them in the yard. But then, when he was soaked through with sweat and shivering uncontrollably, the first dark shape appeared on the brow of the hill. The heavy brood pig raised her snout, then trotted down toward the troughs. Martin made for the safety of the fence and stood there, his hands white on the post. He was sick in the trees after, but the old farmer had been absolutely correct: the herd of pigs cleaned the troughs till there were only a few large bones left. Sick with fear, Martin crossed the wire and retrieved these, the hogs watching with interest, accepting him as one of their providers. Martin put the last incriminating evidence down a chuck hole at the edge of the wood, got in his car, and drove away.

It was a couple of days before the store called about Diane, and a couple more before Martin felt obliged to call the police. The town was small, Diane's reputation was not entirely unknown, and by and large the police were sympathetic. "She'll turn up," said the officer. "Most missing persons do."

Martin agreed. It was not until almost six months later, when her family back in England began making noises, that the investigation started in earnest. Then there were questions, a polite but persistent young officer asked to look through Diane's belongings, and gradually, every so gradually, Martin felt the scales tip as sympathy slid into suspicion.

With that transition, the fantasy of normalcy that had sustained him through the ghastly scenes in the swill shed began to come apart. He was impelled tho think over what he had done, not from any guilty conscience — necessity, for Martin, as for so many others, excused all — but for fear he had made some mistake, left some clue, neglected some essential. He wondered now if he should have discarded some of her clothes along with the cosmetics which he had prudently thrown into the trash, and whether he should not have packed a case and taken it to Boston, perhaps, or checked it in New York, or bought an air ticket, or done any one of a thousand things to throw the quiet, but by now omnipresent, young detective off his train, Worst of all, he began to wonder if there was not perhaps something left in the shed or in one of the troughs.

This thought haunted him. The young detective was forever "checking on his movements" as he called it, and it seemed very likely that he would one day visit the old pig farmer, hear about the wholesome old-fashioned diet of these particular hogs and — But Martin could never go further than that. The very thought was unbearable, suggesting, as it did, that he really had done what he had. So, one afternoon late in the year, Martin did his last foolish thing: he got into his car, taking with him his clipboard and notebook as if he were going to work, and drove to the farm. He had to have a look round. He had to know.

It was colder out in the country; the ruts in the fields were filled up with ice, and the only color in the brown and white landscape was the thin band of rose and gold were the sun, lethargic all day, was dying in splendor, its blood staining the trunks of the trees and the plain unpainted boards of the shed. Martin's mouth went dry, and he delayed, leaning against the wire, sick at heart and unwilling to go on. Then the blue shadows of the dusk appeared, and, sure the pigs would have been driven back to the barnyard, he climbed the wire and crossed the frozen clods of earth to the troughs. They were dry, empty. A fragment of a cabbage leaf stuck fast in one, another had a little long-frozen slip. He went into the shed, lit matches to see into the depths of the kettles, poked in the ashes of the fire: nothing.

Rather than reassuring him, this absence filled Martin with panic. Not so much as a button: they'd been there before him. Even now that smooth and quiet detective would be laying out his evidence, putting buttons and zippers and bones in little plastic envelopes. With a shudder, Martin went back outside. He walked around the troughs, peering underneath, nothing. Chilled with sweat, he got down on his hands and knees and felt beneath each trough, then all along the ground between them. He clawed at the frozen clods of earth until his fingers ached, and then crept back again, patting the cold, ice-slicked sides of the trough: it had to be there somewhere, it had to be.

Deep in his search, he did not hear them until they were pressed close around him, long snouts twitching, small, cold, intelligent eyes watching him with hopeful curiosity. Martin raised his head and saw that they were close enough to touch, their large warm, bristly bodies a solid wall, their evil little hooved feet pawing the ground in hungry eagerness, their eyes filled now with a passionate interest, their narrow jaws open to show the stubby, yellowed teeth.

"No," said Martin with a gasp, "get away." He flung his arm out at them, but the pigs were unconcerned, they pressed closer, eager to be fed. "No," cried Martin, as his chest turned to ice. He clutched the side of the trough and tried to pull himself upright, but his breath failed him. "Please, no," he said, but impatient now, one of the hogs poked him with its moist snout, Martin swung his arm, mad with horror at them, at their eyes, at what they could do, at what he had done, and in this last effort, his heart, long-burdened by its secret, burst.

Martin fell with a cough and a sigh onto the frozen ground. The pigs were puzzled, disappointed. They snuffled at their empty troughs, and, spoiled as they were, it was a full day before they decided that Martin as he was would just have to do.

THE ARCHEOLOGIST'S REVENGE

Nothing would have been managed without the road, but fortune favors the prepared, as well as the brave, and I'd been preparing for years. Ever since the afternoon Eva "disappeared," I've lived for two things, work and revenge.

I'm an archeologist, not a famous one, but I think I can say I'm well respected. Solid and tenured, with the requisite two books under my belt, I've reached a pleasant academic plateau. My specialty is the burial customs in the Late Riverine Archaic, and while the eastern woodlands tribes are not really a glamour area in Native American studies, I have found my researches deeply satisfying — and useful, too, as you will see.

"Useful" is perhaps the proper word for me. I've been a useful teacher, a useful researcher; Jane, my wife, might say I was a useful husband, but a life of pure utility robs the soul. That was where Eva came in; Eva was social danger, emotional extravagance, pure poetry. I adored her from our first meeting, when I walked into the Feingolds' living room, prepared for the usual round of academic gossip and one up-man-ship, and saw her sitting by the fireplace. She was fair and plump, a woman bewitching in that peachy mode the old Flemish painters loved so much. When she saw us approaching, she smiled a big, open mouthed smile and devoured my heart.

"Come meet Eva, Eva and Andrew Donaldson," said Chloe Feingold, who knows everyone's rank, tenure status, dissertation subject, and grant prospects. "Andrew's just gotten the Renaissance appointment in the English Department." She beamed with unfeigned delight at a thin, focused looking chap with lank brown hair and wind burned skin, a poor specimen next to his blooming wife. "And," Chloe added, as if announcing a special treat for us, "he's a Renaissance Man, himself, running a marathon next week."

Fool, I thought, as I shook his hand, what are marathons, what is the Renaissance, that you should neglect this treasure? But he did neglect Eva, though they were moving in, though the old Burdine farmhouse was a wreck, though the lawn was too long for their little suburban mower. Fortune, as I said, favors the prepared. I brought over our riding mower — my wife, Jane, insisted — and while I circled the yard, leaving swaths of hay on the lawn, Eva raked up the cuttings and smiled as I went past. I was as happy that afternoon as if I had been orbiting the outskirts of paradise.

Five years. If you know the nosey, gossipy ways of academe, you won't believe me, but Eva and I had five good years. I even came to love the marathon, particularly the requisite training runs which provided us with hours of happiness. I remember those afternoons in the pasture back of the old farm: summer heat, wild berries, the Glassian repetition of locusts and cicadas, my darling's faintly downey cheeks, the dimples on her knees, a certain blessed avidity. Then fall, the smell of wild grapes and leaf mulch, and spring, spring! after the logistical difficulties of the winter, spring with woodcocks mating, thrushes singing, skunk cabbage and marsh marigolds bursting from the swamp. Each spring, I understood why captives of the old Iroquois and Algonquins were reluctant to return to the stiff Colonial world of floors and chairs, of stays and ruffs and high leather boots.

I would push off in my canoe, paddle along the rim of the large pond, thread my way through the marsh on the little streamlets I came to know so well, and land at the foot of the old Burdine, now the Donaldson's, pasture. Simplicity, itself, when you think about it. I always had excuses: prospecting for fish weirs, looking for campsites, immersing myself in the habitat of the archaic woodsmen. Believe me, I understood them much better after I went hunting for joy in my own canoe, stealing along the pale of settlement to pounce on my own fair darling, Eva.

If my wife, Jane, knew, she was indifferent; wisely so, I think. We had two children, both in college at the time, and our marriage, if no longer inspiring, has its own fidelities and foundations. We understand each other; that's an important point, and Jane has her own interests, the writing of romance novels chief among them. I'm told that her last three are quite the best she's ever done. I wonder if suspicions of my affair inspired her, but Jane keeps her own council.

Andrew was a different sort, possessive but neglectful, the very worst matrimonial combination, and he cast the tolerant, sophisticated spirit of my wife in a very handsome light. Andrew didn't deserve Eva. While he thought his wife was faithful, he ignored her; as soon as he suspected she had a lover, he transferred some of his compulsions from distance running and obscure textualities to interfering with the happiness of others.

I'd have enjoyed having it out with him; physical violence, scandal, statements libelous and actionable sometimes have a deep visceral appeal. But, besides the fact that I had fifteen years on him — fifteen years at least! — there was my family to think about, and, as a very ancient anthropologist once said, the price of a good, or at least a tolerable, wife is beyond rubies. So Eva and I were careful. It is my nature to be cautious, to prepare my ground — you'll see proof of that — but Eva revealed a sly discretion that, considering her spontaneous and uninhibited appetites, was as surprising as it was delightful. For a couple of years, Andrew quite unfairly suspected Gerry DeSentis, a rising young theorist in the English department, and contrived, I'm told, to keep him from tenure.

In certain moods it almost annoys me that I was never a suspect. "Old Bones and Feathers" with his gimpy knee and gray hair wasn't thought to be up to such pranks, but maybe that was just the chauvinism of literary people. I did worry a little when *The Last of the Mohegans* became such a hit; that amazing poster of Daniel Day Lewis rushing bare chested through the forest — didn't that hint at the delights of a wilder, more mysterious, now vanished life? And who should know about such things, if not I, with my head full of rituals and artifacts, of customs and myths, gliding toward my beloved over the black water of the swamp?

Oh yes, we were happy, very, very happy, until one fatal afternoon in mid-April. We'd had a long, wet winter, one of those inconclusive and unsatisfactory seasons too mild for skiing, too wet for walks. Her children were quite small then, and arrangements were difficult. Her husband's graduate students, if good baby-sitters, were eagle eyed and loose tongued, so Eva and I fell back on the Westbrook Mall, where the huge parking lots and food courts allow an anonymous rendezvous. We planned to meet that day in the south lot and take my van for a quick run to the state forest, a mixed deciduous woodland almost deserted in the dreary weather. We would have returned to the mall later, to meet, as if by chance, in the foodcourt, where we could talk back and forth between the little tables like casual acquaintances.

This was a scenario we'd used before with complete success, for neither of us liked to lie. "Where did you go today?" Jane might ask. "I bought some socks at Penney's," I'd say honestly, or "Stopped by the bookstore in the mall. Not a damn thing there but best sellers and weight loss books." And if she mentioned that Chloe Feingold or Pat Meyer had seen me at the mall, I'd say, "Half the university was out today; I ran into Eva Donaldson in the foodcourt."

When Eva did not show up that afternoon, I was disappointed but not worried. She had on occasion to cancel at the last moment: the failure of a sitter, the illness of a child, the odd sprain or strain that brought Andrew home prematurely from his interminable training. If anything, this occasional disappointment and uncertainty added a piquant note to our relationship. I'm a great believer in regularity in marriage, but in affairs of the heart a certain suspense, a certain irregularity in what is, after all, an irregularity itself, opens the way for serendipity.

I hung around the magazine racks for a while, then went home with a handful of novels for Jane. I had supper, read two chapters of the dissertation I was supervising, and went to bed. I had no idea that my life had been drastically altered until the next evening when Gus Phillips called with the news that Eva Donaldson, my Eva!, was missing. I only understood snatches of what he was saying, "car abandoned at the mall," "sitter worried," "Andrew frantic," "police."

"Police," I said, uncomprehending. It's odd how, at certain moments, you're unable to fit together the pieces of the universe.

"Of course, he called the police," said Gus, the half horrified, half delighted bearer of news. "She's been gone over 24 hours. Everyone's alarmed."

Only when I got the whole story again from Chloe Feingold, whose narration had an amplitude missing from Gus's account, did I start to believe that Eva's old Volvo had been found abandoned in the north mall parking lot. "Next to Filene's," said Chloe. "They're having their big white sale at the moment."

I believe she told me some details of the sale, but I had only one idea in mind: that Eva had been harmed.

"At the mall," I said. "The north lot."

Chloe confirmed this, and with every word, my heart sank. We never parked in the north lot, because it was near Computer City, the whole foods shop, and the bookstore, the academic's consumer triangle. We favored the south lot near Home Depot and Sears.

After I had hung up the phone and poured a gin and tonic with very little tonic, I thought about what I'd just been told. I was sure that Eva would not have parked her car in the north lot, and, with a heavy sense of fatality, I wondered if she had driven her car there at all. The mall was barely five miles from her house. Five miles. What's five miles for a marathon runner? And just as if I were an old shaman, dancing before the fire in the long house with my drum and rattles and wolf jaw, I saw Andrew getting out of the Volvo and locking it and slipping down the row of cars; out to the highway verge, over the fence to the bike path, then galloping for home with his elbows flying and his skinny, muscular legs pounding out the yardage. Five miles was nothing: I was sure he'd done it.

And where was Eva? The next afternoon I got in my canoe, not really believing in her disappearance. I thought I could glide across the pond, slip up the little branch of the river and see her waving to me from the pasture. Instead, the field was empty, and I saw something else that had not registered before, the new meadow along the dirt road.

Eva had told me about their plans. A narrow, bumpy track ran beside their yard from the state road back into the Websters' property, which includes part of the swamp and a good spread of grazing land between the Donaldsons' and ours. The plan was to have the strip of scrub, weeds and hay along this old road plowed up and reseeded with wild flowers.

"Easier than a regular flower garden," Eva had said, "and wonderful for butterflies."

Kneeling in my canoe, I could hear her saying, "wonderful for butterflies," and, with that memory of her sunny, open face, of her delight, I burst into tears. I knew she was dead. The place of our happiness was suddenly unbearable, and I was about to paddle away into the swamp, when I looked at the bare plot of earth. It had been harrowed since I visited last, harrowed and, no doubt, seeded with the daisies and coreopsis, goldenrods, and Black-eyed Susans, wild geranium, Indian Paintbrush, blue eyed grass, and clovers that have been blooming so successfully these last few years. I looked at the newly harrowed field, and I'd have bet my life that my darling Eva was lying hidden under those neat rows.

There followed the most excruciating period of my life. I was caught by the discretion which had deprived Andrew of any obvious motive. Oh, the police looked at him all right; it tells you something about marriage that the husband is always a prime suspect, but he seemed grief stricken and, more important, he had an alibi: that same damn field. Old Webster, who's been senile as long as I've known him, swore up and down that Andrew was working on the wild flower meadow the whole afternoon. He heard the tractor. The whole afternoon.

That left the morning. The children were in nursery school in the morning, but they had a sitter for the afternoon because Eva was going to the mall and Andrew planned to do the meadow. He claimed she left just before the sitter arrived, but there was no proof of that. He could have killed Eva, buried her, driven the Volvo to the Mall, run back, hopped on his tractor, and harrowed the plowed field and the new grave into oblivion. That's what I thought he'd done; I was sure of it.

I think the police may have had thoughts along those lines, too. Andrew was at the state police station three, four, five times. But nothing came of it. There was no evidence, no motive. By the time they searched the house there wasn't a clue. He'd had a couple more floors refinished by then — they'd been doing the rooms a few at a time to spare the children the fumes, and the little wild flower meadow was a foot tall and growing lush. Chloe Feingold told me that Andrew showed the troopers around with tears in his eyes. When nothing turned up, he posted a $10,000 reward for information about his wife's disappearance, which suggested that his last book, a reader for undergraduates, was doing better than any of us had expected.

Still, he was a suspect, really the only one. The problem was that the police couldn't give him a motive. I was only person who could provide that — unless Jane had seen more than I'd thought — and I was in a bind. To get at Andrew, I'd have to ruin my marriage and my comfortable relationships with our children — and Eva would still be gone forever.

Perhaps you'll decide I wasn't worthy of Eva, either, and that cowardice kept me silent. Cowardice and convenience. Perhaps I did have a time of cowardice and confusion, but this is to record the fact that ultimately I stirred myself to be worthy of my love and seek revenge.

Just how I was to achieve that satisfaction was not so easily determined. I can't tell you how many spring and summer days I paddled over to the edge of the pasture and tortured myself with memories. I stared at the meadow, flourishing undisturbed, but its soft green and yellow tints gave me no inspiration, no solutions.

I watched Andrew, too. I studied him in the faculty senate, followed his moves at parties, lurked in the swamp while he was mowing the pastures. I took to calling him up, standing nervous at pay phones in the mall, listening to the ring, ring down the line. Sometimes I thought his voice sounded anxious and sometimes tired. Once or twice, late at night, he got angry. I listened without saying anything, waiting, always waiting for the admission, the confession — as if, after all his cares and plans, he was likely to blurt out the truth to a mysterious and silent caller. You will appreciate that I was not myself then.

I actually stooped to a poison pen letter. I'm not proud of that. My only excuse was my desperation: I felt I had to frighten Andrew out of his complacency. I was at the computer lab one night, the big one, not the little departmental lab, and before I knew what I was doing, I'd typed, "You killed her" and printed it out.

I put the message in an envelop and mailed it, then spent the next few days half sick with hope and anxiety. Nothing happened, except that Chloe Feingold told me Andrew was taking everything very hard and invited Jane and me around to have dinner with him. As a result of that excruciating evening, I began to think about my own specialty and how my knowledge might be put to use.

My first attempts were abortive. I made an intensive study of eastern woodland bows and learned to shoot one. I spent some enlighening afternoons with an elderly member of the Naragansetts, and I got so that I could flake a point pretty well. I did not get to where I could see myself skewering Andrew with a brilliant shot to the heart.

I considered Native American botanicals next and worked more hours than I care to remember in the pharmacy lab and in the crumbling shed where Mrs. Margaret Laughing Bear stores dried plants and her musty smelling packets of traditional medicines. I published a couple of papers that were well received, but Mrs. Laughing Bear was dexterous in fending off all inquiries about poisons. Besides, as I began to get a hold of myself, I could see the difficulties of slipping tincture of nightshade into Andrew's cocktail or of feeding him a Death Angel mushroom.

I do think that these fantasies, and others even more embarrassing and puerile, kept me sane. They gave me hope; they kept me from doing something obvious, unforgivable, irretrievable. And then came the road and, all of a sudden, everything fell into place. All my futile efforts, my midnight walks, my sad canoe trips, even those cruel phone calls, had been so much priming of the pump. When the road came, I recognized my chance. All that remained was to proceed in a timely and orderly fashion.

What had happened was that Eli Webster, the senile fool who had given Andrew his alibi in the first place, finally went into a home. The grandchildren wasted no time subdividing the old farm and contracting with a particularly fast and profit hungry developer to transform 60 prime acres into something to be called Webster Estates with a projected 40 houses. Few of us in town were pleased about that and a good old fashioned zoning and development fight ensued.

I pitched in to testify about the archeological value of the fish weirs and the campsite on the property, and I helped Sue LeBonte assemble some of the environmental data on the impact such a big project would have on the watershed. The neighbors were pretty much all against the development, but I found it significant that Andrew didn't get really involved until the business of the road came up.

Access for the new Webster Estates was going to have to be that dirt road along the Donaldson's little wild flower meadow. Nothing could be done, no construction, certainly no heavy truck traffic, until that lane was widened and upgraded. At this point, Andrew went ballistic. I felt I had him for sure.

Like so many other things in small towns, the Webster Estates finally came to a compromise, bigger lots, fewer houses, an environmental set aside. We were to have ten houses, which was more than enough, and over Andrew Donaldson's strenuous objections, the town agreed to widening and paving the road. I was at the council meeting the night the agreement passed, and I went right from there to the University. My book bag was in the car. I took out my texts and my grade book, locked them in the trunk, and went into the building with my empty knapsack.

This was not unusual behavior. I'm nocturnal by choice; I often work late and I make midnight rambles to the Museum for books or records or to check some item in the archives. I remember stopping that night at the museum and looking in at my favorite exhibit: the bark house my students built several years ago as part of our Eastern Woodlands display.

In the light from the hall, the support pillars cast long tree-like shadows over the little bark house, a miniature of the noble halls of the Iroquois.

I had an impulse to go inside, and I did, crouching for a few moments in the cramped space that smells of cedar and bark, mingled with the institutional odors of floor polish and air conditioning. I knew from Mrs. Laughing Bear's shed that it should also smell like dried plants and dirt floors and the residue of fires and cooking fat. I'm not sure what I'd have told the custodian if he'd come by. Certainly not the truth, which was that I was paying homage to people who understood blood vengeance and who were about to help me get it.

After a few moments in the half darkness, I crawled out and relocked the door before descending to Archives and Research, a pleasantly old fashioned room. Below the horizontal windows set high in the walls are banks of good mahogany cabinets where we store our specimens. Most of the collection is pottery shards, but we also have a lot of arrow and spear points, some clothing, a couple of pieces of really first rate embroidery and beadwork, and some bones.

We've returned a number of complete skeletons to the Mohegan and Pequot tribal authorities in the last couple of years, and we're negotiating with the Pequots over some other artifacts. They're building a collection, and I've been trying to interest them in some scholarly activities. I see an endowed chair eventually, perhaps other ventures; with their casino revenue, they've certainly got the money.

By rights some of the skulls in case #14 should be returned as well. They came from federal land and fall under NAGPRA (the Native American Graves Protection and Repatriation Act), but that's a future project. My own favorite, #2456, is from my personal collection and belonged to a woman of the Adena, the mound building people of the central Ohio Valley. I've had her carbon dated. She lived around 1,000 B.C.E., and I've had her skull ever since I stole it from the excavation I was working on the year I received my doctorate.

There's a certain symmetry, isn't there, to my only two cases of professional malfeasance? Beauty must be my excuse: #2456 was a lovely skull, darkened to an elegant biscuit color by the soil where it had lain so many centuries. As I examined it that night in the strong halogen lamp over the case, I saw that her head would have been round, her face broad, perhaps plump like Eva's. I hoped her short life had been happy, as I believe Eva's was. The eye sockets were large; #2456's eyes would probably have been black or very dark brown, instead of Eva's gray-blue, and her hair would have been dark. I think that she was a pretty woman.

Fortuitously, I had put a paper label on her skull instead of numbering the surface of the bone, and, after making sure that there were no extraneous marks, I peeled the tag off and cleaned the little sticky patch that remained with alcohol. Then I wrapped #2456 in a piece of old newspaper and put it in my knapsack.

I had only to wait until the road crew arrived, a matter of considerable vigilance. I went the long way to the University every day in order to be sure the town hadn't yet begun work, and every afternoon in decent weather, I was in the swamp, listening for the sound of graders and bull-dozers — or for the softer, fainter sound of a man digging through tough meadow grass.

At last, the contract went out, and one May morning just as we were finishing exams, I found the road crew had arrived. That evening, as late as I dared make it, I told Jane I was going to take a paddle around the swamp.

"Perhaps I'll go with you one night," she said. "It's been lovely weather."

I had the horrible feeling that she was going to suggest coming with me right then. "Mosquitoes," I said, ashamed of the reluctance in my voice and aware that I was neglecting Jane. "Let me buy some more spray. I'll get that tomorrow. And a paddle. You'll want a paddle, too."

"It's not worth the fuss," said Jane.

"Tomorrow," I said, kissing her cheek. "And I'll do all the paddling."

She laughed and, now reprieved, I made a joke of near disaster. I transfered my knapsack from the car to the canoe and put on my moccasins for luck. I'd been extraordinarily tempted by a pair of embroidered moosehide slippers that night in the museum archives, and I had needed all my willpower and professional pride to leave them in their protective packet.

By the time I got to the Donaldson's, the light was fading. I tied up the canoe to some scrub and walked quietly toward the meadow with my knapsack slung over my shoulder. I can't describe to you my state of alertness that night. I seemed to hear every insect, every bird, the break-ing of every twig, the bending of every blade of grass. Up at the top of the hill, the Donaldson's house was lit up against the lacy darkness of the partially leafed out trees and the radiant pink and lavender sky. It's really a very nice location, but since Eva's death, Andrew had not kept the place up as well. The gaps between the trees along the road had gradually been filled in with a hedge of saplings, shrubs and vines. I was screened by this growth as I approached the work site where the lane was scraped down a good foot or more and piles of earth were heaped along the sides. They had roughly doubled the track, ripping out some of the young trees and cutting several feet into the meadow. I had just about reached this open area, when I heard footsteps.

I practically fell into the only shelter available, a little cluster of maple saplings, poison ivy and bittersweet. A man was walking along the meadow on the other side of the scrub and I was sure it was Andrew. I lowered myself into the vines and grass and waited. He seemed to be checking the work that had been done, tapping the ground here and there with a shovel, but, I didn't dare raise my head for confirmation.

What if he saw me? What to say? Perhaps I should have been tempted by the Museum's polished Algonquin war club instead of those moccasins, but actual physical violence, however satisfactory in the abstract, was out of my plan, perhaps beyond my capacity. Instead, I crouched silently for interminable, mosquito filled minutes until his footsteps faded.

Once he was gone, I moved quickly in the semi-darkness. Weeks before, I had picked out a cluster of large trees. As I approached them, I selected the most substantial heap of bulldozed earth on the meadow side. Taking #2456 from my knapsack, I packed the cranium with soil, then gently fitted it into the raw earth. This delicate operation was probably hampered as much as helped by my professional expertise. It was ten minutes by my watch before I felt it looked right, the skull noticeable but half buried in the sand, clay and rocks, and another five before I had erased the softly rounded prints of my moccasins.

When I got home, I offered to run to the convenience store for some of Jane's favorite ice cream. The pint of pistachio was cold against my arm as I dialed Andrew's number and listened to it ring.

"Who is it?" he cried. For the first time, I responded. I laughed out loud and set down the receiver.

The discovery was in the local paper the next night. I'd half expected to be called at work. It wouldn't have been the first time, for with the density of artifacts in our area, I've run programs for construction companies on the importance of reporting bones and relics. In turn, we try not to hold up work too long while we recover artifacts and map the site. However, the grader operator was a crime, not an archeology, buff. She saw the skull, remembered the Donaldson investigation, and called the police.

"It's just a tragedy," Chloe Feingold told me that evening. For once, I was hanging on her every word. "Of course, poor Andrew is nearly hysterical." For some reason, he was always one of her favorites.

"Surely they don't think he had anything to do with it!" I said.

"Well, of course not!" Chloe said. "But he hasn't helped himself. He keeps saying 'it can't be Eva,' 'it isn't Eva,' putting the idea in their heads, you know. But you can't imagine his state of mind!"

Actually, I could.

"We're recommended our lawyer. You know Hugh Boyd, don't you? He wants that skull examined right away."

"Surely the coroner," I began . . .

"Hugh says it looks old, and I'm just sure it is. Why Andrew had to mention Eva at all is totally beyond me." Chloe said.

"She must always be in his mind," I said.

"Of course," Chloe said impatiently, "but it can't be Eva, it just can't be, and the sooner they get you to date the remains the better. It's important that we all rally behind Andrew."

The dean said something similar to me when he learned that I'd been asked to examine the skull. That was after the police had dug around the road without success; after Andrew, behaving badly, had retreated into shock and mental anguish, and after Hugh Boyd had told all and sundry that his client was being subjected to duress. Though I let Andrew stew as long as possible, I eventually had to give my opinion.

We assembled in a small conference room in the county jail, Hugh Boyd, Andrew, me and the investigating officers. As the seating worked out, Andrew and I were across from each other at the institutional gray metal conference table, an optimal arrangement. This was the sort of single combat I'd envisioned, and I was pleased to see that Andrew had lost his rosy tan and aura of fitness. He looked like a gaunt acolyte of some obscure and fanatical religion, and though he greeted me warmly, I sensed that his nerve was failing. Mine, as you'll see, was in perfect condition.

I laid the carefully repackaged skull on the table and opened my briefcase for my notes. I moved very slowly and deliberately; I had waited in secret for this moment for nearly three years. I think the secrecy is worth emphasizing, for how much of achievement is anticipation, and how much of anticipation is the pleasure of sharing hopes with others?

Andrew winced at the sight of the skull, and I felt myself smile involuntarily, before I cleared my throat and began reading. In essence, I said that the skull was very old and its presence, somewhat anomalous. I speculated briefly about trade routes and the diffusion of Archaic civilization. My lectures are considered first-rate and my introductory classes are always filled early.

"The key thing," said Hugh Boyd, ignoring Eva's disappearance, Andrew's guilt, and my revenge, "is that, as we've maintained all along, the bones could not possibly be those of Eva Donaldson. That being the case, there is absolutely no reason to continue questioning my client."

When the investigating officer had reservations about this, I raised my professional concerns: the possibility of more bones, even artifacts.

I suggested a modest excavation trench. "If we concentrate on the meadow, we won't need to hold up the road work at all," I said.

"No," said Andrew, very loudly and angrily.

I feigned the greatest surprise. "Surely, it would be the best possible thing for you, as well as for certain lucky selected graduate students."

"No," Andrew said. "I won't have the meadow disturbed any further. It was Eva's meadow; she wanted it in flowers." For a moment, I thought he might attempt tears. "I don't know why you even raised the subject. All you were asked to do was to estimate the age of the —" he flapped his hand toward the packet, "— the remains."

Hugh Boyd made soothing noises, but the Lieutenant was clearly interested.

"Of course," I said, "my apologies for even suggesting it, but I'm sure Eva would have wanted this cleared up."

"How do you know what Eva would have wanted?" Andrew demanded. I think right then that he began belatedly to suspect me.

"I know the Dean is concerned," I continued, "and with your tenure reviews coming up . . ." I left this phrase dangling. "Suspicion," I added, "suspicion can have such a negative effect. You can hardly imagine," I told Boyd and the Lieutenant.

"I think everyone will understand my situation has been perfectly terrible," Andrew said. I'm sure I was not the only one to notice that with the notion of tenure, his emotions were suddenly completely convincing. "The Committee, the Dean, everyone . . ."

I laughed, a miscalculation, but I couldn't help it. There's a kind of wilful naivete I find irresistibly comic.

Andrew started as if he'd been struck. "This whole business was your doing!" he cried. He actually stood up at the table. He was right, of course, but I can't say I rate him highly in quickness of perception.

"Control yourself, Andrew. I don't know what you're talking about."

The words poured out, "That skull," "your laugh," "Eva!" — but I'll spare you the full and unabridged text. I remained calm, courteous; I really was extraordinarily calm and courteous that day. I ignored the personal aspersions and said, "There's no reason for you to panic about the meadow, Andrew. For the price of a few aerial photographs we can set everyone's mind at rest. I just thought the process of trial and error would be good for the students."

Hugh Boyd began sputtering, but the Lieutenant — I think that was his rank, trooper ranks are different from city police, you know, — asked, "Aerial photography?"

"You hadn't thought of that? Archeological trade secret, I guess." I was well into my explanation of how ruins, foundation trenches, and graves can be spotted from the air, when Andrew lunged across the table and — there's no other appropriate word here — attacked me.

I still haven't decided whether that was deliberate or not, I mean, a deliberate ploy to suggest unsoundness of mind or just a total failure of self control. In any case, Andrew Donaldson was held for psychiatric assessment, and three days later, I had the painful satisfaction of pointing out a small oblong, visible in a properly enhanced aerial photograph of the meadow. When excavated, this telltale depression proved to contain my Eva's body.

After the trial, I asked for custody of the old skull, although this was a somewhat delicate matter, the state troopers having some suspicions about the source of the original find. Then one of my graduate students became intrigued with the resemblances to known Adena skulls; she wanted to examine both the site and the skull more thoroughly. It was with difficulty that I dissuaded her; in professional conscience, I could not let her build her thesis on a hoax. Finally, as expected, the Pequots got involved. I had some delicate negotiations with their heavy weight lawyer, before they settled for three other bona fide eastern woodlands relics from the historic period.

When interest dies down, I will quietly relabel #2456 and return her to my private collection. Or perhaps I will take her home and rebury her somewhere in the Ohio valley. Perhaps I will do that; I think I will.

Her people believed in an afterlife and provisioned themselves well for it, tempting grave robbers and that better class of thief, the archeologist. But after the great favor she's done me, I don't feel I can leave #2456 to dream away her eternity in my mahogany cabinet. She can even have some grave goods; I have extra specimens that will never be missed. And even if they were, I feel a sense of obligation, for I understand now that even the bones of one's beloved are sacred. I understand that every time I slip into the old cemetery to lay some of Eva's wild flowers on her grave.

STAR OF THE SILVER SCREEN

He'd promised to kill her if she ever left him — and she believed him absolutely. When he'd first whispered it to her over drinks at expensive restaurants or amidst the sexy rumble of the dance floor, she'd interpreted his declaration as love, as devotion, as need. She'd been flattered and reassured; he'd seemed so strong, so passionate and determined.

Now, she knew better. Ben didn't know much about love and nothing about devotion. What he knew about was need and power and control, and he'd known so much about those that he'd gone from an underfed kid selling handfuls of pills and bags of crack to one of the biggest men in the northeast. Big enough so that he handled the money end, the organization end; big enough so that the "product" could have been anything — electronics, imported fabrics, luxury cars, or — his usual response when folks who didn't know better asked what he did — fine imported wines.

That was a laugh, she thought. Where Ben came from a "fine wine" was an unopened bottle of Thunderbird. But he did know a lot about vintages. He was always impressive, the way he could talk about the bouquet and the palate and the fruity blush while the big spenders and society types nodded their heads and raised him a notch with every word. Oh, she'd often watched him in action. First, when she was dazzled by him and later when she was scared; either way, she had to admit Ben was smart. He was the smartest man she'd ever met and every time she thought about that, she gave a little shiver. He said he'd kill her and she believed him — absolutely.

She'd hoped — which shows what kind of a fool she'd been — she hoped that getting so far from "the product" would change him. That the skinny kid who'd become the glamorous and wealthy man would keep changing and that somehow the underpinnings — the sordid overkill and cruelty and stupidity of street life would vanish, presto!, and they could be left with all the things she liked: the city apartment, the country house, parties with musicians, platinum credit cards, Mercedes and Jaguars and private jets. Like Ben, she'd developed her tastes. She'd toned down the flash and bought quality. And if Ben complained a dress was "too plain," she loaded up with jewelry, with beautiful, flawless stones in handsome settings, good as money in the bank any day, because Ben had been very generous.

In the beginning, she'd accepted his presents as love. When he grew more difficult and distant, she extracted them as payment, wages due for slaps and curses, for violent scenes and humiliating demands. Finally, when she ceased to feel anything for him but fear, she bought jewelry for herself, quietly siphoning cash from the almost unspendable money stream that seeped through their lives.

So, all considered, she couldn't exactly say she was unprepared, though she did stay on too long. The bottom line, of course, was his whispered, shouted threat, but there were other distractions, too: trips, cars, furs, jewels; fabulous parties, new clothes, new houses, new rooms, new apartments. Time can be filled up if you only have money, and even when she found herself needing more and more to fill up less and less time, "the product" provided.

She had no real scruples about that. Like a lot of people, she was selectively unimaginative, and she did not find it too great a strain to block out speculations on the overall cost of doing business. She could have been happy — she realized that later — she could have been happy as a permanent thing, if Ben hadn't started drinking. Well, not really drinking, but it sounded nicer to say "drinking." What Ben really did was to become better acquainted with "the product."

That was when she began to be afraid of him, of his sudden rages, his sly paranoia and violent accusations. That was when she began to be afraid of losing everything, not just the swank parties and designer clothes; not just leather seats and satin spreads and damask linen, but herself, her identity. She'd vanished into luxury. She'd thought she'd been growing and developing, but had she? She'd become the woman who lived at the Chateau Blanc, who ate in certain restaurants, shopped at certain stores, traveled in certain circles and appeared at certain parties. That's who she was and who would she be without the Gucci shoes, the Ferragamo scarves, the Channel accessories? She wasn't sure she wanted to find out.

But he said, "I'll kill you," and she believed him because of one night when they were up late in their elegant black and white kitchen. She was heating water for a cup of tea; he was drinking an expensive old whiskey. She had spent the evening watching *Pretty Woman* on video; he had been out with old friends, "product" friends, and he was coming down from strenuous partying, when, without warning — that was the terrible thing — without any warning at all, he spun into a rage and, knocking the pan from the stove, forced both her hands onto the burner.

The next day, he brought her orchids in the hospital. Live, potted orchids that would later flourish in their professionally maintained greenhouse. And bunches of lilies and roses in a crystal vase and a magnificent jeweled evening bag shaped like Humpty Dumpty, that was too heavy for her scorched hands to hold. But he did not say that he was sorry. It was as if he hadn't done anything at all, as if the maniac in the night kitchen had been some other Ben, some other man altogether. When she realized that, she'd become really frightened and understood at last that she had to leave.

All the while her hands were healing, she made elaborate, obsessive plans, but she lacked energy to put them into action until the day Ben frightened her again. Overwhelmed by terror, she ran to the safe for her jewelry case as soon as he went out. The minute she had it in her hands, she knew she'd decided and became calm. She marveled about that later; about how you can get through terror to the other side, like stepping out of a dark, cramped elevator into a big, well-lighted foyer.

She laid the jewelry case on her bed and went into Ben's office, where she rooted through the closet for the heavy leather bag she knew was stashed at the back. She hauled it out, fetched a knife from the kitchen, and forced the catch.

Inside, the casino chips sat in neat plastic boxes, rows and rows and rows of them, red, white, and black with satisfyingly large demoninations stamped on their shiny faces. She transferred the whole lot to a suitcase, replacing them with some heavy cans to make up the weight, and returned Ben's leather bag to his closet. She changed her clothes, loaded the cases into her pretty silver Mercedes, and drove out the gates of the Chateau Blanc without looking back.

It was foggy the whole way to the casino. That's what she remembered afterwards: the ghostly, foggy night with haloed lights and mysterious white voids, and Ben's voice in her ear every minute saying, "I'll kill you if you ever leave me." When she reached the gambling palace — all flash and lights and aggressive architecture — they knew her, of course. How often had she come in on Ben's arm to watch him at the tables, to bring him luck at black jack or to be bored off her feet at poker or roulette? The manager hustled out immediately, obsequious in his tuxedo, to insist that she wait in his office. He offered her coffee and a liqueur and small green cigars while they cut the cashier's check.

Meanwhile, she was like a woman in a dream; she marveled at air so smokey it was visible, a palpable veil irradiated by the fluorescents, and gazed at the banks of monitors, the dozens of watchful eyes that were the visible sign of their suspicion. They might call Ben, she thought, they might call security; instead, a clerk came back carrying a negotiable check with a lot of digits. She slipped it into her purse, thanked the manager, and distributed lavish tips.

The manager personally escorted her to the garage, where he helped with the door of the Mercedes and shook her hand — still tender under her glove. Then she was off down the road, disappearing, literally, into the fog. She had no recollection of where she had driven next or where she had left the Mercedes. Presumably at the airport, but maybe at a bus station. Or Amtrak. She only knew that she'd somehow gotten rid of the car and transferred herself to a Manhattan hotel where she became aware that she was watching a movie on television.

For quite a while, the movie was more real than the room — some sort of suite; than herself — dressed in an unfamiliar pair of jeans and a cashmere sweater; than Manhattan — an implausible rumble punctuated by horns and sirens. The black and white film provided entrance to a simpler, more comprehensible, universe. The soft gray tones did not jangle her nerves like the violent colors of everyday life, where sullen purples, whining citrons, furious reds, and poison greens burned her eyes and made her head ache.

She loved the movie's effortless elegance. The sheen of a streetlight on a bulbous black sedan, the smooth silver and gray patterns of a woman's face, the jagged lights and darks of a man's profile: this was a code that she could read; this was a message for her alone.

And she studied it devoutly, recognizing her story in its hackneyed plot of desire, betrayal, and revenge; reading her fate in the click of high heels, the acceleration of a car, the tense confusion of shots and phones and alarms. But her particular study was the heroine, a tall, straight, beautiful woman, calm and clever, with a lethal snub nosed pistol and an amazing suit. The jacket started with wide shoulders, narrowed to a fitted waist, then belled into a peplum. The skirt was long and gently flaring. With this outfit, the heroine wore high dark heels, a neat, smart hat, gloves — she could have wept with relief when she saw the nearly elbow length gloves — and carried a little purse, dainty, but sturdy. Sometimes the heroine added a scarf, sometimes a fur; whatever the accessories, the look was always elegant and efficient.

Stranded in her unfamiliar hotel room, she saw at once how it all added up; she understood the way it worked — even the old fashioned stockings with their seams. How she admired the discipline of those two straight lines, sure signs of resolve and invulnerability. If she only had stockings like those, if she only had such a suit! Resolve and invulnerability were precisely what she needed, and there, in front of her, was the identity that would provide them. She need only become that straight, beautiful woman to leave the technicolor world behind.

The first thing, clearly, was that magic ensemble, that emblem of another dimension. As soon as the film ended, she called Bloomingdales' and then Sax's. Finally, she obtained something almost right, good enough so that when the boxes were delivered and the clothes spread out on the bed, she felt safe. She felt that she could go out and do the practical things she knew must be done: deposit the check, open an account, sell her jewelry, find an apartment, destroy her credit cards. Start, in short, a new life and obliterate all traces of her former existence.

Later on, after she was settled in a small East Side apartment, she found a dressmaker, a witch woman who understood clothing and armaments and who made exactly what she wanted: a suit with wide shoulders, fitted waist, soutache braid collar and pocket detail, a peplum, and a long, slightly flared skirt. She had it made up in gray. But although that was the screen color, the shade did not translate as well, she thought, to real life. The second version, in taupe, was perfect. Absolutely perfect.

The blouse was to be cream, and they had a struggle with that. Polyester was out of the question, and modern silk, the dressmaker said, lacked body. She agreed, they were in perfect harmony, but, in the meantime, she felt worried and nervous and hesitated to go out. Fortunately, the dressmaker was resourceful; she found some Chinese silk for warm weather and, for winter, an antique satin, as heavy and smooth as the finest ice cream.

The minute she put the whole ensemble on, the blouse, the jacket with the shoulder pads, the flared skirt, the high heels, the hat — oh, what troubles they'd had with the hat, too! — she knew she was safe.

There remained only the gloves, the last detail. She had to search the city for them, through the big department stores, the little boutiques, the luxury importers and vintage stores and flea markets and discounts, because it was not just finding the right style or the right shade. It was finding the perfect gloves, perfect for her purposes, that is; gloves that would complete the costume, that would slide over her damaged hands and take her from the shocks and terrors of reality to the perfect silver shimmer of another dimension.

Success came unexpectedly in a little out-of-the-way leather shop. Imagine a spring day, sunny and cool with the street smell of exhaust and combustion sweetened by the florists' tulips and lilies blooming in their galvanized display cans. The old man at the counter lifted his head when she walked in and, instantly, she felt serene. She knew before he opened the drawer that she would find what she'd been looking for, and there they lay: elbow length gloves of the palest bluish gray calfskin. She bought a dozen pairs and, with them, the freedom of the city. Now that her transformation was complete, she found it possible to walk in the nearby park, to shop at the grocery, to browse along the antique shops and the flower stands, to rent movies at the video shop.

Naturally, she was always on the alert for "her" film, for that special, nameless, half magical, half imaginary movie she had watched so raptly in that strange Manhattan hotel, but it proved elusive. Though she consulted catalogues and books and went downtown to the museums and uptown to the university whenever there were special showings, the tall, resolute woman with the beautiful, enigmatic face never reappeared. She had to be content with echoes in other films: a hint in the music or in the line of a dress, a snatch of snappy dialogue or a sudden, dangerous moment in a city night.

On these forays, she got around the technicolor city by cab, always alone, trusting her costume to inform others who might interrupt her, solicit her, or threaten her that she was not resident in their world. She was a visitor from another dimension, following her own, inviolate script.

As time went on, as she was shaped more and more by her new life, she added other ritual protections to her costume. She shopped daily at the same stores, planned the same menus for each week, bought the same papers and magazines. She paid for everything in cash or with cashier's checks. To the shopkeepers, to the neighbors, she commented on the weather and said, "Good morning" or "Good afternoon," but she never mentioned her name, never revealed her address, never let slip the slightest personal detail.

This caution was advisable, because she knew he'd be looking for her, but it sprang less from fear than from her adaptation to life in another dimension. As long as she followed her script, as long as she was in character and in costume, she felt invisible. Nothing could harm her. Not even Ben.

A year went by, two years. She might have made new friends, she might have gone to another city and started over more or less openly. She might have obtained new documents, secured a court order, taken any one of a number of conventional steps. But more and more the technicolor world seemed alien to her, alien, erratic, and violent. She was quite happy where she was.

Mr. Silverbaum was the first to warn her, old Mr. Silverbaum, who lived on the sixth floor and exchanged courtly "Good mornings" with her when he went out to walk his elderly schnauzer. There had been someone in the hall, he told her in his light Viennese accent, just the previous night. He'd heard a sound and opened the door, expecting his sister who lived in Jersey, and there was a stranger, a man in a dark coat. He'd complained in the strongest terms to the management and to Tommy, the doorman, too.

She listened sympathetically, but being invisible, she was not personally concerned. The Silverbaums were a different matter: elderly antique collectors, they were wealthy enough to be a target for savvy thieves or desperate addicts.

"You were quite right," she said. "You were quite right to complain."

"Of course, of course," he said. "But Madame Cee" — with his fine European manners Mr. Silverbaum had taken the initials on her door and christened her "Madame Cee" — "it is for you I was really alarmed. A woman alone. I said that to Tommy: I said, 'you must be especially careful for Madame Cee.'"

She thanked him and smiled. "I am always careful about opening my door," she said.

She told Tommy the same thing later in the week when he raised the matter. "Mr. Silverbaum told me about the intruder," she said.

Tommy shook his head. "I don't know if it's the same guy that was on Mr. Silverbaum's floor, but Joey's seen someone around back. He called the police twice last week. Well, you know how much that's worth. But I'm keeping my eyes open. I just wanted you to know that. Plus I'm checking the service door regular, but still . . ."

"I'm always careful," she said. She could have reminded him that she got no mail, received no visitors, took no chances. It was not, in any case, a matter of concern. The city was full of thieves, full of the deranged, the homeless. There were plenty of explanations, and she had no intention of changing her routine.

She went out every morning for her papers and for either a bagel or a danish at the little bakery on the corner. She bought flowers twice a week at a flower stand down on Third and shopped for chicken, pork chops, and pasta at the neighborhood Italian market. She always dressed the same way and carried her small, surprisingly heavy purse in one hand, a string bag for her shopping in the other.

She was so regular in her habits that she'd become, in a minor way, a feature of the neighborhood. "The lady in the suit" or "the lady wearing the hat" or, most often, "the lady with the gloves." The shop keepers all knew her and the doormen, too, and when friends or out-of-town relatives visited, the locals would nod their heads at her across the street and remark, "there she goes, the lady with the gloves; we see her every day," and think no more about her.

But should she change her routine, deviate from her route, rewrite her script, there would surely be trouble. The universe would take notice that she had rejoined the technicolor world where everything was uncertain and violent. She would become visible again, exposed and defenseless.

Besides, she'd taken her own precautions. She'd ordered another suit made — there had been some trouble getting just the right fabric last time and she'd had the dressmaker lay in an extra supply — also some light weight fabric gloves for summer in the same pale blue-gray as the calfskin. She had Tommy escort her upstairs if she was out at a late movie, and began to ask the dispatcher for cab drivers she knew. That was only sensible.

But perhaps she was more disturbed than she appeared, for she began to be troubled by dreams. These, while superficially innocuous, proved deeply disturbing. In them she was always rushed for some reason, hurrying out of her apartment and onto the street only to discover that some article of clothing was missing: she'd forgotten her hat perhaps, or her jacket, or — worst yet — her gloves. Or else, she was wearing what she thought of as ordinary clothes — pants, a sweater, a dress — and felt naked and vulnerable. Because of these dreams, she began to dress with extraordinary care and to check her appearance carefully in the hall mirror any time she ventured out.

That's where she was when the knock came at the door. She had just finished her inventory, hat, gloves, purse, when she heard the sound, and froze. The only people who ever knocked on her door were Tommy and Mr. Silverbaum. But Tommy always called first, and old Mr. Silverbaum, who understood her anxieties without ever being told, would even now be calling through the door, "Madame Cee, Madame Cee?" so that she would know there was no reason for concern. She knew this was not Mr. Silverbaum.

When she looked through the peephole, she saw the man in the dark coat, the man Mr. Silverbaum had seen, the man who had been hanging around the back of the building. Just for a moment, she smiled. Maybe his detectives had found her, but Ben had had to come himself. It pleased her that he would be disappointed; he would never have expected her to escape into another dimension.

She smoothed her hair, touched her hat and picked up her bag. Then she unlocked the door and looked into his strange, dark, obsessive eyes.

"Yes?" she said.

It bothered him, she could see that, it bothered him that she was not frightened, that she was calm, that she was indifferent.

His hands were bunched in his pockets; his black coat had a purplish sheen; there was red behind his eyes. Ben definitely belonged to the technicolor world where she had no intention of returning.

"I told you I'd find you," he said. "I told you, didn't I? Do you remember what I told you?" His voice rising, he thrust out his hand and shoved her back into the apartment, the apartment in pale silvery and beige tones, where the tall, straight beautiful woman said, "What do you want, Ben?"

His face was all darks and lights, a craggy, violent pattern. His body was a dark shape against the pale wall and his angular shadow slipped across the rug.

"I told you I'd kill you if you ever left me," he said. "I'd kill you anyway for stealing those chips."

He had a knife in his pocket, a gleaming silver streak that leapt from the dark fabric of his coat. The jagged patterns shuddered and rearranged themselves, and the shot, when it came, was startlingly loud, so loud it echoed along the floor and up a flight and reverberated through the Silverbaums' dining room, so that they stopped drinking their morning coffee to call down for Tommy.

When he got there, the door was open and the hallway smelled of meat and gunpowder. A man was lying in the foyer with blood on his chest and a knife in his hand.

"He didn't know," she said. She was dressed just as she always was in the same suit and blouse and hat and high heels, holding the same little, surprisingly heavy, purse. She opened it now, and held it out so that Tommy could see the pistol. Quite an antique, as far as he could tell, but up to the job, that's for sure, because the man gave a groaning cough and died.

She made the slightest motion of her head, then the tall, straight, beautiful woman walked across the room to the phone and punched in the numbers. Her voice was low and throaty, a voice for dreams, for memories, for alternative dimensions.

"You'd better send a squad car," she said. "I've just killed a man."

GHOST WRITER

Marvin was excited when his agent called. It had been a while since he'd heard from Audrey, whose soft, raspy voice was permanently, if hopelessly, associated in his mind with sales and contracts, and the possibility of fame, if not fortune. Some foreign rights? A chapter in an anthology? Ready cash?

"Can you stop by today?" Audrey asked.

Of course, Marvin said he would, clearing out time that would otherwise have been spent in a fruitless perusal of his notebooks or in research on-line for a now overdue article or in sharpening pencils and tidying his desk and, probably, the way things had been going, quitting early to hit the beach. Instead, he fought the traffic down I-95 through blizzards of snowbirds and the mind numbing exhaust of heavy trucks to Audrey's blue glass office building in the center of Lauderdale.

Audrey Striker had been his agent for six years. Three books, UK rights on one, a modest movie option on another: not bad, not great, about par for the course for a midlist author of more ambition than talent and more talent than luck. What else is new? Another agent might have done better for him but would, just as likely, have done worse. Besides, he liked Audrey's throaty, world weary voice, her greed, her toughness.

She was waiting for him, that was surprise number one, and number two, Cindy, her secretary, was nowhere to be seen. He was being allowed an unprecedented private audience. "Come in, Marv," Audrey called when her office door beeped. She was sitting with her back to the blue tinged panorama of pastel condo and hotel towers, her large, well shaped head awkwardly balanced on her small twisted frame. Her spindly legs were propped up on a footstool. Her cane was beside her, the motorized wheelchair she used for longer distances parked in the corner.

"I've been looking at your latest royalty statements," she said.

Marvin's heart sank. He hoped she had not called him all the way downtown just to tell him that his career was in the toilet. He took one of the handsome leather chairs and angled it away from the bright pastel towers of the city scape toward the comforting expanse of close packed book shelves. He could see the slender spines of his own novels.

"I think we need to make a move in a slightly different direction, and I think you might be right for a proposal I've received."

"What sort of proposal?"

"Completion of a dark fantasy trilogy. I have the contract in hand."

"Sorry," said Marvin, disappointed in spite of himself, "that's hardly my field."

Audrey was undeterred. "We already have a fairly detailed plot outline of the first novel, and rough — I'll be honest — very rough outlines of the second and third. However, with the exception of two characters . . ." She scrambled among her notes. "Ah, here we go. Someone called Lord Ostrucht and the Lady Fergaine must be spared at all costs. Otherwise, you would have almost complete freedom. And," she added, seeing Marvin was about to interrupt, "if the first novel proves successful, as I'm sure it will, you would have even more freedom with the later books. The key, Marv, dear, is speed and quality. Write me a good book fast and we can make a lot of money."

"Look, Audrey, not that I don't appreciate, but I write literate contemporary novels. I don't want a reputation for swords and fantasy."

Audrey gave a smile that marred rather than enhanced her fine, clean features. Nature, Marvin thought, had had a grand design in mind with Audrey and then, at the last moment, smashed it. "Your last novels earned mid four figure advances," she said. "You can't live on that. Think of this as work to support your serious writing. Also, I can assure you, Marv, dear, that your name will never be mentioned. Will never be, must never be; that is a most important condition."

Interesting! Marvin racked his brain to think of who could command serious advances on the basis of rough outlines. The only possibilities were names big enough to scare him just a little. It was one thing to dismiss certain popular works; it was quite another to invent the same sort of audience pleasing junk. "How much?"

"The whole package is 2.5 million. I am authorized to give you a partial advance of $50,000 on signing. On completion of each novel, you and the writer whose name will appear on the jacket split the profits, advance, royalties, everything, fifty-fifty."

The sum was a shock, almost a physical shock, and it took Marvin a moment to digest the possibilities of repairing the Datsun, paying off his credit cards, leaving the Sun 'n Surf apartments.

"Are you on?" Audrey asked.

He could feel a little bubble of exhilaration growing around his heart, but he didn't quite trust himself to decide yet.

"I know you can do it," Audrey said, "and I think you can do it quickly."

"How fast and how long?"

"I need a manuscript of no less than 600 pages; a little longer would be better, but 600 would do."

"Whew!" said Marvin.

"We have a full year. I was able to get an extension," Audrey added a trifle grimly, "on the grounds of ill health."

"And are we sick?" Marvin asked.

"We are drunk, if you must know." Audrey's tone was dryly sarcastic. "We have developed multiple addictions and responsibility issues and a damn bad attitude! I need you to do this, Marv, dear," she said in a different tone. "You and I will earn every penny, but it's a pretty penny, and having invested twenty years of work in — our author — I'm not about to lose the best contract I've ever negotiated."

"All right," said Marvin, "but I'd better have a look at the outline and I'd better read some of the other books — there are others, right?"

"The proverbial five foot book shelf."

Audrey levered herself to her feet, grabbed her cane and limped to the nearest bookcase. She came back with a handful of novels which she laid face down on her desk.

"There will be a confidentiality statement for you to sign," Audrey said. "All the usual. Basically, you promise never to reveal your authorship."

"As if I'd want to," said Marvin.

"But understand, Marv, dear, only your best work will do for this project."

"My best work, my heart and soul." Marvin could already feel himself adjusting to prosperity.

Audrey produced a thick folder of legal documents. She offered the confidentiality statement first, "in case, Marv dear, you should change your mind." This document was as near to ironclad as dozens of "to whits," "whatsoevers," and "to whomevers" could make it.

Marvin signed with a flourish, then turned over the first novel in the stack on the desk. Ah," he said in surprise; he had read some of Hilaire LaDoux's novels and liked them. "I thought LaDoux did sci-fi."

"All the work is on the border of the genres," Audrey said. "Alternate worlds, alternate futures — same old human nature."

"Here's to human nature," Marvin said and held out his hand for the contract.

"You're sure?" Audrey asked. "Please be sure Marv, dear, because there won't be time to get another writer if you change your mind."

"Worry not, sweet Audrey!" He flipped to the end of the document and signed his name. "I'm your ghost."

He left with a stack of LaDoux's novels in a Burdine's shopping bag and stopped at his local liquor store on the way home for some really good beer and a bottle of vintage bordeaux. I'm going to be rich, if not famous, he told himself, and, better by far to be at least one or the other.

Marvin sat down on his minuscule balcony, poured a Bellhaven, and opened *The Cave of the Winds*, the first novel in LaDoux's *Galatan*

Trilogy. He read for three hours, making notes occasionally on a yellow pad as he picked out favorite vocabulary, sentence structures, the little tricks like adjectives grouped in threes and a fondness — a weakness in Marvin's eyes — for beginning with participial phrases.

After dinner, he checked the outline for *Dragon in the Sun*. It was, as Audrey had promised, thoroughly detailed. Ten single spaced pages outlined an epic and dynastic struggle which he found intimidatingly inventive until he realized that most of the events had been lifted from the Hundred Years War in France and the English Wars of the Roses. Okay!

Marvin made a note to himself to begin some serious historical reading — the Borgias should be good for a plot or two, and the Russians, for a series. He was sure that the various Ivans and Peters, not to mention the licentious Great Catherine, could help flesh out the skimpy notes for Dragon II and III

Though Marvin normally worked in fits and starts as inspiration took him, he was at his desk early the next morning. He had a year to produce six hundred pages, which meant, he calculated, roughly two pages a day, the other two months left over for the inevitable mishaps which afflict manuscripts as well as man. He was slightly daunted at the prospect of working up scenes and characters which were not his own, and he dawdled, as he usually did, straightening his desk and hopping up to water the plants and take out the garbage. It was on this latter errand that Marvin had the happy inspiration of imaging, not the novel, but Hilaire LaDoux.

He sat down at his computer and told himself that this new book would be the contrivance of an invented character, a best selling novelist of considerable talent and an unerring popular touch named Hilaire La-Doux. His LaDoux invariably started early in the morning, well before time for the first drink of the day, and tapped out exactly two — no, better make it four, pages a day as good genre writers were known for their productivity.

Hilaire LaDoux would work to something ancient, Marvin decided, and he rejected several possibilities before selecting Monteverdi, his *Orpheus* by preference. Unlike Marvin, who liked to write sitting on his balcony, LaDoux would keep the shades drawn and would wear something elegant and unusual, something Marvin would have to acquire. But for now, semi-darkness and *Orpheus* would have to be good enough. He slid the CD into his computer, heard the chords, exotic with the everlasting strangeness of genius, and began typing: "Trotting along the long, weary, dry road into Balson, Lord Ostrucht saw clouds black as serpents darkening the horizon and laid his hand on the Blade of Zermain. He was alone now, he was the only one left . . ."

Although Marvin took some time to settle into this routine, so different from his own, novelty proved potent. Day after day, Lord Ostrucht struggled with warriors and wizards, with dragons and other chimeras of the mind, searching always for the Lady Fermaine. At first, Marvin stayed close to the original design, but very soon Ostrucht began to develop some new and interesting habits.

Marvin knew that he was really on his way when he discovered one morning that the cliche dragon of one of the planned set pieces had evolved into a yellow tinged mist, so faint as to be almost subliminal. This scarcely noticed alteration in the atmosphere gradually disturbed perception, causing its victims to see the world as horror, as such unrelieved and dreadful ugliness, as to be driven to despair.

"That's very good," Audrey said, looking up from the latest installment of the manuscript. "That's very good, indeed." Like all authors, Marvin needed complements and reassurance, particularly during composition, and she had learned the right way to do this: praise only the book and never, by so much as a syllable, hint that he had a genuine flair for this sort of thing. In fact, Audrey was convinced that Marvin was writing better than ever, that a sort of literate action was his true metier. Instead, she said, "very LaDoux. Hyper LaDoux."

Marvin smiled. "The creation of the character was the key thing — and unexpectedly inspiring."

"Lord Ostrucht," Audrey said.

"No, no, he's quite an interesting fellow, but I meant Hilaire LaDoux."

Audrey looked at him. Yes, now that he mentioned it, she could see some changes, which she had registered without attaching importance to them. An expensive haircut and good clothes were only to be expected from sudden prosperity, but she would not have expected Marvin's choices: a cerise silk shirt, and an Italian silk and wool sweater patterned in mustard, lavender, and sienna, worn with khakis and sandals. Marvin had always been a jeans and t-shirt kind of guy who owned a blue suit for good. He'd added a pair of tinted glasses, too, which shadowed his eyes and made him look subtly different, enough like the real LaDoux to give Audrey a little frisson, because no image of Hilaire LaDoux had been published for years. Well, she wasn't going to worry about that! Whatever works, she thought, and congratulated herself on spotting Marv's potential. "We'll have no problem completing the book," she said.

"No problem at all, and, Audrey, I'm getting so many ideas for volumes two and three. I've started to plant material for future books. Now this scene," he turned the pile of manuscript around and ruffled through the pages. "Here, in chapter sixteen where I've introduced Ranoch, the squire . . ."

"I like Ranoch," said Audrey.

"I'm glad you do, because I see an important role for him in the second volume."

She pulled out a yellow pad and began making notes. When they were finished, she assured Marvin that the publisher would be thrilled, then shook his hand and saw him out of the office herself, as Cindy, who was apparently not privy to the arrangement with Mr. LaDoux, had been sent on an errand.

Marvin supposed that was only prudent, though in his own mind, Hilaire LaDoux came into existence when he put on the very handsome silk jacket that Hilaire wrote in, added the blue tinted spectacles, and slid the Monteverdi *Orpheus* into the CD player. During the less and less frequent days when Marvin took off, wore his own clothes, listened to Talking Heads, drank beer, and loafed on the beach, Hilaire LaDoux, esquire, simply ceased to exist, leaving Marvin to enjoy the fruits of his labor and of LaDoux's reputation.

And after the first volume was published to acclaim and profit, there seemed no reason why Marvin couldn't continue writing about Lord Ostrucht and the Lady Fermaine and their ilk virtually forever. The second volume was finished and Marvin was well into the third before the first cloud appeared.

He was in Audrey's office for one of their now routine private meetings. The latest chapters of *The Dragon's Child* lay on the desk between them, and Audrey was running her delicate fingers nervously over the pages.

"Quite brilliant," she said, tapping the manuscript, "everyone agrees, and you know Marv, dear, I'd be the first to tell you if the books weren't up to par."

He did know that.

"So you'll know this is none of my doing. I'm thoroughly satisfied, and so is everybody at the publishing house."

"What's the matter?" Marvin asked, sensing a problem without really being troubled by it. He had money to sort out problems and people like Audrey to sort them out for him. Since the great success of the Dragon books, their relationship had undergone a sea change: now she waited for his calls and arranged her schedule to suit him. Now it was her plans and her strategy which came under scrutiny as much as his manuscripts.

"Well, it's Hilaire, of course. Jealousy, I'm sure. If I'd thought, Marv, dear, I'd never have let *Dragon* be nominated for any award whatsoever. Never."

"Hilaire?" It took Marvin a moment to remember that there was such a person with volition of his own, a real person whose desires could not be altered by a few lines of type. "He's unhappy? Fifteen weeks on the best seller list, foreign rights, a pot of found money — what more does he want?"

"He's feeling creative again. He feels, well, Marv dear, he feels he doesn't need you any more."

Marvin's first reaction was fury modulating into shock. "He can go to hell! I've got another three novels plotted out, plus some terrific new characters!" It was illogical, inconceivable, grotesquely and monstrously unfair. And besides, he'd been counting on the money.

"He's got an ironclad contract. Look, Marv, dear, I've tried to talk to him, but he claims he's inspired. And more serious, he's determined to cut back on the drinking."

"Great for him. All right, let him write. I still have three good plots and half a dozen new characters."

"His characters," she said. "All his. You know that, Marv."

"So I change the names and we're still in business."

"And who are you?" she asked. "Do you think I can get as good a contract as you can get from selling the outlines to Hilaire? Be real."

Marvin swore there must be some way to indicate that he was the writer behind LaDoux's latest best seller, but Audrey raised the confidentiality agreement and promised to hold LaDoux up for plenty. "I think even a credit isn't out of the question. Something along the lines of 'based on a story by' which will do you good later, Marv. Besides, you can get back to your own writing now, and with what you'll make from the plot outlines . . ."

Marvin was furious, but though he had a lawyer friend go over the contract not once but twice, there was no way out. LaDoux had all rights to the books. As far as the publishing world went, it was Marvin, not Hilaire LaDoux who was an imaginary character, or, rather, what was worse, a middling author with no real prospects.

For consolation, he had a good whack of money for the work he'd done on *The Dragon's Child*, but he absolutely refused to sell anything more, causing Audrey to roll her eyes and to wonder aloud why she hadn't taken to representing sensible people like stunt men and professional wrestlers. Then she sighed and told Marv that he might perhaps change his mind.

"After all," she added, accurately, but somewhat unkindly, "now you have what you've always said you wanted: time and money to do your own writing."

So he got busy. He opened his old notebooks and took up a plot he'd begun then set aside, a story about a talented man down on his luck in paradise: a.k.a. South Florida. Marvin struggled with it for several months, but the story was dead in the water. Oh, the writing was good; Marvin had an easy style that rolled from one paragraph to the next without the slightest a hitch but also without the oddity and flare that can illuminate old stories and make familiar characters fresh.

The very smoothness that had rendered Lord Ostrucht, the Lady Fermaine, and a host of supernatural entities plausible worked against Marvin's contemporary characters. They were just a little bit boring, and, realizing that, he began to find new and creative ways to delay his stints at the computer. When he got fed up with procrastination, he'd throw on his swim trunks and head for the beach: as far as writing went, Marvin was stymied.

Then, one depressing morning, just as an experiment, he got up early, put on Hillaire's silk writing jacket, and dropped *Orpheus* on the CD player. When he sat down to work at the keyboard, Lord Ostrucht was waiting for him, sitting melancholy on the back of his black charger, reading a farewell letter from the Lady Fermaine. Marvin almost wept with joy.

Two days later, when he'd at last obtained LaDoux's address from an unwary new editorial publicist, Marvin was surprised to find that the novelist lived not more than five miles away, along a swanky stretch between the inland waterway and the ocean. Marvin drove out that same night, burdened with a bottle of expensive white French burgundy and uncertain intentions.

Decorative lights lined the waterway side of the narrow street, illuminating boat slips and gazebos and free standing decks where the big spenders could sip cocktails and contemplate hundreds of thousands of dollars worth of marine horsepower. The ocean side was dark with overgrown trees and ambitious plantings. Only a few discreet lights punctuated the shadows, revealing heavy metal gates across nicely tiled driveways or else big signs indicting that trespassing on a job site is a felony in Florida. Since the neighborhood seemed full of folks constructing hurricane bait, there were plenty of these posted warnings.

LaDoux's house was of an older, less ostentatious, vintage, well screened by live oaks, bamboos, and a variety of large and thriving palms — my kind of place, Marvin thought. The flat roofed building was coated with a scabbed and cracked rust colored stucco, vaguely Mexican in inspiration and adjoined by a massive screen made of blocks interwoven with a bright climbing vine. Several soft yellow lights, perhaps candles, glimmered behind this screen, and a weak bulb illuminated the weathered front door. Otherwise, the house, which was handsome in conception, but clearly neglected, remained in darkness.

Marvin stepped out to the sound of surf and of cars and motorcycles passing. He rang the intercom buzzer on the gate several times, and he was ready to give up when a voice, quite loud and very close to him, asked what he was doing and what the hell he wanted. Marvin gave a start. Someone about his own height and weight was standing half hidden by the dappled purple and ocher leaves of a rampant ornamental shrub. The man wore a white shirt and an ascot like a country house extra in an English movie, but what sent the evening lurching in a direction Marvin had not expected was the man's appearance. Marvin immediately recognized their surprising resemblance. "I was hoping to see Hilaire LaDoux," Marvin said. "I'm a big fan of his books."

"Take a look and get out," said LaDoux, starting to turn away. Marvin noticed that he carried a drink in one hand.

"You might want to take a look at me, too," Marvin said. "I wrote your last two novels."

"What are you doing here?" LaDoux demanded, his voice rising. "You're not supposed to have any contact with me. That was in the contract!"

"No," said Marvin, "that was about the only thing that wasn't."

"Audrey should have thought of that," LaDoux said querulously. "Did she give you my address? I'll fire her if she did. No one's supposed to have my address."

"I acquired it elsewhere," Marvin said. "Look, I thought we might work out a deal. Something beneficial to us both."

LaDoux eyed him suspiciously. "What's Audrey been telling you? She's wrong to give you any hope at all. I'll get back on schedule." Marvin decided that he was probably drunk.

"This has nothing to do with Audrey. "I've constructed some interesting plot outlines, and I want to talk to you about them."

LaDoux's eyes glittered. "Plots, plot ideas, used to be my forte," he remarked. "But no more. The Muse has showed me her backside lately."

"So we should talk," Marvin repeated.

"Audrey said you were being difficult. Audrey said you didn't want to sell anything."

"Well, now I need the money."

"Where is this material?"

Marvin tapped his breast pocket. He had a diskette, plus an envelope with few printed pages from one of his detailed outlines. "Pull your car in," LaDoux said. He opened the gate and waved Marvin up the short drive and into the dark and empty garage.

The door clattered down behind them, giving Marvin a moment's trepidation before his host switched on a light. Marvin stepped out with the bottle of wine. He followed LaDoux through the hall and a book and paper strewn dining room that opened onto the terrace and a rustling jungle of palms and banyans. On the west side, a heavy flowering vine cut off the lights and noise of the street with a cascade of foliage and deep red blossoms, while the east was open to the coal black sea, fringed white with breakers along the sand. The place struck him as absolutely perfect.

"For me?" LaDoux asked when Marvin held out the bottle. "Naughty. I'm reformed, on the wagon, learning abstinence." He gave a sour laugh. "We're at the mercy of mysterious forces. "That's the reality of it."

Marvin agreed; he certainly felt that way at the moment.

"Course, a certain awareness of mysterious forces is what pays our bills." LaDoux opened the bottle expertly and poured the wine into two large and ornate glasses. He raised his glass silently and took a long drink. "Not bad."

Marvin said nothing.

"And your problem?" LaDoux asked, after he'd refilled their glasses for a second time. "I assume there is a problem."

"I can't do my own work any more. The only ideas I get now are for the *Dragon* novels, for Ostrucht and his Lady. Even your beautiful terrace with the sound of the sea suggests . . ." Marvin signed. "I've been ruined after writing your novels."

"You wrote them rather well the critics say. Of course, my reputation provided a leg up there," he added.

Marvin nodded. He knew the ways of the literary world.

"So?"

"I thought we might collaborate," said Marvin.

"But I don't need you now, and it's time for you to depart — in the literary sense, I mean." He splashed more wine into each glass. "There's no reason for you to leave this nice burgundy."

"Yet you were willing to buy the outline for the second trilogy."

"The flesh is weak," LaDoux admitted.

"Perhaps you'd like to see a sample."

He looked up with an eager expression and stretched out his hand. He needed help, whatever he said. "Let me see."

"One page." Marvin opened the envelope and handed over the synopsis of the first five chapters.

LaDoux put on a pair of tinted glasses and scanned the copy. "Like this wine, not grand cru, but very nice. And the rest?"

"Good. Audrey knows. She wanted to buy them for you."

"Audrey has somewhat lost confidence in me," LaDoux said. In the silence that followed, Marvin listened to a rustling in the shrubbery and the night wind in the palms. Perhaps Lord Ostrucht should be sent on a sea voyage to some hot, tropical land. "What do you want?" LaDoux asked abruptly.

"To write some of the books," Marvin said.

"But not all of them?"

"Not all of them."

LaDoux stared at him for a minute. "We'll drink to that," he said. "But now I want to see the rest of the plots."

"They're on this diskette." Marvin drew the floppy out of his pocket and dropped it back in. "We'll call Audrey, shall we? Have her come over and draw up a contract."

LaDoux hesitated, then smiled. There was an avidity about him that both encouraged and disgusted Marvin. "Right. We'll call Audrey. To whom we owe so much. Including this whole bloody situation." He stood up. "My office is upstairs. I never do business on the terrace."

Inside, LaDoux switched on the weak hall light and started upstairs. Marvin saw old woodwork, Mexican tiles, cracked and dirty plaster. The main stairs made a steep run to a landing, then turned left. A full moon was shining through the tall window at the top, and Marvin was about to remark on its bright beauty, when LaDoux suddenly pivoted on the landing and kicked him square in the gut. Marvin gasped, his lungs suddenly airless, and grabbed the banister to keep from falling. LaDoux struck him again, in the face this time, sending Marvin tumbling backward down the stair to land flat at the bottom.

He was quite helpless. His lungs were deflated, and he couldn't make his legs work. The stair rose above him like a monstrous wave, down which LaDoux dropped toward him like a surfer. Marvin waved his arms, trying to pull air into his lungs, trying to strike LaDoux, who, clearly not as drunk as he'd appeared, caught Marvin under the arms and dragged him down the back hall. He kicked open the French door and pulled Marvin onto the grass and then, to his rising horror, toward the shore. Out of shock and surprise rose an awareness that he was very likely going to die.

Marvin tried to shout, but his voice was a cracked whisper, lost in the wind and surf. LaDoux hauled him through a low hedge and unceremoniously dropped him over the seawall onto the sand. Marvin tried to get to his feet, but his whole body was focused on acquiring air and his limbs refused to cooperate.

LaDoux adjusted his grasp and started toward the water, but here Marvin began digging his heels and his hands into the soft, deep sand, causing LaDoux to swerve and stagger. It was dark on the beach, too, the few lights dazzling and confusing rather than illuminating. Twice

LaDoux dropped to his knees, but though Marvin could impede their progress he could not stop it. Drops of spray landed on his shirt, as he was dragged through a fishy, salty smelling band of wrack. Then LaDoux splashed into the surf, and cold water shocked Marvin's back.

There were crushed shells underfoot. Unsteady, LaDoux slipped both left and right, almost stumbling on every step. Waves broke over Marvin's head and sloshed down his legs. "The diskette," he managed to gasp. "It's in my pocket."

LaDoux stopped and released one of Marvin's arms, dropping him halfway into the water. Marvin jerked up his head, took a great gulp of air and, as LaDoux fumbled in his shirt pocket, threw himself sideways, pulling LaDoux under with him.

They weren't in more than a foot of water, but the shore was at once soft and gritty, the band of ground up shells unstable beneath them. Thrashing and struggling, they got a little further out, then further yet, and as they swallowed more water and took more blows, they found it harder and harder to get back on their knees, to find their feet.

At last, they floundered into chest deep water, and they were half swimming, half wrestling, each trying to hold the other under, when a big roller crashed into them, separating them and turning Marvin head over heels. As he felt himself dragged out by the current, he forgot LaDoux, forgot everything but the shore, dry land, air. He paddled forward, clawing for ground and, after a second wave broke over his head, felt the rough band of shells under his hands and lurched onto the shore, gasping for breath and shaking with cold and shock.

He crawled onto the beach and fell forward on his face. The waves whooshed and thundered behind him, his lungs burned, the night wind chilled his sore back. He had nearly died; someone had tried to kill him; he had possibly drowned a man. With this, he remembered his danger and scrambled painfully to his feet, but he could not see LaDoux.

Marvin called softly: nothing but the sea and the rattle of palm fronds, and somewhere far away, the sound of traffic, of civilization. He limped to the water's edge and peered into the darkness for what seemed a long time before he saw a whitish something as inert as a log rising and falling in the surf. Marvin waited until he was sure of that inertia, before wading out into the water and hauling LaDoux's body to shore.

Once he had wrestled the corpse up onto the sand, he laid his hand on LaDoux's chest and felt for a pulse. When all signs proved negative, Marvin sat down, put his head between his knees and vomited on the sand. "You've killed the Golden Goose," said a voice in his mind.

An another, even less welcome, thought followed: Hilaire LaDoux was someone whose death would be investigated, whose loss would be news. Marvin's own version of events, so implausible and peculiar that even he had trouble crediting what had happened, would come under scrutiny. He had been attacked, there had been a struggle, and Marvin had survived without anything to prove his story. It did not take a novelist's imagination to see big difficulties, both professional and legal, ahead for Hilaire LaDoux's fired ghost writer.

Marvin stood up, washed off his mouth with salt water, and began to undress, dropping his sodden clothing on the sand beside the corpse. Next he turned to LaDoux, though the body already felt cold, and the slippery feel of the skin, as well as LaDoux's unsettling resemblance, turned Marvin's stomach and made his hands shake.

Finally, after an exhausting struggle, he managed to get his own clothes onto the body and jammed his sneakers on its feet. The diskette, ironically, was still in the pocket his shirt. Marvin retrieved it and set it on the sea wall before dragging LaDoux back to the water. He towed the body out as far as he dared, and when he felt the first signs of a rip current, he let it go.

Back on shore, he bundled up the novelist's wet and sandy clothes. One shoe was missing, and he made a futile search of the sand, before returning to the house. The clothing went into the washer, the remaining shoe in a plastic bag. Up in LaDoux's bedroom, Marvin found a change of clothes and dry sneakers. After he composed a brief note for Audrey, he drove north to the public beach, where he abandoned his car, keys, and wallet. He discarded LaDoux's incriminating shoe in a trash barrel. Then Marvin went down to the surf, took off his borrowed sneakers, and slogged back along the shore to the house. He let himself in, found a bottle of Scotch, and went up to bed.

A day later, Marvin saw a brief about his abandoned car and, within a week, read an account of the recovery of his body. He waited a few days before calling Audrey. By then he knew a great deal more about his new identity: debts, alcoholism, dubious investments, an estranged family, and the absolute impossibility of ever holding a driver's license again.

On the other hand, he had a fair sized bank balance, a spectacular, if deteriorated house, and more important that all the rest, Lord Ostrucht and his lady, for whom Marvin, or Hilaire, as he must now call himself, had wonderful plans. He reached for the desk phone and dialed. "Audrey?"

"Yes, Audrey Striker speaking." Her response seemed tentative; voices are, after all, hard to disguise.

"Hilaire LaDoux. I'm really flying on the new novel, and I wondered if you'd like me to send you the finished chapters."

Again, the hesitation. He could almost hear the wheels turning. "Of course, I would," she said with a fair show of enthusiasm. "But Hilaire, you're working? You're really working? Because I understood you wanted me to find someone to replace poor Marvin — you heard about that?"

"Yes, I did. I can't help feeling a little guilty. He sold me his last outlines, you know. Yes, yes, he cut you out, the naughty boy. But poor fellow! The writer's life is not always a happy one."

"I'd actually found someone — tentatively, you understand. I thought perhaps a woman writer this time . . ." In truth Audrey had been nearly at her wit's end.

"Quite, quite unnecessary," he said briskly. "I've had a genuinely life changing experience. You might say I met a ghost, Audrey, and I can assure you I foresee no more writing problems from here on in."

TABLOID PRESS

Kim is standing there between Princess Diana — tiara, white satin, eyes blue as window spray — and Monica Lewinsky — dark suit, lots of curves, mega lipstick. Though not as nice as Diane's, Monica's eyes are on the blue side, too, which doesn't surprise Kim. She's had a weakness along those lines, herself, named Chris. When she was sixteen and three quarters and bored with school, Chris seemed exciting. Besides the blazing blue eyes, he had a truck, a trailer, independence, a job. Now she knows he's got a pack a day beer habit and a lousy temper from inhaling spray paint at the body shop.

Well, everyone has problems. There's the princess dead with that fat Egyptian: "Diana a Year Later" is the *People* headline; and though Monica looks pretty good in most pictures, today's tabloid screams, "Monica on Suicide Watch."

"What a shame," one old geezer told Kim just that morning, though another one didn't buy the usual and said she'd get more than she wanted on the internet.

Now the woman off pump four in the dark green Jetta wants to give Kim exact change and can't come up with the final thirty cents. She's got her crap all over the counter — pennies, a pen, car keys, kleenex. "I know I've got it somewhere," she says with this loopy, idiotic smile.

And pump two is screwed up, as it's been all week. Some guy in a big Suburban is yelling over the intercom that he's got five-seventy in the tank, and the pump's froze on him. "Yeah, yeah, I'll get it started for you," Kim's saying, when Stu, fat and fortish but agile, hustles behind the counter to stand in her back pocket. He's wearing the baggy gray suit and beige shirt, plus, today, the Tweetiebird tie that he claims gives the customers a laugh. Kim can smell his cologne.

Stu says, "I need some help in the store room, Kim. Let Michael handle the front."

Automatically, Kim looks at her watch; that's what she always does when Stu wants something, she checks the time: 12:35. Lunch is at one, after the trades guys have come in for sandwiches, beer, and sodas, after the high school kids have bought ice cream and diet cokes, and after the elderly morning shoppers have stopped for gas and papers. 12:35: time for her to hump a few dozen cartons and for Stu to try to get his hands down her jeans.

"Michael's gotta leave early today for an exam," she says, thinking quick, because between Stu hitting on her and Chris wanting beer money, Kim doesn't want to stay and can't afford to quit. "Michael's' got early class this semester, so I gotta be up front. And pump two's jamming again."

That distracts Stu for a minute, because he likes to have everything running just right — pumps fast, counter manned, sandwiches fresh, coffee made every couple hours. He's got an eagle eye for the register, too. You have to move fast to get away with anything. He'll count every damn pack of cigarettes himself if he has to.

With this Quick Mart, one in Putnam, another two in Norwich, Stu Gleb should be a rich man, and sometimes Kim tries to imagine what if he was handsome. Maybe bald like he is but attractive, even passable, not so fat, nicer manners. Or maybe elegant with fancy suits, gold jewelry, and a convertible like the rich, wrinkled geezers who pose with blond girlfriends in the tabloids and who set up love nests and get themselves into expensive divorces. What then? Would that be a way out? An escape from Chris and misery?

But Rakesh has told her Stu isn't really rich. Rakesh is the other college student, not at the community but at the state college, and he does some of the books cut rate for Stu. What Rakesh told her was that it's Stu's wife who has the cash. Kim tends to believe that, because Stu is always bitching about money. It's a lousy day at the store after he's been to the casino, and sometimes there are odd phone calls that get Stu upset good.

12:50: pump two's running again; Michael, who doesn't really have an exam, is on the counter; Kim's back shifting cartons of motor oil with Stu, who really should get one of the guys to do the heavy work. Stu's told her he likes her jeans and likes her tank top, and next she's expecting he'll try to get her onto the night shift, when he says, out of left field, like, "Chris still picking you up?"

"You see me with a car?" Kim asks. One of the few smart things she's done with Stu is to impress him with Chris's temper, jealousy, and strength.

"I wanna talk to him next time he comes by."

"Yeah? I'm not working the night shift," Kim says quickly. "I don't care if you talk him into it, I'm not working any night shift."

"Who said I want you working the night shift?" asks Stu. "I thought you said Chris is outa full time work. Didn't you tell me that?"

Kim nods.

"So I'm maybe looking for workers."

That's an idea Kim will have to digest on her break. One o'clock sharp, she takes a cigarette from the pack she keeps in the counter drawer, buys a bottle of juice and a brownie, and crosses the road, because lunch choice between the storeroom or the cemetery is a no brainer. Kim walks through the tall iron gates and down the deeply groved dirt and gravel road. There are graves on either side, neat rows of gray, brown and white stones, trees, too, and further back, the big monuments of the formerly rich, still looking impressive fifty, eighty, one hundred years after.

If it's a hot day, Kim likes to pick one of the ones that look like Greek temples, where she can sit in the shade with her back against the cool stones and have lunch and smoke in peace. But since today the sun will feel good, she picks a brown mottled obelisk that supervises a mess of little individual markers. The obelisk's got Kiernan cut in the base in letters big enough for a highway road sign, and Kim's leaning up against it, drinking her oj straight from the bottle when someone coughs. Kim jumps so quick she slops juice down her top. "Christ!" she says, and a few other things, because her new tank top is white and the stain'll be a bitch.

"Excuse me," says this voice. "You're standing on my grave."

* * * *

When work's offered, Chris is cautious. He's reckless and wild with every other thing, but he approaches work like it's a rabid cat. He wants to know exactly what Stu said and how he said it, and when Kim says, "Why don't you ask him yourself, he's still there," Chris gets all mad and unreasonable. He smacks her one and sulks through dinner, though he does make a call after Kim goes outside with the garbage. Coming back, standing on the step with one hand on the screen door, she hears him saying, "Yeah, we'll see about it, man. Longs you're talking serious money."

Of course, he tells Kim nothing, though she goes as far as to ask if Stu Gleb has a job for him. She risks that much. Chris says it's none of her business and his eyes get mean, so Kim shuts her mouth and figures she'll find out soon enough.

* * * *

Dull day, mist so heavy it feels like rain or rain so light it feels like mist. Kim goes across to the cemetery, anyway; she never misses a day now, though she always says she has an errand to run at the supermarket, that she's got to stop by the pharmacy, whatever. Through the parking lot, dodging cars, carts, delivery trucks, across the street, three lanes, always jammed, then into the cemetery, into what she thinks of as real life, but Kim isn't into irony. She's fallen for happiness.

First, they visit the grave, which is in Maureen's family's plot. Her name was once Maureen Kiernan, which has a nice ring to it, not like Gleb, which sounds to Kim like something nasty. The Kiernan plot is a generous square of lawn with the obelisk at the back and granite blocks on each corner. There are a lot of dead Kiernans under the grass, including the real money man, Joseph Patrick Kiernan, who founded the textile mill that's now a high tech fish farm.

The Kiernan plot is impressive but high maintenance. There's always something to be done, especially around Joey's grave, which has to be kept weedless and perfect, with every dead flower and faded plant removed, with each of the little boxwood shrubs perfectly pruned.

"Did he like flowers?" Kim asks once.

"He liked basketball," Eileen says, "but you can't plant basketballs." Which makes sense to Kim.

After tending the grave, they walk around the cemetery. Maureen always brings a picnic: nice deli sandwiches, cheese pies or slices of meat bits in jelly with fancy French names; pretty cookies and little square cakes with icing all over; grapes or peaches or strawberries big as ping pong balls. There's a thermos of coffee if it's cool; a half bottle of wine or cider if it's warm. Kim and Maureen sit on the porch of one of the Greek temples, which are properly called mausoleums, Kim learns, and talk. They talk about Joey and the grave, first, and then about themselves and their situations, and finally about their need for different lives, for freedom, for escape.

* * * *

This one night, lights sweep across the trailer windows, the neighbor's coon dogs go wild, and, surprise of surprises, Stu's white Cadillac bounces over the ruts in the yard. Stu hops out, his heavy face sweaty. He's got a cigar in his hand and a big charge of nervous energy on his back.

"Hey, Kimmie," he says. Stu never calls her 'Kimmie' at work, and she takes this to mean he's trying to be chummy and friendly. She assumes he wants something. "Your man at home?"

Kim looks over her shoulder. Chris is sitting in front of the tv in the crowded main room. He's got a NASCAR show on and the racing motors produce a steady, whining drone that seems to mellow him out much as anything can. When she nods her head, Stu squeezes past her into the trailer.

"So Chris," he says, and something about the way Chris lifts his head, all alert and interested, tells Kim this is trouble.

"Take a walk," he says.

"In the dark?"

"Go sit in the Caddy," Stu says, tossing her the keys. "Play with the stereo. Check out those dynamite graphic equalizers."

The Caddie has leather seats the color of caramel and nearly as soft, a fancy wood faced dash, and a stereo with enough lights and dials for four, five ordinary boom boxes. Kim finds copies of *Penthouse* and *Convenience Store Decisions* under the front seat, along with a few old newspapers and an empty bag from the donut shop. The glove compartment has maps, a flashlight, aspirin, Tums, an inhaler, and an envelop of photos, mostly showing a boy of ten or eleven, a chubby, round faced little kid.

In several, he's smiling in a red and white basketball uniform with shorts that come down below his knees and a baseball cap on his head. In others, he's all Sunday dressed in shirt and slacks and bare headed, so she can see the dark wavy hair. The boy waves to the camera from the white Cadillac, kneels on the grass to play with a beagle, cocks his arm to throw a football. Kim can see Stu in the fat cheeks and stocky form, but the child's eyes are blue, startlingly blue. Kim flips through the rest of the snaps, quick and not really paying attention, until the final picture, a family grouping, stops her cold. She's looking at the child, the dog, and a tall, blonde woman with the boy's blue eyes. Kim looks at the picture and hears a voice saying, "You're standing on my grave."

* * * *

"I shouldn't be here," Kim says the next day. Just after one P.M., break time, a cloudy day with fall in the air. They're eating these really nice ham and cheese sandwiches with fine crunchy green pickles.

"Why not?"

"I'm working for your husband."

"I knew that." Unconcerned. That's one of the things that fascinates Kim about Maureen, that unconcern, that lack of fear. "I think these should have more onion. I like red onion on a sandwich. Don't you think these need more onion?"

"I never guessed," says Kim, who doesn't have unconcern but would like to acquire it. "What if he shows up? What if he comes to visit Joey's grave?"

Maureen's face changes then and her eyes get dark and hard as if all the grief and anger within are set to come flooding out. "He never comes to the grave. Never, the bastard. He wanted cremation. He wanted to forget." There's a pause. "Stu believes in moving on, in getting on with his life." The words are dipped in acid, coated in bile as thick as chocolate. Kim imagines each syllable being lowered into some internal vat and coming up dripping. "He thinks I'm crazy," Maureen says. "Crazy in general, crazy because of Joey, crazy about the grave."

Kim protests Maureen isn't crazy. Though she is unusual in a wonderful way.

"He'd like to see me in therapy, which would give him leverage, you see, leverage for the divorce. Or, maybe, if I'm in therapy, he'll fight the divorce and try to get me into treatment. That's what Stu would really like. He'd like me in a little clinic somewhere and then he'd have his hands on the business, on everything. He's always sniffing around and saving ammunition for the divorce."

Maureen always talks about the divorce as a kind of object, as a real thing, though it doesn't exist yet; no papers have been filed. But Maureen sees life as a series of separate events and things: the accident, the divorce, the meeting, the grave. She's not like Kim, for whom life slides from one thing to another, so that working for Stu Gleb somehow leads to this thing with his wife.

"I could maybe be something for the divorce," remarks Kim.

Maureen puts her arm around her. "So you could," she says. "But he never comes here. Never, ever. He couldn't face Joey's death and he thinks I'm crazy because I can't forget. He thinks he can spend his way back to happiness; he thinks he can gamble and forget. Well, not with my money, he can't. I can't forget, and I'll see that he won't, either."

Kim is uncomfortable with all this talk about Maureen's husband, especially since he's Stu Gleb and someone she knows. She's just as glad when Maureen asks, "How did you find out?" Her voice is casual but there's interest underneath.

Kim explains about Stu's visit, about the snaps in the car. "He wants Chris to do a job for him."

Maureen's eyes register the fact of the snaps, a kind of visual snarl, then, "What kind of job?"

"I don't know. He hasn't come back again."

"Best find out," says Maureen.

* * * *

But Kim doesn't worry about the job. She thinks some hot merchandise that Stu wants Chris to haul for him like cigarettes up from the south where there's less tax. Or else a little damage to one of the lower volume convenience stores for the insurance money. Maybe just to hang around looking ferocious and unpredictable when Stu expects bad company. Those are the sorts of things Chris is good at, so she's surprised when he comes into the kitchenette one night and starts to clean a gun. Not a shotgun or a rifle, like what everyone has in their neighborhood, but a stubby black thing with a textured grip.

"Get your eyes back in your head," he says.

Kim shrugs. Since meeting Maureen, she doesn't get all nervous and upset about Chris anymore. Kim's figuring to stay out of his way until she manages to be rid of him, so she doesn't ask nosey questions any more; she doesn't bother him when he's drinking or when he's picked up some good stuff. She puts her check on the table and fixes dinner, which makes her, far as Chris is concerned, a together chick. He's starting to tell her so, to let her know that this is for keeps, that she shouldn't think of leaving him.

He twirls the cylinder and takes out a roll of hundred dollar bills to impress her. "I've got a job worth doing," he says. "And I'll need you to drive the truck."

Kim looks at the money and then at him. "What do we have to do, kill somebody?"

She's joking, but Chris kinda nods his head. "We're going to kidnap somebody and hold him for ransom." He says this like guns and kidnapping and ransom's all part of their normal routine. Then he laughs. "And the best part is he's going to cooperate with us all the way."

"Who is?"

Chris doesn't tell her that. He pretends he's said enough already, but Kim can guess and when she tells Maureen the next day, Maureen can, too.

"That dumb bastard," she says.

* * * *

Kim's main thought is to clear the area, and she thinks Maureen may agree, given her own past history. "Chris is crazy," Kim tells her. "He'll be crazier with a gun." Kim sees Florida, or maybe even California, somewhere warm with sand and palms and big hotels looking glassy eyed at white beaches. But, of course, they can't do that. Kim knows without asking that they can't leave the grave, Joey, remembrance.

"You could dump Chris," Maureen says. This is the other alternative, their other fantasy. "You could get an apartment. I'd help you. You could get a really nice apartment."

"He'd come after me," Kim says. "And there's the divorce."

"Yes," says Maureen with this funny smile. "There's the divorce."

* * * *

"I don't see what you need the gun for," Kim tells Chris. "Not if he's cooperating."

"Don't be dumb. It's got to look realistic."

"A knife would do," Kim says. It's in her mind that the gun is a bad idea, that Chris is too impulsive to be trusted, that he will screw up in some spectacular way.

"There might be trouble," he says. "You get less trouble with a gun."

"They'll question me," says Kim. "They'll question everyone who works at the stores. They'll figure an inside job."

"We get the money and we're out of here." Chris sounds so decisive and confident, that, despite her indifference, Kim feels her heart clench. She foresees separation and despair; she sees the truck, the highway, exile from real life.

"All you gotta do is to drop me off," he says so enthusiastically she understands that he is enjoying this, the excitement and importance of it. "I take him and his car. He calls the wife. She gets the money and drops it off. We're all home free."

"Where do you leave the car?" asks Kim. "Where do you leave him?"

"Maybe here. You're at work. You don't have to know nothing."

"I take the truck for the first time ever to work, someone's going to notice."

He doesn't like that. He looks like he might want to make an issue of it, make her agree to what's a purely dumb idea. But he surprises her. "Maybe you start driving the truck to work," he says. "I'm thinking of getting a bike, anyway. I saw this Harley I'd like and I can afford it." He picks his head up, like she's going to give him an argument.

"All right," she says, thinking maybe he'll get a bike and break his damn neck. "I'll start taking the truck. But Stu'll want me working the night shift if I have a ride."

"What do you care when you work?"

Kim hesitates, feeling how events can slide one way or the other. Life's a teeterboard and you can slip off either end. "I don't want to be there alone at night. Stu comes by. I gotta watch him, he's always . . ."

"See you don't give him any reason," Chris says. "But if he tries anything, I'll break his face."

* * * *

Chrysanthemum season. Maureen has two big pots in the back of her car and four smaller ones. The big ones are the size of bushel baskets and have mauve flowers. The smaller ones have white flowers and should stand the winter, Maureen says. Kim helps her pull out the begonias, though they're still pretty, pretty enough so she regrets not being able to take them home. She's getting an appreciation for flowers and sees how the begonias would brighten up the trailer. She thinks about having them on the kitchenette table so that she could look at flowers instead of at Chris all the time.

Maureen digs in the new plants, and Kim brings some water from the faucet down the dirt track.

"So you're driving to work now," says Maureen.

"Chris has this bike he bought."

"Used?" Maureen asks, like she's really interested in Chris and his purchases.

"New," says Kim. And Maureen stops tidying up around the plants and looks at her.

"New." Maureen doesn't say anything else, so that an idea Kim had put aside comes crashing back: mega cash for a phony kidnapping. Maureen frowns and shakes her head. She's quiet all through lunch, thinking this over and when she finally speaks, she says, "Would Chris shoot somebody? In cold blood, would he shoot someone?"

Kim doesn't like to say she has no idea, but she doesn't, though she's lived with Chris for two years. "Why do you ask that?" she says. "What do you mean?"

"I can raise maybe $50,000," Maureen says. "In an absolute emergency, life and death, with bridge loans, twice that much. Subtract a new Harley Davidson and probably money afterwards and how much is left?"

"Chris wouldn't know that," says Kim, but she's already hoping maybe they've been wrong. Maybe Chris has another job, maybe Stu Gleb isn't involved at all.

"Stu knows to the penny. He knows our money isn't liquid." Maureen has to explain this to Kim, how money can be liquid or not, how it can be tied up.

"So why is he doing it? Why is he doing this thing with Chris?" Kim asks.

"This is going to be Stu's version of the divorce," Maureen says. "I think he wants to get his hands on everything; I think he doesn't care about the ransom at all."

"You have to tell the police," Kim says.

"And what would happen to you? They'd guess how I found out."

"I could leave," Kim says. "I could get out of town."

"If that's what you want," says Maureen. "But I have a better idea."
* * * *

Chris goes out on the bike the next night and soon as he clears the yard, Kim begins looking for the gun. She told Maureen "no problem," but after she searches under the bed, the bedside table, Chris's footlocker, the shelf above their coats, the medicine cabinet, even the cupboard by the door where they put canned goods, Kim starts getting nervous. Outside, she checks the truck over like a sniffer dog but can't find a thing. Back inside, the phone rings.

"Find it?" Maureen asks.

"Not yet. I thought you didn't want to call."

"I'm at the gas station. Would he keep it in the bike?"

"He might. He's got those carrier things. They probably lock."

"You'll have to check," says Maureen.

So there's Kim with bullets rattling in her jeans pocket and the whole trailer turned upside down, when Chris roars into the yard.

"Cleaning," she says.

"Don't be crazy. We'll be outta this dump soon."

"How soon?"

"What you don't know won't hurt you," he says and laughs, as if he thinks he's pretty funny.

Within minutes, the phone rings again. Kim knows it's Maureen, she just knows it is, but Chris picks it up, listens a minute, then swears and says he doesn't have time for any damn opinion poll. Kim lets out her breath.

After dinner when she carries out the garbage, Kim tries the catches on the motorbike's carriers. She tries again later on the excuse that she's left a sweater in the truck, but what she finally has to do is to get up a half hour earlier than usual the next morning. Chris is still asleep when Kim gets the bike keys out of his pocket and goes outside barefoot, half frozen, and shaking with nerves to unlock the carrier. There's the gun, black and ugly and serious looking.

Kim thinks of Joey's accident and freezes. In her mind she hears Maureen saying, "I always kept the gun locked up, always, always locked up, but Stu wanted it handy. 'What good's a gun you can't get to,' he'd say. Safety, that was his thing, but it wasn't very safe for a little boy, was it?" Kim remembers how Maureen's eyes went wild and dark, how she wept and said, "There were bits of bone on the wall, bits of bone."

So Kim is reluctant to touch the gun, though Maureen went over the whole process with her, two, three times. Kim stands there, dithering, until there's a sound — a car somewhere — and she breaks open the chamber revealing neat, shiny bullets with round brass ends. Out they come and in go the ones Maureen brought her. Close up the gun, wipe it, and put it back quick with the oily rag on top.

The carrier latch snaps loud enough to stop Kim's heart, but there's nothing, no reaction, no door opening, no face at the window, and all she's got left to do is to slide the keys back into Chris's tumbled, greasy jeans and fix herself an early breakfast.

* * * *

Two days, three days, nothing happens. Kim's beginning to think that maybe there's another deal, that maybe Chris has pulled a fast one, that maybe they'll be okay after all.

Maureen wants to know if she's sure she changed all the bullets, and when Kim says "yes," Maureen tells her, "Wait and see."

But Kim's still jumpy, wired with nerves, so Maureen says, "Don't worry; we've defanged them." Maureen seems pleased about that and confident. "There's not a damn thing they can do to us now."

* * * *

A yellow wash from the neighbor's security light and Chris shaking her shoulder. "Get up," he says.

"What is it? What time is it?" Kim's thinking fire, flood or a racoon in the trailer.

"Let's go," he says. "This is the day."

She gets up and dresses, her hands shaking, though Chris has been defanged, though the gun is harmless, though no matter what Maureen does — calls the police or raises the cash — nobody gets hurt.

The kitchenette reads 5:30 A.M. "You're way too early," Kim says. "Stu won't be at the store before 7:30."

"Who said we were going to get him at the store?" Chris asks.

"You said I just needed to drop you off. You said . . ."

"Listen, I trust you," Chris says with this awful heavy certainty. "We're in this together."

He puts his arm around her shoulder and they go outside. She expects him to drive, but he motions her behind the wheel and gives her the keys.

"I'll tell you where to go," he says. "Keep the lights off until we hit the road."

The sky's beginning to gray, but Kim nearly hits the boulder at the driveway end and has to put on the low beams. It's a relief to get onto the main road and have light. Chris sits beside her, giving orders without any real direction, until they reach a country road, all winding and stone walls. After a mile or so, he has her pull in at a drive with fancy carriage lamps on either side.

"Cut the lights," he says. Kim has to wait a few seconds until she can see to ease the truck along the circular drive to a three car garage. An attached breezeway with long windows and a glass door connects to the house. Chris pulls on a ski mask and takes the gun out of his jacket pocket. "Keep the motor running," he says.

None of this is quite real to Kim, though she can feel her hands, which are freezing, and the clammy, coldness of the shirt against her back, and a stiffness in her feet. She's really in need of sun and heat and someplace different, but the situation, itself, is like something on tv, like a film, a drama, a still picture in the tabloids: "Celebrity Home Invaded by Masked Intruder," something like that.

When Kim hears the tinkle of breaking glass, she wants to push on the horn and alert the house. She also wants to put the truck in reverse and get the hell out. Instead, she hangs onto the wheel with both hands and tells herself that everything will be all right: crazy at the moment, but without permanent damage. Kim's still telling herself this when the shots start, one, then two, three, four, close together. She piles out of the truck, stumbles across the gravel drive, and races to the house where lights are coming on, and there's this indescribably bad, scary atmosphere.

"Chris," she shouts and then, "Maureen! Stu!" Though that's careless, not prudent, dangerous, as is running down the hall toward the light, toward the master bedroom, toward Maureen, who, gun in hand, is shrugging her way into a bathrobe. Maureen has a rigid, unfamiliar expression on her face, as if the darkness that used to live behind her eyes has come out into the light for good.

"What's happened?"

Maureen recognizes her then, recognizes the voice, the face. "Don't go in there," she says, meaning the bedroom, where Kim can now see objects, bundles like, lying on the floor. Bundles she somehow knows are Chris and Stu. Kim starts to cry.

"Don't do that," says Maureen, touching her shoulder like the old Maureen, the real Maureen, glimpsed for that second then disappearing. "You don't have time. Go down the field track to the highway and hitch a ride to work."

"I'll be late," wails Kim as if this is all that matters.

"Tell them Chris went out early with the truck," says Maureen. "You don't have to know anything else. But get out of here. You've got to get out of here now."

* * * *

Kim walks out the glass doors and takes a moment to see the palms and the crowded strip of sand at the edge of the water. Outside the hotel air conditioning it's really too warm for her nice receptionist's blazer, but green's her best color, and it only takes a few minutes to run to the coffee shop, crowded with delivery guys and workers and other hotel staff on breaks. Kim returns greetings, friendly waves: she's been around long enough to know people.

Coffees, one with, one without, plus a bagel, a donut, extra sugar. Kim's already collected her order when she checks the magazine rack and feels time stop for a moment: Princess Diana on the cover again, midnight blue silk, a jeweled necklace broad as your hand, eyes as blue as Maureen's when she stood on the edge of the grave with all the mauve and white mums and handed over the envelop.

"You'll need," said Maureen. "To get started."

Kim took it; there wasn't anything else to do, not if she wanted to leave, to start again, to get away from scary bundles and awkward questions and Maureen's wild eyes.

"Maybe you'll come back," said Maureen.

And though Kim said, "Maybe," at the time, she knows she never can, she never will, because Maureen's crazy; Stu Gleb was right about that. Just the same, standing in her green hotel blazer just across from the sand, Kim can't help feeling grateful, and nostalgic, too, about the cemetery and picnics and real life.

MY DEMON LOVER

My mother always warned me, "be careful what you wish for," and I should have listened, because what I got from my wishes was both unexpected and alarming. But I'm getting ahead of myself. Let me take you back to when I was seventeen and plump. Nothing excessive, I realize now, just definitely on the high side of the size chart. Plump, with problem skin no amount of tetracycline or Cover Girl could solve, I was young, awkward, and a bit lonely. I wanted not just sex and excitement, but romance with a capital R; I was looking for the other side of my soul.

Along the way, I became addicted to the more extravagant templates of romance like Heathcliff and Romeo, men who lived and died and killed, killed, too, for love like Carmen's Don Jose, demon lovers, every one. I had a taste for the excessive and the improbable; I wanted a spectacular love, the sort that is unreal and unlikely. I wished for it, ached for it, and, ten years down the road when I'd almost settled for what was reasonable, available, and likely, I got my wish.

I was slimmer then. Well turned out, in fact, because I was working as the evening Weather Girl at WFAX, our biggest state channel, pulling in a 20 share and double figure ratings. I was expected to give the evening forecasts, exchange banter with the studio anchors, make happy talk about sunny days, and put on a serious face when meteorological disasters struck.

Not, you'll perhaps agree, the most promising media position, but one that suited me and which I made my own. Please believe that I am something of celebrity, far better known than either of the anchors. In fact, I possess the best sort of celebrity: glamour combined with authority.

Before *moi*, the station entrusted its meteorological duties to a succession of good, gray trustworthy father and uncle types, who were losing their hair and clogging their arteries. That tells you right away where television's head is, doesn't it? The weatherman has to be trusted, even though it's far easier to check the weather than most other things in modern life. Better, I say, to have a sleazy, unreliable type at your weather desk and save the solid citizens for important things like renovation companies and auto body shops. But there you are: "image, it's everything."

My own image is definitely upscale. Nothing I'm going to tell you makes sense unless you have that clearly and firmly in mind. When I decided on TV, on media as a career, I studied what worked and isolated a certain gloss, a certain presence, a certain style. Although my competitors were attractive, more attractive, really, with their impeccably styled hair, perfect teeth and pretty clothes, they were all white bread, interchangeable, forgettable. I aimed for impact and a more substantial image. The Joan Collins of *Dynasty* was my pattern: big shoulders, big hair, big eyes, a certain sexual authority.

Weather "Girl" didn't really suit what I had in mind, but, thanks to managerial timidity, I had to proceed gradually: think Vanna White morphing into Margaret Thatcher. I slowly added bigger shoulder pads, smiled less, pronounced more. I didn't just read the weather, I predicted it, no "ifs," "ands" or "buts."

My anchors would get nervous.

"So Nadine" — I don't think I've mentioned that along the way I changed from "Nancy" to "Nadine" — "what about my golf game? Any chance of sun this weekend?"

You know the right answer as well as I did: (Giggle) "Well, Arnie, there's some hope, but pack your umbrella." I dispensed with such wishy-washy pap: "Leave your clubs in the bag, Arnie," I told him. "It's going to pour."

And it did, because, you see, I really know weather. I really do. I have a talent for it. Sure, anyone can learn to read the satellite pictures, interpret the charts, track storms. And if you can't, there are plenty of people with pocket protectors and cathode pallor who'll tell you all about them. I do my homework, of course, but I have something else, a real feel for a falling barometer, a nose for a storm. On tough calls, I'm right maybe eight out of ten. Good enough so that the superintendents call when school looks dicey and WFAX supports me even when I disagree with the big national services.

You'll understand my position now: I'm a recognizable demi-celebrity and a bona fide authority. No simpering and studio banter for me. I'm there to give the weather forecast: to tell you how things are going to be, to predict a future which I already know.

I'll admit this minor stardom grew my ego. It certainly spawned some backbiting and rug-pulling media gossip. But with ratings like mine, I could smile at criticism and take up personal appearances, charity work, community service. Even politics didn't seem too farfetched. I was contented, well paid, good looking. I'd almost forgotten that I'd ever wished for anything else.

Then, nearly two years ago, I attended the local Opera Guild's fall fund raiser — have I told you about my appearance for the Opera in *Die Fledermaus*? I was one of the New Year's Eve revelers and, in the jail scene, when the inmates sent out to learn the forecast, I came on and brought down the house. I wore a wonderful period costume, deep purple with a black coq feather trim that made me think the eighteen-nineties would have been my ideal era: a little more rump, a little more bust, a little more tummy, a lot more drapery. Some of us have good frames for drapery, for bustles and flounces. When I put that dress on, I felt I could rule the world, I really did.

Anyway, the Opera fund raiser pulled in all the climbers and strivers: nouveau culture hawks, dutiful old Yankees, Italian-American construction moneybags, plus a smattering of politicians, gregarious and avaricious, eager to show the flag and to prospect for a little wealth of their own. I was being gracious on demand, joking about my "operatic career," and swapping hurricane stories with Dave Griffith, a lecherous downstate exec possessed of deep pockets and gubernatorial ambitions, when a slim, dark man with a bulging forehead and untidy black hair squeezed around the drinks table and laid his hand on my friend's arm.

"Dave," he said, "Hugh Spencer."

"Hugh! How could I forget! Great to see you. Hugh's a genius," my friend Dave said.

Hugh did not dispute this, although he did not strike me as promising. He wore an exceptionally ugly and ill fitting gray suit, an almost threadbare white shirt, and a narrow green tie. He had a lean, pale face and dark, curiously opaque eyes, as if the windows of this particular soul were shuttered tight. Otherwise, his only remarkable feature was an exceptionally wide, white forehead that was over scaled for his thin mouth and narrow jaw. He looked like Edgar Allan Poe on Valium.

"Absolutely a genius: he does video games — and business presentations to die for!" Dave exclaimed and started growling like a sports car revving up. Oblivious to the reactions from other guests, Hugh added a few high-pitched squeals. Drinks sloshing, arms waving, they began a little symphony of sound effects before collapsing in merriment.

"Brilliant," said our gubernatorial hopeful. "Hugh's presentation really changed our old gray image."

"Varoom, varoom," said Hugh. "That was a Lambroghini, you know."

"Really!"

"Vintage. There's nothing like the sound. The sound carries the image there, just picks it up and takes it to another plane."

Hugh's face grew animated as he described his work. His black marble eyes glowed, giving his white face the lean and hungry look of a Cassius dreaming of knives and power or the mad intensity of a drugged up poet burning with verse. But even as he talked to my friend, the politician, I could feel Hugh's focus shifting my way like an overdue weather system.

"This is Nadine Johanson," Dave said. "WFAX weather desk. The gal who called that killer snow storm last December."

"I know, I know," said Hugh, as he shook my hand. "You're the reason I turned up today."

Dave laughed. "I didn't know you were such an incorrigible ladies man, Hugh."

A film of sweat streaked across Hugh's brow.

This was not what I'd anticipated. It's true that I've never desired the ordinary, but I'd expected my long desired, completely imaginary prince to be handsome, suave — presentable, at least.

"Ms. Johanson is perfect for my new heroine," Hugh said. "She's perfect for the Dark Queen."

"Queen," I liked; I was not so sure about his "new heroine." If you'd asked me at that precise moment, I'd have said I preferred an inconclusive flirtation with Dave Griffith to electronic immortality with Hugh Spencer.

"Another game!" exclaimed Dave. "Listen, not before we get our stockholders' presentation finished! I tell you, Nadine, this guy can just blow a meeting away!"

"I've been working on the new game a while now," Hugh said. His eyes turned opaque again, like limousine glass.

"You've heard of his last one?" Dave asked me. "*Stone Tower*? This guy could have retired on *Stone Tower*."

"My nephews love *Stone Tower*," I said.

Mega sales for sure! I couldn't help regarding Hugh differently, but that dreadful suit suggested he'd done something stupid about the copyright. You can't trust geniuses for business, can you? I'd retained that much from English Lit.

"My second effort," Hugh said. "Nice things in it, but this new one is something special." He turned to me, his open face as innocent as a schoolboy's. "You were my inspiration."

Dave laughed. Dave, I should tell you, is basically a good old boy type jerk. Because of that, he's going to go a fair way in politics, but not as far as he'd like. I can predict that with confidence.

"Really," said Hugh. "Your show was a revelation. The clothes, the hair, the tone!"

I was up there with the Lambroghini. Varoom, varoom!

"I saw you as the Dark Queen right away, and once I had her, everything else followed."

"I'm flattered," I said.

"You perhaps would like to see it, the game, I mean, *The Dark Queen*." He spoke shyly, but even then I could feel that he'd be persistent. There was something different about him. He was a nerd with attitude, a geek of genius. I wondered what else might be hidden behind those shuttered eyes.

"Well, some time," I said, looking at my watch, the busy person's hint. A minute more and I would have been out of there. Gone. Captured by Naomi Silverstein, the Opera Guild Chair, or Muriel Nucci, the chorus director, who'd told me I have a nice alto and wanted me to help with a benefit. I was surrounded by the movers and shakers of community culture, courted by politicians, recognized by all, safe, in a word, from the subtle temptations of the imagination.

"No time like the present," exclaimed Dave, who is singularly lacking in perception. "Listen, my kid, Patsy — you met Patsy at the shareholders meeting," he prompted Hugh. I didn't need any reminder. The last time Dave brought the little brat with him to the station, she'd pawed through all my makeup. "If Patsy ever found out Dad passed on a chance to see one of your games pre-publication, I'd never be forgiven." He brayed with laughter, clapped Hugh on the back, and draped one of his long arms over my shoulder.

Hugh smiled politely, his secret, closed eyes sliding back toward my face.

"Come on," Dave said. "This'll be fun. You only like opera when you're on stage. Lead on, Hugh."

I saw Dave's agenda plain as day. Any time we met, he wanted to invite me for lunch, a quick drink, a semi-innocent get together. "What about your wife?" I asked, scanning the crowd for Caroline. "This will take a while . . ."

"A half hour," Hugh said eagerly. "My office is right down off Franklin."

"Practically next door!" exclaimed Dave. "Besides, I can leave Caroline the Mercedes. You're not running the Corvette in this weather, are you, Hugh?"

"Too cold for her now," Hugh said.

It always annoys me when men refer to cars as feminine.

"Hugh's got a vintage Corvette convertible," Dave said. He growled again, and to the imitation of much horsepower, we bade farewell to the Opera Guild and stepped from the permanent twilight of the hotel suite to the cold, brilliant afternoon sunshine.

Hugh's company was in an old factory block. Though Hugh, himself, seemed permanently disheveled, his BMW was new, and his large workrooms were equipped with a fleet of top of the line Mac Workstations. A corkboard the length of his office was covered with notes, photos, and drawings for various works in progress.

"Hey, here you are!" said Dave, examining a row of photos. I was standing before the studio's satellite map, full face, both profiles, a better grade of mug shot.

"What awful snaps," I said.

"Off the television screen, I'm afraid," Hugh apologized. "We've captured some on video and that's better. I wish the Opera had taped *Fledermaus*. Still, we redraw everything, anyway."

He switched on one of his machines and called up a file. "This is better, don't you think?" The monitor bloomed with purples, pinks and lavenders, as a woman with dark, flowing hair filled the screen. She was a Queen of the Night wearing a vaguely military costume and a crescent moon in her hair. I could definitely see a resemblance.

"Wow," said Dave. "Way to go!" And he growled again.

In the face of my own interior image, my secret self-portrait, Dave's brand of sexuality was suddenly terminally boring. You know those exercises in beginning art and writing classes: make a mask, describe yourself as your favorite animal, do an abstract portrait that represents your inner self? Well, everything I'd tried to make myself was floating on those glowing pixels, and I couldn't take my eyes off Hugh Spencer's computer screen.

"Do you like it?" asked Hugh, in a soft, insinuating voice. I could feel the invitation.

"She's remarkable," I said. When our eyes met, I smelt the burn in the air and felt an atmospheric disarrangement.

"Wow," said Dave. "You sure this is a kids' game? Safe to buy this one for Patsy?" And he laughed again.

"It's an adventure, puzzle game like *Stone Tower*," Hugh said, dead serious. He did not seem to pick up double entendres. "*The Dark Queen* is the object of your quest. If you can find her, you win the game. But she's also part of the complications. She can help you if you make the right decisions along the way, or she can turn malevolent and bounce you right out of the game."

"Like weather," I said.

"Exactly. She's a sort of magic weather goddess," Hugh said.

His gleaming eyes transformed his face, and I realized that in this un-expected shape, in this unpromising situation, I'd gotten my wish. At that moment, I should have heard my mother's warning, but it was too late. I was a prisoner of my imagination, caught by the habits of a long fantasy life. Hugh and I got rid of Dave and went out to dinner. We wound up a late and extravagant night back in my apartment.

That's how our affair started, and, while it lasted, it was brilliant. Have you ever been to the big science museum up in Boston? The one with the colossal Van de Graaff generator? Bang! And a lightning flash! Think 100,000 volts and let your imagination go but don't expect the details from me. Passion's a saleable commodity these days, and I have something else planned for the material.

It will suffice to say that we were happy for a while, as people are who attain what they think they've always wanted. I'll amend that. We were unusually happy, because we reflected each other, and, in the most seductive of mirrors, saw ourselves as we had dreamed we'd be: a little larger and more important than life. Isn't that the true agenda of romance?

He worshipped me; I could live with that. What was more difficult to abide was *The Dark Queen*, character and game, both of which gradually took on sinister overtones. I was perfect, you see, for the Queen, for the game, for his interior fantasy. Perfect already. Pay attention here: already is the key word.

I don't know how many of you have had experience with Perfection: the Ultimate Challenge. Forget the marathon, presidential fundraising, the Iditarod: perfection's what really stretches the sinews, because it's static. Perfection can only decline, and poor Hugh had already convinced himself that he couldn't finish *The Dark Queen* without me. Me, that is, as I was the day we met.

To illustrate the difficulties that developed, we have to move forward almost exactly one year — I know the date, because I again had the Opera Gala on my calendar. That autumn, I'd felt a certain shift in taste coming, a psychic isobar, and I decided on a new look, a new hairstyle. In the media business, these are commercial decisions, you understand, and extra important the older one gets. I decided shorter, neater hair was required and probably lighter, too. Brenda, the stylist, concurred

"Smart," she said. "A lighter, younger effect."

"Yes," I said, when she'd worked her magic, "yes, I think this will do." The studio brass approved, the public response was favorable, but Hugh was devastated. I'd broken his heart, derailed his project, betrayed The Dark Queen. He went on and on before attempting manual strangulation and, when he discovered I outweighed him by 30 pounds, tears, remorse, hysterics. I'd gotten my demon lover, all right.

We broke up soon afterwards. Hugh had genius, but I have common sense. A couple of well-placed bruises could have hurt my career, and Van de Graaff generators, although spectacular in every way, can become wearing on a daily basis. I told him this was the end. Ready to be older and wiser, I changed my locks, my phone number, and my parking garage, even as Hugh prepared to realize my fantasy. Though his pursuit added a certain edge to life, be assured it was inconvenient.

He was diabolically clever. He broke into my computer and into my apartment. He left messages on my desk at work and obtained a CB that interfered with my stereo. I would be relaxing with Tchaikovsky — *Swan Lake*, maybe — I hadn't totally lost my taste for lush strings and ghostly romance — and there would be Hugh's voice, desperately yearning, "Nadine! Nadine! Come back!" as if I were one of the enchanted swan maidens, or, I suppose, in my case, swan matrons, though that doesn't have quite the same ring.

But I must not stray from the point, which was that eventually he wore me down into sympathy and foolishness. Hugh called me late one afternoon — he was amazingly ingenious in procuring my phone number. He wept, he pleaded, he apologized, he promised. His masterwork, *The Dark Queen* was almost finished. It was on the cusp and needed but a single touch to bring it to completion, to perfection. Perfection : I should have shuddered at the word.

If he could see me for an evening, a half hour, a few minutes, a few minutes was all he needed, a few minutes of inspiration. And to say good-bye, we needed to say good-bye, we needed to end better. It was his fault, but he repented; he was sorry. He desperately needed to say good-bye and then he'd leave me forever. He would. You can see that Hugh had plenty of inspiration when he really tried.

"All right," I said. "I'll meet you."

"I'll pick you up," he said. "We'll have dinner. A farewell dinner. A celebration for The Dark Queen."

I said that sounded all right. We drove to a romantic inn near the shore, a pricey, ancient Yankee place with faded chintz, wide boards, candles in pewter sconces — even a blazing wood fire, because it was a cold night, too cold for the Corvette convertible. Hugh looked happy. We toasted the game, our past, and our new, rational friendship in which we would meet once a year.

"What date?" I asked. "The anniversary of the day we met?"

"No," he said. "This date. Every year on this date, no matter what."

I liked the idea. I like obsession and romance, even a touch of danger, so long as they don't interfere with normal life. "Every year," I agreed. "Here?"

"Yes," he said, his eyes like black fire, like glistening slivers of the hardest, darkest anthracite. "Here, along the river."

Our glasses clinked; I'd had my hair tinted dark again for our meeting, and he was delighted with the firelight rippling over my violet moire silk. In his own way, Hugh was fascinating and charming, too, as long as I was the Dark Queen and perfect. We had a couple hours of genuine happiness, and when it was time to leave, we shook hands over the table and kissed in the parking lot. There was snow in the air and a dusting of white on Hugh's BMW.

"Good luck finishing your game," I said as we sped through the night. The river and the shore are quiet and dark that time of year.

Hugh looked at me, the look I had seen that first day at the Opera Guild reception, the look of Cassius, the assassin. "The game is finished," he said. "The game has been finished for a week."

"Surely not," I said. "You insisted on this meeting, because . . ."

"The computer game is finished, but not our game," he said.

I don't know about you, but I like the portentous better in books than in life. I believe I said so.

"The game ends in death," Hugh said. "The Dark Queen, the Queen of the Night, the Queen of Spades, she's always death."

He'd pushed the BMW almost to escape velocity, and as we careened around a curve, I saw the black glisten of the river ahead and forecast the future. I saw our car leaving the road: I saw us flying over the verge and flipping down the steep bank into eternal darkness. I saw that, and I grabbed the wheel, twisting us away from the water and *The Dark Queen* and Hugh's madness and sending us across the road toward the trees and the utility poles on the other side.

He shouted and wrenched the wheel free. I had no doubt then. I got my hand on the ignition and turned the key just before there was a terrible, spine-shattering jolt. Air bags mushroomed to fill the compartment with gas and nylon, and, in their smothering embrace, I found pain and finality.

That was the end of my demon lover: the driver's side hit first and even the best German engineering with air bags cannot protect against a 70 year old ash hit at 90 miles an hour. The whole left side of the BMW sheered off, and I was lucky that my unlocked door was sprung in the impact, because a trucker hauling fish up from the coast was able to pull me out into full-fledged celebrity and scandal.

Of course, in almost every way I've been altered for the worse, although I'm an even better weather forecaster than I was before. All those plates and screws and bones with pins in them have made me an exquisite human barometer. Let me tell you, I know storms intimately now.

But when the plastic surgery's complete and the orthopedic therapy is finished, I'll be back. The cosmetic surgeon promises to make me more attractive than ever. He has this image, this idea in mind. He's cute, sexy even, without bad habits that I can see, but a man who wants to turn you into his ideal is half way to being a psychopath. I think I'd be better off with the orthopedic surgeon, who finds me fascinating, replacement parts and all, or the lawyer who helped me sue Hugh's estate and institute libel actions against some of his defenders. I've been astonished at how enterprising and malicious some of Hugh's friends have been and how creatively they've blown up a few indiscreet phone calls.

But I have the ultimate response and intend to make a good thing out of notoriety. Perhaps I've not mentioned that I preserved every scrap of correspondence, including e-mail? I made sure that my answering service kept all Hugh's messages, and I had every word on my answer machine transcribed. Money in the bank with all the interest in Hugh Spencer, and I'm publishing as soon as possible.

The Dark Queen is still flying off the shelves, propelled by sensation and disaster. And quality, too, for Hugh really was a genius. With its infamous suicide pact loop, *The Dark Queen* is "archetypal," "Jungian," "cutting edge," "the first game for grown-ups," to quote the reviewers. Hugh's gruesome, spectacular, and ambiguous end hasn't hurt, either.

"His life and art," said one recent commentator, "encapsulated the searching anguish of the end of the twentieth century." That's as may be, but I do sense a certain fin de siecle appeal, and I'm beginning to see young women dressed as the Queen of the Night.

So I'll survive nicely. My memoirs are in the works, and even pre-plastic surgery, I'm becoming a fixture on the more daring talk shows. I intend to be bigger than ever — and not just in the local media market, either. But some nights, I still go home to turn on the computer and rendezvous with the Dark Queen, my alter ego, my danger, my apotheosis, and also with Hugh, who's no longer a danger and a nuisance but a romantic genius whose quirky talent pervades his work and whose fateful passion rumbles through the foreboding music that accompanies The Dark Queen.

I confess that other men seem somewhat insipid since my demon lover attained his ideal form. It cost me a lot to get him, but obsession can tolerate a few bionic parts, and I'd find it very hard to give up Hugh, my ideal Hugh, now. He haunts my imagination, and though I'm moving on, with possibilities on every side, there are autumn days when I think of the night stars and black water and imagine a rendezvous with Hugh down along the river.

THE MAN KALI VISITED

I am at the inquest and a sallow faced man with short hair and a blue striped suit is warning me to tell the truth, the whole truth, and nothing but the truth and asking me to state my name and occupation. I am stumbling over my words and forgetting American idioms and remembering irrelevant slang from Bombay, because I am feeling hopelessly and irredeemably foreign. Not only is the "truth" in this matter slippery and elusive, but the court does not seem ready for the "whole truth";, and "nothing but the truth" may be impossible.

"My name is Neena Dasgupta and I am office manager and secretary to the publisher of *Skin Magazine*." *Skin Magazine* runs photographs of pretty women with no clothes on and stories about sexy women by young men of minimal talent and maximal imagination. Its publisher, Mr. A, was my employer and my salvation. Thanks to *Skin Magazine*, I went from being the discarded wife of an ambitious graduate student to an independent woman on a good salary.

"Will you tell the court where you were on the afternoon of September 9th, 1993?"

"I was at the offices of *Skin Magazine* until 5:30 P.M." Very nice offices, too. I helped with the design. Modern and airy but with interesting colors, cinnabar, ocher, deep pink and turquoise; colors of the subcontinent; colors for moments of nostalgia and reflection.

"Can you describe that afternoon for the court?"

"It was a most ordinary afternoon. We were laying out pages for the November issue, and I personally was getting Mr. A's schedule organized for the next few weeks."

What this means is planning everything for him, paying the bills, answering his correspondence, dealing with the lawyers, two ex-wives, his elderly mother, and his neurotic Doberman's veterinarian. Although insufficiently appreciated by the puritanical American public, my poor Mr. A was a creative person. He wanted to distill sex into pictures and to distill women into beauty. Perhaps those were wrong desires, yet from my point of view, they seemed quite traditional. Our temple sculptors have been turning naked men and women into images for centuries. But in this new and different climate, it is natural for people to keep their clothing on. And so instead of grottos and temples full of beautiful sculptures and paintings, we have *Skin Magazine* which pays me, as I have mentioned, very well to be keeping Mr. A's schedule straight and seeing that his printers are paid and checking that all models are old enough or are accompanied with permission forms signed by their mothers.

"'Mr. A' is Mr. James Rembrandt Addison?"

"That is correct."

"And Mr. Addison was in the office that afternoon?"

This is, for anyone who knew Mr. A, a foolish question. Where else would he be? *Skin Magazine* was life as he was wanting to live it, where all women are beautiful and sympathetic, all men are attractive and successful, and the dull stretches and sharp edges of life are covered by a mist of desire. This was childish, of course, but we are all as childish as we can manage. What is sad is that we cannot contrive to be children forever, not even in fantasy.

That is what I have learned from this matter, but I do not think the judge wishes to hear my ideas. He is an elderly man with a red face and white hair. I am thinking that he has grown old listening and judging, which must be a so tiring life. I am guessing that he will not want complications in the simple case of a fatal heart attack.

That is definitely how Mr. A died. No "foul play" of the ordinary sort. He was completely alone, I am sure. Of course, I would willingly have stayed with him and supported him in the face of immaterial, as of material, threat, but he would not permit that. To let me stay would have been to acknowledge the situation, the implications, the dangers, all of which were complicated, elusive, and unusual.

I decide not to attempt this part of "the truth." Instead, I say, "He went out jogging at one as usual and he had a reservation for lunch at 1:45 at La Caricole. He returned at 2:45 and worked on slides and picture selection until 5. Mr. A always had the final say on pictures."

"The office closes at five?"

"Yes, but Mr. A often worked later and I sometimes stayed late, too, if there was a shoot scheduled."

"Why was that?"

"Mr. A, Mr. Addison, was always very proper."

There is laughter in the court and the judge is displeased. You are seeing here an illustration of my point: the "whole truth" is not required because it is not welcome. But Mr A, who took sexy photos and published soft porn, never told a dirty joke, fondled a model, or made raunchy remarks. He could be very sweet, but all his sexual energy was going into his pictures. Which were always of a perfect woman in a perfect situation. Which were pictures. Only. If you are understanding my point.

"Please go on Ms. Dasgupta."

But I must be careful. I am tending to drift off onto the realm of "whole truth" which is dangerous. I must stick to "nothing but the truth," which I like because it tells what I must leave out without committing me to exactly what must be put in. "Some of our younger models have been known to lie about their ages," I say. "Mr. Addison always felt it important in uncertain cases to have an older woman in the studio."

"Yourself."

"Yes. All the other staff are very young and neither Toby nor Mark, the assistant photographers, would have been quite suitable." Most unsuitable, in fact. When I am at a shoot, I wear my large gold earrings and drape a scarf over my head and carry a clipboard and see that they sign everything in sight: permissions, waivers, statement of age, contract, model's agreement, etc, etc. We have never had any trouble.

"And what time did you leave on the evening of the 9th?"

"I wanted to finish up some correspondence, and I was still working at ten to six when Mr. A asked me to leave."

"He asked you to leave?"

"He said there was no need for me to stay." Of course, I had been intending to stay; the correspondence was just an excuse. I believed that she was coming and I was afraid for him. But that, too, is an unpalatable "whole truth." For Mr. A, too. Or perhaps it was just too late for him. Maybe it was too late from the first day, the first day she arrived at the office.

"And what sort of mood was he in?"

"He was looking forward to shooting a favorite model. I think he said she was scheduled for 6:30."

"Do you know who this was?"

Now here is a difficulty, a case where the "whole truth" and "nothing but the truth" are in conflict. "Nothing but the truth" is obviously safest, and I hear myself say, "I believe it was to be Ms. Kal."

"You believe?"

"That was the name written in his calendar, yes."

"The mysterious Ms. Maria Kal. The Ms. Kal with no known address."

The judge is again displeased. He feels that it is unbusinesslike that we have no address for her. I could explain that manifestations rarely have addresses in the modern sense, although they may have localities. Indeed, they may have localities. Ms. Kal's, I think, is around our business. I think she was attracted. And why should that be surprising? For millenniums we have tried to attract spiritual forces: flowers, incense, sacrifices, dances, songs, prayers, rituals spiritual and sexual. We call the forces and sometimes they come. But they do not leave an address; they do not present social security cards or sign waivers or fill out W-2 forms. They come, like Ms. Kal, invoked but unbidden, and in surprising forms.

It was late, I remember. Six P.M. or maybe 6:30. The July issue had just been sent to the press, and Mr. A had been working, working at the last minute as he always does, checking this, changing that, driving the retouchers mad with his demands for perfection. And I am, of course, reassuring him and calming them and closing doors when tempers are getting high and talking to the printer and being, as Mr. A is always telling me, indispensable. So we are at 6:15 P.M., say, on that June evening, the evening of the solstice, the longest day, the shortest night, a significant day with the warm breezes, the perfect sky. Toby and Mark have gone home; Lydia has made the last coffee of the afternoon; the building's cleaners are running vacuums and polishers in the halls. I am tidying up and getting my purse ready to go when there is a knocking at the locked office door.

I am thinking to ignore it and then it comes again and, such ill luck!, I open the door. There is Ms. Kal as I saw her: a handsome woman of indeterminate age. Older by ten years than our models, though how old, I can't say. Perfect skin, wonderful figure, magnificent hair, but mature eyes. Our models tend to be perfect but half formed, all the better to take on the suggestions of the photographer, to be the receptacles of fantasy and desire. In contrast, Ms. Kal was mentally fully formed, her intellect aged and bottled in bond like the premium whiskey that advertises in *Skin*. Thirty? Maybe, though forty was not out of the question. Way, way too old and yet impressive! Perfect in her own way, splendid black hair, pale caramel skin, green eyes: a northern princess carrying the blood of warriors and maharajahs or the most wonderful nautch dancer ever imagined.

She would see Mr. A. I am explaining that he is so busy, so tired, that our models are booked so far in advance and only through certain reputable and famous agencies. And she is smiling, smiling without showing her teeth, which I know will be sharp, and making little impatient gestures like a fine horse, and walking toward Mr. A's office and, before I can stop her, putting her head in and calling him out. I am hoping, hoping, he will send her on her way. But instead, he makes a little sound as if he'd just sucked in his breath – and hers with it. "Come in," he says. "Come in. I've been waiting for you." I am feeling very cold because this is not true in the business sense: no appointment, no phone calls, no letters, no contacts. So he can only mean that she is the one he has been waiting to shoot; she is the one who is looking exactly right with no retouching; she is desire and sex and woman all distilled and perfect.

"You have no address for this woman?" the judge asks again.

"Alas, no. I did not wish to interrupt their first conversation, and she was never on the books."

She came, she went. Always late, always at the last second, always on the spur of the moment. A curious and vivid phrase, that, and so right for her. Mr. A would prepare to work late, to shoot her picture into the wee hours, to work til dawn in the darkroom — and then to sulk all day the next day because he had failed. There was always something wrong with the film, with the light, with the always so mysterious inner workings of the camera. Despite an obsessive, heart-breaking persistence, Mr. A never did succeed in getting a usable picture of the absolutely unique Ms. Kal.

"But she did come to the office more than once?"

"I only saw her once. It was my understanding she came several times." This, I am thinking, is safe to say. And quite true.

The judge shakes his head. He is still trying to make sense of a sense-less situation. "I have a description given by Mr. Toby Bell, one of the assistant photographers on the magazine. He has testified that he saw Ms. Kal one night when he returned to pick up a camera which he had left on his desk. He describes her, if you remember, Ms. Dasgupta, as slim, blonde, extremely pretty and about seventeen years old."

"That is not the woman I saw. And Mr. A, as I have explained, would not have been photographing a young woman of 'about seventeen' alone in the studio at night."

"On the other hand, your co-worker, Penny Rohmer, may have seen her leaving the offices. Ms. Rohmer describes a fashionably dressed African-American with very short hair."

"I do not remember any such model."

The judge is not pleased with my memory. As the keeper of the calen-dar, I should be more accurate, more precise. I should have the full name and address for Ms. Kal and a consistent description of her. I shrug and draw my scarf around my shoulders. I am not venturing onto the "whole truth." I have my green card but not my final papers. I am a "resident alien" who must be mature and logical, not a tabloid-crazed citizen who can safely spot Elvis or go joy riding with Martians.

"Now, on the night in question, did you see Ms. Kal – or whoever the model was – arrive?"

"No, I did not." Though I knew she was coming, though I feared the consequences. Mr. A's ambition had become an obsession. He was dropping all his other work, even neglecting his true and only love, the magazine; he was forgetting the joys of fantasy and letting Mark and Toby shoot the November photo spreads. A great mistake, I was reckon-ing. They lacked Mr. A's so fatal imagination; they lacked his style and flair. But he could think of nothing else but Ms. Kal. Would she return? Could he succeed? Her photos would be the crown of his career, the ar-tistic summit of his ambitions, absolutely unprecedented and, of course, worth a fortune. Meanwhile, I was telling him that she was bad luck, a dangerous woman, a manifestation to be avoided at all costs. Poor Mr. A was alternately laughing at me and drinking bourbon straight out of the bottle in his darkroom.

"All right, Ms. Dasgupta, will you tell the court what happened when you arrived at the office the next morning."

I feel the tears in my eyes and begin to shake. I was truly very fond of Mr. A, and I am still uncertain whether I am under Ms. Kal's sentence or protection.

"The witness," the judge says, "can have a minute to compose herself." When I am composed, we go on.

"Just take it slowly, please, Ms. Dasgupta. What time did you arrive at *Skin Magazine*?"

"About 8:40. It depends on which bus I catch. Sometimes I am as early as 8:30 and sometimes it is almost nine o'clock. I go in and do a little work and then I am opening the office at nine for the others." I could explain a good deal about the office routine, and I would like to do so. I could tell how I open up the shades on the west side and close the blinds on the east. How Lydia starts the coffee machine that wheezes and groans so that Tony and Mark are making rude remarks. How I turn on my desk radio to the classical station and listen to Monteverdi or Bach, so soothing, so regular. Instead, I must tell about seeing the red light above the darkroom door.

"This was unusual?"

"The red light is only on when someone is working in the darkroom. Mr. A worked at night but rarely until nine in the morning. And Toby and Mark did not have keys." But I was not thinking then about Toby and Mark, I was thinking terrible thoughts and remembering terrible memories of the ignorant old village festivals for the goddess with their rivulets of blood and the smoking corpses of headless goats. The goddess of the dawn feeds on blood; the patroness of sex bears our death.

"Please continue," the judge says.

I am surprised to be in the big square courtroom with the so white walls, the green tinged lights, the brown seats. I had been in the office, our pretty airy office with the colors of the subcontinent, ocher, cinnabar, turquoise, and pink, knocking on the door of the darkroom, calling, imploring, begging, then warning that I must be opening the door, the sacred darkroom door never to be opened when its red light is on. I turn the knob, push the door, and blood colored light washes over darkness. I see the shape on the floor and fumble for the switch and then in an instant, I am seeing and understanding everything. Poor Mr. A, my benefactor, employer, and friend, is lying on the floor, his tongue out, his face a hideous mask of fear and horror, his bodily fluids mingling with puddles of developer and fix. I put my hand on his chest and touch his wrist and his jugular vein, but Mr. A has already been transformed, swept away on the great wheel of earthly illusion. Perhaps he is even now being reborn in Bombay or Brooklyn, screaming into life with all his old sorrows and pleasures forgotten.

I stand in the darkroom, knowing I must be calling the police and 911 and preparing to tell "the truth," "the whole truth" and "nothing but the truth." But first, I am having a look around. There are strips of film, developed film, hanging up against the light, and I can make out images of a nude woman of extraordinary beauty, images which were waiting, I think, only for me and which are fading now with unnatural rapidity, fading and twisting, and going back into the chaos of all things before "truth" and "whole truth" and "nothing but the truth" got separated and distinguished from lies and untruth and indeterminacy.

On the floor lies a single print, the first, perhaps, of the negatives Mr. A had been developing, the print that would have crowned his career and made his fortune. I pick it up carefully, because it has lain in the water and chemicals and is creased and stained. I turn it over and even though I am expecting the worst, I am frightened. The voluptuous Ms. Kal has been transformed into the dark goddess with her long red tongue, her necklace of skulls, her girdle of human hands, her black and terrible body, at once the womb and tomb for every thing living now and in the future, through every incarnation.

In the windowless courtroom, I tell the judge "nothing but the truth': how I found Mr. A, how I screamed, how I ran out to call 911.

"Now Ms. Dasgupta, I know this is difficult for you, but these next questions are very important. Were there any photographs?"

I am so glad he has asked me something I can answer honestly. There was one photograph, which now resides wrapped in a piece of fine silk under a garland of flowers in my bedroom. The photo I managed to secret out of the office under the noses of the so busy crime scene technicians, investigating officers, coronor, and photographer. But there were other photographs and I am pleased to say, "Oh, yes. There were photographs of Everly Chique for the November issue. They were hanging up to dry and some of her slides were still on the light table."

"Ms. Chique is employed by Hot Stuff Videos, Inc., I believe."

"Ms. Chique has extensive video credits, yes. She is scheduled to appear in our Skin Flicks feature for November."

"According to the office records, these photos were taken on September 6th and 7th. Is that correct?"

"That is correct. Toby was shooting those. He is still learning, but Ms. Chique is very experienced with photo sessions."

"Now I want to be clear about this. There were no other photographs, negatives, roles of film in the darkroom?"

"Oh, yes, Sir. As I am sure the police have been reporting. Some blank negatives, some torn up papers. Nothing useable, alas, and all the time poor Mr. A lying dead on the floor."

"The police on the scene described him as lying in a pool of liquid with several flat plastic pans around him. How does that fit with your recollection."

"It is fitting perfectly. He had obviously been working developing something. Perhaps he was discarding the results. Perhaps there was a flaw in the film. I am thinking a roll of film had not come out."

"Did you remove anything at all from the darkroom, Ms. Dasgupta?"

"No, I did not." Now I am lying. You see how treacherously one slips from a decent approximation of the truth to out right lies? But what should I say? That I removed the photograph that killed Mr. A, a now fading but still dangerous representation of the goddess whom I know as Kali and whom Mr. A knew as Ms. Kal? That would be the "whole truth" but what good would it do us? I am thinking "nothing but the truth" with one exception is what I will be sticking with.

"And did you bring anything into the darkroom, Ms. Dasgupta?"

"Some flowers. For the dead." It is appropriate to be ending with truth and a lie. Or with a truth that is not the "whole truth." They understand flowers for the dead. That is very appropriate and how often have I been sending expensive flowers to the funeral service of this person or that for Mr. A. But they might not comprehend flowers for the cruel goddess, who may be lonely in this cold and alien land, who may yet visit me.

Now the judge is rebuking me for tampering with the crime scene, though my actions were understandable and, he believes, innocent. I sense it will be all right. I will keep my green card; I will get my final papers. I must be, I think now, under the protection of the goddess, for he is saying, "Thank you, Ms. Dasgupta. That will be all," and I am stepping down from the witness stand.

THE VIEW FROM ABOVE

Although Philip said the parasail would be a good thing to try, something to mark her recovery, Callie wasn't so sure. She wasn't a great swimmer and the gliders can go pretty far out from shore. Up high, too, but Philip, her brother Phillip, said, "That's the point, Callie. The whole point is that you're doing something you wouldn't normally attempt. It's sort of a test to mark a new stage in your development."

A new stage of development was certainly a welcome idea. The last one hadn't been so good, what with confusion and imagination and things not being what they seemed at all. That was a bad spell, a very bad spell, which ended after a series of steps, that had seemed logical enough at the time, with Callie gagged and bound with duct tape on the ground in a city park.

Of course, finding herself there was a shock. She thought anyone would agree with that! And when the police asked, it had made sense for her to say that she'd been tied up, because she'd been abducted, because she'd been forced into a car. By a man, by men, with a knife, a gun. That's how things go when you lose the thread of life.

Callie remembered staring at the dirt, unable to move, tape hauling at her hair, at the skin of her wrists, and asking herself, How did I get here? That actually was a quote from a Talking Heads song she liked, the one where David Byrne keeps repeating, *same as it ever was*, and doesn't recognize his wife or his house or anything in his life. The song has a good chorus and a beat that could almost carry Callie over whatever questions she had at the moment.

Of course, without the distractions of music, Callie had to do her best to think how she'd gotten into such a mess. "There was a man," she told the police, and they wrote her answer down in their little notebooks to use against her later. But though she'd feared and anticipated disaster, she still had to give them more, like how tall the man was, how dark or light, and what kind of hair he had. Before she knew it, life had gotten away from her again. She was in terrible trouble and making difficulties for everyone from the man they arrested to Philip, who had to come and explain about medication and the way things escaped her sometimes.

So maybe the parasail idea was a good one after all. She was feeling much better, without lost time and mysterious difficulties, and her probation was going well. She was on probation, because, really, there hadn't been any knives or guns or men, either. It appeared — though Callie couldn't admit this because she didn't remember — that she had tied herself up and staggered around the park until she reached the clump of beach plum trees.

She couldn't think why she'd done that. It didn't make much sense, but it was the sort of thing that happened to her whenever she lost the thread. According to the attending psychiatrist, she was prone to self-dramatization and delusions, but Callie felt that phrasing was inaccurate as well as unkind. Rather, she had confusions, which she accounted for with little stories and explanations that sometimes, admittedly, got both her and other people into trouble.

With the parasail ride, though, she would be doing something unusual and a little dangerous for real. She would be going out over deep water, which scared her, and also going high, which, Philip said, would give her a different view and a different perspective. Callie agreed that might be useful, and on Thursday afternoon she showed up at the beach, just as she'd promised Philip.

With the harness attached, her life vest on, a multitude of instructions absorbed, Callie gripped the aluminum frame and took a last glance at Philip's smiling face.

"You'll love it, kid!" he said encouragingly; oh, he was a good brother.

The tow boat started up. Callie felt the tug as the sail caught the air, then she was being jerked across the sand and over the white, curling line of the surf, where she was lifted by the invisible air, caught by a mysterious current like the ones that had taken her to the store for duct tape and to the park for disaster.

Faster than she'd imagined possible, Callie was high above the surf with panic in the wind. "Please, please stop," she called, but the engine was too loud, and the boat was already beginning to throw a white wake as it bounced across the breakers near the sand bar. In a few minutes, the parasail was out where the blue in-shore water turns dark green, where there are sharks and dangers, and Callie had tears her eyes as she lurched against the wind. She couldn't imagine why Philip had suggested this crazy stunt or why she had agreed.

She'd fall, she knew she would; the tear line would snap, and, despite the harness and the straps and the frame, she'd plummet into the surf. Or the tow-rope would break and she'd be carried up on a thermal, wafted out to sea, and never be found again.

Things were definitely escaping her, when Callie commanded herself to get a grip, to breathe and concentrate. She had to do that now sometimes. She had to breathe in and out and concentrate until the world came back into focus, as if she was a camera with a bad mechanism.

The first thing was not to look down. Looking down was bad, emphasizing as it did, the great height and the dizzying surge of the waves and numerous possibilities for violent death. Whenever she looked down,

Callie imagined dropping like a stone and being covered in water and never breathing air again.

But she was better. It was clear she was better, and the proof came as she was dangling from the glider frame and remembered how to rise and fall. Yes! Straighten up and she rose; lean forward and the big sail visible above and ahead began to drop. Callie started to relax over the ocean, and by telling herself, breathe, breathe, breathe, she found that she'd gotten under control. Not, maybe, the surest control, but okay.

There she was up a couple of hundred feet in the air, and she was okay with that, which meant she was definitely better, which was what Philip had wanted her to understand. I am someone who can go parasailing and not panic, she told herself, I am someone who can look into deep water and see the world from above and still hang on. That's progress.

Although her arms and shoulders were getting tired, Callie was not actually scared any more by the time they started back toward the beach. The boat was still quite far out, but the wind pushed her in toward the sand bar, visible at low tide as a long, pale streak in the water.

As the shadow of her sail swept along the water, Callie saw children playing in the shallows, and several swimmers churning along in the deeper water between the shore and the bar. A fat man with a hairy chest bobbed on an air mattresses, and, strung out along the bar itself, visitors stood up to their knees in water, staring over the ocean.

At the farthest end of the bar, just where there was a wide breach in the sand barrier, were two men with a woman about her own age, a blond in a red tankini. The two men were tanned, one with a lot of wet black hair and the other going bald; Callie saw a distinctive little patch of hair, as neat and geometric as a corporate logo, right on top of his head. You do get a different view from above, she thought; this was the different perspective Philip had wanted her to have.

The trio in the water were splashing and laughing and having a good time, a real life ad for a Florida vacation, when suddenly one of the men pushed the woman in the red tankini, and the other lunged to grab her feet, creating a churning patch of white water.

Far above, Callie caught another air current that swung her back out over the open water. Dangling under her glider, she was disturbed by the scene, alarmed, even, but more annoyed than worried: men, except for Philip, could be such boys! But when the boat brought her in closer to shore, she was quick to look back at where the trio had been frolicking in the surf. All Callie saw were the two men. The woman had disappeared.

Of course, she would have been mad at them for pushing her like that, for frightening her, Callie thought. The woman would be swimming back to shore, and Callie strained her neck trying to spot her, but there was no one gliding through the water. Well, not a swimmer, then, the woman would be wading and probably struggling a bit through the deepening water, for the tide was turning. Callie twisted her head and tipped the frame, but there was no sign of anyone in red, no one.

On the sandbar the two men were still standing, casually, as if nothing had happened, but Callie was sure that something had happened. The woman was gone, and the water was now up well over the men's knees.

She called down to the boat, waved one hand, tried to get the boatman to circle back, but her time was up, he was heading straight into the beach.

Philip was waiting to see her land, a dicey business of watching the sand and coming down at a run. Callie wobbled and almost tripped, touched one side of the frame to the ground, but came to a stop unhurt.

"You did great!" he called. "Fun, right? Was I right?"

"Oh, Philip!" Her voice was a wail. "A woman's disappeared. I think she was drowned in the water. They pushed her down and held her under." As she struggled to get out of her harness, Callie saw Philip's smile fade.

"No, really, really," she said and turned to the boatman, who had hopped out to help his assistant steady the sail. "Didn't you see what happened?"

The parasail operator, a short, stocky fellow with a marked accent and a lot of curly black hair, shook his head.

"When we came in close to shore near the sand bar," Callie said urgently, "right on the bar there were two men and a woman. Didn't you see them? How could you have missed them?"

The man gave her brother a look and shrugged. "I gotta focus on the boat, on keeping the ride smooth. I got no time to be looking at who's playing in the water."

"They weren't playing. I thought they were playing at first, yes, but they weren't. One pushed her, one of the two men, and the other one held her under. I saw him grab at her feet, then there was a lot of splashing and white water."

Philip had a t-shirt which he put over her shoulders. "You better go get changed, Callie," he said, looking uneasy and disappointed. "It's easy to get burned over open water."

"I didn't imagine it was anything. But I saw the splashing and then nothing," she said. "The woman just disappeared. When we came back, she was gone. Completely. She was blonde and wearing a red tankini."

"So are you," said Philip, and Callie could tell just what he was thinking.

"I'm not making this up," she said. "We have to go to the police or the lifeguards, at least to the lifeguards. We can ask them, if you don't believe me. They were watching the water the whole time. They'll have noticed if the woman in the red tankini swam back in, if she came out on shore, if she's all right. Maybe they were just horsing around," Callie said, trying to let him know she was being sensible and rational. "Maybe the angle I had, maybe that made it look worse than it was."

"I'm sure that was it," said her brother. "I really hoped you'd get a little clearer perspective."

"Oh, I did, I did, Philip. I was frightened at first, but then I got used to it, and it was wonderful until the end, until they pushed her, until they drowned her. I know they did. We've got to go to the police." Callie could hear her voice rising, could feel the day slip sliding away from Philip and the boat and the latest parasail customer to the pale streak of the sandbar and the woman wearing the red tankini.

Philip drew her over to one side and spoke quietly. "You know what the police will say," he said. "You know how they'll react."

Oh, she did, she did know. She'd be in some computer, on some record somewhere; they'd know all about her, and yet you could be right and be doubted, just as easily as you could be wrong and be believed.

"Then the lifeguards. It won't take us long to go down and check with them. Please, please, Philip," she said, and eventually, he nodded and drove her back to the parking lot at the other end of the beach, because she didn't want to go alone.

"I don't know how you'll find the right life guards," he said when they reached the wide white sand with its skein of pastel colored guard huts. "The sand bar runs nearly the whole length."

"I'm trying to remember the color — was it lavender or green? The guard huts are all different. I think I caught a glimpse of lavender."

Philip said nothing but his expression was eloquent.

"Well, I was looking at the sandbar, at the people, at those two men. I wasn't paying attention to the guards!"

"My point exactly," said Philip, but Callie refused to give up. They slogged along the soft, hot sand from one station to another. At each, she asked about a woman, a blond woman, "about my age I'd guess, in a red tankini. Out on the bar with two men. Did you see her come back in? They pushed her into the water and held her down. Yes, yes, I saw it." And she would explain about the parasail, about the view from above, about getting a new perspective, while Philip stood a few feet away looking sad and worried.

Callie knew just what he was thinking — and the guards, too, for they insisted they'd seen nothing. Sure, they had been watching the sand bar area, but they'd had no reports of a problem. "You're getting one now," Callie said. "I'm reporting a problem," and so on until the guards would ask if she could pick out the two men. Were they on the beach? And if not, what did she expect the life guards to do?

Then Philip would tell her she'd done all she could, and they'd move on, over his protests, to the next post, where the questions would start all over again. The beach was half deserted by the time they reached the last possible hut and began the trek back along the access road between rows of beach plum. Callie was in tears, walking fast, head down, full of bad thoughts and the sort of confused misery that had marked the last, bad stage in her development.

"Come on, Callie, admit you were wrong. They were just horsing around. Who would drown someone on a public beach in high season?" Philip asked. "You did the right thing, but let it go. Come on, I'll buy you lunch. A late lunch, how's that?"

"I want a drink," she said.

"Yes, and a drink, too," he said, though early drinking was normally something he discouraged.

There was already music coming from the waterside restaurants when they arrived at the familiar stretch of cafés, restaurants, and clubs. Philip and Callie sat at a sidewalk table and ate big salads and drank white wine and listened to a keyboard man and a percussionist who would have been too loud indoors but were about right with sound of the traffic and the crowded sidewalk.

"I feel I should do more," she said. "I feel I should call the police."

"Callie…"

"No, look, it's reasonable. I saw — well, I think I saw — someone killed. All right, I know, I know, I was high up, but that's the thing, Philip," she said, leaning forward. "Don't you see — they didn't think to look up. The way the light was, the shadow of the sail was much further out. They never looked up. They thought they were invisible. They didn't see me."

"That may be true, but Callie, would you recognize any of them again?"

She shrugged and poured herself another glass of white wine and thought they'd have another bottle. She wanted, she needed, to get her head in a better place altogether. "She was blond," she said.

"Thanks to good hairdressers, so is half the city."

"And the men were tall. One had long dark hair. And the other was going bald. In a quite distinctive way."

"Great," said Philip. "Look around you." He waved his hand toward the street, the other tables, where, admittedly, there were tall, dark men and balding men and a couple, at least, who looked plausible. "What good will that do the police? And Callie, it will only get you into difficulties. You do know that, don't you?"

She did, absolutely, but she couldn't leave the topic alone. As she began to feel more and more irritable and depressed, Philip urged her to go home.

"You'll feel better in the morning," he said, but Callie contrived to quarrel with him. She wanted to stay downtown, to walk under the trees, to lie on the sand, to dance in a noisy club, to get very drunk. She was better, yes, she was, but she'd had a bad day, a terrible day, she needed to relax.

Eventually Philip gave up, and much as she loved him, Callie was glad to see him go. Philip was big on new perspectives, but he wasn't always much fun. After he left, Callie wandered along the street. She had a drink with a visiting German and told him the whole story over a couple bottles of Red Stripe, but he only understood half of it.

"I'm telling you, they pushed her under, they drowned her," she said, loudly enough for the nearest dozen tables to hear. When he laughed and pawed her arm, Callie put down change for a tip and left.

She stopped outside a club where she could hear the loud thump, thump, thump of Miami, the kind of beat that accelerates your heart, just what she needed. And when she saw the man with the baseball cap, the same man who'd been in the restaurant — she thought it was the restaurant, but maybe it was the bar with the dumb tourist — she smiled, because she liked chance meetings. Seeing the same people passing in the street or sitting near her in cafés gave her a friendly feeling, as if the whole city were out in search of a good time.

The man caught her glance, winked, and gave a little wave; he'd noticed her, too, and Callie smiled again. She was sure he could dance; she was sure he could just by looking at him.

Inside the club, lights flickered off the walls and ceiling, spattering the floor with shadows, changing the shape of the world, providing a different perspective. Thunder from the drums, the thin, rainy tish, tish sound of cymbals; Callie moved her arms, moved her hips. The man in the baseball cap was right with her, dancing in front of her, behind her, showing off fancy moves until they pranced out into a treed courtyard where there was an open air bar. Ambulating toward the drinks, Callie thought that you didn't need a parasail to get a different view. You did not. This struck her as funny and she started to laugh.

"What's so funny?" the man asked.

She shook her head and waved the question away. He brought her a drink and one for himself. Rum based, very strong, but when she was in one of her moods, Callie had a high tolerance for alcohol.

"I'm getting a different perspective," she said. "From the one I had earlier today. When I was gliding over the beach."

Right away, he was interested in that, more interested than Philip or the parasail operator or the indifferent and complacent lifeguards. "You should tell me all about it," he said, and she told him some of it.

Then Callie said, "I want to dance," and she went back to the floor, leaving her drink on a table.

They danced a long time, mostly together, though Marcus, that was his name, Marcus with the Yankee cap, had to make a phone call at one point, and Callie moved out alone on the packed floor and collected new perspectives.

Late, very late, Marcus said he had to leave. He and a friend had a boat, a big powerboat, and they were supposed to head to the Keys in the morning.

"That's now," said Callie, "it's morning now."

"So I have to leave," Marcus said. "Can I drive you home first? Or maybe you'd like to see our boat? It's really beautiful. A beautiful boat for a beautiful lady."

"I'd rather dance some more," Callie said.

"No, no, the boat," he said.

And she laughed and said dancing, but they both knew she'd go to the boat.

"We can dance on the boat," he said and that settled it.

Callie had only a hazy notion of the drive to the marina, where Marcus led her to a powerboat large enough to be called a yacht. The tide was changing, and the boat shifted gently on the swell. The vessel had several decks, and it was as gleaming white as porcelain.

"Wow, some boat," she said.

"The cabins are beautiful," Marcus said. "You want to see them?"

Callie shook her head. "I can't stand being below in boats. I've got to be on deck." She saw a ladder leading to the top deck and climbed up. There was an oblong stretch of fine, varnished teak, furnished with the nicest deck chairs. Callie flopped down in one and looked up at the sky, dark and orange tinged toward the city, but already graying out over the Atlantic. The breeze was damp and cool. Marcus climbed up to find out where she was. "Okay?" he asked.

"I'm going to lie here and get a new perspective," she said.

But really what she did was to fall asleep until the pale, early light woke her. Slate colored clouds were visible to the east, and the city was a thin gray and pink line to the west. They were at sea, and down below on the main deck, some man, not Marcus, was saying something about getting going. He seemed to be anxious and in a hurry.

Callie dimly remembered that this was a friend's boat. She didn't like the idea that she was at sea with a stranger, with two strangers, really, for she could scarcely say that she knew Marcus. Realizing that she would have to make arrangements to be put ashore, she went to the railing to check the lower deck.

"It's almost dawn," said a tall man with a distinctive little patch of hair right in the middle of his balding head. Callie had time to think that yes, you do get a different view from above, before she heard Marcus say, "We can take care of her any time now; we're in deep enough water."

TO BEAUTY

We all worked late in those days, and many nights we wound up at a little restaurant-bar called Le Zinc. The technical staff favored a burger joint next to the Video Palace, but all the writers and "content providers" went to Le Zinc, not so much for the food, which was mediocre French, but for Morgan, raconteur extraordinare, who presided behind the bar. For us frustrated writers, Morgan was a gift. He was a small, neat man, once handsome, who had declined in early middle age to a dapper non-chalance. I never saw him fussed, not when there was a minor kitchen fire, nor when one of the waiters had a breakdown in the middle of dinner hour, nor when customers had too much to drink or else felt they hadn't had quite enough. Morgan had seen, as he put it, "a Mexican tornado," and he was disinclined to trouble himself for anything less.

He did have one curious habit, which was revealed to us only after we had become regulars, entitled to linger, drinking extra cups of coffee, arguing over articles, and planning the next issue of our on-line maga-zine. Late at night, as Morgan cleaned up the bar, washing and drying the steins and glasses, we'd try to get him started on a story or on one of the long, funny, circuitous jokes he knew. One story remained untold, however, though we were sure that it was a good one, since it was in conjunction with his habit, late at night, of pouring himself his one drink of the evening. This was a straight up shot of old whisky, rum, or tequila and the signal that Le Zinc was about to close.

Morgan would raise his glass, "To Beauty," down his drink and tell us that it was time to go home. No amount of teasing or questioning secured us the story behind "Beauty." As generous Morgan was with convoluted tales of dubious schemes, race track scams, angling babes, and small time thugs, all sprinkled with French or, I should say, Frenglish phrases in honor of Le Zinc, on the matter of Beauty he was resolutely silent.

I'm not sure he'd have told me either, if I hadn't hit a bad patch. Things hadn't been going well for me at home, work was boring, and I'd decided to try my luck out west. My defection, as it was considered, left me isolated at the magazine. I wound up alone at Le Zinc the last night I was to be in town. Morgan told me the story as a going away present.

I remember that it was a terrible night: not just snow but wind and blowing snow, not just wind and blowing snow, but sub-zero cold, and, on top of everything, ice underfoot where the slop and rain of a few days earlier had turned to glass. While I was on my soup, the lights went out, and we ate by the light of the table candles, the waiters working with flashlights tucked under their arms.

Everyone was laughing and cheerful. The darkness, the candles, the white storm glow outside made for a giddy kind of intimacy. People called back and forth across the room, teasing and flirting. Late, with the restaurant emptied, the waiters putting on their coats and joking about getting lost in the blizzard, Morgan poured himself an extra good Scotch and toasted Beauty.

"She must have been special," I said.

"She was the most beautiful woman in this world," Morgan replied, "and my lucky angel."

"You mean your guardian angel," I said, forgetting that Morgan was always precise in his language.

"This was a lucky angel," he said. He came around from behind the bar and sat down with the last sip of Scotch to tell me the story. "Those were the days," he began "when I was troubled with le vice."

I raised my eyebrows.

"I'd just graduated from high school and was working as a pizza delivery man; I had no money to speak of, no prospects, no education. I was dying of boredom, literally dying, until I discovered the track and betting, the football spread and our neighborhood bookie. My life got interesting in a hurry."

I said I could imagine.

Morgan sighed. "A teenage kid lacks perspective," he remarked. "A few thousand — well, more than a few thousand — dollars. That was the end of the world for me. My dad had bailed me out once when I was in the hole for a couple hundred, but he wasn't up for four figure loans. Dad drove a bus; my mom worked at the school cafeteria. I was supposed to be saving money for the community college. You can see the picture."

I could. "What did you do?"

"I took the shopper's trolley to Tijuana and didn't come back. Crazy, huh?" Morgan shook his head. "I had adventures, let me tell you, mostly connected with little Mexican tracks and razor-eyed Mexican gamblers. Pretty soon I was in worse shape than I'd been back home, though at the time it didn't seem so bad, since my losses were all in pesos."

I agreed that the peso is not the dollar.

Morgan made a rueful face. "Enrico didn't see it that way. I owed him a few hundred thousand the night he knocked on the door of my room with a pair of Aztec executioners. My man Enrico threatened to kill me first, pounded me around second, and then, as if this was a real favor, proposed I work off the debt with his cousin Vincente.

"I wasn't keen on the arrangement, even considering the alternatives and my physical state of the moment. But Enrico had already purloined my passport and California driver's license, both of which he intended to sell. I pleaded for the passport, at least, and pointed out that I had a job bussing dishes at one of the local hotels, a ptomaine palace which he knew only too well.

"I remember how he pursed his mouth and shook his head. Have I mentioned that he had a noble head, fit for an old coin or a corrupt bench? What I required, Enrico said, was a high wage job, a professional position, and he knew just the thing. He made me pack my clothes, and with an Aztec on either side of me, we departed in Enrico's black Lincoln Continental. We were off to visit his cousin, where I traded le vice for le crime, because, to save a long story, Vincente was a professional thief, pickpocket, and purse snatcher."

I must have looked surprised.

"Don't do him an injustice. Vincente was un artiste, a man of great skill and considerable strategy, though slovenly and unprepossessing. He looked like a small timer fresh from central casting, which was one of the reasons he required an assistant, or rather, two, for we were three in the gang: Vincente, *moi*, his apprentice of the moment, and Magdalena."

I guessed that she was Beauty, but Morgan shook his head. "Though any man would say that Magdalena was attractive, sexy, really, and, unlike Vincente, she was always presentable. Her role was to process stolen credit cards."

Here Morgan allowed himself a nostalgic sigh. He had an appreciation for all the skilled trades, a genuine admiration which enabled him to keep good waiters and cooks long after they had outgrown the modest ambitions of Le Zinc. "Magdalena knew to the dime how much she could charge, and to the minute how long to run a card. She could size up a fence as well as Vincente, and she had a very good eye for items of value."

"Even the patron, who did not pass out compliments lightly, considered her first rate, and to watch her work a store with a stolen credit card . . ." Morgan shook his head. "It was a shopping master class, I can tell you."

I expressed surprise that this pair needed any assistance.

"Risks must be taken in any profession," Morgan said sagely, "and those at the bottom, like those at the top, prefer to have some expendables. Besides, I was neat and tidy and becoming bilingual. I could look like a tourist; I suspect that I looked innocent. Hell, in that company, I really was innocent.

"My job varied. I might scout a hotel lobby or distract a mark. It was my job to ask a prospect the time in order to see what sort of watch he was wearing, or to bump someone on the street and keep apologizing until Vincente got the wallet or opened the purse. After I got a bit of skill, we sometimes reversed roles. Vincente would distract a tourist, while I grabbed the goods. He wanted me implicated, you see."

"He sounds like someone out of Dickens."

"Very like, and with a Dickensonian twist, which Magdelana let slip once by accident. She and I became quite friendly," Morgan added with a sly, satisfied expression. "One night she told me that my dexterous patron was also a police informer, who betrayed his apprentices in order to keep on the good side of the law."

"You were in real danger."

"You bet! Mexican jails are the stuff of nightmares. So even though Vincente rarely left me alone and never allowed me any cash, I began looking to get away. Then, just when I had devised a tentative, desperate, and almost sure to fail scheme, everything changed. Vincente rolled up one morning with a green Ford Fairlaine: we were headed for Guadalajara to work the crowds coming in for a big *Copa de Libertadores* match.

"He was in high spirits. Everything would be *mucho grande*; the tourists would be like fleas on a coyote with Atalante supporters in from Mexico City and all the visitors up from South America. I'd see Magdelana strut her stuff in the swank malls of Guadalajara, and he, Vincente, would demonstrate unimagined feats of skill and genius. I might have caught the fever, myself, but for Magdelana's warning. As it was, I was alert to the dangers of getting deeper into Mexico without what Vincente would have called 'a prudent exit strategy.'

"The patron noticed my lack of enthusiasm. 'Money for us all,' he said. 'Perhaps enough to pay off your debt.' 'Really?' I asked. 'All things are possible,' Vincente replied, laying a paternal hand on my shoulder and making me think of the long arm of the law.

"There was no alternative: I had to go. And I certainly brightened up when I saw the city, big, handsome, and bustling, brimming with new possibilities. Vincente had perhaps anticipated my reaction, for in the days before the match, he kept us busy reconnoitering the four star hotels and practicing our trade among the clients of the fancy goods and antique shops in the artisan villages.

"Then the crowds arrived for the match, the teams, the journalists, the commentators, the fans, and we prepared for action. I was delegated to brush Vincente's one decent suit and press his shirt, while Magdalena trimmed his hair and touched up his shave. I put on my dark trousers and jacket. As spruce as can be, Vincente and I were dropped off at one of the best hotels, while Magdalena, looking elegant and tense, pulled away in the Ford. We had ten minutes before she returned.

"We breezed though the lobby and right into the restaurant at the front. Vincente paused a moment by the little podium with the menus, his small, sharp eyes scanning the room. Then he asked the hostess to seat us toward the side and gave me an impatient poke in the back. He'd spotted our target; I was oblivious: I'd seen the Beauty.

"She was sitting in the center of the restaurant, a very young and shapely woman with golden brown skin, long, slim legs, and nearly waist length blond hair. She had dark eyes, so brown they looked black, and smooth, perfect features that blended the best genes of three races. I remember to this day what she wore: a pale suede skirt, a cream silk blouse, high delicate sandals and enough gold and diamond jewelry to fill a case at Tiffany's. This goddess had come to earth with two other young and pretty women. They were leaning over the café table, laughing and talking, but the Beauty sat quietly picking at an omelet, a slight, somehow sad smile on her face, as if she loved her friends but was bored with everything in life. Oh, how I understood that feeling!

"Will it surprise you," Morgan asked, "to know I would have died for her on the spot? Performed wonders, risked any danger? That in some profound way I had left rational life behind? The next thing I knew, Vincente was tapping my arm and nodding in the way he did when we were set to go. And then, I noticed, what I should have noticed first thing, and would have spotted instantly if I had not been bewitched: the Beauty had left her purse under her chair.

"I shook my head. You will think badly of me," Morgan said, "that I did no more than hesitate. I think rather badly of myself; it's a good illustration of how conditioning can overcome our better instincts. When he saw me frozen there, Vincente clenched his fist, rolled his eyes, strove, in short to wake me from my dreams of bliss and heroism. Then he stood up and I followed him, my heart pounding as it always did, adrenaline flowing, fear putting me outside of myself. I watched Vincente approach the table, feign surprise, and address one of the Beauty's companions, his voice so loud and jovial as to be almost unintelligible.

"Time slowed down. I had an unforgettable glimpse of Beauty's rounded, golden arm, of the emerald ring on her right hand, of the meal chit already signed beside the bread plate. Surprised and puzzled, graceful as birds, the young women raised their heads toward Vincente, and I scooped up the purse and tucked it under my arm. In the seconds before the alarm was raised, I slipped past the hostess and the bell staff – a mere shadow at the corner of their eyes, or, if they noticed at all, just another bellman off on an errand or one of the dark clad waiters.

"Vincente was right behind me. He was like an alligator, alarmingly fast despite short legs. Down the steps, under the portico, past a taxi just pulling in, around a clothes rack which one of the bellmen was loading with garment bags. Vincente hopped off the foot high curb, skipped through the traffic, and reached the other side of the street just as Magdelana pulled up. We slid into the Fairlane, ignoring the barrage of horns behind us, and she hit the accelerator before we had the doors right shut.

"Vincente swiveled around to watch for any sign of pursuit, while simultaneously shouting directions and instructions at Magdelana. She had never been in Guadalajara before, and she was always more comfortable as a shopper than a chauffeur. Vincente had her switching lanes and swerving this way and that until, in panicky exasperation, she pulled into a side street, jumped from the driver's side and hopped in back beside me.

"I mention all this," Morgan said, "to explain how it was that we noticed nothing amiss. Vincente, who might have known — and would, at the very least, have understood the ramifications instantly — was occupied with the traffic. Magdalena took inventory of the credit cards, while I counted the cash and attempted to palm some hundred peso bills for my own use. Our haul included a foreign passport, some store credit cards and, in a little red envelop, a key.

"I held it up for Vincente's inspection. 'Not like a hotel key,' I said. He glanced back in the mirror. 'That's a safe deposit box key; we can't do anything with that,' he said. I smiled because it had been the Beauty's. I put the precious souvenir, how precious none of us guessed, in my pocket.

"Vincente broke out a cigar in celebration. It was only much later in the day, when we'd already made two more successful forays, and Magdalena had filled the trunk of the Fairlane with watches, gold jewelry, leather goods and electronics, that Vincente recognized disaster.

"We were back relaxing in our hotel when Vincente's cell phone rang. It was his brother Enrico, and Enrico was very, very upset, along with every gambler and bookie in the country: the big game was threatened. 'Why, why?' Vincente asked. He listened to the answer in a silence which Magdelana and I recognized as increasingly ominous. Then he swore long and creatively, denying, so far as I could tell that we were even resident in Guadalajara, never mind gainfully employed there. When he hung up, his face had turned to lead.

"He cleared his throat and, with an attempt at casualness, asked Magdalena what name had been on the Beauty's credit card. Then he asked what I had done with the key. My heart sank at the thought of losing this token, but before I could invent some excuse Vincente grabbed my throat and threatened to have my gizzard – he habitually employed colorful phrases. When I produced the key, he smiled and wiped his mouth. 'And the purse?' he asked. This was such a silly question that I was momentarily silent. 'The purse!' he screamed. I told him that we'd thrown it away, of course, for this was absolutely standard operating procedure.

"'You threw it away,' Vincente corrected. 'You threw it away. Do you realize we will all be crow's meat if that game isn't played?' He mentioned a name that meant nothing to me, then threw up his hands and slapped his forehead theatrically. He would never again employ a gringo. 'El Gigante, you fool! The great and temperamental striker! The greatest player in the hemisphere. Maybe in the world! This is terrible. His club is owned by the *drogas*. This is worse. And worst of all, worse beyond imagining, the pretty lady with the purse is his *chicha*, and the key, the key my stupid young friend, must unlock something of exceptional value!'

"I had been in such a waking dream since seeing the Beauty that this revelation came as a dreadful disillusionment. I can't exactly say what I'd hoped for, but my heart froze at the mention of *drogas* and football stars. Indifferent to Vincente's anger and Magdalena's alarm, I asked bitterly, 'What if we find the bank?'

"Vincente slapped me. 'It's got to go back,' he screamed. 'Otherwise El Gigante doesn't take the field. If he's not on the field, all bets are off. If all bets are off, we'll be on the run from every gambler in Mexico. The great man wants everything back. Everything, key, money, cards. And the purse! We should have saved the purse as well'!

"He was quite distraught about the purse, but in the end Magdalena convinced him that the actual bag could not be as important as the contents, not even to the unreasonable El Gigante. Vincente sat on the bed and fixed me with an evil stare. 'You snatched it; you return it,' he said. I pointed out that I'd probably been seen, that the bellstaff would all be on the alert, that my imperfect Spanish would scarcely allow me to talk my way out of trouble.

"Vincente glowered at me and said nothing but that I would do it or that, as he put it, his protection would be withdrawn. Then he and Magdalena went into a huddle, making frantic plans in rapid Spanish, while I thought gloomily of Mexican jail cells and the bad types who dwell therein. It would be like Vincente to clear himself with both touts and cops by fingering me.

"I asked Magdalena about this later as she was straightening my tie, preparatory to my venture into the lion's den. She shrugged in response. 'You must go to the hotel,' she said. 'That's for sure.' 'And afterwards?' 'I'll pick you up, of course.' She paused. 'Or you can make other arrangements.' I knew then that Vincente did not expect my return, that he was sure I'd get caught, that he did not care much either way.

"Magdalena, who had more appreciation for my personal charm, gave me a couple hundred pesos along with a huge bouquet of flowers and a brown paper package containing the contents of Beauty's purse. We went out to the car together, while Vincente stayed barricaded in our room. 'We could drive north,' I said to her. 'How far do you think we'd get?' Magdalena asked. Of course, she was right.

"All the way to the hotel, I felt sweat on my forehead. I rehearsed what I'd say to my folks — if I was allowed to call my folks, if I dared to call my folks. I was all too aware that I hadn't called them when I could have called them, that I'd let them down, that in some ways I could never go home. I was ashamed and frightened and then fatalistic: my life was over at eighteen.

"'Get out,' Magdalena said. The car had stopped. The entry portico of the hotel shaded the windshield, a smiling bellman opened my door. I walked into the lobby, dazed as a deer in headlights.

"I had strict orders to leave the package and flowers for immediate delivery to the Beauty, emphasis on immediate. *Pronto*, Vincente had told me a dozen times, *pronto, pronto*! I made my way through a cluster of dark men in team track suits and warm up jackets, all laden with gym bags and crowded by eager fans, to the high marble topped reception desk. I expected to be seized at any second by some indignant bellman. Instead, I was utterly ignored.

"The receptionist on the phone was switching at top speed between Spanish and English. Another was sorting out some difficulty for a stout, self important guy with a scrub brush mustache who alternately consulted his cell phone and his clipboard and was satisfied by neither. The manager, dark, suave, impeccably suited, spoke in deferential tones to a group of noisy and expensively dressed Latin tourists, the women with big hair and stiletto heels, the men with wild, open shirts and gleaming hair pomade on complicated 'dos and sideburns. I stood, awkward with the flowers and package, glancing around at the lobby, the bellmen, and the fatal restaurant where I had seen the Beauty, and, I realized, her room number.

"'In and out, quick, quick,' Vincente had said, but Vincente was going to turn me over to the police or to El Gigante's dangerous supporters; my immediate future included nameless back alley horrors or some ghastly lockup. In such circumstances," Morgan said, "it behooves one to attempt some gallantry, some *beau geste*! I went to the elevator and squeezed in at the last moment beside two guests and a cart full of luggage.

"I got out on nine and walked the rest of the way up to the Beauty's floor, the eleventh. When I eased open the stairway door, I spotted two big guys in green tracksuits lingering near the elevator: Vincente had given me certain valuable life skills. I checked the nearest room number and scuttled along the hallway to 1147. Before I could lose heart, I knocked.

"No answer. I had not considered that she might be out. With a fearful glance over my shoulder, I knocked again. This time, I heard a sound, and then someone asked 'Who's there?' in Spanish. 'A friend,' I said. 'A friend returning lost property.' There was a pause, before I heard a soft sound near the door, which, a moment later, opened.

"I was standing three feet from the Beauty, who had a puffed and darkening eye and a swollen lip. 'You've been hurt,' I cried. 'What's happened? Who has done this to you?'

"There are times, after all, when one is saved by a spontaneity which reveals the heart. She grabbed my arm, pulled me inside, and locked the door behind us.

"'Who are you?' she demanded. I held out the package in return. 'It's all there, money, cards, key. Everything but the purse.' She tore open the package, dropping money and cards in her haste to find the little red envelope. She snapped it open, took out the key and held it up to examine it. 'You've saved my life,' she said.

"'You should leave him,' I said. 'He isn't worthy of you.'

"She gave me an odd look. 'And you're a thief,' she said.

"You know, until that moment I had not really seen myself that way. 'I've had bad luck,' I said, 'I had no choice.'

"She gave that particularly sweet and sad smile which I've remembered ever since. 'Who's had choice?' she asked. We stood there for a moment, looking at each other, understanding, if not everything, a great, great deal. She went to the bureau and returned with a handful of large bills. 'Take this,' she said, 'and put every penny on Atalante.'

"I was alarmed. 'Things will be all right now,' I said, fearful for us both. 'El Gigante will surely play now, won't he? And your team will win.'

"When she shook her head, I understood another of the reasons that she seemed sad. 'It is not to be. El Gigante will play, but the team will lose. It is already decided.'

"I kissed her hand and suggested such mad things that she laughed before she told me I had to leave. I took the stairs two at a time, all eleven flights, swaggered through the lobby and out under the arch of the portico. The Fairlane was nowhere in sight. A bellman opened the door of the first cab in line, and I left, a free man.

"I kept back enough cash for a room and dinner, but followed the Beauty's instructions with the rest. That night, I watched the match from a bar stool in a smoky cantina. The game was tense and scoreless for eighty agonizing minutes. Knowing little of the sport, I focused on El Gigante, a rangy, hawk nosed man with brown skin and wild shoulder length black hair, who seemed bigger in every way than any other player on the field.

"He was graceful, despite his massive torso and brutal expression, a fluid, unhurried presence, who could, when an opening presented itself, move unerringly toward the goal. Even with reasons to dislike him personally and fear him professionally, I could see his quality.

"Five minutes from the end of time, the visiting keeper bobbled a save and a tiny, stocky man from Atalante sent a rebound into the back of the net. My companions in the cantina, were divided, patriotism clashing with prudence: almost to a man they had bet on the visitors. Atalante pulled everyone back onto defense, and the match was in injury time before El Gigante took a wobbly pass and charged in alone on goal.

"Was his timing a hair off, did his foot slip an inch or two? He drew back one of his thick and powerful legs and shot the ball no more than an inch wide of the net. The close up camera showed an impassive face and proud, contemptuous eyes. At the time, I felt only relief. Now, you know, I take a more sympathetic view. I think that, being a genius of sorts, El Gigante was even less lucky than the Beauty — and certainly not as lucky as me.

"I slipped out of the cantina and caught a cab. I had the driver wait while I collected my winnings, then went straight to the bus station. I was as rich as I was ever likely to be, and I figured that something could be worked out at the border. As it was," Morgan concluded with a smile, a smile which, I noticed for the first time, held a hint of sadness.

"What about El Gigante and the Beauty?" I asked. "Did you ever hear of them again?"

"El Gigante played in Spain, before returning home to offend the *drogas* and get gunned down in the street. Perhaps he'd had enough of thrown games or perhaps he grew less skillful with age. I never heard what happened to the Beauty, whose generous spirit saved and changed my life."

"Perhaps she got away from El Gigante and his dangerous friends," I suggested.

"My profoundest hopes for her," Morgan agreed. He put a drop more whisky in his glass and raised it again. "To Beauty," he said, "Now we must call it a night."

IDEAS IN MY HEAD

You know that old saying, "Don't try to put ideas in my head?" I've had an interesting example of that, and I can tell you that once certain ideas get into your mind, they lodge there like grit. You can't get them out and you can't leave them alone; pretty soon, you can't think of anything else.

That's the way it was with Jack and me. Once Herbie had planted the suggestion, there was nothing we could do about it. And anyone who knew Herbie, that's Herbert A. Rothberger to those of you outside the business, probably wouldn't blame us at all.

Where was I? Alien ideas in the brain are seriously distracting and some days I have problems putting my thoughts in order. Which is a laugh, being that Jack and I are professional wordsmiths. Arsen and Dutton — you can ask around — everyone knows us. We're not maybe your top of the line scriptwriters and script doctors — no auteur stuff, no Oscars on our shelves — but we've had a couple of pilots made and we've written for most of the top cop shows and hospital dramas and we've both made major money in the soaps. Several film scripts too — one of them made — I want you to see we're pros.

Nonetheless, even pros get the blues in the form of rejection slips from baby-faced execs with their feet on their desks and your script bound for the shredder. Jack and I'd hit a run of bad luck, which is why we wound up one wet day — a bad L.A. omen right there — in the offices of Distracting Productions, the bailiwick of Herbert A. Rothberger, AKA Herbie, pitching an action yarn.

Slipstream was a solid piece of work with a nice role for the child phenom of the moment, a moppet with blue eyes and blonde hair named Ashley Button. I kid you not. She was known around the studios as Cuteas, as in *cute as* a button, and she was a serious talent with a good memory and precocious eyes.

Our plot was watertight. That's Jack's doing. His dialogue is ready for the bin, but his plot construction is a thing of beauty, and I think Herbie got to him before he got to me. I think so.

Anyway, we're sitting in Herbie's big office beside a Nordic track with zero miles on its odometer and a spidery Bowflex that looks carnivorous, and a decorative secretary who's probably not as dumb as she looks. I usually do the talking so I launch into our spiel: "A big time hijacking goes bad when the cargo turns out to be nuclear fuel rods. The robbers go on the lam with the representatives of a rogue state behind them and both the CIA and the FBI bringing up the rear."

"Think the X Files without the aliens," says Jack. "Advanced paranoia."

Maybe wrong to mention a Fox show to Herbie, who had, I seem to recall, a death feud with the network.

"So what the hell is it?" he says, not waiting to find out. "Is this a heist picture?"

"Yeah, a heist picture, but not just a heist picture, because, see along the way, they're spotted by this little girl, who gets her father involved, plus we've got the subplot with the agents, kind of a father-son or brother-brother thing going..."

This goes nowhere with Herbie. To Herbie, *Moby Dick* is a fishing story, pure and simple.

"Heist pictures are dead. With Tom Cruise, maybe. Cast of unknowns and the little blonde brat — no way."

"We don't have to cast unknowns," I says.

Herbie snorts. He has a particularly repulsive nostril clearing snort like a pig with a fly up its nose that brings his own porcine nature front and center.

"You guys bring me a Tom Cruise, a Cate Blanchett, a Will Smith picture, I'll be the first to let you know."

See the kind of guy we're talking about here? Gratuitous, right? As if he wasn't resident in the B Picture universe himself.

"However," I says, "this is a heist picture with a difference. And the script's like a clockwork toy." I start to describe the novelties and beauties, the many ingenuities that Jack has concocted and which I have adorned with razor sharp dialogue.

"Heists are dead," says Herbie. "Plus there's no romance. How're you going to pull in the date audience with no romance?"

"All right, all right," says Jack, who's quick off the mark plot-wise. I can see the wheels turning in his mind, clear as one of those old clocks with glass front and back so you can see the gears moving. "There's the kid, we start from the kid, all right, and we add..."

He doesn't even get the sentence out before Herbie says, "No kids. Kids are for Oxygen, Lifetime, housewives in the afternoon. Forget the kid."

"Forget the kid," Jack repeats.

"I wouldn't touch the kid for an Oscar nomination — her mother's poison and her dad's a lawyer."

"We make her an adult," says Jack.

Herbie purses his lips. "A hot babe?"

"Combustible," Jack says.

"Maybe with a thing for one of the robbers?" I suggest.

"Yeah," says Herbie. "You try that and get back to me." His hand's already hovering over his intercom button.

Jack and I get out onto the street. We've forgotten umbrellas and it's pouring. "Remind me never to buy a gun," Jack says. "I wouldn't trust myself."

We go back and rework *Slipstream*. Cuteas has transmogrified into an eighteen-year-old bombshell who's definitely trouble. She's friends with one of the heist team, a fact her FBI agent father only belatedly registers. "We got parental angst, we got family, we got high drama," I tell Herbie when we see him next.

"And we've sharpened up the suspense," Jack says. "The guys on the heist are really pawns of terrorists. They don't realize and when they do…"

His film eminence frowns. "People don't want to be scared," says Herbie. "They want to be scared, but not of something that could really happen to them."

"You want *Godzilla*," said Jack. "You want *Creature of the Black Lagoon*?"

"Listen, I'm trying to help you guys." Herbie's all offended. "What's her name, the broad with the father complex —"

"Heather."

"Heather's a dumb name, Heather's been overdone."

"We can change the name," I says.

"So change it. She has possibilities. Fuel rods — who the hell understands fuel rods? See what I mean? That's why I say, heist pictures are dead."

"Slice of life? A smaller drama?" Jack asks. "Father daughter conflict — straight laced agent versus rebel daughter? Heist in the background?"

"Some small pictures have done well lately — good return on investment," I says.

Herbie agrees to look at the rewrite.

By this time, we're beginning to sweat. Jack's been borrowing from me and I've been pawning stuff acquired in my palmy days. We buckle down, anyway. Like I say, we're pros all the way. We lose most of the heist except the actual theft and focus on the conflicting loyalties of the father and daughter.

"We've got a different angle on the perpetrators, too," I tell Herbie at the next meet. "No more professionals. Small timers, desperate men. There might even be a role for a good kid actor — one of them has a sick child. See, it's desperate men on both sides."

Herbie listens to all this. At least this time, we get through the whole pitch. "You know, you guys got no sense of the times," he says when we're done. "Sympathetic criminals — tricky at best. Okay if they're rich, get what I mean? You redo *Topaki*, professional thieves, glamour guys — women love outlaws — you're okay. Poor and desperate — no way. Throw the book at them. Where've you been?"

Back to professionals. Back to square one, but we don't mention. "That can be done," I says. I'm thinking that we have most of what's needed back in version one.

But that's not enough for Herbie. He basically doesn't like the heist at all.

"Suppose it goes wrong even earlier," says Jack. "Suppose our juvenile female winds up a hostage? Ropes and bondage," he adds — Herbie's tastes being well known.

"I'll look at it," he says, and then as an afterthought, he adds, "You get it done fast, drop it off at my house. I'm out of the office a couple of days."

This sounds like interest, so, back at the computers, Jack and I pull three straight all-nighters. Now the daughter is hanging out with a trucker whose unwittingly been assigned the nuclear cargo. Missy's with him in the truck when they are hijacked at a rest stop. He gets shot — we debate over his fate — and she becomes expendable, but maybe irresistible, supercargo. Lots of opportunity for cleavage and noir close-ups; heavy breathing in semi-darkness — Herbie stuff all the way.

Jack and I exchange high fives and figure we're home free. We messenger the script, and sure enough we get called back into his office pronto, but when we start talking about the fine points of the new story, he's suddenly not sold. That's Herbie — New England weather in Southern California — the worst of two worlds.

"It's all right," he says, "it's a picture. But I'm thinking chick kidnapping's been done, know what I mean?"

We do, having hit every cliché in the book as per his own request, because Herbie demands the sure thing. We'd had a script for Cuteas — a genuine talent; we'd had topical suspense — ripped from the headlines, no less, but that was too much novelty for Distracting Productions. So we went the other way and here we sit while he has second thoughts.

"Now," he says, like he's just come up with inspiration, "you got a guy kidnapped, man against the elements, that kind of stuff, I'm maybe hearing you."

Man against the elephants, I think, elephants being a herd of Herbies with loud ties and black shirts and elegant little patent leather loafers with no socks. I'm getting up from the table before I cross some verbal

Rubicon, but Jack's into the challenge — he later told me he was desperate; he'd maxed all his credit cards and he was ready to run with whatever Herbie threw his way.

"Yeah," he says, "no heist, no nukes, we heist a guy. A young guy — get the girlie audience."

Herbie shakes is head. "Stale. You need a guy in his prime. Harrison Ford of a few years ago."

"More than a few," I mutter, but Herbie doesn't notice.

"All right, all right," Jack goes, "guy in his thirties, maybe."

"Forties," says Herbie, who's closer to fifty, I'm thinking.

That limits the pool of actors — and raises the price, but I can see this is personal for Herbie. He's got a stake in this, something beyond the usual profit margin for Distracting Productions.

"You want a kidnapping story," I says. "With a man the victim?"

"Kidnapped but not the victim," Herbie says. "Not the victim. Where you guys been? Audience surveys pass you by? We're sick of all these girlie men."

"Our perpetrators bite off more than they can chew?" This plot line's been around since O. Henry's "The Ransom of Red Chief." Not that Herbie reads.

"Yeah. You got it."

"Diamond merchant, maybe?"

"Too ethnic," says Herbie.

"But he's got portable goods on him. There's your motive."

"I got to plot this for you?" asks Herbie. "They hold him for ransom —"

"Requires an organization," says Jack, thinking out loud.

I realize we could use our heist prep scenes if we modified them a little.

"Smart has organization. Dumb's different. These guys grab him and go. They're operating seat of the pants," says Herbie.

"This is a farce?"

I get a look of thunder. Herbie lowers the boom. Reaches for the death ray.

"Look," he says, "This is real. This is reality, today's mean streets. Danger on every corner."

"Yeah, but the plot's got to be plausible. You got a big executive, ransom worthy, he's got the bodyguard, he's got the chauffeur."

"Look," says Herbie, "not all of us run scared. I drive myself unless I gotta find parking."

Jack gave me a sideways look. I think that was it; right then, I felt the idea. You know, you can feel an idea coming. Like with a story, you don't have an idea, and then you still don't have an idea but you have this feeling that one is in the vicinity, that you just have to watch and wait and you'll find yourself sitting down at the computer and typing in Scene I. That was the sort of feeling I had when Jack looked over at me.

"Gated property, though," Jack says. "Like yours."

We've been to Chez Herbie, where we were checked and double-checked and scrutinized by little glowing lights — and recorded, too, probably. All this to keep down the covetousness of the general public, which might cast a longing eye on the velvet lawn, the topiaries, the roses, the marble fronted palace, the soigné assistant, and the shrewish, if very desirable looking, blonde wife.

Herbie gives a snort of exasperation. "You get him at work."

"Most executive offices are better protected than your private homes," Jack said.

"There's always a weak point," says Herbie.

"Garage?"

"You got it. The monitoring in this one isn't worth shit. They got a fortune worth of trash compactors and air filters but they're cutting corners all the time on the monitors."

"Problem is their car, though," I said. "And even a rental —"

"Maybe they walk," says Herbie. "Maybe they drive both cars. Christ, I thought you were the writers and I was the producer. You get this done, I'm going to take a writing credit. You get him in the garage, see, and you wrestle him into the back of the car."

"Nobody wrestles Harrison Ford into the back of a car," I observe. "Not in his heyday."

"Have to whack him good," says Jack.

"No damage," says Herbie, "not so soon. Drug him, maybe. Save the blood for later."

"We talk about this a while. Then Jack and I get our marching orders. Back to the script one more time. We're really punchy but we rack our brains and study garages until we finally come up with a story that's ingenious, real quality, but at the same time, no good. We know all too well what Herbie wants now: man against the elephants, ie., middle aged, overweight CEO outwits the lowlife and emerges triumphant.

Still, we need money, we need money now. We put aside a clever, if brutal, plot involving a quick killing and a trash compacter and ditch a script loaded with smart lines to bring our CEO home in glory. We call the office and once again Herbie's secretary tells us to drop it off at his house.

"I don't like this," says Jack. "Something here smells funny. Totally funny. It's like he wants to keep this out of the office. What's he got going here that's not strictly flicks?"

"Beats me," I says. As it turns out, our professional imaginations didn't run as fast as Herbie's. "He doesn't like it, we pitch our other solution."

Jack looks at me. "He gets one more chance, this is it."

And I don't say anything, though I know what he's talking about and though silence bespeaks assent. Call it a *folie à deux*. Or *tres* — I got to include Herbie somehow.

We get the call late. Herbie's pleased. The script's crap, but Herbie's pleased. As writers, we don't feel great, but we need the cash.

Jack puts on his lucky Toledo Mud Hens hat, and we hustle off to Distracting Productions as lights come on in the City of the Angels. Upstairs, Herbie is alone, his decorative secretary departed. I don't see any sign of our script, which I take as a bad sign, but he says, "So you got it done. Not bad at all."

We're expecting our contract, but Herbie starts talking about his financing difficulties, certain problems with his stake in a special effects action flick that ran over budget. "I love this, don't get me wrong; I love this," Herbie says.

"You could have told us a month ago," says Jack.

"A month ago, I didn't love the script," says Herbie. "You understand this business. Things change."

We let him have it then, but Herbie didn't budge. The script was "great, super; ideal for his purposes" and "maybe in the spring his finances will allow, etc, etc."

Jack and I go slamming out of the office. "We've been had," says Jack, "but I don't know what his game is."

I'm no wiser, and there we are swearing up a storm and kicking along the sidewalk when Jack says, "I forgot my hat."

Personally, I never want to see Herbie again, but that hat's a classic and Jack can't write without it. To save time we cut back in the side door of the garage and we're tearing up the ramp when we see Herbie, suitcase in hand, heading for his black Mercedes. He's whistling as if he hasn't a care in the world.

"Hey," says Jack. "I gotta get my hat out of your office."

"No time," says Herbie. "I'm in a major hurry."

"It's my Mud Hens hat," Jack says. "I gotta get it."

"Tough." Herbie opens his trunk with the remote, throws in his luggage, and reaches for the door.

I've never seen Jack move quicker. Next thing I know, he has Herbie's arms behind his back. Herbie's struggling and shouting, and I clock him one and then again. He deserves it. Jack's trying to trip him up, but Herbie breaks away and I stick out my leg. Crash, Herbie bangs into the side of the car and he kind of staggers and makes a lunge again for the door. I don't know yet if I hit him or Jack, but in all the confusion Herbie falls, bam, onto the cement and doesn't get up.

He's out cold. So much for man against the elephants. The garage is suddenly very quiet; I can't even hear the traffic on the Strip. That's an effect often used in thrillers of the psychological persuasion, but which surprises me.

Jack and I look at each other. "What are we going to do?" he says.

"He comes to, we don't work in this town again."

That's a consideration. But I take a closer look at Herbie and suddenly I feel sick and hopeful at the same time. "I don't think he's coming to."

Jack disputes this, claiming esoteric medical knowledge.

I check again and shake my head. "He's not coming to."

We look at each other for a moment, then bang. That's what I mean by ideas in your head. We've plotted this out. And when somehow the situation jumps from the page to the VIP section of Herbie's garage, we know what to do. Without thinking whether this is a good idea or a bad idea, we pick up his keys, grab Herbie the Inert and drag him to the back, where, yes, indeed, there's the trash compactor chute. Jack punches in the numbers; he always does his research, right down to trash compactor access. With the over-the-top plots we cook up, you gotta have the details right.

Just the same, I'm in a sweat until the thing starts to grumble and the door slides open. One, two, three, heave! Herbie with his patent leather loafers and his mean disposition disappears with a soft thud.

"What about his car?" I ask as Jack wipes the key pad and the handle.

"Leave it. We gotta get that hat, though."

Up the back stairs, down the hall. I'm drenched with sweat and I can hardly breathe. Doing stuff like this is seriously different from even the most vivid imagining. At the door, I pull my shirt cuff over my hand and when Jack turns the key, we open the door, adrenaline bathing every cell, alert for alarms and sirens. I think I'm going to pass out before Jack grabs his hat, and we get ourselves downstairs and onto the street. It feels like we've hit a worm hole and accessed some parallel universe, because everything looks the same but feels different.

Nothing is quite real to us; we're light and new. At the same time, any thoughts about the garage and Herbie and the sound of the compactor bring certain details up to more reality than we can handle, number one being the script we followed. This is burned soonest and wiped off our computer disks, and we make an effort to erase the plot line from our neurons as well.

All this ultra caution blows up when we remember that our earlier copies made their way to Chez Herbie. Crisis time. Whatever fiscal or domestic machinations Herbie had in hand, he'd made sure his wife had access to our work. What for?

We're clueless, but anyone who looks at the script's evolution from heist to accidental kidnapping to executive kidnapping would sure have questions now. Especially the bereaved Mrs. Herbie.

By the end of the week, Jack and I are little more than sweat-soaked nerves. I get so that I'm hallucinating LAPD cruisers and I about leave my skin every time the phone rings. The longer — inexplicably longer — we wait for what seems inevitable, the worse it gets, and I think we'd both have been committable but for a lucky spell of hurry up work on a soap pilot.

By the time we come up for air, the Rothberger case is on the back pages. A few months later it's stony cold. Herbert A. Rothberger disappeared from his office, leaving half a million dollars skimmed from Distracting Productions in the trunk of his Mercedes. No one has heard from him since.

A year later, Jack and I have almost convinced ourselves none of this had anything to do with us, when we get a call from Leonie Rothberger. Major panic attack, but we can hardly snub the new — and able — head of Distracting Productions.

Next afternoon: same office, different secretary; no more Bowflex and Nordic track. Mrs. R ran to a nice line of Asian porcelain and modern furniture. She had a big mane of blonde hair and a vaguely predatory air. A fat pile of familiar looking scripts sat on her desk.

"I've been going through the files," she says. "Herbert had a number of your properties."

"We'd been discussing some projects with him at the time — of his —" I'm at a loss for words, so I add, "So tragic for you," though she hardly looks consumed with grief.

"*Slipstream* is a nice piece of work. I'd like to option it."

Well, well! It's nice to be appreciated even by the dangerous Leonie Rothberger. We have a good meeting about casting and production and she offers very fair terms. At the end, she puts her hand on the rest of the scripts. "What do we do with these?"

"We were under a bad influence at the time," says Jack. "I think the shredder's the best place for them."

Leonie Rothberger gave a faint smile. She's not a woman to reveal her emotions, but — scriptwriter's eye — I pick up on that. "The wisest thing for your reputations." A little pause; a warning? "Kidnappings and ransoms are so overdone."

"And maybe for you, too," I says.

"He'd have taken the money and run, if he hadn't been — intercepted somehow." She looks at us very steadily. I guess right then that she has a good working theory of whatever Herbie's game was and maybe also who did the intercepting.

I don't trust myself to answer and neither does Jack. After a beat, Leonie Rothberger switches on an industrial strength shredder and starts feeding in the scripts. "I hate to do this to gentlemen with imagination," she says as our writing turns into packing filler. "But it's for your own good."

"Ashes to ashes and pulp to pulp," says Jack.

Mrs. Rothberger gives a feline smile. "Amen to that," she says.

THE PARADISE GARDEN

On the day his buried his poor, mad, tubercular mother, Dwayne assumed his dead father's name, hung the American Lieutenant's military tags around his neck for luck, and left the Philippine refugee camp. After extraordinary hardships and dangers, he reached new and strange California, where the casual offer of assistance to an elderly Mexican with a flat tire secured him employment. When Dwayne Nguyen proved trustworthy, hard working, and substance free, he was promoted to be the old Mexican's driver and apprentice and came to work in the paradise garden.

That was not its official name. The ordinary eye takes things as given, namely that this was the six acre lot around the Spanish style mansion of one Lennart Barber, an extremely wealthy exporter of agricultural chemicals, now living in semi-retirement. The eye of one raised amidst squalor and grief by madness and scholarship saw things differently. The orange trees, roses, bougainvillaea; the hibiscus, camellias and olive trees, the profusion of flowers and the dark thickets of shrubs were the perfect setting the glittering courts and warrior queens which his scholarly mother had told him about night after night in their tent. And as paradise gardens must, this one had a thorny and desiccated heart: a magnificent collection of cactuses, which were the old Mexican's special pride.

He had an impressive expertise with these succulents, and although Señor Barber had a habit, indeed, a policy, of making frequent, complete, and inexplicable changes in staff, the proprietor of Rodas Landscaping was exempted time after time. His great skill — and perhaps his near blindness — caused the whirlwinds of dismissals and expulsions to pass gently over him. In this way, old Jorge Rodas came to know more about Lennart Barber's affairs and nature than many who considered themselves his acquaintances or even his friends.

This information was to prove useful to his apprentice, a young man of good intelligence but eccentric education, and also to the young woman who stepped out onto the terrace one hot afternoon. Señor Rodas, having made his inspections and given his orders, had retired to rest in the potting shed, leaving Dwayne to see to the weeding and watering.

The young woman's name was Amelia. She was twenty-one years old and she had arrived from the Philippines six months before to marry, sight unseen, Lennart Barber as an alternative to other, less reputable, means of improving her family's finances. She was almost beautiful and unfailingly polite. Besides Tagalog, she spoke some English and good Spanish. Her other qualities were as yet hidden from her husband, but they were perceived almost instantly by Dwayne Nguyen, who looked up from a thicket of floridabundas and fashionable English roses to see her standing by the wall of the terrace.

She was wearing a little white dress that left her brown arms bare, but Dwayne glimpsed the golden armor beneath the fabric and, although normally the shyest of men, raised his straw hat in the same courtly gesture Señor Rodas had perfected.

"How hot it is," she said in Spanish. She was already becoming used to air-conditioning and sea breezes and finding the summer days scorching. "Would you like some water, a cool drink?"

Although Dwayne was neither hot nor thirsty and although Señor Rodas discouraged familiarity with their customers, he answered her, not in Spanish but in Tagalog. "How very kind of you. I would like a drink of water."

The result was more than he could have dreamed: her eyes filled with tears, and Dwayne, who had never had so profound an effect on any young woman, felt his heart turn over. She went into the house and brought him water, a beautiful, shining, colorless column in its own plastic bottle, and handed it to him so that she could hear him thank her in her own language, and watched him drink it, so that he could tell her it was refreshing. He understood. One's own language is water for parched ears. When he apologized for not speaking Tagalog better, she shook her head. "Beautiful," she said.

After that, Señora Barber came out early every day so that she could pick her flowers while Rodas Landscapers worked in the yard. She always consulted gravely with Señor Rodas about which blooms might be picked without disturbing the overall display, and she began to show interest in the cactuses, although she confessed honestly to him — honesty and straight-forwardness were among those qualities as yet unknown to her husband — that the desert garden did not appeal to her in the same way as the roses and other flowers.

"Yes, that is quite natural," old Señor Rodas said. "Flowers are the proper setting for the young and beautiful. But these desert species, Señora, are the plants for our maturity and old age. Now they are my favorites, as they were the favorites of the Señora who planted them many years ago." So great was his love of the cactuses and other flora, that he began taking both his apprentice and the young Señora Amelia through the collection almost daily, pointing out beauties and peculiarities, and teaching his pupils the proper Latin, Spanish and, if he knew them, English, names. When she spotted plants from her homeland, Señora Amelia, in turn, would tell them the names in Tagalog for the pleasure of hearing her native speech.

In this way, they became great friends, and when her husband was away, Amelia would often ask Dwayne to help her pick the flowers or else she would come out to work in the potting shed with the old man, for, as she confessed the house virtually ran itself.

But when her husband was home, Señora Amelia was never seen outside except by the pool. They never heard her singing in the garden or saw her perched on the terrace to eat lunch in front of her portable television set.

One day even after Señor Barber had departed for Bangkok or Buenos Aires or Abijan, Amelia did not appear in the garden. Señor Rodas frowned and seemed anxious and irritable, although normally he took no notice of the comings and goings of his employers. "It is none of our business," he would remind Dwayne, if his apprentice mentioned that old Señora Rothstein had an oxygen tank or that Señor Burns had dented his car again.

The following day, there was still no sign of Amelia. She did not even wave from the terrace or send Felice out for flowers, as she'd done when she had the flu a couple of months before. Señor Rodas shook his head and looked so concerned that Dwayne took fright. When he went up to water the flowering plants on the terrace, he began to sing, very softly so that Old Rodas would not scold him, a little Tagalog song he'd learned in the camp.

He had not finished the second verse before he heard her feet on the flagstones. He did not look round, but kept on watering until she said, "You are mean to call me when I did not want to come out." He turned and saw her bruised face and the blotches on her golden arms. Señor Barber had betrayed her trust, and her loyalty was about to be transferred. Dwayne understood that deep in his heart, in the same compartment that had recognized her true nature. But, consciously, all he felt was a stunned anger, a rage against the universe. "What happened?" he asked.

When she told him, he said, "You must run away. You must leave." Paperless himself, his mind was dominated by the idea that she had documents, that she was legally married to a citizen, that she was a free agent. But there were complications.

"My sisters," she said. There were five other children, three of them girls. The family was desperately poor, and her parents, she said, did not see the sense of keeping girls in school when they could be earning good money.

"In the bars," Dwayne guessed.

"In the brothels," she said brutally. "I need money. He provides — but only a little at a time."

So there it was. She walked in the paradise garden the next few days and studied the cactuses with Señor Rodas as if nothing had happened. But on Friday night, she stopped her little white sedan in front of a convenience store where Dwayne was waiting, nervous in a new blue and white shirt which he had bought in the strip mall after work. They purchased a take out from the Manilla Express, a hot, spicy taste of home, drove to the beach, and ate their picnic on the sand, watching the great Pacific rollers beach themselves at the edge of the continent. That was the start of their affair, the affair of a shy scholar incognito and a disguised warrior princess.

After three weeks, Señor Barber returned for a couple of days. Once again, Amelia disappeared into the big silent house, but, this time, it was Dwayne who was nervous, so nervous that Señor Rodas shook his head. "Be careful of them," he said. "Be careful of Señor Barber. He is not to be trusted."

"And her?" — he'd almost slipped and said "Amelia." "What about Señora Barber? Is she not to be trusted?"

Señor Rodas' seamed and wrinkled face grew sad. "It is for the Señora to be very careful," he said, but the cautious gardener was not moved to speak further. Meanwhile, the two young people had a period of happiness, for Señor Barber, as was his custom, left again abruptly.

During the following weeks Dwayne found it remarkable — although it confirmed his apprehension of her nature — that his beloved never showed the slightest fear of discovery. When he asked her one day, she shrugged. "All he requires of me is obedience," she said. "And his only order is not to open his office closet."

"His office closet?"

"He has an office at home," she said. "There's a closet where he stores valuable papers. Or so he says. He works in the office a lot. It even has a television set, and I think he watches movies there when he wants to be alone."

Dwayne thought of the bruises and asked, "And do you go into this closet?"

She seemed genuinely shocked. "Never. I've never even set foot in the office. Why should I do such a thing when my husband orders me not to?"

"But he has beaten you," Dwayne said.

"That is what frightens me. Whenever he comes home, he asks me if I have been in his closet. I have not and he should see that the room is untouched, but he does not believe me. And after a day or so, he convinces himself that I am lying. It's as if he really wants me to open that closet."

"Yet he has ordered you not to," Dwayne said.

Amelia shrugged. "Either way, I must be beaten, for being innocent or being guilty, because there is some subtle thing he wishes, but I cannot determine what it is."

When Señor Barber broke her hand on his next visit home, Dwayne felt his mother's madness leap within him. He was ready to kill the Señor and damn the consequences, but Lennart Barber had already departed for Chicago, en route, Amelia said, for South Africa. He would be gone two weeks; she had seen his tickets. Still, she would not leave. There were her sisters. Simone was particularly pretty. "The most beautiful girl in Manilla," Amelia said with at touch of bitterness. "I must keep her in school another year so she will be able to get a decent job. Another year."

In despair, Dwayne put some of this before Señor Rodas the next afternoon as they worked in the gardener's own little nursery. "Another year,' she says! What will happen to her?"

"In another year, she will be dead," the old gardener said. "She is not the first."

Dwayne stopped pouring perlite into the pot he was preparing. "What do you mean?"

"Not the first wife. Or the second, or the third."

"He is old enough to have been married before," Dwayne admitted. He did not want to take in all the implications of what Señor Rodas was saying.

"Certainly. And has been. But this is since I started to work in his garden. Three." He held up three fingers for emphasis. "All like our friend, the Señora. Young, pretty, foreign. Poor girls, acquired mail order, postage due. Without friends. You understand what I am saying?"

"What happened to them?" Dwayne asked, his mouth dry.

"The first one — I don't know. I had just started working for the Señor then. The garden was much neglected: cactuses dying from overwatering; damage of all kinds left unattended; weeds everywhere. And imagine the roses." His expression was eloquent. "I never saw the young Señora, but when I heard she was dead, I went to pay my respects to him. He seemed surprised that I had spoken. Then unconcerned. It took him a moment to find the right emotion. You've known such people?"

Rather grimly, Dwayne allowed that he had.

"We have to learn to be human," Señor Rodas said philosophically. "Cats have to learn to be cats; dogs to be dogs. Why should we be different? That day, I could see Señor Barber struggling to find sorrow, to find regret. Then he found them and his face turned sad. She died in a boating accident,' he said. I told him I hoped God would comfort him."

"And the second wife?" Dwayne asked in a soft voice.

The old man shrugged. "Disappeared. Went home, apparently. There was a quick divorce. Or so we heard." He looked completely unconvinced. "As for the third wife, she was killed in a robbery.

"A robbery?"

"She disturbed the robber and was beaten to death. It seemed to be a professional job. No fingerprints, valuable things taken, security system wires cut. The Señor was away in San Francisco at a conference."

"This robber was caught?"

"I don't think that robber ever will be caught. But you can see my point. The Señor is an unlucky man, who attracts unlucky women."

"But none of them could have been as nice as Señora Amelia," Dwayne burst out.

"Not the two I observed, anyway."

"Any man could be happy with the Señora," Dwayne said.

"But Señor Barber is not."

In despair, Dwayne revealed that he knew more about the Barbers than he should have. "She says he seems almost disappointed by her obedience," Dwayne concluded.

"She is clever," said Old Rodas. "She sees it all, poor thing. He is tired of her now." He thumped the pot smartly down on the table to settle the soil. "The Señor wants her to disobey him so that he has an excuse to kill her."

When Dwayne repeated this to Amelia, she thought for a moment before her eyes darkened and she nodded.

"Either you must run away or we must kill him," Dwayne said.

Amelia did not answer immediately but began pacing restlessly back and forth on the terrace. The little lights strung in the trees twinkled and paper lanterns big as pumpkins made artificial moons against the cloudy night sky. He had not been to the paradise garden after dark before, and his fear and desperation were sharpened by the beauty of the lights amidst the trees.

"There are my sisters," she said. "And you have no papers." So she had known that all along.

Dwayne felt a wave of nervous desperation, out of which came another idea.

"The closet," he said. "There may be something important in the closet. Something that will give us power."

She decided instantly and, gripping his hand, led him into the house. They walked down marble and tile halls past big, lavish rooms with the distant city lights winking through the windows. When they reached the office, she caught her breath, then turned the knob. "You see," said Amelia as the unlocked door opened.

Inside, the room was perfectly ordinary, a rich man's rosewood paneled version of Señor Rodas' paper cluttered annex to the potting shed. But instead of the smell of fertilizer and earth, Señor Barber's room had the sad, distinctive odor of musty, closed up places never intended for the light of day. There was a desk, files, a half empty bookcase, and, mounted on a cart, a large screen television set and a VCR.

Amelia looked around curiously. Dwayne, nervous, went directly to the closet and tried the door.

"He keeps it locked."

"We will get a screwdriver to pry it open."

"If you and Señor Rodas are right, there must be a key," she said, and within minutes they found several, including one which opened the closet door. Inside was a set of shelves, some holding padded books and some with boxed video tapes.

"Porn," suggested Dwayne.

She picked up several of the tapes and thought momentarily of the video shops, the flashy clubs, the crowded sidewalks of night time Manilla. Desperation and her beauty might well have taken her in that direction. "No labels," she remarked. "And there are no pictures on the slip cases."

"Maybe really nasty stuff."

Amelia set down the tapes and picked up a pastel leather book. It was a wedding photo album, and she went pale when she recognized the bridegroom. "It is a Señora Barber," she said, holding the book so that Dwayne could see one of the photographs. The bride was young with long dark hair and delicate East Asian features, enough like Amelia so that he was almost poisoned with fear.

"So there were more than three," said Amelia, as she opened the other books. The earlier wives were blonde, pale Americans. In their wedding albums, Señor Barber looked young and handsome.

"Señor Rodas says that your husband has never learned human emotions."

A shadow passed over Amelia's face. "We should see what is on the tapes," she said.

They might have been fooled if Señor Barber had taken the trouble to rewind his treasures all the way. They might have been deceived by footage of parties and trips and "cheesecake" shots of bathing beauties. But Señor Barber's obsession had a cruder edge. The very first tape they played began toward the end with a grainy image of a woman's torso laced with blood. In his shock, Dwayne did not at first recognize what he saw. The dark splotches seemed to distort the geography of the body, and for a disorienting instant he remembered the first video he had seen in the camp: an old American musical, wonderful and peculiar, as stylized as the dances known to his mad mother. Then he heard Amelia draw in her breath and knew this was real blood and that all his fears for his princess were well founded.

It did not take Amelia and Dwayne long to discover the fates of the other disappeared wives. Fast forward, sudden stops, an avalanche of horrors. "There is one left for you," said Dwayne. He put in the last tape and felt the rising wind of madness, for there was Amelia, waving at the camera, climbing out of the pool in her bikini, sitting on a bed in a short nightgown. That this was happening here, in the lavish house, in the paradise garden, here, where there were not the excuses of war and hunger, somehow made everything worse. He could not endure to see any more.

"He likes pictures," she said, not completely calmly. "He has no shame. He wanted me to see all this."

Dwayne stopped the tape. Amelia's image wavered on the screen, then faded to black. He hit the rewind button and rewound the tape. Then they pushed everything back into the closet and left the office, where they couldn't breathe, where life seemed disgusting, where evil, like the devil in paradise, had presented them with the ultimate questions. They could not even think clearly until they escaped to the kitchen. They poured beer into Señor Barber's thin, elegant glasses and washed the taste of blood and evil from their mouths. After a few minutes, Amelia turned on her little portable television and began to click nervously through the channels.

What to do, what to do? Neither of them thought of the police. They both knew that men with badges and guns must be approached, if approached at all, only through powerful intercessors. And they had none, not even wise Señor Rodas being right for a matter of this gravity. As for flight, there were the sisters and Dwayne's lack of papers, and something else which Señor Barber would never have guessed: a kind of anger, a ritual madness, a thirst for battle. It took, perhaps, a man like Dwayne, raised to be the scholar-counselor of a warrior princess, to understand. Now he sat at the polished black stone kitchen table and sipped a Heineken and waited for the decision which he would help bring to fruition.

Amelia did not speak for a long time. She looked straight at the set, clicking the buttons on her remote one after the other. At home, Dwayne thought, they could have consulted an astrologer, someone wise in the ways of days and times. Or perhaps one of the chanting Buddhist priests whose yellow robes had gone shabby in exile. Or Father Peter Hernandez, who said mass in the camp and who, like Dwayne's mother, suffered moments of madness. Since they did not know where to find similar spiritual powers in California, Amelia consulted the glassy square of the tv. Guns and screams and car chases suggested one course of action; cruise ships and airline ads and Serengetti lions, another. But there were always the sisters, Simone and Annamaria and Francesca, and dancing women with their hair flying and tough streetwalkers with long, unsteady legs suggested their fate.

Suddenly Amelia gave a cry of triumph. "There! It is the number!"

Dwayne saw it was the number 800, a good number because free. And the digits added up to 22: his very age: an auspicious number.

"The number for criminals," Amelia said. "For reporting crimes. For telling the world." She looked at him, her eyes fathomless. "And maybe for money," she said. "Money for papers. And for my sisters." She took a deep breath. He could see her trembling, then her gold armor began to glisten, and Dwayne heard the trumpeting of elephants, jeweled and painted, ready for battle.

Amelia picked up the phone and punched in the auspicious number.

Two days later, after he had lied to Señor Rodas for the first time so that he could drive with Amelia to Los Angeles; and after she had disappeared, brave as a lion, into a big white building clutching one, but only one, of the tapes; and after all sorts of fears and a handful of cash money, part of which had already gone for a convincing new California driver's license complete with his picture, the television people came to the paradise garden.

Their lights were hot and bright, a soundless bombardment; their growling trucks panted exhaust, and cameramen, loaded like infantry, rushed the building. Dwayne held the door for them. "Rodas Landscaping," he said and answered questions in Spanish.

Sound technicians brought pole mikes and clear parabolas to catch the breath of souls, and cable strewn photographers muscled in video cameras. From the doorway, Dwayne watched Amelia, small and resolute, surrounded by big, red faced Americans with letters on their shirts, letters familiar from the tv. Dwayne wanted to be beside her as her lover, as her scholar advisor, but he knew that he must remain invisible to these men and women with their all-seeing cameras and curious mikes. He knew that much, so he thought of his father, the brave black Lieutenant, and tried to protect his princess with ferocious looks.

Now she was listening to the producer, a slim man in an open necked shirt. He gestured with his clipboard.

"You've got to search," said the man. "You gotta make it look as if you're just discovering everything."

Amelia glanced back at Dwayne, who poured all his love and courage into one silent glance. She caught her breath and straightened her back:

she was a woman in a million. Then she set off down the corridors of the big house, followed by the noise and lights of the television crew, who kept stopping, despite her urging, despite her urgent gestures, to photograph the huge living room and the sprawling bedrooms — deeper and deeper, down corridors of marble and rosewood to the office.

From his vantage point in the hall, Dwayne saw her begin looking as they had looked that night, opening the file, then the drawers, then the final last small drawer at the back. She held up the keys, unlocked the closet and stood silently aside so that the camera man could focus in on the wedding books.

"Pick one up and open it," said the producer. "Right, good, get in on that Timmy. Jesus Christ, he's got enough of them. Yours? Is yours here?" he asked Amelia.

"I'm still alive," she said.

"And they match?" the producer asked now. "Same gals as in the videos?"

"No doubt about the ones we checked," said his assistant.

"Copies of everything for the DA. Best we can do. Get this cut for the Thursday night show. All right, how's the light on that?" And so on.

At first, Dwayne was perplexed to see them shooting things over and over again, but then he was reassured. This was right; this was proper where such great evil was concerned. These, he realized, were the California priests and astrologers, and this was the way they recreated reality and made something new and different which was tv-real and harmless. Yes, he understood why the filming went on and on until it became boring, became routine.

When Dwayne saw that Amelia was in good hands, he drifted back to the front yard to examine the trucks, to inspect the cables and equipment that lay behind the great glassy eye of the tv. He was standing in the shrubbery with his clippers, watching everything and pretending to work, when Señor Barber's white Honda turned into the drive. For a moment, Dwayne was immobilized with shock and fear. Then he remembered his mother telling him how crafty and patient General Guyen had thwarted the great Kublia Khan, and realized that even he, Dwayne, had underestimated Amelia.

She had insisted on this day, though the tv people could have come earlier, though Dwayne had urged her to get everything done as soon as possible, though he had been haunted by the thought of Señor Barber's premature arrival. Amelia had assured them all that the Señor had two more days in South Africa. Now Dwayne saw that, like the old general, she had laid her stakes in the river, and here was her husband, not floating on a doomed war boat, but arriving to a yard full of television trucks and cars while cameras ran in his secret office.

Señor Barber should have turned his car around. But he hesitated, surprised, genuinely surprised, because his wife's qualities had remained unknown to him, and he had never given a moment's thought to the gardener's silent, and probably illegal, assistant. He was still in the car, his mind racing, when one of the security people laid on specially for this particular shoot, pulled in behind him in a noisy junker.

Señor Barber jumped out, waving the pistol he was, indeed, licensed to carry, demanding to know what was going on. The guard, whose preferred language was Croatian, had been sensitized to guns back home and produced one of his own. At the first shot through his windshield, the security guard fired three times. Señor Barber, with his imitations of human emotion and his passion for video, fell back onto his driveway and poured his blood down the grooves of its patterned cement.

His last moments were recorded, the camera crew rushing from the house before the cry went up for 911 and emergency services. Señor Barber exhausted an obscene and profane vocabulary which was sucked into the magic parabolas even as his blood stained image was shrunk to be made tv-real and harmless, a process that struck Dwayne as miraculous. He marveled at the strange rituals of California, rituals which, though unfamiliar, were completely comprehensible. With that comprehension, Dwayne began to relax. The world, for so long terrifying and strange, was, after all, intelligible. His mad mother with her rebels and scholars and warrior princesses had prepared him for the paradise garden where, Dwayne knew, he would always feel at home.

THE HELPFUL STRANGER

She wouldn't have done it if it hadn't been for the smile, which warned and excited her and frightened her into action. How to describe? Not a friendly smile, nor the automatic, good business professional smile, not even the nervous smile of someone trying to make a good impression and suspecting that he's failing; none of those. It was something else, Dana thought, a quick bearing of the teeth, as if he anticipated biting into something he shouldn't.

As soon as she saw the smile, ideas jumped in Dana's mind and she came all alert. Later, of course, she felt a little guilty, but she'd been in a desperate spot, herself. For all she knew, she might have had a funny smile, too, and she could almost understand how the whole situation had developed from an ordinary Saturday.

That morning, she'd set out in her ancient hatchback with her bike hanging on the rack just the way she did every Saturday, which was the best day of the week, the day which belonged to her, Dana, absolutely. Friday, the end of the school week was good, but Friday night belonged to Bruce, her fiance. They went club hopping or to a concert or a movie, and that was nice. Bruce was fine; she liked going out with Bruce, but still, Friday nights she was expected to get dressed up, mentally and physically.

And Sunday was okay. She would rest up from Saturday's ride, read the papers, perhaps take a short spin or a long walk with Bruce, but by three, certainly by four, o'clock, the long shadow of the approaching school week began to descend. There were papers she'd put off doing, and lessons to be planned. As Sunday drew to a close, Dana would feel the leaden feet of dread returning. She was responsible for five classes of eighth graders who gave no quarter, and she didn't want to go back to school.

But Monday morning at eight-thirty, she'd have to put on a bright face, take a deep breath, and tell herself that an adult of twenty-three could control a group of thirty young barbarians. She could, she could, but by 2:15 P.M. every day, she was exhausted and depressed. Intellectually, she understood that she was too inexperienced for so many difficult pupils. Emotionally, all she could think was that it was only October. The idea of the whole year ahead of her, and of years and years after that, filled her with panic. I'm not cut out for this, she thought, and wondered if she would be able to finish the semester.

Her mother had no doubts whatsoever. "Dana's a natural," Mother always said. "Just ideal for a teacher." Dana's father had no opinion on the subject, which was all right, since his wife had opinions enough for two.

Dana had been marked out for a teacher while she was still in high school, and from the safe confines of the Ed School, teaching had seemed nice enough work. She'd been attracted by the neatness of the lesson plans, the tidy structure of the day, the orderly progression of information and skills which was blown away by the rush of wild, active, profane, raunchy "learners" who turned up every Monday morning, bright eyed with energy, while Dana dragged herself to her desk, exhausted.

From that moment, each week was like a long grade that Dana had to gasp her way up, arms and legs straining, then, just when her chest was about to burst, the top of the hill: Friday and the descent ahead. Dana would clear the last steeps, which were lunchroom duty and the horrors of her sixth period class, before the final bell brought an eruption of books, papers, backpacks, and shouts. The kids surged out in a wave, shoving each other in the halls and banging their lockers, before disappearing behind the poisonous exhaust of the waiting buses. Dana would gather up her books and papers, and discard her untouched lunch bag. As she headed for her car, she would feel her spirits revive with the prospect of Friday night and two whole days off.

Saturday was her day. Sometimes Bruce would want to do this or that, but she was dexterous about putting him off. Sunday they could go to his folks' for dinner or watch the soccer in the park or work on his boat. Saturday was hers, and usually she sat down at her kitchen table with her trail guides and maps as soon as she got home on Friday. Then, before meeting Bruce for dinner, she would go over her bike, oil the gears, check the tires, pack up her jeans and wind breaker, fill her water bottle, and check that she had provisions for a picnic.

Saturday mornings, she carried her bike down the two flights to the driveway, put the rack on the back of her car, and set out for the bike trail of choice or some pretty country town where she could ride for hours along the quiet roads, feeling the dreadful awareness of being teacher, fiancee, fulfiller of expectations drop away with every mile. That was the routine and she was determined to hang on to it, though Bruce sometimes complained and her mother had been fussing lately.

"There was that hiker — strangled. When was that, Bob?" she called through to Dana's father. "Not long ago, I know that. And there was another young woman killed in one of the Connecticut parks. It's not safe on your own. Take Bruce with you. He can get a bike. It would be something nice for you to do together." Mother was very keen on togetherness where Bruce was concerned.

Dana had murmured about Bruce being busy, about an old soccer injury, plausible excuses, but, really, she needed Saturday for herself, without eighth graders or Bruce or her folks or his. Dana felt that she could not get through the week without spending Saturday on her bike, which let her find the place she'd been needing to reach all week, the place where she could look around and decide if any of this was what she really wanted from life.

Her latest discovery, the old rail line trail through the state forest, had been a satisfactory route, so pleasant that Dana regretted she wouldn't be able to ride that way again. The road bed was a little soft in spots but well cleared with easy grades and very pretty. She had seen deer and a beaver, met a nice chap on horseback, passed a round faced woman driving a pony with mesh head cloth to keep off the flies from its face. The threatened rain had not arrived, and the cool weather, the swift moving clouds, the brilliant reds and yellows in the swamp all made it a good day, a happy day.

Dana felt the first faint hint of returning anxiety when she reached her car in the parking lot beside the forest's shallow lake. It was after three, and Saturday was beginning to run out. She drank some of her bottled water, secured the bike on its rack, changed her shoes, and turned the key for the engine. The old Subaru whined and rumbled, but as soon as Dana started backing out of the lot, the engine sputtered and fell silent. She tried again, but the starter ground without success. I couldn't have flooded the engine so quickly, Dana thought, but no matter what she tried, the motor refused to engage.

She sat tapping the wheel, feeling the pleasure of the day slip away: she would be late home to Worcester; her mother would start in again on the safety issue and nag Bruce to get a bike. And if Bruce got a bike, he'd want to come on Saturdays. To avoid thinking more about this unendurable eventuality, Dana decided to call Triple A, but she found no one home at the ranger's house and no public phone in the park. She was preparing to set off on her bike when a door clicked open, and a man wearing jeans and a navy wind breaker got out of the dark SUV on the other side of the lot. Though she'd been aware of the vehicle, Dana had not realized anyone was behind its heavily tinted windows.

"Need help?" he called, his voice light, neutral. He was tall and lanky with a trucker's cap over his short, dark hair. Despite the tinted windows and the now rapidly spreading overcast, he wore mirrored glasses, and silver reflections of clouds and trees kept Dana from getting any sense of his personality.

Prudence whispered, take down your bike and ride to the highway. But it was getting late; Dana had no idea how far it was to the nearest phone and, once she called, she'd probably have to wait an hour for a mechanic. "My car won't start. I'm going to have to find a phone to call Triple A," she said.

"You should carry a phone," the man said as he crossed toward her. "They're so cheap now." He stopped just on the other side of her bike rack.

"Sometimes you don't want to take calls," Dana said.

He smiled then, a curious, significant, warning smile. Dana realized that she registered the smile only because she had been teaching eighth graders, who lack adult skill in hiding their emotions.

"I have a phone," he said quickly, eagerly. "Why don't you make the call, and I'll take a look under the hood."

"I'd love to call, but I don't want to take up your time," Dana said. She didn't want him to be helpful and so create a sense of obligation.

"I've got time," he said. "I've been sitting looking over the lake, just kind of waiting. I'm lazy, while you've been out riding, keeping healthy." Dana thought she heard a distasteful touch of irony in his voice.

"It was a nice day, a nice day to be out." If she'd learned nothing else in two months, Dana had learned how to evade provocation. She was not going to argue about the healthy life.

"That's what brought me out," he said. "I only come out on nice days. I like to look at the water and feel the calmness of it." He went back to his big dark vehicle and produced a phone. When she took it from him, Dana felt the damp imprint of his hand on the plastic case. What did he have to be nervous about?

"Want to pop the hood for me?"

He seemed a perfectly nice, helpful man, but Dana felt a sudden aversion to turning her back on him. "The car's unlocked. Just reach down at the side for the hood. I'll call and then I'll try to start the engine."

He looked at her as if he knew just what she was thinking. "Have the number?" he asked and smiled again.

Dana nodded. She reached into her day pack and pulled out her wallet, watching him all the time. But that was silly, really, because she was in a public, if lonely, place, with the Triple A operator on the cell phone. Dana gave her location and directions. The Triple A woman thought the mechanic could get there in twenty minutes, surely in half an hour.

"They're coming right out," Dana told the man. "You don't need to bother."

The hood sprang up and he fixed the little metal support bracket to keep it open. "It could be something as simple as your battery," he said. "Or a loose connection."

"The battery is brand new," Dana said.

"You can get a dud battery," he said. "Lot of the stuff today is just crap. They think we'll buy anything, and half the time they're right. Screw the Great American Public is the name of the game."

Dana sensed, rather than saw, his bright, fixed gaze behind the shiny glasses.

"We can see through them, though. We got the tools to check this out." He went back to his truck, emerging a couple minutes later with a volt meter to pronounce her battery functional. "It's not the battery."

"The Triple A people said twenty minutes. Fifteen now," Dana said. This, she thought, was a plain enough hint, but he paid no attention. "Connections look okay, but won't hurt to tighten them up." He fiddled with the wires on the battery for a moment, then asked her to try the engine.

Dana slipped into the car, closed the door and turned the key. The man listened to the various whines and rattles and shook his head. He dropped the hood and came around to lean on her door. He had a number of ideas for what might be wrong, distributor, water pump, other mysterious Subaru organs.

"You've been very kind," said Dana. "I'll just wait for the mechanic. I don't want to keep you."

"I've got nothing much to do," he said. Despite this wistful remark, there was an impersonal, almost mechanical, quality to his voice, as if he'd learned what to say without feeling the words. "Besides, they may keep you waiting quite a while. It's real quiet here this time of day. Not the best place to be stranded." He put his hand on the door frame near the lock button and Dana regretted having rolled the window down. "I like to help people if I can," he continued. "I think that's the right way, don't you? To be helpful?"

Dana agreed, though she knew it would help her considerably if he would go back to his truck and let her wait alone for the mechanic. "I almost forgot your phone," she said, handing it out the window to him. "You're right, I should get one. I know Mom will be worried."

He handed the phone right back, all pleasant and above board. "You'd better call Mom," he said. "Let her know what's happened."

Dana took the phone and opened it, then tapped on the case without punching in the numbers. "My mother thinks it's dangerous for me to cycle alone."

"Perhaps your mother is right," he said. "Now, take me. I could be anyone, right? Someone who sits all afternoon watching the lake could have anything in mind. You can't always be lucky as you are today."

Dana suspected he was trying to frighten her, though that was a silly idea when he had just handed her the phone. Annoyed, she punched in the numbers smartly and told her mother what had happened.

Her mom's voice rose in her ear. "Where are you calling from?"

"Some guy's loaned me his cell phone. I'm in the parking lot." Dana explained about calling Triple A.

"I'll phone Bruce," said Mom. "He'll have to drive down and pick you up."

"Don't do that," Dana said too quickly, at least, she felt she'd spoken too quickly, as if she were not eager to see Bruce, as if she were making up excuses. "I may be real late. I'll call him from the garage."

As usual, her mom had advice and suggestions and was willing to discuss what should be done at length.

"I've got to go," Dana said. "I've got to give back his phone."

"What's his name?" Mom asked.

"I don't know," said Dana. "He was in the parking lot and saw I couldn't start the car."

"Ask," said Mom, and Dana raised her eyebrows, because he'd loaned her the phone and been helpful and really all she had against him were his creepy mirrored sunglasses and his eagerness to help.

"Mom wants to know your name." Dana smiled ruefully to let him know this wasn't her idea, but when he hesitated, she understood it was a bad sign.

"George," he said.

"His name is George Anderson," she told her mother. Anderson was the first surname that came into her mind, and Anderson would be good enough, because Dana was pretty sure George wasn't his given name, either. She closed the phone and handed it over.

"Mom feel better?" he asked, giving her a sly look, as if they were conspirators, as if she had become complicitous in a way, which Dana supposed she had.

"Yes, thank you." Very formal, very careful.

He smiled again and opened his mouth to ask this or that, when Dana heard the sound of a truck bouncing into the lot. "Ah, there's Triple A. Thanks so much for the phone." She opened her door to deliverance and waved for the mechanic, who pulled up in a red wrecker with another man riding beside him in the cab.

The garage mechanic was slim with punkish blond hair and good looking despite his oily coveralls and grease blackened hands. His much older companion had a racy shock of swept back gray hair, black rimmed glasses over friendly dark eyes, and the last traces of a drawl. The two of them heard whole story, opened the hood, repeated the stranger's investigations, and agreed the battery was fine.

Rather than taking Dana's hint to depart, George hung around, answering questions before Dana could respond and amplifying her remarks. He's trying to make them think he's a friend of mine, she thought.

"No trouble before?" The mechanic asked.

"No. The car's old but ultra-reliable."

"Yeah?" He and his companion exchanged glances. "There has been some trouble lately in these parking lots."

"Cars tampered with," his friend agreed. "Not just petty vandalism."

"Really?" Dana tried to remember if she'd seen the SUV when she arrived at the lot. Of course, George could have arrived at any time, seen the rack, figured she'd be gone for a while. But however disagreable, none of that mattered now. She'd be out of the lot in minutes and on her way home.

"We'll have to take it in."

Dana nodded and produced her card. "Have you room in the truck for me? I'll have to call someone to come down from Worcester and pick me up."

The mechanic shook his head regretfully. "The garage is closed. We'll just leave the car until Monday. I was on my way home, giving Joe a lift, when I got the call. Perhaps your friend here . . .

"Sure, Dana, I could run you up," George offered.

"No, I couldn't think of that. It's more than an hour. We just met in the lot," she told the mechanic, who did not seem to take in either this information or her implication.

"Drop you in Putnam, how's that? I'm on my way there, anyway." George was all eagerness, all enthusiasm. "Save these good folks some trouble. I'll drop you in Putnam and you can call for your ride from there."

"Would that be all right?" the mechanic asked, and Dana did not feel able to say, I don't want to ride with this stranger.

"Great," said the gray haired man. Joe, that was is name. "Ellie'll sure be happy to see me home early for once." He and the young mechanic laughed about this.

George smiled and opened the passenger door of his van. "I'll have you home in no time," he said.

Dana got into the van. Dark blue fabric seats, a vaguely unpleasant, musty odor, a coffee container. A woman's sweater lay on the back seat. Dana fastened her seat belt, and George started the engine. He waited until the mechanic had cleared the parking lot, then he backed out and turned, not toward the highway, but up the forest road.

"I like the back roads," he said.

"I do too, normally, but I need to get home."

"Won't take long. I know all the shortcuts. You can go a long way on these back roads. Goodwin Forest to the Natchaug and up though the Bigelow Ponds to the Massachusetts border."

"Is that where those hikers got lost?"

"That's right. City people are inclined to get lost. Like you, maybe. Maybe you're a city person and would get lost, but not me."

Dana chose not to answer. The heavily tinted windows darkened and flattened the early fall landscape making the familiar look exotic, surreal. Maybe that was why Dana felt uncertain about her emotions: she was nervous and yet alert, almost excited. She was doing something her instincts warned her against, something out of her usual pattern, something that suggested change and escape and an alternative to Monday mornings.

George drove from one narrow secondary road to another until the the asphalt ran out altogether. They were on a bumpy dirt track, when he abruptly pulled over and stopped. Ambiguity vanished, and with a jump of her heart, Dana thought, I've made a serious mistake.

"I've got some cigarettes in the back," George said. "Want a cigarette?"

Dana shook her head. Her eyes were irresistibly drawn to the truck keys. When he goes to the back of the van, she thought, I could slide over, I could put the truck into gear.

George smiled as he shut off the engine and dropped the keys into his pocket. Dana heard him open the back of the van. I could open the door and run into the woods, Dana thought. She turned around to see where he was and met his eyes.

"I know this place to buy cheap cigarettes on route 6," he said. He was opening the rear passenger door when Dana heard a car. She saw the state insignia, the close cropped head of the trooper.

"You folks having trouble?'

"Nope, just getting out some cigarettes," George said.

"I had trouble," Dana said. "I had to hitch a ride when my car wouldn't start. There really should be a public phone in the Goodwin parking lot."

"Fortunately I had my cell phone in the van," George said. "Best thing in when you have a breakdown."

"We're being extra careful here around dusk," the trooper said, as if he hadn't heard her, as if he hadn't picked up on her complaint, her alarm.

I'm invisible, Dana thought, I'm invisible and no one else sees my situation.

"We're on our way out, but we thought we'd take the scenic route," George said. "Woods sure are pretty this time of year." He got in the van and started the motor. The trooper lingered until they pulled away.

"Your tax dollars at work," George remarked as the cruiser's tail lights slid into the distance.

"Yes," said Dana, but she was thinking to herself, I was lucky.

George took a right turn onto a tarred road that wound further into the forest. "So what do you do?" he asked.

"I'm a teacher," Dana said.

"I'll bet you teach English."

"That's right."

"You do!" He was delighted. "I knew you did,"

"How did you know?" Dana wasn't sure she was pleased to have been marked so soon by her profession.

"I've just always liked English and books — Stephen King and Poe, I liked Poe a lot."

"I teach "The Cask of Amontillado." The students like that as much as they like anything."

"I liked "The Telltale Heart" and the "The Masque of the Red Death," too," he said. "We read them in high school. About the only stuff I really did like."

"It's hard to get my kids to read anything."

"And how is school teaching? Do you like it?"

"Not much," Dana admitted. "I'm not much good at it. At the kids part, at controlling the kids. The rest I'm okay with."

"Yeah, well control," he said. "We all want to be in control, don't we?"

"I don't know," said Dana, "I don't seem to have much taste for it. With school teaching, I'm becoming a big fan of self-control. That's what my kids need."

"Control is important," he said. "Keeping control, being in control. Now me, I like to feel in control."

"Maybe you should have gone into teaching," Dana said. Instead of me, she thought.

"Funny, I thought about being a teacher. I could have done that. I could have done the control bit; I just couldn't stick the school bit. Sometimes in college, things happen. You know."

"Yes," Dana agreed. She'd met Bruce in college and taken education courses and the rest had just happened.

At the edge of the forest, George turned onto the state road and headed east on route 44. Yes, they were going toward Putnam, that was right, Dana saw the signs. There was nothing wrong with George except her over active imagination; he was just lonely or bored, one of those unfortunates with marginal social skills, who do not have quite the right sense of humor, who say odd, spontaneous things and make people uneasy.

Dana felt relief, and something else, an irrational kind of disappointment: she would have no excuse about Monday. She would have to go back. How much nicer it would be to keep going, how much better if George had been someone different, perhaps a romantic lead right out of a screwball comedy, instead of an unhappy, creepy man. To avoid thinking such things, Dana asked, "And where do you work?"

"I'm independent," George said. "I install vinyl windows all over eastern Connecticut, southern Massachusetts.

"You must travel around a lot," she said.

"Yeah, I'm always on the move. I like that, being able to go here and there. With the interstates, you're here in the morning and five hundred miles away by night. If there's poor hunting in one place, there's opportunity elsewhere."

"I think I might like a job with traveling." She hadn't thought of that before, but it was true. She liked seeing new places, meeting new people.

"I hadn't figured you for a traveler, but you never know about people, do you? See why we need to talk more? I think we need to get to know each other better. We'll stop and get a drink and talk about jobs and Poe. I know this neat bar . . ."

"I need to get home." But now Dana spoke without any real conviction. She was out of danger and there was no need to be in a hurry.

"You don't want to get home that badly," he said as if he could read her mind. "If you did, you wouldn't have been out three, four hours on the bike."

There it was again. That social awkwardness. Not the right thing to say at all, and it made Dana wonder if that was just a guess or had he been in the parking lot all the time she was riding in the forest?

"What about you?" she asked. "You've been out all afternoon, too. Is there no one waiting for you at home?"

"Naw. I'm on my own."

"Sure you are," she said and glanced toward the back seat.

He turned and looked full at her, surprised or maybe annoyed.

"The sweater," Dana said. "Pink and purple stripes with some embroidered flowers. It must look real nice on you."

"Oh, that belongs to a friend. Not even a friend, just a hitchhiker I picked up. She left it behind, forgot it, I guess. I figure I'll see her again. I think you always see people more than once."

"Always?"

"Yeah. I can always see her again. If I want to."

They were up to speed on the main road, whipping along toward Putnam, and Dana began to shiver in the chill from the van's air system. She had her jeans in her day pack but she'd left her coat in the car.

"Cold?" he asked.

"A bit. I need to change."

"I'll stop if you want. There's a little park just up the road. You can change in the back."

"No, that's all right. We don't want to meet a second helpful trooper." She gave a little laugh to signal this was a joke and after one of those curious two second pauses, George laughed too.

"I can change into my jeans in Putnam," Dana added. "There will surely be somewhere. A McDonald's or something."

"When we stop for a drink," George suggested and he reached into the back seat and pulled up the sweater, which was thick and had a distinctive, rather disagreeable smell of perfume and sweat. "Just about your size," George said.

"Maybe not my color." Dana noticed the soiling around the cuffs and an odd, rusty stain. But though she disliked the thought of putting the sweater on, she was freezing, and she draped it around her shoulders.

"She had hair like yours," George said in a reminiscent tone. "Kinda reddish brown and curly. Your hair is not as curly." He sounded regretful.

"The sweater needs a clean but it must have been expensive. I'm surprised she left it behind."

"Well, we got kinda wasted at this bar I know. I'm not much of a drinker myself," he added. "But for conversation, you need a drink. With some people, you need more than one."

"What do you talk about with hitchhikers?"

"This and that. Like us, what have we talked about? Poe and jobs and control and what we really want. That about it?"

Dana agreed it was.

"Now we've never met before, have we? But we have some things in common; I feel we have some issues in common. So, a couple beers, we'll know a whole lot more about each other, we'll have a kind of contact we didn't have before — just like with my friend the hitchhiker."

He gave her the strange, predatory smile and this time two ideas that had been floating in and out of Dana's mind came fully to the surface: George was dangerous and she could make use of him. Dana suddenly felt the way she sometimes did riding alone along a new trail, uncertain about who or what she might meet. She felt the potential threat, and with it, a conviction that she could manage danger which made her feel almost unbearably jumpy and excited. "Sure," she said. "But in Putnam. That way, I can call and we can have a couple drinks before Bruce comes down to pick me up."

"We'll have a couple drinks first," George said. "Then maybe you won't want to call Bruce."

Dana knew enough to laugh and George took this endorsement at face value. He grew quite expansive and talkative. He told her more about vinyl windows than she wanted to know and asked her about her students. It could have been a normal conversation except for her sense of fear and excitement and her feeling that his opaque personality had become transparent to her.

It was full dark when they reached Putnam with its winding streets and century old brick factory buildings and cheap, modern facades. Streetlights glowed an anemic orange behind the dark glass, and black water poured over the old mill dam.

"I really want to change," Dana said, as they drove into the antiques district, full of lighted store fronts and old fashioned shop signs, a little pocket of prosperity in the defunct mill town. "I don't want to go anywhere in bike shorts."

"You have the legs for them," George said.

"Thanks a lot, but it's nearly 40 degrees."

"You should put on the sweater. It's really a warm, nice sweater. It would suit you fine."

"When I can change," Dana said. "I don't want to get it all sweaty." in She had her belt off before George stopped the van a small municipal lot. She returned the sweater to the back seat and opened her door.

"The bar's right down the street," he said. "You can change there."

"I feel funny going inside a bar in shorts."

"Not quite proper for a school teacher?"

Thank God for some stereotypes, Dana thought. Looking up and down the street, she spotted an antiques mall in what looked like an old factory building. "What about there? I'll bet they have a ladies room."

"Sure." He locked the van doors. "Change and then you'll call, and we'll have a couple beers."

"Yes," she said. She hurried across the street and he followed her.

Inside was more crowded than Dana had anticipated. The antiques mall was getting ready to close; customers were lined up at the counter. Another group of shoppers, laden with packages, stood in the middle of the long aisles of booths comparing notes as if fearful of having missed some treasure and reluctant to leave. Dana passed oriental vases and screens, nineteenth century paintings and folk art figures, art deco knick-knacks, colonial tables, Victorian bureaus, 1930s mirrors. Postcards, dolls, quilts, a nightmare attic of fusty furniture, tools, ornaments, and clothes. All things for people to buy, but, really, Dana though, things that others had wanted rid of, things they had been glad to escape.

At the back of the building, she was directed downstairs by one of the dealers, a skinny, dust colored woman surrounded by old toys and rocking horses and metal banks. On the lower level, Dana found more narrow aisles with bedsteads by the dozens, chairs, some with seats missing;

bureaus, tables, lamps, mirrors, picture frames, some with hideous pictures; antique sewing machines, carpenter's tools, and kitchen goods. The lavatories were tucked in the rear behind a couple of lacquered screens and a plaster angel. In the women's room, Dana struggled out of her bike pants and threw them into the trash basket.

Although her mind had been alive, positively jumping with ideas, she had not known what she would do until she threw away her bike pants — new, expensive, nicely padded. She pulled the jeans out of her day pack and struggled into them and found a dry turtleneck and put it on in place of her damp t-shirt. She opened the lavatory door cautiously, but no, George, all innocence — or all confidence, was upstairs. She had only to get out, and trusting that there must be a back way, a window, a place to hide, even, she started down the aisles, past pool cues and lace and lacquer boxes, dishes and the breakfronts they'd sat in; souvenir mugs and wooden trays and victrolas and old cigar boxes and tobacco cans. Then, just as her heart had begun racing with nerves, a sudden cool draft issued from a narrow, half open door behind piles of headboards and disassembled beds. Dana climbed three steep stone steps to the October night.

A bus was waiting. The antique fanciers, laden with small, precious boxes and bags, were embarking, while the driver stowed larger items in the luggage rack underneath. He did not notice Dana climb on board and head for the lavatory at the back. When she emerged half an hour later, the big charter was rolling south down the interstate away from George and Bruce, her mother and father, and five classes of underachieving eighth graders.

Of course, Dana felt guilty, even about George. When she read he'd been questioned, she almost called, though she told herself it was unnecessary: George was completely innocent and there wouldn't be a shred of proof, not a shred. Still, it was odd that the only person she felt she should call was George, but Dana didn't have to agonize for long. When the police searched George's van, they developed an interest in the stained pink and purple striped sweater, not to mention the handcuffs they found and strands of reddish, curly hair which happened to match some from the corpse of a hiker strangled near the Massachusetts border.

Of course, Dana faced the temptation of thinking that she was special, that George — who really wasn't "George" at all, but she couldn't think of him with any other name — wouldn't have harmed her. Dana realized this idea was foolish, and she hoped that George was wrong and that they wouldn't meet again. She wasn't special but lucky, just as George had been lucky two or three or however many times — the police were unsure and still investigating — before he met her and became unlucky.

So Dana had been right to trust her instincts, very right, and at the moment, her instincts told her that she was better off where she was, and, indeed, she felt that in her new surroundings she might be happy after all.